A WORLD TO WIN

A WORLD TO WIN

Mary Lancaster

Published by
Bladud Books

For my husband.

First published in 2006 by Mushroom eBooks.

This Edition published in 2007 by Bladud Books,
an imprint of Mushroom Publishing, Bath, BA1 4EB,
United Kingdom

www.bladudbooks.com

ISBN 9781843194392

Discovery

April – September 1847

CHAPTER ONE

I first saw him in Vienna.

Sometimes now I think it was in Vienna that I first saw anything at all, but that's not strictly true. Actually, I first saw clearly in London, at the mature age of twenty-seven, by the simple expedient of purchasing a pair of spectacles — and all at once I was enchanted, amazed by the beauty of everything, the sharpness, the detail that suddenly became so clear to me!

I suppose this euphoria might account for the very odd thing I did in London, but at the time I could only wonder why I had never bought them before, how I could have let so much of my life pass in a dull, myopic haze.

Well, it was easy really. As a child I was ashamed of my constantly worsening disability and hid it lest I be thought stupid. Needless to say I kept my secret and was still thought stupid, which just shows the pointlessness of vanity. After that, as a young girl, no one would let me have spectacles on the grounds that gentlemen didn't want to marry ladies so disfigured — apparently it gives us a daunting air of intelligence. Myself, I can't help thinking that neither do gentlemen wish to marry ladies who cut them dead in the street and ignore them at parties simply from not being able to see who the devil they are.

I speak from experience, incidentally. By the ripe old age of twenty-seven, I had only ever received one offer of marriage, an engagement from which I was freed with embarrassing speed. Just as well, for had I married, I would not have been in the position of looking for a genteel situation in London, never have bought my spectacles, never have answered that fatal advertisement, and so never have found myself in an opulent private hotel room, being interviewed by Count and Countess István Szelényi for the post of governess to their two children.

It was at this interview that my spectacles really came into their own. I was still fascinated by the newly discovered details of people's features and expressions, but when I first encountered Count István and his wife, I was completely bowled over by the sheer sharp beauty before me. As I said, it's the only excuse I have for my odd — my *bad* — behaviour.

The Count stood up as I entered the room and approached with a faint, formal smile. Of course, he wasn't really seeing me: nobles of Count Szelényi's rank do not *see* governesses, even if they deign to interview them.

Tall, dark, splendidly built and impeccably dressed, he was younger than I had expected and handsome enough to have turned to jelly the knees of any impressionable young lady, even one used to the joys of perfect vision.

"Miss Kettles?" he said, and naturally his voice was charming too: low, cultivated and exotically accented.

"Count Szelényi?" I countered, inclining my head with a little too much pride — I found it very hard to behave like a governess.

"Yes, I am István Szelényi. This is my wife. Please sit down."

I sat, casting a glance at the lady while I did so. As befitted the wife of so magnificent a nobleman, she was both elegant and beautiful. She was sitting by the window, relaxing against her chair back in a way that would have appalled my Aunt Edith, but somehow she still exuded aristocratic splendour, her fashionable morning gown of pink silk billowing in luxuriant flounces around her chair. Aloof and superior, she managed to acknowledge me by the slightest nod, but she never said a word throughout the entire interview, contenting herself with occasional glances at me from under her long, blond eyelashes. They were secretive glances, almost suspicious, and it struck me that she looked so at all women who came in contact with her husband. Obviously I set her mind at rest — well, I have never been much of a threat to Beauty — for she raised no objection to my engagement.

"You are a little younger than I expected," Count István began, civilly but with no trace of hesitation.

I said, "I am twenty-seven," and looked straight into his fine, grey eyes. I saw no recognition there. I felt none myself.

"May I ask what your experience is?"

"To be honest, none," I told him flatly. I think I smiled.

He sighed. "Then perhaps you will tell me what qualifies you to take charge of my children?"

"I have been well educated," I returned calmly. "I know my arithmetic, history and geography. I can play the piano-forte and sew. I have Latin, French and Hungarian..."

"Hungarian?" he pounced. I knew he would.

"Hungarian."

He leaned back in his chair, regarding me thoughtfully. "That is unusual in an English lady, is it not?"

"I dare say, but I am Scottish," I said pedantically, adding by way of explanation, "My mother's family were Hungarian."

2

Again, I looked straight into his eyes. But he only smiled faintly. He doesn't know, I thought, and felt laughter bubble up inside me. It was a bitter sort of mirth, but it still made me reckless, so I choked it back, and waited.

"That is fortunate for us," he observed. "In Hungary, people of our class tend to speak in French, but I do not forget I am a Magyar. I would have my children grow up with a thorough knowledge of their own language, as well as French and German — do you have any German, Miss Kettles?"

"A little," I said cautiously. He nodded consideringly. Again there was a pause.

"Do you have references?" he enquired at last. I delved into my reticule for the required letters. The Count accepted them, read them quickly, occasionally casting a quick, almost curious glance at me. "Your father was a minister of the church?"

"Yes," I answered, feeling my heart bump. "He died some three months ago. To be frank it is why I am now in need of a situation."

And how he would have disapproved of this one! I shuddered to think of what he would have said. I hoped the dead did not really watch over us.

The Count nodded. "Of course. I understand. These gentlemen speak very highly of you."

From the corner of my eye I saw the Countess give me a slightly longer look. The Count leaned forward to hand the letters back to me. I took them without comment.

He said, "May I ask what brought you south to London?"

Before I could help it I shrugged. Aunt Edith wouldn't have liked that either. "Partly a desire for change," I said honestly, "and partly because I was told there is a greater variety of situations to be found here."

"I see," said the Count. "You realize what this post would entail?"

"Yes, I think so. I would be teaching your son who is seven and your daughter who is six."

"Of course, but we would require you to do so in Buda-Pest," he said a little drily. "Also in Vienna when I have to attend the Emperor, and in my father's castle in Transylvania. It is all a long way from home."

"I have no home," I said quickly and then, disgusted by the pathos of such a statement, I added, "I have nothing to keep me here; I have always wanted to see the world, and I need a situation." I smiled faintly. "I am told Transylvania is incredibly beautiful."

How fortunate I would now have my spectacles to appreciate it.

The Count said, "Mmm." He stood up. "Our tour here is nearly over. We plan to leave London at the end of this week. We will travel as fast as possible to Vienna, where we may stay some time before going on to Buda-Pest. I move around a lot, Miss Kettles, and my family go with me. You may find it tiring caring for small children in such circumstances, but I shall expect them to be taught just the same."

I nodded. He glanced at his wife, but she was gazing out of the window and didn't turn.

"Then you accept the post at the salary stated?"

With every ounce of sense I had, I knew that this was madness and that I should stop before it went any further. But I couldn't help myself. After all, the salary was extremely generous.

"Yes," I said brazenly. "I accept. I have just one question however. Your advertisement mentioned a 'replacement' — why did your previous governess leave?"

I told you I was feeling reckless. Such blatant curiosity could easily have cost me the situation. Perhaps I was trying to lose it, knowing in my heart I shouldn't even be *thinking* of it. However, it was the Count who looked embarrassed. He half-turned, tidying some papers on the table before him.

"She did not choose to leave," he said at last. "She — er — died."

I blinked. "Oh dear," I murmured. "How — daunting."

The Countess lifted her head, and I saw her china blue eyes were full of laughter — a mirth not entirely free of malice.

I never liked children. You may think governessing an odd choice of occupation in the circumstances, but I had long ago worked out that it was all I was fit for. I was reasonably well educated — for a woman — and of respectable family. I could sew only slowly and badly, despite what I had told the Count, and I had had great difficulty in keeping house for myself and my father let alone for a family of strangers. So I had either to sponge upon my father's family or become a governess. With regret, I chose the latter.

Even more regretfully, I contemplated the dead governess, my predecessor, and tried not to wonder what appalling acts perpetrated by my charges had driven her to the grave. For I was under no illusions about the position of a governess in a wealthy household. Despised by both family and servants and universally regarded as inferior to the children to be taught and disciplined, it would be very easy to find the situation intolerable. I had resolved to seek what entertainment I could from it — and then the Devil prompted me to answer Count István's advertisement. Which, as I began to say some time ago, was how I came to be in Vienna and to see Lajos Lázár.

I was only presented to my charges on the morning of our departure from London. They were called Miklós and Anna. The boy was small and slight, delicate looking, with his mother's secretive eyes; the girl was plump and prosperous. Both stared at me flatly when I smiled at them — I particularly hate when children do that — though they answered me politely in French when their father introduced us in that language.

Their politeness lasted all the way to Vienna, and in the end I was glad to see it go. Initially suspicious of them, especially on account of my predecessor's demise, I was greatly relieved on that swift, exhausting journey to find them biddable, well-mannered children — a trifle precocious, perhaps, but intelligent and interested. Their grasp of languages was especially impressive: they spoke French and Hungarian with equal fluency, interspersed with odd phrases in German.

However, by the time we reached Vienna there was another nagging suspicion in my mind: that they were just too well behaved to be children at all. Either they were lulling me into a false sense of security — in which case I should look out, or follow my predecessor to the grave — or they were sick and I should report the fact to their parents.

I felt rather sick myself as I unpacked my meagre possessions in Count István's elegant Vienna house. The elegance had not yet impinged upon my brain, only my own tiredness and that nagging worry over the children. I thought I was getting another headache.

Still, I revelled in my solitude and the stillness of my quiet bedchamber. I felt quite joyful at the prospect of staying in one place for several days.

"Travel," I said to my one evening dress as I hung it up in the wardrobe, "is, after all, overrated."

I had longed for years to see more of the world, and now that I had — admittedly at a cracking pace — I was ridiculously disappointed, harassed by a vague sense of insecurity that had very little to do with my menial position or the strangeness of the Szelényi family. It had more to do with glimpses of poverty, faces turned towards me with want and discontent and hardness in their eyes.

My sombre thoughts were interrupted by an abrupt knock on the door. I nearly screamed with vexation for I dearly wanted a few hours' peace. Instead I stayed silent, hoping I would be presumed asleep, but the knock came again, accompanied by a double-voiced giggle that was unmistakable for all its rarity.

Surprised, I crossed the room and opened the door. Two small nightgowned figures erupted past me in a medley of mirth and garbled words, from which I deduced that they had escaped from Zsuzsa, their nursery-maid — it wasn't difficult, Zsuzsa's attention was easily distracted by anything male and over the age of sixteen — and for some reason come to say goodnight to me.

"That's very kind of you," I said, eyeing them dubiously as they dived on to my bed. My heart was unwilling to be touched. "You've never done this before."

Heaving herself in to a sitting position by leaning on her brother's head, Anna grinned at me.

"We thought you might be lonely," she said disarmingly.

"I haven't had time to be."

"We wondered," Miklós chimed in, emerging flushed from under his sister's elbow, "what your name was."

"Miss Kettles," I said primly and, I hoped, repressively.

"Don't you have another name? Frau Weitel did."

"It was Marta," Anna added. "What is yours?"

"Katherine," I said, surrendering to the inevitable.

"We could call you Miss Katherine," Anna offered in friendly spirit, "only it's even harder to say than Miss Kettles."

I found myself admitting, "My friends call me Katie."

"Oh, that's *much* better!" cried Miklós. "Can *we* be your friends then?"

I opened my mouth, and closed it again. "If you're good," I said, taking off my spectacles to wipe an imaginary smudge.

"Why do you wear these?" the girl asked.

"To see."

She stared. "Can't you see without them?"

Suspicion returned. I could imagine all sorts of future catastrophes resulting from this conversation.

"Certainly I can." I put the glasses back on and regarded her fully. "They help me to see *even better*."

Anna looked quite awed, but Miklós was holding out his hand to me.

"Can I try them?" he asked. I contemplated him for a moment, eventually deciding it would be the lesser of two evils to get it over with now. I took the spectacles off again and helped the boy hold them over his eyes. His face screwed up alarmingly.

"I can't see anything at all — it hurts!"

"That's because they are *my* spectacles," I said, taking them back. "They only help me. Do you know, I think you should run back to bed now before Zsuzsa reports your escape to your mother."

"Very well," Anna said reasonably, "but will you take us to the Prater tomorrow, Miss Katie?"

"Perhaps," I said, pulling them both off my bed and pointing them firmly in the direction of the door.

"Please — we'll be very good — even Frau Weitel took us once... " She broke off in surprise as her brother's outburst of laughter interrupted her. "What?" she demanded.

"Katie Kettles! Katie Kettles!" he chanted gleefully. "What a funny name!"

His sister regarded him pityingly. "I think it's a very nice name," she announced, no doubt with an eye to tomorrow's expedition to the Prater. I watched them go, still arguing and giggling. The politeness had vanished for good, I suspected.

When the door was closed behind them and the patter of their running feet had receded into the distance, I sat down in front of my bedroom mirror and began to unpin my hair for the night. The looking glass was the most ornate I had ever been able to call my own, however temporarily.

Unfortunately, my eye was caught by its own reflection and I examined myself critically. My straight brown hair was straggling free of its pins; my skin was too pale and there were large, dark shadows under my eyes. I resembled nothing so much as a refugee from an infirmary.

On the other hand there was no sign now of my headache, and as I peered closer I thought I detected a slightly brighter light in my eyes. My eyes, I should say, I have always regarded as my best feature: unfortunately they are so weak that either I can't see out of them, or my spectacles hide and distort them.

Dissatisfied, I sat back and thought instead of the children. I sighed, for I suspected myself of softening towards them. Well, it was an interest in life, and those had been sadly lacking in recent years.

"Watch your back, Katie," I told myself severely. "Remember they are still the Enemy!"

CHAPTER TWO

During the time we stayed in one place, the Enemy's lively good humour persisted, so I grasped my opportunities and unashamedly picked their brains about the family. I confirmed that they were somewhat in awe of both parents, that they liked living in Vienna and Buda-Pest, but liked best to be at Szelényi Castle in Transylvania, with Grandpere.

"So you get on well with your grandfather?" I enquired, carefully neutral.

"Oh yes," said Anna. "He's quite fierce, but he likes us."

"I hope he does. Who else lives in the castle?"

"Aunt Katalin," said Anna, "and Uncle Mattias — but sometimes they live in Pest too. Like Aunt Maria."

"Don't forget Aunt Margit," Miklós added, and they giggled — at Aunt Margit, I inferred. Further digging elicited the information that Aunt Margit was dotty, but that this was all right because she was only Papa's half-sister.

I looked forward to Aunt Margit.

While in Vienna I saw as little of the Count and Countess as I had on the journey. The Count was busy on important Court business — he was the Emperor's best friend according to Anna — and the Countess was equally busy on no business at all. She only once found the time to spend an afternoon with her children, and that turned out to be momentous in many ways. It cast the Enemy into raptures, causing them to ignore their paid governess; it opened their governess's eyes to the precise depth of their worship of their beautiful mother — as well as to the illogic of petty jealousy in lonely spinsters; most of all, it gave me a few precious hours of freedom.

It was not exactly a gracious proposal on the Countess's part. Glancing back at me over her shoulder, a child clinging to either elegant sleeve, she said carelessly, "Do you want the afternoon off? You look as if you need it."

Needed or not, I jumped at it as my one chance to see Vienna unencumbered by my small enemies. Pausing only long enough to check my state of health in the mirror — I was in fact less pale than a week ago — I grabbed my old bonnet and sallied forth into the city.

I had a truly wonderful afternoon, for Vienna is one of the most relaxed and friendly cities in the world. Even the street corner loafers are decidedly unthreatening. Greatly daring, I spent part of my generously advanced salary on a new bonnet, which I wore at once — it was a rather frivolous affair of straw and green ribbons, not quite suitable to my position — and then wandered happily through narrow streets and grand avenues, watching the people and browsing in dark little book shops. I treated myself to *The Count of Monte Cristo*, which I had heard to be a rattling good yarn, and was just contemplating beginning it over a cup of delicious Viennese coffee, when the most momentous event of the afternoon occurred.

I was just walking, enjoying the people and the sunshine and my own anonymity, and reflecting on the good fortune that had brought me here. Then, as I rounded the next corner, I was pulled up short by the sight of a large gathering of people directly in front of me; I had been so lost in reverie that I had not been remotely aware of the low murmur of the crowd or even the loud, passionate voice speaking over it.

Intrigued, I moved closer. I could see a young man on some sort of platform haranguing the attentive crowd with much gesticulation. He looked like a student. Those I could see of the audience seemed to be mostly poor working people, factory hands and shop workers or the unemployed, with a scattering of the more respectable who might have been clerks or teachers.

Though I could not make out what the young man was saying, I had a distinct feeling that it didn't much matter since such large gatherings were illegal in Austria for any purpose. Nervously, I contemplated skirting the crowd and going on my way, but curiosity was ever my downfall.

I paused at the edge of the mob, straining my ears and craning my neck to see better, both in vain. The girl beside me — she was little more than a child and might have been a seamstress or a shop girl — shifted her position and bumped into me. She apologised at once, so timidly that I smiled reassuringly and took the opportunity to ask, "What is going on here?"

"The young man is making a speech," she answered helpfully.

"What about?" I asked.

"I don't know. I can't hear."

"We could move nearer," I suggested.

"It's better to stay on the edge of the crowd," she said with devastating simplicity, "in case the soldiers come."

I looked around me uneasily — I had a respectable position to keep after all — but this *was* my sole afternoon of freedom, of exploration and adventure. Prudence never really had a chance.

"Well, if I'm to be arrested," I said drily, "I'd rather know why," and began to ease my way through the throng towards the speaker. The crowd parted for me easily enough, even when I came right to the front, for there are few people who cannot see over my head.

"Heavens," breathed an awed voice in my ear, and I realized the timid girl had followed me after all.

The speaker was standing on a large, old wooden table which looked as if it had been carried out from the coffee-house across the road. My German was not yet good enough to understand all he was saying, but it was definitely a political speech, and a disgruntled one at that. I sighed, rather disappointed, and examined his face and dress instead: both were pleasing if unremarkable.

Much more remarkable, I found, was the other young man sitting on the edge of the table, idly swinging one leg. He was shabbily dressed and rough looking, with dark blond hair too long to be tidy and skin well browned by the sun. A working man, I guessed, with political aspirations.

"Do you know him?" my new acquaintance whispered, seeing the direction of my gaze.

I shook my head and whispered back, "Do you?"

"No, but I know who he is. That's Lajos Lázár."

I looked at her blankly.

"The radical," she said, amazed by my ignorance. "He writes articles in the liberal newspapers and he's a lawyer for poor people."

I blinked in some surprise and re-examined the subject in question.

"He doesn't look like any of the lawyers I've ever met," I said dubiously. He looked, in fact, inherently disreputable: young, lean and hungry.

"He defended my neighbour's son," the girl said simply.

I doubted he would be an asset to a man in the dock, but I kept my opinion tactfully to myself. By this time, I could see that one or two people were becoming decidedly irritated by our constant whispering — one huge man in a dirty black cap was glaring at me quite fiercely. However, my informant was not to be stopped there.

"*And* he's the one who got Ehlberg released."

I was obviously meant to know who Ehlberg was, and after a blank moment I did remember over-hearing the name in several whispered conversations during the last week. I gathered he was some sort of political prisoner who had just been released, to the joy of a few and the amazement of many.

By the time I had registered the implications of that, my companion was musing a little wistfully on her hero. "He's got such an attractive face, hasn't he?"

"It's an *interesting* face," I allowed. He had a wide, mobile mouth and prominent cheekbones, and etched around his eyes and forehead were surprisingly deep, weary lines. "Is he a friend of the speaker?"

"Probably. He might even speak himself."

She seemed quite excited by this. I, however, felt a stab of unease. I really was in rather unsavoury company, I suspected. To confirm it, I turned my attention back to the speaker, and listened with some disfavour as he did his best to stir up men and women who would suffer far more than he for any crime he incited them to commit.

I disapproved of rabble-rousing. Once, with my father, I witnessed a "small" hunger demonstration in Glasgow: I saw the ugliness, the desperation of the mob, and I saw the callous brutality with which it was squashed. I had no desire to see it again, anywhere.

I had already turned to my companion, ready to bid her a brief good-bye, when that odd instinct that tells us we are under observation made me look beyond her, straight into the eyes of the radical lawyer sitting on the table.

He showed no signs of embarrassment at being caught so vulgarly staring. Instead, he smiled, a slightly upward quirk of the lips.

I didn't know whether to be outraged or simply to smile back. As a respectable lady, the former would have been wiser, but he had one of those vital, arresting faces that somehow compels collusion.

However, before I could make up my mind, the speaker himself demanded his attention by flinging both arms out towards him and crying, "I give you my friend, Lázár!"

Shouts of applause greeted this. Lázár's smile died; his eyes released mine. Casually, he swung up on to the table, coming lightly to his feet beside the student — who clapped him heartily on the back before jumping down to lean on the table, facing him.

Lázár held up his hand for silence — and received it. Beside me, my companion held her breath. Well, he was an oddly imposing figure for one so shabbily dressed.

When he spoke, his voice was almost lazy, though deep and pleasing to the ear, with an accent at once unusual and familiar to me.

"He's Hungarian, you know," whispered my young companion.

I nodded: Lajos is the Hungarian for Louis.

He began: "I don't think Hermann has left me anything to say, but..."

The "but" was treated as a huge joke by the crowd, who roared their appreciation until Lázár, carelessly good-natured, again held up his hand for silence. Still half-poised for flight, like everyone else now I was quiet and waiting.

He stood at his ease on that rickety old table, much as if he was entertaining a party of friends in his own home, and began to speak easily, quietly, without any of the elaborate gesticulation or passionate outbursts indulged in by the student. Lajos Lázár did not harangue: he *conversed*, with friendliness and humour; he gave his opinion and answered questions that were thrown at him civilly enough but quite without awe by his avid audience.

It was this original impression of calm good sense that held me, at first from surprise and then from interest. So, though I had truly meant to leave, I didn't. I stayed to listen and that was fatal.

Of course, I still could not understand all that he said, but I grasped that he was urging some kind of unity against the injustices of a government that left so many poor and powerless in the hands of so few.

It didn't sound unreasonable.

I found myself straining to catch his meaning until gradually even the words themselves hardly mattered. It was the honesty, the *feeling* behind them that was important. And despite his deceptively casual manner, this man was deadly serious. There was anger in him, and a kind of restrained passion, and permeating everything, an air of excitement, a *knowledge* that soon we would be able to change things.

The emotion flowing from him began to sweep me along with it. I remembered the pinched, discontented faces of the poor that had stared at me so accusingly all across Europe, and I knew suddenly that I was wrong to bury my head in the sand. I knew that a better world had to be worth fighting for.

My breath caught in my throat. I felt *uplifted*, as if by a revelation.

And then I was dropped again with a bump. For, as Lázár listened to the rather unclear question of someone behind me, I saw his eyes shift suddenly beyond the crowd and stare at something in the distance, something he continued to watch as he spoke.

"I'm sorry. I'll have to answer you a bit later. There is plenty of time, so don't panic, but the soldiers are coming. You have to disperse now."

In Glasgow that day, I had never imagined that I would be one of a mob run down by soldiers.

My heart was lurching unpleasantly, even though Lázár was proving his point of "plenty of time" by continuing to stand on the table with an incongruous air of leisure, while the crowd, curiously silent now, pushed and swarmed and dispersed itself with agonizing slowness.

Still half-bewildered, I looked around for my youthful companion, but she had already fled. I was sure we both regretted my boldness.

Taking a deep breath, I moved decisively onwards, mingling as sedately as I could with the other scurrying, buffeting fugitives. As I passed the ridiculous platform, I heard someone cry urgently: "Lajos, for God's sake get down from there! You know it's you they really want!"

Involuntarily, I glanced up towards Lázár. He had crouched down on the table to speak to the student, but over the young man's head his eyes uncannily met mine. Again I beheld that funny, upward tug of the lips.

Someone pushed against me; I stumbled, and tore my eyes free, hurrying away with the melting crowd until I wondered where in the world I was.

It was fully half an hour before I could force my hands to unclench enough to hail a fiacre. Blindly, I stared out of the window at the passing houses, aware only of the scene I had just escaped, and of my own unforgivable reactions.

Oh, I allowed him to be convincing. I even admitted that he would be a positive asset to a defendant in court. It was just a pity he chose to waste, to *abuse* his undoubted talents in such a mean, unproductive way as this afternoon. Some part of me was still spellbound by his performance — no doubt the fault of my spectacles which continued to provide me with an all too fascinating, new view of the world — but the thinking part of me, the important part, angry at my common weakness, wished that I had jumped up there beside him and warned the people against him, for I knew him now to be a very dangerous man.

Regardless of rights and wrongs, I knew that if people followed him — and, God, how easy it would be! — it could only lead to violence.

CHAPTER THREE

Two days later, we left Vienna.

I was dreading the resumption of travel, but as it turned out we took the steamship up the Danube to Buda-Pest, and I found this to be a much more pleasant way to move around. So did the children. Though they had made the same journey several times before, it still excited them wildly, causing them to dash about from rail to rail, trying to chase each other and engage the crew or other passengers in conversation. It took the combined resources of Zsuzsa and me to prevent them leaping over the side in sheer high spirits. Their parents, needless to say, were relaxing below.

When the children's behaviour had calmed down to the extent of being no longer life-threatening, Zsuzsa wisely felt unwell and also retreated below. So, while the ship chuntered and puffed along the river, I sat the children down on a bench and read them a story. Peace lasted until we reached Pressburg — where the Hungarian Diet, or parliament, met — and took more people on board. The children watched the whole process of landing and departing with an intentness that bordered on supervision.

I watched too, for I was in Hungary now. The city seemed to be a handsome place, dominated by a square, strangely austere castle which glared down from the hill above the town.

When the crowd on the quay had waved us all off again, quite impartially it seemed, and we pulled away from Pressburg, on through flat, sandy countryside, I asked the children if they would like to go below.

"Oh no. We like it best on deck," Anna assured me. "We can watch the captain up there on his box."

"To make sure he doesn't do anything wrong?"

They giggled at that, and we decided to stroll round the deck — with the emphasis on "stroll". Nearly everyone we encountered smiled at the children. Some even nodded politely if distantly to me — my situation in life being all too evident, despite my frivolous new bonnet which, incidentally, had gone quite unnoticed by the Countess.

Needless to say, Anna and Miklós got quickly bored with this sedate behaviour, so I allowed them brief forays between myself and the rail. They were instructed not to run, but I watched them rather nervously all the same; horrible visions of explaining their loss overboard to the Count and Countess kept popping in to my head.

I quickened my pace as they bounded suddenly out of sight, only to discover when I caught up with them that they were doing nothing more dangerous than engaging yet another total stranger in their bright, precocious conversation.

Their victim this time was sitting on the deck floor with his back resting against the ship's rail and a book open on his raised knees. Such an unusual posture in an adult was bound to attract their interest.

I hurried over.

"Miss Katie, we've found Lajos!" Anna greeted me happily in French.

"Indeed?"

Their unconventional new companion turned his face up to me and smiled, a slightly upward quirk of the lips that was both peculiarly charming and immediately recognizable.

My breath caught. I knew a moment of pure panic, because of what he was and where I had first seen him, but then, ruthlessly, I squashed the upheaval and tried to look as staid as possible — I do that rather well.

He came to his feet with the same easy, casual movements I remembered.

"Mademoiselle."

Now I was looking up at him. Of little more than medium height, he was still considerably taller than I, slight in build and dressed carelessly enough to be called shabby with some justice. His eyes, I realized with surprise, were a warm, dark brown, contrasting oddly, though not unattractively, with his light hair.

"Lajos lives near us in Transylvania," Miklós informed me. I blinked behind my spectacles, but could think of no suitable comment. Lajos Lázár was still looking down at me.

"You were at the meeting," he remarked, "on Tuesday."

"No," I said coldly, regarding him with considerable suspicion. People do not remember me from crowds without very good reason. "I was *not* at the meeting. I merely stumbled across it in ignorance."

"Do you know Miss Katie then?" Anna asked with interest.

"No," said Lajos Lázár gravely, "but I would like to."

13

"She's our governess," Miklós said, with an air of pride that would have touched a less stony heart than mine. "From England — well, Scotland."

Lajos Lázár held out his hand. It was brown and sinewy and rough. Primly, I put mine in to it.

"Lázár Lajos," he said. Hungarians, I should point out, put their surnames first.

"Katherine Kettles," I responded politely, and slid my hand free. In fairness, he showed no signs of wishing to retain it. Men don't, as a rule.

"Are you going to Buda-Pest, Lajos?" Anna asked.

"Yes. Are you?"

"Oh yes. Will you come and see us there?"

At this point, Anna's amiable if impractical plans were interrupted quite unexpectedly by her father.

"Miss Kettles!" his voice thundered behind me. I think we all jumped, except Lajos Lázár. I certainly did.

"Sir?" I said neutrally, turning to face him. I would only once see him more furious than he was that afternoon. He was rigid with anger, his cheeks livid, his normally cool eyes flashing dangerously.

"A word, if you please," he ground out.

I took the silent children's hands and went to meet him.

"Take the children below," he ordered, "and then you may explain yourself."

I have never relished being spoken to in such a way, but in truth I was then too curious to be angry. Obediently, I took the children to an amazingly revived Zsuzsa, and rejoined the Count where he stood on deck, leaning against the rail farthest from Lajos Lázár.

He did not look at me as I approached, but began to speak immediately. "What do you mean by allowing my children to consort with that man?"

"I beg your pardon. I didn't know you would object, and they did appear to know him."

"Unfortunately, in the freedom of Szelényi, these things sometimes happen," he said bitterly. "But I will not have it, Miss Kettles! They are to have *nothing* to do with him — do you understand?"

"Perfectly," I said equably and he glanced at me with quick surprise, as if he had thought I would object. "They are your children, sir. "I am only the paid governess." Despite my tone this seemed to calm him a little. He almost smiled, so I ventured, "May I know why you object to him?"

"He is — unsuitable." The Count was tight-lipped again. "He is a peasant, rude, loud-mouthed, immoral and extremely stupid."

It was, I reflected, a fairly comprehensive denouncement, though I doubted if one could be a lawyer, however poor one's clients, if one were merely a stupid peasant. But then, since I knew Lázár to be, on the contrary, quite dangerously clever, I had already discounted the Count's opinion in its entirety, only wondering exactly what had provoked it. However, I simply nodded and was already leaving him when another thought occurred.

"Do the children know he is out of bounds to them?" I asked, and when he looked at me uncomprehendingly, added, "I was wondering if they acted out of disobedience or misguided friendliness when they spoke to him?"

The Count laughed, a harsh, short sound. "Oh, misguided, certainly."

"Then you wish *me* to explain to them that he is — unsuitable?"

"Of course," said the Count coldly.

Of course. The Szelényis had very fixed ideas of suitability — not all of them correct, as I well knew. For the first time I felt a hint of sympathy for the young radical. And then, was I not myself guilty of dismissing him in much the same way as the Count, simply from one half-understood speech? A man who helped the poor could not be all bad.

As evening approached, the unexciting, flat landscape on either side of us gave way to a low range of hills and later, more spectacularly, to mountains so close to the river's edge that they seemed to rise up out of it.

I abandoned the children to Zsuzsa — she was not the only one who could be diplomatically unwell — and settled myself in a quiet corner of the deck to drink in the beauty around me.

It was a wonderfully clear, balmy evening, causing the mountains to stand out magnificently against the darkening sky. I did not see how I could possibly sleep that night. There were few people on deck now, but somehow I was not surprised when someone came and stood beside me at the rail.

"Good evening," said Lajos Lázár, in English, oddly enough. "May I join you, or have you been forbidden to speak to me?"

I glanced at him uneasily. "I haven't, but the children have." All the same, my daring in talking to him at all was causing a distinct flutter in my stomach.

"A pity."

I was still determinedly watching the mountains, waiting for the next spectacular view as we rounded the river bend, but I felt his eyes on me. I suppose I was an odd sight in my drab dress and frivolous hat and spectacles — though I have to say I had never valued my glasses as much as then.

I knew I should make a civil excuse to abandon him — after all, I didn't want to lose my post just yet, and the Count's unequivocal view had been made quite plain to me. Anyone could see us here.

Yet when he said idly, "Have you been a governess for long?" I found myself answering promptly, "For nearly one month."

"Do you like it?" There was a note of genuine curiosity in his voice.

I shrugged. "They are good children in their own way."

"Is István a very demanding employer?"

His English was excellent, I reflected, and unlike the Count's almost without accent. On the other hand his manners appeared to be informal to a fault: I was sure Count Szelényi would not relish being referred to by his Christian name, not by this 'unsuitable' personage. My curiosity concerning his connection with the Szelényis grew apace. I glanced at him again. He leaned one arm on the rail, half-turned towards me, watching me with his disconcertingly direct gaze.

I found myself answering him truthfully, "No, not at all. My friends led me to believe that if I took a post as governess I would also be unpaid seamstress, secretary and general slave, so I suppose my life is actually remarkably idle."

"I think you'll find István's household already has plenty of seamstresses, secretaries and slaves, without recruiting you."

"Obviously I have taken an excellent post."

"Why *did* you take it?"

"Badness," I said on a sudden choke of laughter, quickly suppressed. "Curiosity. Necessity."

His lips curved slightly in the characteristic half-smile I remembered. Turning my gaze quickly back to the mountains, I pulled myself together and instinctively went on the offensive.

"And yourself, Mr. Lázár. Is there much demand for lawyers in Transylvania?"

Too late, I realized my mistake: without questioning others, I could not have known his profession. I bit my lip, but he answered easily, "Oh, plenty. Every landowner needs a legal adviser. Unfortunately, most of them do not value my advice."

"Why is that?" I asked lightly. "Aren't you a good lawyer?"

"It's not my legal skills they question. They object to my politics. They are afraid I shall incite the peasants to rise up in revolution against them."

I curled my lip. "So they forbid you to come within a hundred miles of their property?" I suggested rather insolently.

"Something like that."

"And Count Szelényi — does he feel the same way?"

"I'm sure he does, but he has a problem in keeping me away. My parents live on his property."

I looked at him in surprise. Stupidly, I asked, "What do they do?"

"My father works the land," Lázár said frankly. "He is a farmer."

I took this in slowly, eventually connecting it with Count István's contemptuous denunciation: *"He is a peasant."*

It seemed I was correct in my initial opinion of Lajos Lázár. He was indeed remarkable. He smiled slightly, and I had the uncomfortable feeling that he was reading my thoughts. I looked away, downwards at the river flowing past us.

More seriously now, I asked him, "Is it hard for you to find work?"

"I find more work than I can handle, but I suppose none of it is very lucrative, if that is what you mean. I have a permanent position as assistant to a lawyer in Pest. Kecskés is — sympathetic to my cause, so providing all my work is done in the end, he gives me leave to do more or less as I please." He shifted his position, turning more fully towards me. Unexpectedly, he added, "I wish you didn't disapprove of me quite so much."

"Mr Lázár," I said drily, "we are both well aware that my approval or disapproval makes absolutely no difference to you whatsoever."

He smiled slightly, his eyes unblinkingly on mine. "You're wrong," he said after a moment. "Besides, I want everyone on my side."

"I suspect you have a long way to go."

"True."

"And anyway, what makes you think that *you* are right, and all the people who oppose you are wrong?"

"Observation," he said promptly. I shouldn't have asked. "Come, Miss Katie, you are an intelligent woman — you cannot pretend that poverty and injustice do not exist, or that they are acceptable?"

"Of course not," I said coldly, even while I flushed at his unexpected use of the children's name for me.

"Well, it is equally obvious that they cannot be eradicated by perpetuating the same old political system we have now."

"I think more is likely to be achieved through existing systems than by agitating the people!"

"In Britain, perhaps," he allowed, straightening his back and placing both brown, working man's hands on the rail, "but here there is never any progress; in Transylvania even last century's land reforms were never implemented! Meanwhile, the Hungarian Diet meets every few years and achieves absolutely nothing because it opposes the King-Emperor's schemes on principle. The Lower House traditionally opposes every reform proposed by the Upper, and vice-versa, even when their proposals are exactly the same! Why? Simply to maintain their own power! Even when they finally agree on a principle, it is rarely, if ever, put into practice because the nobility runs the administration. In effect the nobles own the peasants as their subjects, and have so many privileges that for the most part they are reluctant either to abandon them or to extend them to others less fortunate."

He paused, then disarmed me totally by adding apologetically, "I'm sorry — I didn't mean to preach to you."

I smiled involuntarily. "I'm sure you can't help it! Besides, I didn't know about the Diet."

"Hungary is a backward country. We need political and social modernization, economic progress, land improvements; yet we only stagnate because the wealthy — that is, the nobility — are afraid to change things that have always provided well for them in the past."

"*All* of the nobility?" I asked, thinking of Count István and his father.

"Not quite. A few see the need for reform — even your employer on his

17

better days. Some, like Miklós Wesselényi — who went to prison for his beliefs — and Count Széchenyi, have been arguing the case for years."

By now I had forgotten the unwisdom of speaking to him, of being seen in his company. Frowning, I asked, "But what exactly do you mean by reform?"

"Ah," he said ruefully. "What *I* mean is not the same as what Count Széchenyi means. His ideas — capitalism, the ending of serfdom, a wider franchise — are only the beginning of what I believe to be necessary."

This was dangerous ground. I didn't really want to know the extent of his radicalism.

"It's your country," I said hastily, "but even so, stirring up the people as you did on Tuesday can only lead to violence, and in the end I believe it would change nothing."

"I wasn't trying to stir up the people, only to *wake* them up."

"It's the same thing."

"On the contrary. I don't want to hurt, Miss Katie, only to educate."

"*Educate?*" I scoffed. "You were *haranguing!*"

He smiled faintly. "Surely not. No, I really mean 'educate'. Some friends and I teach classes for workers, for poor people and the illiterate..."

"That's not 'education'," I interrupted indignantly, "it's 'indoctrination'. That I do find despicable. To take poor, uneducated people and fill their gullible heads with your nonsense..."

"Why are you so determined to quarrel with me? We teach people to read, Katie."

I dropped my eyes. "Oh."

"It's the first step," he said. "A basic right. Only when people can read can they learn properly for themselves. Until then, they must believe those who can, whether that is you or I or Prince Metternich. If I had not been able to read, I would never have known the existence of other forms of government, like Britain's or America's, never have heard of the Great Revolution in France."

"I suspect your country would have been better off if you hadn't," I said, rallying briefly.

"Touché," he acknowledged. "Am I preaching again?"

"Yes!" But still I couldn't leave it there. I glanced at him sideways. "So, revolution by education — is that your aim?"

"Yes. I believe it can be managed without violence."

"You are sanguine. And will *you* manage this revolution?"

"Oh no. I don't think I'm the right man for such a job."

"No? But I'm sure you know one who is."

He smiled and shrugged. "Perhaps."

Sometimes my own perception surprises me. I laughed. He watched me for a moment, still smiling a little in response, then asked, "Have I convinced you?"

"Of the righteousness of your cause? I reserve judgement. I am a newcomer here, after all, and a foreigner. But I'm afraid I very much doubt your bloodless revolution, however noble your motives or intentions."

He nodded. "It's a start."

I blinked. "Mr Lázár, I'm only an impoverished governess. Why are you trying so hard to convert me? Do you wish me to murder the Szelényis in their beds? For I give you notice — I won't!"

"I'm relieved to hear it."

I regarded him. "Am I to convert the Count's heir to egalitarian principles?"

"You are free to try, of course, but it might cost you your position."

"I should think it would."

I turned away at last from his humorous gaze, and for the first time in nearly an hour noticed the scenery. The mountains were further back from the shore now and we were coming close to a town with elegant towers and domes.

"Waitzen," said Lajos Lázár.

"It's beautiful," I said, meaning everything.

I felt him nod beside me, but he was silent, and that too suited my mood. Together we watched the town go by. The mountains, still some distance away, were more beautiful without it. I was almost afraid to move and disperse the dream. The man beside me stirred. I felt his hand touch mine lightly, briefly, yet the unexpected shock broke into my peace.

"Look," he said, and I turned quickly, following his gaze to the other side of the ship. I was amazed, for on this east bank of the river everything was flat, a dark, vast plain as far as the eye could see.

"How extraordinary!" I exclaimed.

He did not respond, so I looked at him, my mouth already open to speak again, but I closed it, for he was watching me with an odd intensity that made me only too aware that he was in fact utterly unknown to me. His rough, angular face was strangely attractive in the moonlight, and that made it worse.

I caught my breath. The flutter of panic I had felt when he first approached me returned now with a vengeance. I knew an instant of confusion, a dangerous tug of attraction.

"I must bid you good night," I said, a little too abruptly.

"Of course." He straightened his body from its relaxed pose against the rail. "Thank you for your company."

It seemed a peculiar civility in him, but I almost believed he meant it. I smiled a little uncertainly and began to walk away, but his voice stayed me. "Miss Katie?"

I glanced back over my shoulder.

He said, "I hope we meet again in Buda-Pest."

"I don't see any reason why we should," I said, and knew that already I was regretting it. Lajos Lázár was a little *too* remarkable for my peace of mind. For anyone's.

"You can usually find me at the Café Pilvax," he offered.

19

I smiled over my shoulder. "Thank you," I said sweetly, "for the warning." And I walked resolutely away. I was pleased to hear his soft, surprised laughter following me on the breeze.

CHAPTER FOUR

I knew to expect something wonderful of Buda-Pest, because my mother had told me — and I was not disappointed. As if I was coming home, I drank in the ancient, brooding splendour of Buda, with its great fortress on one side of the river and the new, bustling beauty of Pest on the other; and between them, the Danube itself, wide and majestic with tiny green islands scattered picturesquely into the distance.

As we drew in to the quay, the steam-ship let off a great whistle, a salute promptly returned from the shore, causing the children to jump up and down with delight. It also caused swarms of people to dash on to the quay. There was colour everywhere: the shore appeared to be full of superbly uniformed soldiers — who later turned out to be merely servants in livery; exotically dressed noblemen glinting with gold and jewels strode among peasants in pig-tails and gaily embroidered shirts selling their wares from huge baskets. I revelled in the sheer ostentation; my Presbyterian soul was tactfully subdued.

Naturally the children and I watched our arrival from the deck. Somewhat to my surprise we were joined by the Count and Countess. I had supposed their rank entitled them to be first off the ship, but I soon discovered that this was not their intention.

I saw the Count lift his hand in salute to someone on the shore, while the children swung in my hands like wayward puppies on the end of a leash.

"Uncle Mattias!" cried Anna suddenly. "Look, look, it's Uncle...!"

I should like to think it was my sharp tug to her hand that stopped her yelling like a diminutive fishwife, but I suspect it was her mother's chilly glare.

Though I tried, I could not make out which of the waving crowd were Szelényis. However, I had not long to wait, for barely had the ship tied up when two young people leapt up the gangway ahead of the officials whom they had presumably suborned earlier — a tall, well-built young man, dark and good looking and rather romantically dressed in a blue frock-coat laced with gold; and a very lovely, willowy young lady who moved with impossible grace inside her fashionably cumbersome petticoats. Both were laughing as they all but ran aboard and straight towards us.

It was fortunate that no one noticed me watching the greetings between these newcomers and my employers, for quite without warning I felt a lump in my throat that was almost bile, and the thought that kept going round and round my head, not just with bitterness but with utter rage, was, "*What a loving family. What a close, loving family.*"

The fact that their affection was obviously genuine only made it worse. This was what should have been my mother's, what my mother had been deprived of, coldly and deliberately.

It was the tight pain in my head that brought me back to my senses. Deliberately, I looked away from the family to the quay, forcing my muscles to relax, my eyes to see the cheerful throngs, and gradually, almost to my surprise, the pain subsided to a dull, manageable ache.

I wondered if the busy officials would allow Lajos Lázár ashore, or if he would have to swim for it.

I realized that I was laughing to myself at this entirely imaginable picture. Almost at the same time, I felt myself to be observed. Looking round quickly, I met the gaze of Count István's beautiful young sister who, I remembered, was called Katalin — curiously enough, for it is the Hungarian version of my own name. Unexpectedly, she smiled, even took a step nearer me.

"You must be the new governess," she said in French.

I inclined my head.

"Welcome to Hungary," the girl said with simple friendliness, and I, surprised by the unexpected courtesy, could only murmur, "Thank you, Mademoiselle"; but already she was turning back to her family.

People were going ashore now, greeting friends and family, directing the gorgeously attired servants about luggage. I found myself watching the departing passengers, but I saw no sign of my acquaintance, the amiable revolutionary. Only as we finally prepared to disembark ourselves did I catch sight of him, already on the quay, the centre of a noisy group of young men who were enthusiastically shaking his hand and clapping him on the back amid much noise and laughter. They had already begun to walk away by the time I noticed them. He didn't look back.

The Szelényi palace in Pest was even more magnificent than the house in Vienna. Of course, it was newer, built on spacious, classical lines, with elegant columns on either side of the front door, and a tall wrought iron gate — solely ornamental from all I ever saw, for it was never locked — to discourage the unwashed from wandering too close. It was run by a vast army of maids and wonderfully liveried menservants under the strict eye of an Austrian housekeeper unimaginatively called Frau Schmidt, and a fierce, charming old Hungarian simply known as Ferenc, who had once really been the soldier he still resembled.

I quickly discovered the sternness of these two to be a façade assumed solely for the benefit of the lower servants. Unlike their counterparts in Vienna — who had seemed more embarrassed by me than anything — Frau Schmidt and Ferenc never showed me anything but kindness and a friendliness that sprang originally, I'm sure, from compassion. However, my own gratitude for such unexpected consideration made me respond with uncharacteristic warmth, and the friendship between us was soon genuine.

So, although I ate with the children in the school room during the day, I dined every evening with Ferenc and Frau Schmidt in the housekeeper's private sitting-room, enjoying increasingly comfortable gossips; after which I would repair to my own cramped but comfortable quarters to while away the remains of the evening, reading novels or writing letters home to Aunt Edith and to the friends who were my only regret in leaving Scotland.

I suspect these letters were full of surprised glee at landing in so comfortable a position, with employers who barely noticed me, let alone plagued me with extra duties or excessive supervision.

I think it was the third day after our arrival when, not long before noon, a maid appeared with the request that I bring the children to the blue salon.

Having delivered her message, she scuttled off, which was most inconsiderate of her when I had not the remotest idea where to find such a room. It was Miklós who led the way along wide, scented and polished passages, past innumerable closed doors and wildly over-dressed footmen, until we finally arrived at the correct apartment — a spacious, elegant drawing-room decorated in a tasteful China blue, with a highly polished wood floor and a scattering of small, expensive Persian rugs. Here I made the acquaintance of yet another Szelényi, Maria, Count István's older, married sister, now Baroness Mirányi.

She and her sister Katalin, together with another most striking young woman, were visiting the Countess. While Baroness Maria hugged the children and questioned them about various things, I watched her rather curiously. Like all the family, she was handsome, a tall, statuesque lady who, I suspected, revelled in the description "formidable". There was nothing of Katalin's rather charming air of frailty about Maria. She was as strong as Count István. At the very least.

Eventually, her busy eye fell on me.

"This is the new governess?" she enquired in French.

The Countess turned her beautiful head towards me, looking slightly surprised to see me there. "Oh yes. Miss Kettles, from England."

"Scotland," Miklós corrected promptly.

Baroness Maria inclined her head graciously. I returned the gesture.

"You seem rather young," she observed.

"I am getting older."

She blinked. "I hope you have the proper talents — and experience — to teach my brother's children?"

"Really, Maria," the Countess said lazily. "You don't imagine we would have employed her if she had not? Her credentials are excellent. Sit down, Miss Kettles."

I had never been a weapon between sisters-in-law before. I decided to savour the experience.

Since Katalin politely gathered in her spreading skirts, I sat on the sofa beside her. The children hung around their mother, quiet but clinging — I had never clung so to my own mother, but then she had not left me to be brought up by other people. From this position, to my silent disapproval, they were somewhat casually introduced to the third visitor, Baroness Teréz Meleki.

I knew that name already from household gossip. She was the Countess's best friend, a wealthy widow and a quite famous hostess in political circles. I studied her with interest, for it was said she held pronounced liberal views and possessed great influence among Hungarian politicians, including the great reformers Kossuth and Count Széchenyi. It was difficult to tell her age, but though she lacked the Countess's classical beauty she was nevertheless a most attractive woman: her movements and her speech were languid to a fault, yet somehow she exuded power and intelligence. Naturally, she didn't so much as glance at me.

"So what are your plans for this afternoon, Elisabeth?" Maria was asking the Countess, who wrinkled her forehead distastefully.

"I have promised to call on Sofia Zolnay," she said, as one doomed.

"Oh dear," drawled Baroness Meleki, half pitying, half amused.

"Precisely, but I couldn't avoid it. I was hoping you might come with me, Katalin, to preserve me from annihilating boredom."

Katalin's unquiet hands suddenly stilled in her lap. "This afternoon? Oh, poor you, but I can't, Elisabeth. I promised the children I would take them on a picnic to Buda Hill."

This was news to me. It appeared to be also news to the children, whose expressions of joy were not unmixed with surprise. However, if the Szelényi ladies could not tell when one of their own was lying, I was not about to point it out to them.

"But you aren't dressed to go out, Miss Kettles," Katalin exclaimed in alarm when she eventually appeared in the schoolroom. "Aren't you coming with us?"

My suspicion grew that there was more to this outing than the desire to avoid Mme Zolnay.

"If you wish," I said equably.

"The children wish it too — don't you?"

Flatteringly, they assured me they did, so without fuss I fetched my pelisse and my bonnet — on which I was gratified to see Katalin's gaze linger just a little too long — and we set off.

Travelling in Hungary is an experience. The coachmen there believe in wasting no time on any *gradual* build up of speed: one moment you are still, the next you are jolted into flying motion. Flung back against the luxurious cushions of the Szelényi carriage, I made involuntary noises of alarm. Katalin only laughed.

"László is gentle," she said ominously. "You should travel in a fiacre."

Even in foul weather Pest looks bright, vital and handsome, and today the June sun displayed it in all its glory: wide, paved streets and large, curiously empty squares surrounded by white stone houses which dazzled me at first by their splendour; and modern shopping thoroughfares with brightly painted boards hanging over each shop to proclaim its purpose. Hurtling past these delights, we sped eventually down to the harbour area, where Katalin, in friendly spirit, pointed out the new chain bridge being built across the river to Buda.

"It was Count Széchenyi's idea," she told me. "He's our great reformer."

"It looks magnificent," I said with some truth.

"It will be when it's finished."

"But how do we get across now?"

"By the Bridge of Boats!" Miklós said gleefully.

I had visions of leaving the coach in Pest and hopping across the river from boat to boat, but in fact they were joined by rough, uneven planks over which vehicles could bump their way quite easily. Though the bridge was guarded by a toll house, László blithely drove us past it without stopping or even slowing down.

"Don't we have to pay?" I asked naively, looking back over my shoulder for angry pursuers.

"No," Katalin said simply. "Nobles don't pay tolls."

Of course they don't. Only the poor pay taxes here. Relaxing, I allowed myself to admire the river scenery, dominated, it seemed, by the huge fortress of Buda, at which Miklós now pointed excitedly.

"Papa is in there!" he exclaimed.

"Is he?" I said doubtfully.

Katalin smiled. "He is actually. He sits on the Vice-Regal Council which meets there."

I didn't need to ask what the Vice-Regal Council was. It was a kind of privy council consisting of important nobles who advised the King and implemented his orders — or at least such of them as they saw fit, for all Hungarians seemed to be rebellious by nature: it was just a matter of degree.

I hadn't known that István was on the Council. It seemed the Szelényis were a more important family than I had imagined...

"Shall we walk round the ramparts?" Katalin suggested to the children, "and you can show the views to Miss Kettles."

"Can't we have the picnic first?" said Anna.

"Oh no — you'll enjoy it much more after your walk."

Though this was meant to be a treat for the children, Katalin was being very firm about the order of our afternoon. I soon discovered why.

She airily dismissed the coach — leaving me to carry the picnic basket — and hurried us up to the castle ramparts, which had been converted into very pleasant walks with quite extraordinary views across the Danube to Pest and the vast, sandy yellow plain surrounding it. From here I could see the shape of the whole town, the neatly laid out squares and crescents of the inner city and the sprawling, yet cramped suburbs. I could even make out the scurrying, ant-like figures of the bustling citizens. I was impressed.

Nevertheless, we seemed to be the only people around. Anna and Miklós danced between Katalin and me, chattering and questioning, but Katalin was obviously distracted, answering vaguely, if at all, and leading us on at a cracking pace.

I could have done with consuming the contents of the basket before lugging it with me on a route march.

However, relief was in sight, in the shape of an army officer in a plain, white uniform, dawdling — *lurking* — in our path. Somewhat to my surprise, as soon as he saw us, he took his hands out of his pockets and came purposefully towards us. The mystery of Katalin's desire for our company — especially mine — became instantly clear. It was a Man. I should have known: with a girl of Katalin's beauty and charm there was bound to be a Man.

He did not seem to see the rest of us, but went at once to Katalin, who paused, flushing attractively and smiling straight into his eyes.

"Katalin," he breathed.

She recovered quickly, glancing surreptitiously at the children and me. With a creditable, if entirely futile, attempt at aloofness, she said, "Captain Zarescu! What a surprise."

I choked back my laughter as I saw the Captain take in the presence of two small children and one dowdy spinster. My visions of a dashing seducer from whose evil clutches I would eventually be forced to rescue her, were then dashed entirely, for the wretched man actually *blushed*.

Unless I have read all the wrong books, evil seducers do not blush.

I looked at him with more interest: tall and thin to the point of lankiness, he was raven-haired and fine featured with huge, deep-set dark eyes that were somehow unbearably sad. I could see his attraction.

"We're going to have a picnic," Katalin was rattling on, almost desperately. "Perhaps you'd care to join us?"

"Thank you, I'd love to," the Captain replied promptly, then hesitated. "That is, if there is enough to go round?" He spoke Hungarian fluently, but with an odd accent that was new to me. Assured of our abundance of victuals, he politely offered to carry the basket. I gave it up gracefully, and for the next fifteen minutes allowed myself to be used as planned — to occupy the children while their aunt occupied the Captain.

Our picnic, when we eventually stopped, was quite informal. We sat on a rug which Captain Zarescu took out of the basket and spread on the ground for us, and the children took great delight in setting everything out, while I admired the new view, stretching this time over the ancient walled city of Buda to the blue-tinted mountains beyond. In contrast with Pest, Buda seemed quiet, almost still, nestling cosily into the foot of wooded, vine-laden hills.

All this while the Captain looked slightly bemused, though not displeased at having to share his assignation with two small children and their governess. Of course, by this time, Miklós and Anna had charmed him and enrolled him in the massed ranks of their friends.

I regarded Katalin thoughtfully over my cheese, wondering just how she would prevent the children telling anyone who would listen — including their parents — about the jolly picnic with Aunt Katalin's friend the Captain.

She met my gaze briefly, at once pleading and conspiratorial. Of course, the children had nothing to tell, I realized. As far as they knew, we had met the Captain by accident, and nothing could be more open and respectable than this gathering. It was *my* silence she needed — and she knew it.

I couldn't quite understand her reason for making secret assignations at all. Captain Zarescu seemed quite unexceptionable to me: well-mannered, intelligent and obviously ridiculously in love with Katalin. I expected he was poor.

I decided to forget my role as silent governess for a while, and asked the Captain where he was stationed.

"Here in Buda," he answered.

"Have you been here long?"

"About a year, I think...?" He glanced automatically at Katalin for confirmation.

"A year and two months," she said with a smile.

"Is this where you met?" I asked casually.

"Oh no — we've known each other for ever! Alexandru's — Captain Zarescu's — family live quite near us in Transylvania."

That was a surprise; but it gave me another, not entirely improbable idea. "I don't suppose you know someone called Lajos Lázár?" I suggested.

The Captain's eyebrows flew up. "Why, yes, very well! Do *you* know Lajos?"

"Hardly. The children introduced us on the steam ship from Vienna."

"Oh dear," said Katalin uneasily. "István wouldn't like that."

"He didn't. But I don't suppose his objections extend to all M. Lázár's friends."

I smiled innocently as I said it, but they were busy exchanging unhappy glances. Count István obviously did have objections to Captain Zarescu, whether or not they had anything to do with the disreputable Lázár.

Having thus cast a blight on the proceedings, I swallowed the last of my cheese and reached contentedly for an apple.

I don't enjoy being used — not without permission. I consider it rude.

CHAPTER FIVE

"Miss Kettles," Katalin burst out, almost as soon as the schoolroom door closed behind Zsuzsa and the children. "I have to speak to you."

"Yes?" I sat down at the recently cleared tea table, regarding her expectantly and not entirely seriously over my spectacles. She walked slowly towards me.

"This afternoon — you — you suspect I planned it, to meet Alex — Captain Zarescu."

I sighed. "It's none of my business."

She sank into the chair opposite me, frowning. "I know I was wrong to drag you into it..."

"I would rather be asked."

"Of course. I'm sorry." She looked at me from under her long, tangled lashes. "Will you tell my brother?"

I said again, "It's none of my business."

"It's not even as if he's my guardian," she said eagerly. "I have a perfectly good father..."

"And would *he* approve?" I asked sardonically.

She opened her mouth, then closed it again and sighed. "No."

"I thought not. Oh, don't worry — I have no occasion to speak to either of these gentlemen about you. Why on earth should I?" Katalin almost sagged with relief, so I took the opportunity provided by her temporary weakness to satisfy my own curiosity. "I *would* like to know why you need to meet him secretly," I said as neutrally as I could. "Why is he so objectionable in your family's eyes?"

"Don't you know?"

I shrugged. "I suppose he is poor. And if he is a friend of Lajos Lázár, I presume his politics are — er — radical."

She sighed. "Both are true. *And* his father is a priest."

"So was mine," I said, amused.

"No, you don't understand. He is an Orthodox priest. Alexandru is Romanian."

Bewildered, I heard the tragedy in her voice. "Is that bad?" I asked naively.

"It is when I am a Magyar. Magyars despise Romanians as dirty, ignorant, lazy peasants."

I blinked. "I don't believe anyone could so accuse Captain Zarescu!"

"Of course not! He is a gentleman in every sense of the word! It is only antiquated prejudice. And, of course, the fact that Alex supports the Romanian nationalist movement makes it worse..."

"You mean you are forbidden to speak to him simply because of his nationality?"

"I may speak to him, I suppose, but I certainly may not marry him." Her tone held bitterness now as well as profound unhappiness. I felt an uncharacteristic wave of sympathy.

"You wish to marry him?"

"More than anything in the world. But they wouldn't let me, so all I can do is snatch clandestine meetings, like this afternoon's." She sighed again. "Do you think I'm behaving badly, Miss Kettles?"

"Yes, I suppose you are," I said, after a slight pause, "but to be honest, I don't see what else you can do that isn't worse."

Her face lit up with a quite enchanting smile. "I *knew* you would understand! I liked you as soon as I saw you! I can't think how István came to employ anyone so sensible!"

I shrugged. She was silent then for a time, deep in thoughts that were clearly not all pleasurable. At last, she looked at me again and took an audible breath. "I have no right to ask this of you, but — would you — perhaps — occasionally bring the children, and come with me to meet Alex? You see, I'm afraid Maria and István will get suspicious if I go out alone too often, and the children are such a wonderful excuse — there could be no talk against me if Alex and I were seen together with *you*, and them..."

I met her gaze steadily. "No," I said. "You have no right."

"But will you?" she persisted.

I looked away, considering. I had my own reasons for wishing to disoblige her father, but I rather liked Katalin and encouraging her affair was likely to lead only to her greater hurt. On the other hand, I suspected she was already in far too deep to avoid pain.

"How did you meet him?" I asked at last.

She smiled. "He used to come to Szelényi when I was a child. He went to school in Kolozsvár, you see, and became friendly there with Lajos Lázár. The Lázárs are our people. Alex stayed with them sometimes at school holidays, and that was when Mattias and I were always hanging around Lajos, whenever we could escape from the castle — pestering him, I dare say! But he was always kind to us, and patient; he told us lots of things about the countryside and the animals, things we never knew. Lajos was different then: less — frightening."

I was intrigued to hear that he frightened her; I wondered if István's excessive dislike stemmed from the same cause.

Taking off my spectacles and calmly polishing them on my skirt, I said neutrally, "Exactly how terrifying *are* Mr Lázár's politics?"

"Oh, impossibly! He is a *republican*, he would abolish the king, the nobility, break up the Empire — he'd abolish the Church itself! Have you ever heard of the Young Hungary movement? They are *outrageous* radicals, aiming at nothing less than revolution — they say the poet Petöfi is their leader, but Lajos is certainly one of them!"

Rather surprised by this passion, I put my spectacles back on and regarded her.

"And Captain Zarescu?"

"Oh no. Though I suppose he has some sympathy, feeling so strongly about the injustices of society. Anyhow, after we grew up, we didn't meet for years till one evening we ran into each other in the theatre foyer in Pest. I knew him at once — it's funny how instantly pleased I was to see him. Without thinking, I asked him to call — after all, he is an officer — and he did. Maria was polite to him, but I was advised not to encourage his *encroaching* ways — can you believe that?"

I could.

"Fortunately, Mattias began flirting with radical politics at university, and he met Alex in the Pilvax Café — which is where they all congregate to talk and swap their forbidden books! — and he used to bring him to the house sometimes."

She paused again. The Pilvax Café, I thought irrelevantly, was where one could usually find Lajos Lázár. Clearly it was a den of political vice, and to be avoided at all costs. Which was a pity in some ways, for although — naturally — I thoroughly disapproved of the enigmatic Lázár, I would not really have been averse to seeing him again. Accidentally, of course. It was true he disturbed me in some ill-defined way, but he also intrigued me, and I confess I wanted to know his opinion on a number of points, not least this of Magyar prejudice...

Katalin was saying, "There's no more to tell really. I fell in love with Alex and he with me, and when Mattias began to get wind of it he stopped inviting him to the house."

"His liberal politics didn't extend that far?"

"Only in thought," she said, with a touch of contempt. "In practice, he wouldn't dream of allowing a Romanian priest's son to marry his sister. I can't forgive him for that, you know. Whenever I remember it, I can't bear to look at him."

She glanced at me from under her lashes again. It was a charming trick — I'm sure men everywhere would have offered her the world for a look like that. "So will you help me?"

I, however, am female. And in any case I have always been immune. I regarded her thoughtfully.

"Why don't you just run away together? Marry him in spite of their disapproval."

Her eyes widened a little; she smiled. Her head even lifted as if she imagined herself proudly defying her family for love. But in the end, the smile died, and she shook her head ruefully.

"No; we couldn't. For one thing, my father would put a stop to Alexandru's career prospects. He's extremely vengeful about such things — I must tell you about my eldest sister one day..."

"Oh?" I said calmly, though my heart was hammering in my breast.

"Sofia. She was my half-sister, I never knew her, but Margit, my other half-sister remembers her. *She* ran away with a man my father disapproved of, and he *never* forgave her. He never spoke to her again, cut her off without a penny. And you see, that's my other reason — I'm not really *suited* to a life of poverty."

I pulled myself together. "Not even to be with him?"

"Oh, I'd try, but I know I would behave badly, and in the end, I'd drive him away. I have seen what irrational meanness can do to a marriage, to affection. *I* would do that, and I couldn't bear it."

I wasn't sure whether to despise her poor spirit or admire her unexpected insight. In the end I said only, "What happened to your half-sister, Sofia?"

"I don't know. He never speaks of her, but Margit thinks she's dead."

I looked away. "Do you never think to find out?"

"No," she said with devastating simplicity. "None of us knew her, except Margit. She chose her life, as I must choose mine. I hope she was happy."

How magnanimous, I thought bitterly, but Katalin was already repeating urgently, "So *will* you help me?"

I shrugged. "As well be hung for a sheep as a lamb," I murmured.

"I beg your pardon?"

"Very well," I said hastily, "I'll do it."

"You angel!" she cried, enraptured. "My dear Miss Kettles — oh the devil, I can't call you that now we are conspirators! May I call you Katie?"

"If you wish," I shrugged, but she was already dashing ahead.

"I'll move back here tomorrow — I usually do when István is home. Maria drives me mad after a few weeks."

I could believe it. My own endurance was considerably less.

"So," said Katalin brightly, "that should make everything easier."

Easier, I wondered, for whom?

Well, my life may not have been simplified by the shouldering of Katalin's problems, but it was certainly made more interesting.

We had a positive spate of educational outings: to the new national Museum, to the beautiful old Matthias Church in Buda, and to the observatory on the Blockenberg Hill. We also went on a few rather less improving visits to The English Lord, which sold the best bonbons in the two cities. On all these expeditions, Katalin came with us, and at some stage was always joined by Alexandru Zarescu. They had very little privacy for lovers, but for the moment at least, just being together seemed to make them happy.

What the family thought of Katalin's sudden penchant for the governess's company, I never found out. Frau Schmidt never said anything either, but as time passed and she came across Katalin in the school room more and more often, her expression of surprise was not entirely free of disapproval. Katalin, naturally, never noticed.

Then, disaster struck.

I was waiting for the children to finish the work I had set them, occupying my time by gazing out of the window at the sand storm rushing down the street. Pest is subject to these commotions, when the sand blows off the Great Plain and into the town, sometimes totally obliterating the streets for minutes at a time. The storms leave little piles of sand everywhere — even inside the house if you're not fast enough in shutting the window, as I had learned from experience.

I enjoyed watching this phenomenon, so I was not entirely pleased when Katalin came bursting in to the schoolroom. Naturally, the children were immediately distracted and I had to speak to them severely to make them continue, before dragging Katalin to the other side of the room to let her tell me her problem.

"He can't come today," she said tragically, waving a letter in front of my eyes and then snatching it back as she recalled the private nature of its contents. I hadn't known they wrote to each other as well — they really were indiscreet.

"Can't he?" I said with a touch of impatience. "Never mind — it's happened before. You'll see him tomorrow or the next day instead."

"No." She shook her head; tears were glistening on the ends of her lashes. "He's going away."

"Away? Where?"

"Oh I don't know — Vienna, I think. Only for a few weeks, but it seems so *long*, Katie!"

"Well, *when* is he going?"

"Tomorrow morning. He says I can send him a letter tonight at the Pilvax Café..."

The Pilvax again. Meeting place of radicals and revolutionaries. I gazed a little blindly at the children, trying to talk myself out of it. At last I said, "Where had you planned to go tonight?"

"Oh, some party, but I've already cried off. I can't face it. I said I had a cold."

She wasn't a very credible liar — I had never seen anyone look healthier. I regarded her thoughtfully. "Then you could go to the Pilvax," I said.

She stared back at me. "Go to the..." she began in amazement, and broke off. "Seriously?"

"Seriously. Who would know you?"

"Mattias if he's there! But no, he's going to that party with István and Elisabeth."

"Well then," I said reasonably.

31

I heard her breath catch. "I could, couldn't I?" she murmured. I nodded, and she seized my hand. "You'd come with me, Katie?"

"I suppose I'd better, to save your honour."

Her honour, at the expense of mine, I thought wryly. At least in my own eyes.

I had dinner as usual with Ferenc and Frau Schmidt, excusing myself early on the grounds of letters which had to be written. I was becoming an adept liar.

My one evening gown was quickly donned. It was no longer new and, as Aunt Edith had pointed out when I had insisted on buying it, it was quite impractical, being made of cream-coloured silk, but I had always liked it for it was both simple and elegant in shape, innocent of the excessive flounces so much in fashion, and with only moderate petticoats. And, now that I seemed to have recovered my health and spirits, its paleness brought out the colour in my cheeks in a way I thought not wholly unattractive.

In a fit of vanity, I threaded a bright red ribbon through my hair, and was rather doubtfully admiring its effect in the glass when Katalin burst into the room, resplendent in her plainest evening gown — which, of course, cast mine into the shade in any terms you can think of — and holding a velvet cloak over her arm.

"Are you ready, Katie? Do hurry!"

I met her eyes in the mirror and sighed. "Do you really want the entire household to know that you left the house with the governess at this time of the evening? I think that might be carrying eccentricity too far."

"Oh."

No doubt her maid had dressed her too, in the full knowledge of her "cold" and her refusal to attend tonight's party.

"Quite," I said. "Can you — er — *creep* out? Wait for me round the corner and we'll find a fiacre."

In Buda-Pest, fiacres are rather smart vehicles drawn by two surprisingly small horses. Unfortunately, in the spring and summer they are open carriages, so we had to trust in the darkness and Katalin's hood to hide her memorable countenance.

"The Pilvax Café," I told the driver as we got in, and he seemed to know where I meant.

We bounded into motion, leaving my stomach well behind. It was only a short drive, which caught me unawares, for I had just had the belated thought that two unaccompanied ladies entering such a place — exactly what sort of a place was it? — might well be leaving themselves open to unwelcome interest or even insult.

However, situated in a broad, tree-lined boulevard, it looked respectable enough from the outside. Katalin showed an irritating tendency to cling to me as, typically, she left me to pay the driver.

"Do you think we should?" she whispered.

"He's your lover," I said baldly. "Make up your mind."

I almost thought she would back out; I found I was holding my breath, but as the fiacre sped off in a cloud of dust and sand, she straightened her shoulders and marched forward. I couldn't help feeling it would have been a shocking anti-climax to have crept cravenly home.

A liveried doorman bowed to us respectfully as he ushered us in. Though I looked at him quite hard, I could see no speculation or disapproval in his face, so I murmured thanks and swept past him.

Both coffee-house and restaurant, the Pilvax was a large, open hall with vaulted ceilings, bright and well-lit. Tonight it was busy, but I was relieved to see the company did not consist solely of men. In fact it seemed to be quite unexceptionable, even fashionable, despite the few threadbare coats I spotted in among the sartorial elegance.

A waiter hurried to meet us.

"Captain Zarescu?" I asked him, since Katalin appeared to be temporarily dumb.

"Certainly, Madame, this way, if you please," he said cheerfully, and much to my relief. He led us towards one of the long tables, at which a group of young men sat with the remains of a meal and some wine, and various pieces of paper scattered about. With the aid of my invaluable spectacles, I picked out the Captain quite easily.

He was idly playing with the stem of his glass and smiling faintly at the man next to him when the waiter spoke to him. Not unnaturally, his face expressed surprise as he looked up at us — but that was nothing to his amazement when he saw who his uninvited guests were.

His chair ground on the floor as he swung it back and stood up. Two strides brought him to us and his hand was almost crushing Katalin's.

"Why, what is this? What brings you here?"

Meanwhile I was quickly scrutinizing his companions. Some of them glanced at us with only minor curiosity; some didn't even stop talking. They were a mixed looking group, but only Captain Zarescu was in uniform. The others were plainly and rather casually dressed for Hungarians, without any of the emblems of nobility which I had become used to.

Lajos Lázár, I had realized at once, was not among them. I didn't know whether to be relieved or disappointed, but something had gone from the evening.

Katalin was saying almost brokenly, "You're going away. I was distraught — and then Katie had the idea that instead of sending you a letter here, I should come..."

The Captain shook my hand warmly. "You are a good friend indeed, Miss Kettles. Come, will you join us here? Shift up there, Petöfi, make way for my guests!"

The young man thus addressed glanced up from a spirited argument with his neighbour, and immediately came to his feet. He was a slight, good-looking youth with curly black hair and extraordinarily sparkling dark eyes; but uneasy bells were already ringing in my mind — was Petöfi not the name of the revolutionary leader of "Young Hungary"?

"Allow me to present Sándor Petöfi," said Zarescu, confirming my suspicion. "He's our greatest living poet — or so he tells us."

Either by accident or design, this sally cleverly glossed over the problem of Katalin's identity, for by the time we had all duly smiled at the joke and been divested of our cloaks and ushered into seats between Zarescu and Petöfi, the moment for introductions was past.

"I've never met a poet before," I said cautiously to my new acquaintance, "or, at least, not a good one."

"I am *very* good," grinned Petöfi. "Though I will be better yet."

"What kind of poetry do you write?"

"Oh, whatever I think about. I write about the people, about my country, about injustice — perhaps you have read some of my work?" he asked confidently.

"Not yet," I said tactfully. "But I would very much like to." One has to be civil.

"I would send you some," Petöfi said regretfully, "but unfortunately, I leave Buda-Pest tomorrow."

"Petöfi is off in pursuit of love," Captain Zarescu explained, pouring some wine for Katalin and myself.

"They mock me," Petöfi complained.

"Nonsense — we're trying to keep your spirits up."

"My spirits *are* up. Parental opposition is only there to be overcome."

I glanced meaningfully at Katalin, murmuring, "Good luck."

Remembering the reason for our visit here, I turned back to Petöfi to allow the lovers some private conversation. It was no strain. Petöfi was an immensely charming young man who spoke with enormous, nervous energy and a rather stringent wit, though permeating all his conversation was a sound lack of respect for authority. However, he was serious about three things. One was his love, a lady called Julia who resided in Transylvania and whose parents disapproved of Petöfi's suit on the grounds of his poverty and lack of definite prospects. Julia herself was apparently impervious to these faults and as determined to marry as he.

His second serious love was literature, which he discussed with great enthusiasm and knowledge, and his third the rather nebulous concept of the Hungarian people. After some time I was both baffled and dazed by him, but in an odd way I found I liked him.

However, since this was to some degree Petöfi's farewell dinner, I felt a little guilty about monopolising him, so eventually I turned away and touched Katalin's arm.

"How long should we stay?" I murmured.

"Just a bit longer," she said brightly. Her self-confidence had returned with a vengeance. I sighed and looked around me. Between me and the door were a lot of people eating and drinking. Huddles of young men were in serious conversation; others were in gales of wine-induced laughter. I wondered what Aunt Edith would say of it. I knew exactly what my father would have said, God bless his Presbyterian soul. Even after several months, it's odd how grief can hit you again out of nowhere with the same, devastating force. Appalled, I fought to control my weakness. I was aware of a slight commotion by the door, so I concentrated on it blindly, slowly blinking away my emotion until the blur cleared, and through it, standing by the door, I saw Lajos Lázár.

CHAPTER SIX

He was with another young man, exchanging greetings with the noisy group by the entrance, the same half-smile I remembered on his full, rather sensual lips. He was dressed almost in the same way too, certainly no better, and the same battered bag he had carried on the steam-ship was slung over his shoulder.

I heard someone at our table say, "Petöfi, there's Lajos now."

At that, Petöfi immediately broke off his conversation and stood up, stepping round the table and shouting out uninhibitedly, "Hola! Lajos — over here!"

I watched as Lázár lifted a hand in quick acknowledgement and began to make his way towards him.

Petöfi said, "I thought you were going to miss my farewell!"

"Farewell?" Lázár repeated, carelessly taking Petöfi's outstretched hand. "I thought you had decided not to go abroad after all."

"I'm not going abroad. I'm touring Hungary."

"Ah. You're going to Transylvania."

"Naturally! I *will* marry her, Lajos, whatever you think. Won't you wish me well?"

Lázár's rather serious expression relaxed into a smile. "Of course I wish you well, you idiot, and all the luck in the world."

Petöfi grinned and suddenly embraced his friend; and over the poet's narrow shoulder, Lázár met my interested gaze.

I pushed my spectacles more firmly on to my nose, forcing myself to wonder dispassionately if he would remember me. It seemed he did. Released, he clapped Petöfi lightly on the shoulder and then, although I saw him acknowledge Zarescu and register the improbable presence of Katalin, he came straight to me, holding out his hand with casual courtesy.

Wordlessly, I put mine into it, felt again the pressure of his strong, brown fingers and the same strange, electric excitement his touch had produced in me on the ship. Shaken, I found it hard to meet his dark, direct gaze.

He said gravely, "It's good to see you again." I managed to incline my head with a trace of my old mockery. "Even," he added, "if only in the guise of Katalin Szelényi's chaperone."

I lifted my brows. "What did you expect?"

His fleeting smile came and went. "I never know what to expect of you, Mademoiselle — it's one of the reasons I like you."

I felt the colour creep into my cheeks — I am unused to compliments, however unconventionally given — but fortunately he released my hand as he spoke, and turned to greet Katalin, who had been struggling between relief at escaping his attention and indignation at losing precedence to the governess.

With interest I noted that he did not embarrass her by shaking hands. I also saw that it was she, not he, who was made nervous by the encounter. Watching her face as she returned his civilities, I realized that she was indeed afraid of him. He was out of his *place* and threatening hers in a way that Zarescu — however he might have agreed politics with Lázár — never would, nor could.

A waiter appeared with more glasses and another bottle. At the other side of the table Petöfi talked to the young man who had come in with Lázár. I heard him say, "What the devil were you two up to, Vasvári?"

"Don't ask," the other advised. "And if anyone else enquires, we were here all evening!"

I was aware of Lázár throwing himself into Petöfi's vacant seat beside me. Suddenly, I felt both exultant and afraid. I wondered vaguely if my hand would shake when I picked up my glass. It didn't.

Lázár reached for the bottle and poured himself some wine. I took a sip of my own, declining his polite if silent offer of more. He tipped half the glassful down his throat in one quick, surprising movement, and I felt his eyes on me. I forced myself to meet his gaze.

Unpredictably, he said, "You look very beautiful tonight."

Warm blood flooded into my face and neck. Part of it was shame, for I had *wanted* to look pretty.

"Nonsense," I retorted. "I look as I always look."

"Not quite. I've never seen you before without that dashing hat."

Unexpected laughter bubbled up. "It *is* smart isn't it?" I agreed cordially.

"Does it annoy your employers?"

"To be honest, I don't think either of them notice what the governess wears. Which is probably just as well." I took another, more confident sip of wine.

"And Katalin? I gather you have been recruited as chief conspirator?"

"I felt sorry for them."

"You'll lose your position," he warned. "Neither of them is known for discretion."

"I know. I'm teaching them."

"By coming to a place like this?"

"It may be busy, but I'm sure no one who comes here has ever *heard* of Katalin."

He looked amused. "The odd liberal-minded aristocrat makes his appearance, you know. I can see at least two from here."

"Oh dear," I said, genuinely alarmed, "and I thought I was being clever."

"I shouldn't worry. Most people only see what they expect to. Your Hungarian, by the way, is excellent."

"So is your English," I said, reciprocating civilly. "My mother was Hungarian. What is your excuse?"

"I went to England a year or so ago. And Scotland." There was a kind of humorous challenge in his eyes as he added provokingly, "I thought your people, on the whole, more egalitarian in spirit than the English."

"*A man's a man for a' that,*" I murmured, smiling faintly.

"*For a' that and a' that,*" said Lajos Lázár in almost perfect Scots. "*Their tinsel's show, and a' that, The honest man, tho' e'er sae poor, Is king o' men for a' that.*"

I put down my glass. "Mr. Lázár, you never cease to amaze me."

"I try."

I regarded him, a million questions jostling for priority inside my head. After a moment, I took a deep breath and said, "Mr. Lázár. May I ask you an intrusive, personal question?"

His lip twitched. "I thought you'd never get around to it."

I ignored that. "How did you manage to become so well educated?"

"I read a lot," he said flippantly.

"I mean in the beginning."

"I went to school and I worked hard."

"That doesn't give you a degree in law."

"No, the University of Pest gave me that."

"Is it usual for — for..." I broke off, floundering.

"For peasants to go to university?" he suggested. I looked at him uncertainly, but he didn't seem to be in the least offended. "No, it's not usual. I had help. Count Szelényi, István's father, paid my fees. He also let me share István's tutor for a couple of years before."

I stared. "So you and István were actually educated together?"

"For a time."

I frowned, taking another sip of wine. "Is that why he dislikes you so?"

"It's one reason."

"You were cleverer than he was."

"And younger. And a peasant."

Suddenly I could imagine István as an arrogant boy, bewildered and humiliated by the superior intelligence of the rough, precocious upstart thrust upon him. His behaviour concerning Lázár made much more sense to me now, though it raised another question.

"I don't understand *why* Count Szelényi did all this for you."

"I asked him to."

I said carefully, "He's not known as a biddable man." Nor a compassionate one. Who knew that better than I?

Lázár reached for the bottle and refilled his glass. This time he didn't ask, but simply refilled mine too. For the first time, I thought he was reluctant to speak. At last, he looked back at me.

"I had force on my side," he said lightly.

I took a sip, meeting his gaze over the rim of my glass, perversely reluctant to leave the matter, when he so obviously wished it left. "What force could a peasant boy have against a great lord?" I enquired sardonically.

He shrugged. "A threat. Blackmail, if you like."

I felt my eyes widen.

He smiled. "Are you shocked?"

"Yes, I believe I am," I said, finding my voice with difficulty.

"Well, he could afford it, and my father certainly couldn't. Don't you want to know what I threatened him with?"

"No," I said firmly.

"I wouldn't tell you if you did. He kept his bargain, after all."

"So you're not completely amoral?"

"Far from it. I have lots of morals: it's just that they lapse slightly from time to time." His lip twitched again. "On the whole, I am extremely trustworthy."

"Trustworthy?" Petőfi interrupted suddenly at my side. "How can you say so when you've just stolen my chair?"

"You said you were going to Transylvania."

"Not till tomorrow, damn you! Trust you and Zarescu to monopolise the most charming ladies in the Pilvax."

"You must make allowances for Zarescu — he's being sent to Vienna tomorrow."

"Well, that will teach him to be a government lackey," said Petőfi tolerantly.

"Precisely," said Lázár, pushing the bottle past me towards the Captain. Katalin was looking indignant, but her lover only grinned as he poured himself some more wine. I gathered it was an old joke.

The rest of the evening passed in something of a whirl. I seemed to be surrounded by several simultaneous discussions ranging over the literature, philosophy and politics of many countries; and I quickly became fascinated, as much by the erudition of these very young men as by the speed with which they threw ideas around and their bewildering shifts between intellectual debate and witty banter. Away from their company I might have reservations about their particular brand of idealism, but here among them I found it oddly attractive. I even found myself drawn into one of their hectic discussions, for though I had never felt my ignorance quite so much, I have always been able to think for myself. At one point, I even grew quite heated, which is hardly the image of myself I generally choose to portray, but no one seemed to think the worse of me for it — in fact, I found Lajos Lázár on my side and felt curiously proud.

I noticed too that Lázár himself, although not the loudest or the most frequent speaker, was always listened to by the others, even Petöfi, whether or not they agreed with him.

When we finally rose to leave, Zarescu came with us. Lázár, who was then taking vast quantities of pamphlets from his bag and giving piles of them to various acquaintances, only glanced up at the Captain's call of farewell and waved. I couldn't help but feel a little piqued by his casual attitude.

And then, moving towards the door, I found myself hoping suddenly that there were no secret police in the café, though I could think of few better places for them to work, judging by the highly seditious nature of the evening's conversation — much of it had been to do with radical French writers whose works were forbidden in the Empire but which were still intimately known by Lázár and his friends.

A moment later, I had more personal cause for anxiety, for as I prepared to follow Katalin outside, I felt a light touch on my arm. Turning quickly, I found Lázár there.

"A gift," he said, with his fleeting smile, and I felt his fingers on mine, pressing them round a thickness of paper. Before I could even register the shock, he was hurrying back to his friends.

This time I went first into the house, blithely ignoring the porter's inquisitive gaze. I met Ferenc on the stairs, but if he was surprised, he chose not to show it. I only bade him a cheerful good night and went on up to my bedroom.

Once there, I cast off the concealing cloak and lit the candle on the desk. I opened my reticule and took out the pamphlet Lázár had given me. Slowly, I sat down in the pale, flickering light and began to read.

It was a curious document entitled, "In defence of work" by L.L. The title page was fully printed, but the inside pages had only printed decorative borders; the actual words were written by hand. An ingenious method of eluding the censor while producing work that looked both eye-catching and respectable.

Lajos Lázár wrote as I had heard him speak — with a powerful fascination. It was clear, intelligent, humorous and totally absorbing. Even I, staid and disapproving, actually *enjoyed* reading it. It began as a defence of the dignity of the working man and his right to work, pleading for better living standards and education; then progressed to a moving comparison of a poor, honest labourer, exhausted by his efforts to acquire a meagre crust for his family, with a fat nobleman wallowing in more money than he knew what to do with and which he had done nothing whatsoever to earn. And by the end, it had become a hilariously cruel denunciation of that nobleman as a useless parasite, and a spirited demand for the abolition of all unearned wealth and privileges from the king's downwards. It seemed no one escaped his criticism. Even I began to feel guilty.

"Phew," I murmured, as I finished reading. I wondered if Lázár could go to prison for this. It seemed likely. And there he was in the Pilvax which was *known* as the haunt of radicals, blatantly handing these round like cakes at a children's party.

And how long had it taken him to write them all by hand? Even with help. There had been hundreds in his bag!

For a long time, I stared blindly at the leaflet, thoughts chasing each other round my head. At last, the candle began to gutter, and I moved to light another. Then I put the pamphlet carefully away inside "The Count of Monte Cristo", which I replaced on the bookshelf beside my bed. I thought I should probably have burned it.

It must have been shortly after this that the Countess, in an erratic sort of way, began to command my presence when she occasionally took Miklós and Anna visiting with her — thus enjoying all the benefits of her children's company without any of the attendant trouble.

I can't say I enjoyed these morning calls to the splendid palaces of Pest, but at least I was permitted to see, if not actually meet, some of the cream of Hungarian nobility, including the great reformer, Count Széchenyi. At this time, he was still a towering figure in Hungarian politics, although he was already somewhat eclipsed by his rival, the more flamboyant and extreme Kossuth. I thought him a melancholy man, and not entirely stable.

I also 'saw' Count Batthyány, who was the Opposition's choice for leader of the Upper House in the forthcoming Diet which was to meet in the autumn. Naturally, he was encountered at the home of the dazzling widow, Baroness Teréz Meleki. A balding man with a magnificent beard, he had both presence and wit.

As the Countess sat down beside him, her friend said, "The Count was just telling me how important it is that Kossuth be elected as Deputy for Pest."

"Indeed? How interesting," said the Countess, quite patently bored. Not for the first time I wondered what on earth these two friends had in common: the one living for politics which sent the other straight to sleep.

"And of course, he is right," Baroness Meleki drawled, smiling at Batthyány in such a way that I was reminded of a beautiful but predatory cat — had

Frau Schmidt not hinted at something scandalous in her private life...? "We all know Kossuth is the only one with enough drive and popularity to succeed."

"He'll be elected," Batthyány said confidently.

"I understand he is also the choice of the young radicals. With *their* support, I suspect he can't lose."

At that, I pricked up my ears, for I had often wondered what influence, if any, Lázár and his friends actually had.

"Ah." Batthyány regarded her doubtfully. "I don't think we really want to encourage such a connection. It would too easily drive away influential moderates — such as this lady's respected husband, for example." He indicated the Countess with a gallant bow.

"Oh nonsense, Count. Elisabeth, surely the support of a few writers and poets would not turn István against Kossuth?"

"No," said the Countess flatly. "István can't bear the man under any circumstances."

In my corner, I choked back a laugh. I felt oddly proud of her: she was certainly not influenced by her company! Baroness Meleki, however, looked quite irritated.

Batthyány only smiled benignly, saying, "I have hopes of bringing him round. Kossuth is a hard-working man, you know, and I believe only he can put us on the right course to reform."

I wondered. I recalled that first conversation with Lajos Lázár when I had mockingly asked him if he planned to lead his revolution. I wondered what he thought of Kossuth in the role. However, I soon had more immediate things to think about, for in the carriage going home that afternoon, the Countess surprised me again.

In fact she deprived me of speech by saying suddenly through the children's chatter, "Do you know what ails my sister-in-law?" Appalled, I could only stare dumbly at her. "I mean Katalin," she said impatiently, fortunately misreading my hesitation. "She is out of spirits. Nervous. I was wondering if you knew why."

I had always suspected that someone would notice Katalin's state sooner or later. Yet I hadn't expected it to be the Countess. "She spends an inordinate amount of time in the schoolroom," she went on. "And I can find no reason for such an unlikely haunt unless she is pouring out her woes to you."

I pulled myself together. "She talks to me, yes," I said uncomfortably. For the first time that I could remember, the Countess was holding my gaze.

"Is she still hankering after that Romanian officer?" she asked bluntly.

I blinked. "Yes," I said truthfully, "I believe she is."

The Countess looked away, out of the window. "It won't do, you know."

I said nothing, for I was feeling so guilty that it was all I could do to stop myself from wriggling. It was one thing to help Katalin, even to go against her father. It was quite another to *deceive* the people who employed me and who had certainly never done me any harm. Besides, rather to my surprise, I had developed a curious sympathy for the Countess; she seemed vaguely unhappy, drifting discontentedly from place to place, without aim or object or the ability to change. Even her affection for her children was frustrated by the custom which dictated they be brought up largely by servants.

"It won't do," she repeated.

"I know," I said quietly.

How had I got myself into this position? By my own foolishness, and not all of it had been good-natured...

CHAPTER SEVEN

That Sunday, I found myself high in the hills above Buda, sitting on the terrace of a tiny, secluded inn, sipping sweet, local wine while the warm breeze blew my hair against my cheek, and I idly watched Lajos Lázár flick through the pages of a book.

As if to rub salt in my wounded conscience, the Count and Countess had generously granted me the whole of the day to myself, while they took the children on an overnight visit to friends in Pest County. Ungratefully dismal, I had thought I might go to church. I was still slightly confused as to how I had got here instead, but I had long since stopped worrying about it. Rather, replete after a simple, hearty lunch, I leaned back in my seat, sighing contentedly, letting the peace of the place flow over me.

It had been Zsuzsa the nursery maid, already dressed for travel and looking conspiratorial, who had brought me news of my visitor that morning, even before I had put the last pin in my hair.

"There's someone to see you," she had whispered, regarding me with a new respect. "In the Little Room." I had time for a quite startling vision before she added, "Do you know where I mean? The small room on the ground floor, next to the servants' stairs."

Relieved, but still curious, I followed her out and hurried downstairs to greet my visitor. I presumed it was Captain Zarescu unexpectedly returned, or someone with a message from him, though why it should come to me rather than Katalin herself, I was at a loss to understand.

I found the Little Room easily enough. It was an excellent place for a secret meeting, being quite unused by the family and close enough to the servants' quarters to enable easy access — or departure — from there. I opened the door quietly, and was immediately brought to a halt by the sight of Lajos Lázár. He was perched on the curly legged table which stood in the middle of the room, idly swinging one foot and reading a book which lay open on his knee. He looked up as I came in, and smiled.

"Good morning," he said, closing the book with a tiny snap.

I recovered quickly, shutting the door behind me. "I had not realized," I said sarcastically, "that you were on visiting terms with the Szelényis."

"I'm not," he agreed, "but I have friends in the household. I grew up with some of them."

I should have known. "Including Zsuzsa?"

"I pushed her into a pond when I was six. When I was ten, I stole oranges for her."

"And now you are — what? — twenty-eight...?"

"Twenty-five. Yesterday."

"Happy birthday," I said politely. "So now you are so old, *she* runs errands for *you*?"

"I regard it more as a favour than as an errand." He slid his hip off the table and came towards me.

Curiously, I asked, "Don't you find your place in life rather — confusing?"

"No," he said simply. "But I'm sure others do. I brought you this." Wordlessly, I took the proffered book from him. It was a slim volume bearing the legend *Petöfi Sándor,* and a little further down in Hungarian, *The Village Hammer.* "I think you'll find it entertaining — and not too politically offensive."

"Thank you," I murmured, "but you know, I could have bought a copy..."

"Keep that one; I have another."

I looked at him uncertainly. I wasn't quite sure what he was doing here, but looking at him now, in his threadbare coat and untidy neck-tie, as disreputable as he had ever appeared and somehow larger than life, I knew beyond doubt that I should have nothing more to do with him. He may have been only twenty-five years old — yesterday — but I already knew that he was a dangerous man. And dangerous to me.

He stood so close that I was aware of the smell of him, a warm, clean, male smell mingled with faint tobacco and something elusive. His body was very still and his rather secretive dark eyes regarded me intently.

My breath caught, but fortunately by then I had become fascinated by the unusually tired lines on his young face: they seemed much deeper than before, the shadows under his eyes much darker.

"Don't you ever sleep?" I asked curiously, taking him by surprise. He blinked; his lip twitched, and he leaned lazily back against the table.

"Sleep? No," he said casually. "Not much."

"Because of your wretched cause?"

"No, I just don't need to. According to a physician friend of mine in Vienna, I'm an insomniac."

I stared. "You mean you can't sleep at all?"

He shrugged. "An hour in a night maybe, sometimes two, sometimes none."

I remembered the few hours I had lain awake over the years, worrying, agonizing, grieving, unable to find the release of unconsciousness. "How — *awful*," I said, low.

"It's not all bad — I have far more time than most people, which gives me an unfair advantage in lots of things: studying, for example."

"So that's how you did it," I murmured, almost to myself.

He looked amused. "Partly. I am also strong-willed, but boredom in the night was certainly a motivation."

"But how can you work if you're tired?"

"If I'm tired, I sleep. I didn't realize you were so maternal."

"I'm not. I take a scientific interest." He smiled at that; and more easily now, I smiled back.

He said idly, "Zsuzsa tells me you're not going into the country with István."

"No, I have a whole day of freedom!"

"What will you do with it?"

"What would you recommend?" I asked unwisely.

On the way we had talked of many things, for my unlikely companion knew an amazing amount about lots of different subjects, contriving to make them all funny or fascinating. I felt much as I suspected Katalin had all those years ago, following the young Lázár around the Transylvanian countryside, drinking in his words.

Once he had mentioned something about collecting messages from his fellow villagers among the palace servants, to take back with him to Transylvania.

Surprised, I had asked, "Are you going soon?"

"Tomorrow, if I can."

"So quickly?" I said involuntarily, then bit my lip. I could feel his eyes on me, so I roused myself to say mockingly, "What will you do at home? Rouse the peasantry?"

His lips quirked. "The peasantry is roused already — I've lived there a long time. No, my aim is to see my family, and to help with the harvest."

From then on, I had stopped being surprised by anything he said. Now, with the ease of much longer acquaintance, we were discussing Petőfi's poem, *The Village Hammer*, reading parts of it to each other, smiling over its jokes and appreciating its cleverness, till we lapsed into a brief, companionable silence.

Into it, I said quietly, "I have also read your — piece of work."

"Ah yes," he said deprecatingly, tossing Petőfi's book on to the table between us. "My magnum opus — at least for this month. You needn't tell me what you think — I know you disapprove."

"I think you write very well," I said frankly, "and I think you should be a lot more careful. How many people saw you handing these things out at the coffee house?"

He shrugged. "The police know all about the Pilvax. They won't touch me."

"Aren't you being a little arrogant?"

"Just practical. They could have arrested me any time in the last two years, but they won't do anything until I become a bigger nuisance free than I would be in prison. I can make an awful lot of noise if I choose to, and no one wants the 'common people' to be incited."

I glanced at him, half-doubtful, half-fascinated. "Is that what would happen if they arrested you?"

"It's what they're afraid of. Shall we walk? There's a wonderful view from the top of this hill." I rose readily enough, and then realized he was smiling to himself, as if at some pleasant memory.

"What?" I asked resignedly, though I was in fact intrigued.

"I was just imagining the faces of the Vice Regal Council. Vasvári and I delivered some of my leaflets to their chamber, that night you were at the Pilvax."

I closed my eyes, wondering how quiet — and how dull — the world would be if he were silenced for good.

By the time we returned to Buda — in a friendly peasant's cart — and found a fiacre to take us back to Pest, the light was beginning to fade, and with it my unexpected joy in the day. The quiet wonder had gone; reality was returning to haunt me. Discontentedly now, I stared out of the window as we bumped over the bridge of boats. With panic, I realized I was fast losing the chance to talk to him about anything important.

Taking a deep breath, I said abruptly, "What do you think about Katalin and Captain Zarescu?"

"I think they're making each other unhappy," he said surprisingly.

I looked at him. "But do you think there's any chance of her father letting them marry?"

"I doubt it. He might have been induced to swallow an impoverished Magyar officer, but a Romanian is too much. The prejudice is deep."

I frowned, shaking my head. "I must say it's one I don't understand."

He shrugged. "It's just the negative side of the nationalist feeling that makes you proud of your country: you despise — or fear — other races. It's not new and it's not peculiar to Hungary."

"So you approve of nationalism?" I said, recklessly.

He stirred, turning to face me more fully. I felt his knee brush my skirt. My eyes were caught and held. "Come to the Pilvax with me," he invited, "and I'll tell you."

I blinked. "Certainly not!"

"Why?" he asked at once. "You've been before."

I had, but with Katalin. The Pilvax was too well known, too *public* — what would people think if I went there alone with him?

"That was hardly the same thing," I snapped.

"Why not?" he asked, and of course, I couldn't answer. He reached out and took my hand. I wished he wouldn't touch me. "Come — I'll buy you supper, or just coffee if you prefer."

It wouldn't do. I didn't want to lose my post, and though I told myself I only wished to keep it till I met old Count Szelényi, that wasn't strictly true. I didn't want to stop teaching the children, my rather delightful enemies; I didn't want to lose Katalin's friendship, or abandon my interesting observations of the Countess. I didn't want to be sent home in disgrace, and if this was somehow confused with the man beside me I didn't want to think about it. No, this was one time I would not be swayed.

I shook my head. "No," I said firmly, drawing my hand free with an odd reluctance.

He sat back. Deliberately provoking, he said softly, "Oh dear, and I believed you were an independent woman, impervious to other people's prejudices."

Stung, I looked out of the window. "I could lose my position, Lajos."

"Unlikely. I think you are just ashamed to be seen with me."

I was furious at this aspersion — not least because there might have been a grain of truth in it. I turned back to him consideringly. "I suppose," I said sweetly, "you might consider another tailor."

That surprised a laugh from him, but he persisted. "So you'll come?"

"For five minutes," I said recklessly. I have a perfectly sound brain. Sometimes I wonder why I let it be so easily overruled.

Lajos shouted the change of direction to the driver, and then lapsed into silence for the rest of the journey. I didn't mind; I had plenty to think about. But when the fiacre pulled up outside the Pilvax, he didn't get out at once. Instead he sat looking at me, and I saw with surprise that he was serious and a little rueful.

"I'm sorry," he said quietly. "That wasn't fair. I wanted to see if you would do it, but you're right — it would be foolish to risk your post by being seen here with me. I'll tell the driver..."

"No." His eyebrows lifted in surprise. But with his admission, my doubts about the scheme had somehow vanished, perhaps because he was caring for my reputation after all. And I, perversely, now chose to consider it worth the risk; the sparkle had come back to my day.

"I would very much like a cup of coffee," I said calmly.

His lips curved upwards. "You're a strange creature," he observed. I sighed. "No," I said wryly, "just contrary."

For a brief instant his smile broadened as he reached over to open the door but then, before he could get out, it was suddenly wrenched from his hand and some one else climbed in, forcing Lajos to fall back into his seat.

I was too paralysed by shock — and then by fear — to make a sound. Another man followed the first, in equal silence, closing the door behind him and then plucking Lázár's bag off his shoulder. Almost more bewildering was the fact that Lajos did not react. He simply dug his hands into his worn pockets, and watched the two intruders opposite us by the pale light of the street lamps, one slight and bespectacled, the other large and burly, as they wordlessly opened his satchel and rummaged inside.

Outraged, I tried to demand an explanation, but the words stuck in my throat as my first, instinctive assumption that these men were robbers began to wobble precariously.

"I hope," Lajos said conversationally at last, "that you have proper authority for this."

Police, I thought with a powerful jolt of fear for him. Dear God, what did he have in that wretched bag today?

"Every authority we need," the first man snapped. His companion threw the contents of the bag down on the seat between them, one at a time — a newspaper; a large, dull-looking book; a sheaf of papers, quickly rifled and discarded; a half-eaten piece of bread and cheese, gingerly removed between thumb and forefinger.

"Sorry," Lajos said apologetically. "If you'd given me warning, I'd have cleaned up for you. Incidentally, if you come across any of my underclothes in there, I'd be grateful if you'd spare my blushes and leave them where they are."

I stared at him, unreasonably indignant at this light-hearted reaction. His eyes were on the two men, watchful but quite unafraid, and slowly I felt my own fears begin to subside. Perhaps, tonight, there was nothing there to incriminate him...

The empty satchel was flung impatiently on the floor. Lajos looked from it back to the policemen — if such they were.

"It might help if you told me what you were looking for," he observed lazily.

"This," said the first man curtly, taking something from his pocket and tossing it contemptuously on to Lázár's knee. Involuntarily, we both looked. The street lamp was shining obligingly down upon it, an eye-catching little pamphlet entitled "In Defence of Work" by L.L.

My breath caught. My eyes flew instinctively to Lázár's face, and then, though no one seemed to be aware of my existence, I was suddenly afraid that my behaviour would give him away.

"Ever seen this before?" the large man sneered.

Lajos glanced up at him and smiled. "I forget," he said with such blatant untruth that I cringed.

"You forget," the first man repeated, and caused fresh alarm by turning his glinting spectacles upon mine. For the first time, I considered my own compromising position in all this, and cravenly wished that I had never agreed to come. "Perhaps the lady remembers?"

"The lady," said Lajos, before I could speak, "is of much too high a rank to bother with such trifles. Besides, her friends would really hate her to be harassed."

To my amazement, the policeman turned away from me, apparently content to leave it there, as if he had expected to find a lady of rank with him — in disguise, I could only assume. I wondered who in the world he thought I was.

The larger policeman leaned towards Lajos. "You're not as clever as all that," he said softly. "Sooner or later you'll make a mistake — and we'll be there, Lázár, we'll be there."

The tone of his voice as much as the warning made me shiver, but Lajos only sounded amused. "I don't doubt it."

They left as quickly as they had come, and my breath escaped in a quite audible rush.

"Sorry," Lajos said casually, and I glared at him.

"No you're not."

"Well, I'm sorry they chose tonight when you are with me."

"On the contrary, it's as well they did choose tonight!" I exclaimed. "What if it had been the last time I was here, when you were *loaded* with those wretched pamphlets!"

Too late, I remembered the driver, who was no doubt fascinated by the whole scene, and bit my lip with mortification; but Lajos Lázár only smiled lazily, beginning to gather his things back into the bag, half-eaten bread and all.

"They don't move so quickly. Come, shall we go inside? I think you need a drink!"

I didn't deny it. I only wondered if I was actually insane going anywhere with him after what had occurred. Standing in the street, I shivered in the warm evening and watched him pay the driver, who grinned and winked with unexpected approval before he whipped his horses into plunging motion.

"Does this happen to you often?" I couldn't resist asking.

"Hardly ever." He shrugged. "A couple of times in Vienna, but never here before."

He took my arm, moving towards the café door.

"Then why now?" I demanded. It seemed to my shaken, law-abiding British soul that he wasn't taking this nearly seriously enough.

"I expect because I annoyed the Vice-Regal Council," he said carelessly. He glanced at me and his lips quirked. "Don't look so worried — they were only trying to frighten me, probably so that I'll stop agitating for the Opposition before the elections. If they had really wanted to arrest me, they wouldn't have waited all these weeks. Still," he added thoughtfully as he ushered me into the coffee-house, "I wonder who set them on to me?"

Someone on the Vice-Regal Council who had particular cause to hate him.

"Count István?" I suggested.

"I shouldn't think so. He doesn't like me, but we did grow up together."

He sounded certain, even indifferent, and yet the thought crossed my mind that he didn't want it to be István. However, before I could dwell on this new curiosity, I became distracted by the many long glances being cast in our direction.

As I had rather fearfully suspected, entering the coffee-house this time was quite different to the last. For one thing, I had felt anonymous then, and Katalin, for all her beauty, was not important here. Lajos Lázár quite obviously was. The same sort of people who had ignored us on that occasion now looked at me quite hard, which was just what I didn't want, not only for the sake of my reputation, I should say, but because I felt dowdy. My bonnet might have been pretty enough, but my workaday cloak and dress — never things of beauty — were now frankly drab.

This time too, Lajos chose not to stop to speak to his acquaintances, though he raised a casual hand in acknowledgement of the many greetings called to him. Nor did he sit with his friends, but guided me to a quiet, empty table, and even held the chair for me to sit.

The waiter brought wine and a light supper, leaving Lajos to serve them. I decided to have one glass of wine. I felt I needed it. Then, nervous in front of all those inquisitive eyes, I reverted hastily to the subject of nationalism.

Lajos picked up his fork. "Well, Hungary consists of far more peoples than just Magyars. We have Romanians, Slavs, Croats, Serbs, Slovenes, Germans... If we quarrel among ourselves over which race deserves what, then we all lose; but united, we *could* scare the wits out of Metternich and his cohorts in Vienna. I'd say out of the King-Emperor as well, but I believe he has none."

"We can't all be geniuses," I said drily.

"No, but if we wish to rule an Empire that spans half of Europe, I believe we should have at least common sense."

He had a point. "Go on."

He shrugged and took another mouthful of wine. "To be honest, I'm not sure how far to push the nationalist issue. For myself, I don't find race in the least important, but most people do."

I swallowed the blatant calculation in this statement as well as his surprising uncertainty, watching him gaze into his glass for a moment. Then he drank some more wine, and I asked carefully, "What does Mr Kossuth think?"

"Kossuth? He has sympathy with all nationalism, I suppose, but only up to a point. As far as he is concerned, the races historically subject to the Magyars must remain so. And I'm not convinced they'll put up with that for any social or political benefits." He paused, regarding me. "What do *you* know of Kossuth?"

"I know you support his candidacy for Pest in the Election."

"I don't recall telling you that."

"You didn't. *Baroness Meleki*" — I couldn't help adopting that lady's languid, slightly affected pose and tone of voice as I spoke her name — "Baroness Meleki is of the opinion that he can't lose with the support of you and your friends."

"I'm sure she's right," he said, amusement dancing in his dark eyes.

"*Count Batthyány* on the other hand, believes you would only hamper him, on account of repelling moderates."

"When did you move into such exalted company?" he enquired.

"Oh, I haven't. I'm allowed to watchit from time to time. So what *do* you think of Kossuth?"

"That he'll go further in my direction than most of his colleagues, and could be pushed further yet."

His single-mindedness took my breath away. I leaned forward curiously. "Exactly what influence do you have, Lajos? Apart from holding sway with the common people. Do you have the vote?"

"By birth, certainly not; only nobles can vote. But it could be argued that I am by education one of the *Honoratiores* — an honorary noble, if you like."

"So you *can* vote?"

"I certainly *will* vote. We all will, and use all the influence we can muster."

I smiled, half-sardonic, but half-admiring. "And as you said, you can make an awful lot of noise."

"I intend to."

For some reason his words sent a shiver through me. I found myself avoiding his clear, direct gaze, looking instead around the room at the other patrons who seemed, fortunately, to have lost interest in us. In the distance I recognized the youth Vasvári and one or two other faces from my previous visit. Then there had been an atmosphere of boyish recklessness in the café which I had found curiously beguiling, but now it was the earnestness in so many of these young faces which most struck me. They were as serious and as determined as Lajos; and with a jolt I realized that already they had power enough to frighten the authorities — why else would the police be trying to intimidate Lajos? Suddenly it seemed to me that the revolution they dreamed of might not be so far away after all. It could happen at any time, and surely with the autumn elections and the new Diet, they would find their opportunity...?

Suddenly fearful, I turned back to him, saying urgently, almost breathlessly, "How far are you prepared to go, Lajos? To achieve your revolution? Would you really be prepared to *die* for it? To let others die for it?"

He looked at me in surprise, but his eyes were clear and honest. "Yes.

There comes a time when you have to make a stand, whatever the consequences."

"And that time has truly come?" I asked, staring.

"The time has long passed, but when the *opportunity* comes, we'll be ready to seize it." His face relaxed, and he touched my hand. "Don't look like that. I told you on the steam-ship I believed it could be done without violence. I still believe that, but you asked how far I'd be prepared to go, and that is my answer: as far as necessary."

"Katalin's right," I said slowly. "You are frightening."

I hadn't planned to be in Vaci Street the following morning. It was Katalin, inspired by news of Captain Zarescu's imminent return, who decided that his birthday present — a rather beautiful watch which she had left in the jeweller's shop to be engraved — must be collected immediately. And it was I who, in an effort to contain her indiscretion over this gift, volunteered to fetch it.

The shop's proprietor was a middle-aged Jew with romantic tendencies. I almost blushed at his arch comments as I admired the engraving and handed over a horrendous amount of Katalin's money. Vaguely, I wondered if anyone bothered to keep a check on her spending.

I was positively relieved to escape into the street, the watch carefully stowed away in my reticule, but as I moved through the elegant shoppers, I suddenly saw a figure so familiar and so unexpected that it caused my heart to lift.

Lajos Lázár stood by the kerb, talking to someone in an open carriage, his foot resting casually on the step. Involuntary pleasure that he had not yet gone — a pleasure oddly confused with the warm, disturbing kiss of farewell he had most improperly pressed into my palm on parting last night — gave way to curiosity as I went instinctively towards him. Surely the crest on that carriage was familiar? It was. It had stood outside the Szelényi palace on a number of occasions. Its owner turned her beautiful head and laughed, and I recognized Baroness Meleki.

"*Au revoir,*" he had said to me, the lamplight glinting on his fair hair, shadowing his smiling face. "*I'll miss you.*"

My steps faltered, and even as I wondered why it should surprise me that they were acquainted, I saw her reach out and touch his cheek in a tender, unimaginably intimate gesture.

Abruptly, I whirled away from the unbearable sight, crossing almost blindly among the passing traffic. I found I was holding my breath, fighting with an emotion of quite frightening strength, an emotion I was eventually astonished and appalled to recognize as jealousy.

CHAPTER EIGHT

"My God, what a miserable, Gothic pile!"

The thought came unbidden out of the daze of pain and weariness as the coach thundered through the huge, iron gates. It was my first view of Szelényi Castle, and I was seeing it in the dark of a new moon. The children had been asleep on either side of me for some time, and even Zsuzsa's head was nodding; my own head throbbed alarmingly, so I was in no condition to appreciate properly the splendour of the black, imposing castle on the hill, towering and stark against the night sky.

The journey had been a nightmare in almost every way, for the roads outside Buda-Pest are more dreadful than you can imagine, and they grow gradually worse the further away you go. Jolting and bumping our muddy way eastward, I had developed an almost permanent headache which constantly threatened to turn into something far worse. I felt I was living on my nerves, for I knew that at last I was about to meet the old Count; I was about to face the outcome of my foolish behaviour in London.

The only joy in it all had been the scenery, which grew increasingly spectacular as we went on. My mother had told me of Transylvania's beauty, but I still wasn't prepared for the wonder of it. I had my first glimpse of the country from the top of the mountain pass which forms its border with Hungary. Standing by the coach with the children, my hand had reached involuntarily for the support of the cross which marked the official boundary, for the view simply took my breath away. Behind us were the cold, bare-looking mountains of Hungary, disappearing into a vast plain. Before us lay Transylvania: a wonderfully deep mountain gorge, hung with vibrant, green and yellow woods, giving way to a spectacular succession of hills and valleys, each more lovely than the last.

I suppose Transylvania lacks the wild grandeur of the Scottish Highlands, but in the next few days I came to realize that I would not swap my present location for any. Its gentle, almost fairy-tale beauty, its innumerable wandering streams and picturesque castles, held a far stronger appeal to me. For hours at a time, I could forget my headache and my plans, and just glory in my surroundings.

Occasionally, of course, my peace was interrupted by Zsuzsa's cheerful chatter or by her disparaging remarks about the natives.

"Look at him!" she uttered once, with quite startling contempt, pointing out a raven-haired Romanian peasant to me. "The stupid Vlach with his dirty shirt hanging out!"

It was true he wore his shirt over his trousers, rather than tucked neatly in, but it was obviously a deliberate custom and I could see no more dirt on his shirt than might be merited by a day's work. Zsuzsa was very much a child of her people, and accordingly she despised Romanians. Of course, she was of peasant stock, but it still gave me some clearer idea of what Katalin and Zarescu were up against.

Captain Zarescu had returned to Buda-Pest only days before Count István had informed me of his decision to leave as soon as possible for Transylvania. I had managed to hide the confusion of feeling this news aroused in me, but Katalin, needless to say, was openly furious: no sooner was her lover restored to her than her family conspired to drag her off to obscurity. I wondered if the Countess had had any part in this sudden decision, in order to remove Katalin from the source of her danger. If so, she had stirred up a hornet's nest, for Katalin simply refused point blank to move.

"How can you stay here without your family?" I had asked reasonably.

"I have friends who will be glad to have me stay with them. I have certainly no intention of giving up Alexandru's company for that of my ill-natured father and my dotty sister! To say nothing of Teréz Meleki who contrives always to make me feel like a gauche schoolgirl!"

My fingers had grown very still on the needlework I was attempting. I looked at her. "Baroness Meleki is going too?"

"Oh yes, haven't you heard? It's to be quite a party. Colonel von Avenheim, István's crony, is there already for a visit before he takes over the garrison at Vanora. And Teréz is to come with us — or with *you*, since I won't be there — though for the life of me I can't think why she wants to!"

I could.

Apparently, so could Maria, for I was privileged to be present with the children when the Countess had informed her of the extended party. "That woman," she had said disgustedly. "I don't know why you associate with her, Elisabeth."

"She amuses me," said the Countess, patently bored.

"It won't be you she's seeking to amuse at Szelényi," said Maria with grim humour. "It will be that jumped up peasant boy from the village."

I looked carefully at my hands. So it was not only true, but well known. I had begun to hope I had leapt to the wrong conclusions from my brief glimpse of them in Vaci Street. No wonder, I thought, that the police had so easily believed in my "rank" that night. They had thought I was Baroness Meleki. Lajos had protected me with her name, as clearly as if he had spoken it. And I had actually mimicked her in front of him...!

"Lajos Lázár?" said the Countess. "Oh no, I think that's quite over, don't you? Besides, doesn't he spend all his time here or in Vienna these days? Being a thorn in István's side."

"No," said Maria uncompromisingly. "He's always there in the summer when we are. Curious really: I should have thought he'd have left all that behind him..."

Katalin had held out for several days, during which the Szelényi palace was in turmoil from the flaming rows she conducted with her brother. The house had been full of loud voices and slamming doors, until the servants took to creeping around with nervous expressions on their faces, and even the children became reluctant to leave the schoolroom.

And then, suddenly, the fighting had ended. Katalin gave in gracefully; her family was all smiles again and the household breathed a collective sigh of relief. Even Mattias, who had taken to eating and sleeping elsewhere, returned to the palace.

However, none of them would have been so pleased if they had known the reason for Katalin's abrupt capitulation, which was simply that Captain Zarescu had been granted leave and would be in Transylvania barely a week after ourselves.

*

Now, finally arriving at Szelényi Castle, Zsuzsa and I stumbled out of the coach carrying a child each. Miklós didn't look very substantial, but he weighed an awful lot that night.

I remember passing through a doorway, and liveried menservants taking the children from us. I can see now, as clearly as then, the vast, stone hall, eerie in the candlelight, and the enormous marble staircase reaching out of it. Zsuzsa and I were both silent as we trudged up in the wake of our noisy, cheerful employers. I didn't think I was capable of speech — or even of thought, which was no state in which to make the acquaintance of old Count Szelényi.

I heard István say, "Father," and involuntarily I looked up. Through the figures ahead, and the shadows, I could see a tall, frail-looking old man, bent with age or illness or both, embracing his vigorous son. My foot faltered, and I felt Zsuzsa's steadying hand on my arm. We climbed on.

At the top of the staircase I stopped, because I couldn't get past the people being formally greeted by the old Count. As Baroness Meleki was introduced, I became aware that Zsuzsa had slipped by and was gone. I stayed, because I didn't know where else I could go, and took the opportunity to study the old Count.

I had waited so long to meet him, I no longer knew what I expected. His body was indeed frail, but even in the poor light I could see the fierce, hard life in his eyes, under drawn, bushy white brows; and the voice which so courteously welcomed the Baroness was very far from feeble.

It was a tall, soldierly man who first noticed my presence — oddly enough since until then I had been entirely unaware of his. He took a step towards me with a faint, shy smile.

"You look lost among all this commotion! Allow me to introduce myself — Karl von Avenheim, Colonel..."

"How do you do," I murmured mechanically, but his attention to me had drawn that of the old Count.

"Who's this?" he demanded. "István, where are your manners?"

István turned with some surprise to me, and then back to his father. "It's our new governess. Peter! Show Miss Kettles to her chamber at once — her..."

But the end of his order was quite lost in the roar of the old man which made everyone jump. "*What*? I will not have that name spoken in this house!" he thundered, after which there was a short, amazed silence.

Then István spoke, at his coolest and driest. "That is unfortunate, sir, since we shall then have to find some other way of addressing the lady. Peter, if you please."

I found a liveried manservant before me, and followed him rather blindly. As the talk started up again behind me, I heard Maria say, "What on Earth is the matter with her name? Come, let's get out of this draughty hall..."

I glanced back over my shoulder. I was sure the old Count was staring after me. I was glad.

*

I woke to the sound of shutters being thrown back, and to bright sunshine on my face. I could hear the singing of birds, the distant voices of men talking, and somewhere closer, the whine of a dog. The pain in my head was quite gone.

When I opened my eyes, I saw a maid tip-toeing out of the room. I struggled to sit up. "What time is it?" I asked, and the girl jumped, whirling to face me with a startled, half-frightened countenance.

"Eight o'clock, Miss. There's coffee and toast by the bed, but I didn't like to wake you."

"Oh thank you," I said, reaching at once for the reviving brew.

"Will that be all, Miss?" she asked and scuttled out almost before I had replied.

Terror is not normally one of the emotions I inspire in people. I was almost intrigued, until I realized that her fear was not aroused by me at all, but by the terrible old man who couldn't abide the sound of my name.

Washed and dressed, I chose to finish the last of my toast while admiring the view from the window — it looked on to the stable yard, but to the left, beyond it, I could see clearly to the hills. I found myself sighing with unreasonable contentment.

Below me, the stable boys were calling to each other while they worked, brushing down the horses, clearing out the stalls. They were Magyar peasants — I could tell that now from their appearance and dress. As I watched, Mattias Szelényi strode into the yard with a cheerful greeting, going at once to the skittish chestnut peering over the stall door.

Mattias had been my most unexpected informant on the journey. During my first sensible discussion with him — conducted on the porch of a very modest inn one evening after dinner — I had learned that although it was part of the Hungarian Crown, Transylvania was governed separately. It had its own Diet which met in Kolozsvár, and where all the resident races were represented — all, that is, apart from the Romanians, despite being the majority. I could see how someone normally as placid as Captain Zarescu might be so incensed by this injustice.

I had another thought too. "So which Diet is your brother involved in?" I had asked. "I assumed it was the one in Pressburg."

"Both. We have lands in Hungary too, and István is quite revoltingly wealthy in his own right."

I cast him a quizzical glance. "You don't approve of wealth?"

He grinned. "I do if it's mine. But seriously, I believe those like us who have so much land, also have a duty to improve the lot of the peasants who live on it. Besides, we'll never have a modern, thriving economy until we get rid of the feudal system and drag ourselves into the nineteenth century."

I found I liked Mattias, now I had discovered him to be something more than the careless, hedonistic student I had once imagined. In fact, I was ridiculously *comfortable* among these people I had come to hurt...

We did our best, the Enemy and I, but that first day at Szelényi, our hearts just were not in the serious business of education. The sun was shining too enticingly. They wanted to be outside or with their grandfather, or both; I was consumed with the desire to explore, both outside and in.

Somehow we got through until lunch, which was served in the schoolroom; but while the children ate obediently, their eyes kept straying to the window — I know because I was looking all too often in the same direction.

Fortunately, we had a visitor, a thin, untidily fluttering lady of uncertain age who slid into the room with a smile that was both warm and fearful of rejection. However, I had never yet seen my charges reject anyone, and this newcomer was no exception. They spilled out of their seats with loud cries of "Aunt Margit! Aunt Margit!" and cast themselves into her delighted arms.

After a tactful moment, I stood up with the vague but benevolent intention of preserving their aunt from suffocation, but her eyes met mine over their bouncing heads, and she smiled at me, the same timid, almost dog-like smile I had seen when she first came in.

"Miss Kettles," she said breathlessly, "How nice to meet you! I'm Margit Szelényi..."

I prised the children off her and sent them sternly back to their food. "How do you do?" I said at last. "I'm sorry: I find their affections quite uncontrollable sometimes!"

Margit's eyes searched mine, back and forwards from one to the other, and I found I was holding my breath, waiting for the recognition that must surely come now. She was after all Sofia Szelényi's *full* sister. But she only twittered, "Yes indeed. Isn't it nice?" and dragged her hand haphazardly through her wispy, grey hair. "And are you comfortable, dear? Do you like your position?"

"Why, yes thank you, I do..."

"So glad. Oh dear, please don't let me disturb your lunch. I'll sit with you a while, if I may..."

She duly did. Somewhat dazed, I agreed with her that the roads in Transylvania were appalling, and that we all must be tired, and then the children told her all about their doings in Buda-Pest.

"Goodness," she said once to me, "you *have* been busy."

"Their minds are very active," I said by way of explanation.

"Yes indeed. So are their little bodies... It quite exhausts me! But of course you are... How old are you, dear?"

My lip twitched. "Twenty-seven," I answered gravely.

She nodded. "Yes indeed — and you have such a nice name... it's one of our best family names, you know, Katherine..."

"Will you take us riding this afternoon, Aunt Margit?" Anna interrupted, surreptitiously purloining a morsel from her brother's plate. I put it back.

"Oh bless you, no. I don't ride much now. My arthritis, you know... But perhaps you could take Miss Kettles out and show her around? With Mark, of course..."

"Oh yes!" cried Miklós. "You'd like that, wouldn't you, Miss Katie?"

"I would," I confessed, although I hadn't ridden for years, not since my father had been minister of a small church in Perthshire. I turned to Margit. "Should I ask their parents' permission, do you think?"

Margit looked surprised, then I thought she almost preened. It seemed her opinion was not often sought. "I should just go," she whispered. "Even my brother would not want them studying *all* day on their first day back..."

Accordingly, while Margit scuttled back into the bowels of the castle, we put the books away and sallied forth to the stables.

Szelényi was joyously beautiful. Situated high in the foothills of the Carpathian mountains, it just bordered on the spectacular. The castle itself, an impressive building dating back to mediaeval times, stood at the top of the highest hill for miles around, looking down on forests and farmlands and vineyards, and a scattering of villages all owned by Count Szelényi.

With Mark, the Head Groom, and the children as guides, I was shown the glories of the scenery and led past fields which seemed to be farmed in strips by several different tenants. Harvesting had begun. I saw men — and some women — working in the fields, sweating under the blazing sun. They were mainly Magyars and Szekelys, a related race peculiar to Transylvania. None of them looked terribly prosperous, and some looked positively miserable to my searching eyes, as they bent their bare backs to the toil. Sometimes I saw them pause in the distance and watch us; if they were close enough, they touched their foreheads, and the children waved, much as they did to anyone else they knew.

Yet the eyes which observed us were not friendly: some were shielded or stolid; some were almost glitteringly hard, though whether this came from hatred or from the difficulty of their lives — or both — I could not tell. They greeted Mark amiably enough, but I remember feeling glad that I was with the children and not with their parents.

This was one aspect of the country my mother had never mentioned: the poverty, the alienation. I supposed it would have seemed normal to her as it did to the other Szelényis. Briefly, I thought of Lajos and the young men in the Pilvax: if it was normal to them too, at least they knew it was not right...

Surreptitiously, almost nervously, I kept a weather eye out for Lajos as we rode. For some reason, I was afraid to come across him here, to see him in his peasant role, as if he would be somehow altered by his surroundings. But then, wasn't he already changed in my eyes? My idealistic, slightly dangerous friend had become merely Teréz Meleki's low-born lover.

*

Visitors arrived at the castle the next day. I knew because I saw them from the schoolroom window; a handsome young couple, talking and laughing in the formal garden with István and Katalin. As I watched Elisabeth and Mattias coming out to join them, Miklós said behind me, "That's Baron Acsády, our neighbour. And his sister. She's called Ruth."

I looked at him, contemplating a reproof. Guessing this, he grinned at me, quite unabashed.

"I've finished," he claimed. I went to see for myself.

It was with some relief that I abandoned the children to Zsuzsa later in the afternoon, for I was now so determined to explore the castle that I couldn't concentrate on anything else. Making the most of my brief liberty, I set out with something of the same euphoria I had felt in Vienna the day I had bought my new bonnet, for I had already discovered the castle's régime to contrast quite unfavourably with the laissez-faire attitude prevailing in Pest.

The trouble was, the old Count kept to traditional customs which meant that the whole household dined together — family, secretaries, stewards, governesses, even the village priest — thus severely curtailing my liberty.

If my mother could have seen me last night, dining in the ancestral hall...!

It was, in fact, a daunting place to eat: huge, high-ceilinged and full of shadows and draughts, even on such a warm, summer evening. Like the rest of the castle, it was furnished with massive seventeenth century tables and cabinets, the walls hung with rather ancient looking tapestries and even more forbidding portraits of long-dead Szelényis.

I had sat appropriately near the foot of the table, beside the priest, Father Ránoczy, a youngish man with a startlingly sardonic glint in his keen eyes. Opposite us had been the steward, who said little, but smiled too much.

I suppose, on the whole, it had been a jolly meal, with Katalin and Mattias keeping up an amusing barrage of banter, while Teréz Meleki flirted genteelly with her elderly host. István had been suave and erudite, his wife decorative and bored, but it had been Margit Szelényi who had drawn most of my attention: positively *twittering* in a flurry of half-finished sentences, she had jumped visibly whenever her father spoke to her, which he seemed to do only to deride her or to order her to be silent. My dislike of the old man grew.

Naturally he had never so much as glanced at the governess while we ate, though as we left the dining room, and parted for the evening in the hallway, he did honour me with a ferocious frown, as if he had just recalled my obnoxious name.

The memory of that made me smile now, as I closed the door on a huge library which far outshone the one in the Pest house. Moving on, I found places as diverse as a still-room and a billiard-room, from which I quickly retreated in fear of being discovered there by a stray Szelényi. Various servants I encountered in the castle's long corridors looked at me a little curiously, but none questioned me. As a result I felt somewhat inhibited about asking for directions when I inevitably became lost, and went on until I found myself in a dark little passage which came to a dead end. Fortunately, my eyes eventually discovered this end to be a door. Without much hope, I tugged the handle — and to my surprise, it flew open, flooding me with low, evening sunlight.

I stepped outside, into the same stable yard I could see from my window. So, at least I was no longer lost! However, before I could congratulate myself too much, I realized I was being observed with amazement by Mark and a group of stable lads crouched together in the middle of the yard. They had been examining something on the ground which now, since my unexpected arrival, appeared to hold only the attention of one man with his back to me.

Mark said something, and then this man too glanced round, his eyes screwed up against the direct sun. With inexplicable shock, I recognized Lajos Lázár.

He was dressed as most of the peasants were, in faded black trousers and a loose, white shirt, open at the throat. The familiar half-smile dawned on his lips as he looked up at me without apparent surprise.

"Hallo," he said casually, and rose smoothly to his feet. "Were you looking for me?"

"No," I managed to say uncompromisingly. "Just looking."

Mark too was standing now, and I saw that the object of their attention had been a small, black puppy of decidedly mixed parentage. It danced after Lajos, eventually skidding to a halt by my feet and scratching itself vigorously with one hind leg, after which it launched itself at me, barking out its instant affection — or at least curiosity — in a small, high-pitched canine voice.

My smile was quite involuntary as I bent to pet the dog. It tried to lick me and scratch itself at the same time, without loosing its balance. I laughed.

"Is he yours?" I asked as Lajos's shadow fell over me.

"No, he's Mark's."

I glanced up. Mark materialized beside Lajos, woodenly explaining. "The pup's got an itchy skin ailment — I asked Lajos to bring me up some ointment for him." And he passed me with a nod, heading into one of the out-buildings.

I straightened, shifting my gaze from Mark's broad back to Lajos's watchful eyes. "So, you are an apothecary as well?" I said, lightly mocking.

"That's my mother's skill. I'm merely the messenger. How are you?" Unlike most people, Lajos asked that question as if he was genuinely interested in the answer. I smiled, unreasonably glad to see him again.

But then it struck me that the ointment for the pup was just an excuse for him to be at the castle, that he was really here to see Baroness Meleki. I could live with that, since I had to, but I had no intention of being used to carry messages between them, so, with sudden alarm that he might ask me to do so, I moved away, saying hastily and a little incoherently, "Don't let me detain you — I'm sure you are very busy..."

But he was walking beside me across the yard, his loose, easy strides keeping pace with my urgent steps. "It's you who seem to be in a hurry," he observed.

"Oh no, I was just exploring the castle," I murmured, feeling foolish. I slowed, glancing up to meet his half-amused gaze. His lips parted to speak, but before he could, a boy rushed into the yard shouting, "They're coming back!" and Mark reappeared at the door of the outbuilding just in front of us.

"Lajos, you'd better clear out now," he warned, "or lie low in here — that's the family almost back from their ride."

"Why, are they going to arrest me on sight?" Lajos asked humorously.

"No, but that ass Acsády's with them—" He glanced at me, "Begging your pardon."

"Beg Acsády's," I suggested, "but I shan't tell."

Mark almost grinned. "The thing is, he doesn't care for Lajos."

"He's not alone," Lajos added. "But in this case, neither does Lajos care for him. Still, I don't want a fight, so I'll take myself off."

"Good," said Mark, going back inside.

Lajos lifted his hand in careless farewell, strolling away across the yard. But it seemed he was too late. Already I could hear the clatter of horses' hooves, the sound of cheerful voices and laughter. A moment later, the party rode into view, and instinctively I moved backwards into the doorway after Mark.

Apart from the old Count, the whole family was there, together with Baroness Meleki, the two Acsádys and Colonel von Avenheim, the gentlemanly new commander of the garrison at Vanora. Caught in the midst of them, Lajos paused and stood still as the horses carelessly walked or trotted past him. I was used to thinking of Lajos as the danger to *them,* but now, seeing him stand there, so slight a figure among the rich, powerful people he had made his enemies, I was shocked by the fear that suddenly crept through me. He looked — defenceless.

CHAPTER NINE

I felt Mark's brief, respectful touch on my arm. "I'd stay here till they've gone," he breathed, and I obediently stepped further back into the shadows, from where I could still see a good part of the yard. I appeared to be in a tack room.

Mark went out, calling orders to the stable lads, and in the ensuing bustle of dismounting and unsaddling, I hoped Lajos would escape unnoticed. But Mattias Szelényi, no doubt with the best of intentions, put paid to that.

"Evening, Lajos!" he called cheerfully, as he dismounted and gave the reins to one of the boys. From my shadows, I saw several people turn and look at Lajos. István appeared slightly irritated, but not particularly angry, so I presumed he was used to running across Lajos on the castle premises; Baroness Meleki also stared deliberately, though I was sure she had seen him as soon as she had entered the yard. However, it was Baron Acsády who caught and held my attention. Still astride his big grey horse, he cast his eyes at Lajos and immediately I saw his thin lips curl in one of the most unpleasant sneers I have ever seen.

Lajos, with much his normal manner, lifted his hand in acknowledgement to Mattias and to the party in general, and began to go on his way. But suddenly, Acsády's horse was in his path. "Why, *Monsieur* Lázár!" he said mockingly. "You do indeed move in the best circles these days. I didn't realize, István, that *Monsieur* Lázár was one of your guests."

"A guest of the stable boys, perhaps," István said drily, and I heard one or two laughs, distinctively Baroness Meleki's. I began to feel indignant on my friend's behalf. Lajos himself stood still, looking up at Acsády unflinchingly, but I could tell from his posture that he was wary. István moved towards them.

"He's a popular man," Acsády marvelled. "Why, only the other night, I hear, he was the guest of the tavern-keeper at Szelényi. I hear also that you and I, among others, were the butt of his crude, peasant wit."

My heart sank into my shoes.

The rest of the party had dismounted, and now stood around watching expectantly. I had the impression they were awaiting entertainment.

Lajos said, "I'd like to stay and repeat all my old jokes to you — some of them are really quite good — but unfortunately I'm expected elsewhere. So if you'll excuse me..." He moved to step round Acsády's horse, but a touch of the Baron's heel pushed the animal again into his path. My discomfort was turning into anxiety.

"Oh no, I don't think we can excuse you so quickly," Acsády mocked. "I understand you are valuable company these days — at least to traitors and criminals."

"Let him be, Acsády, he's not that bad," Mattias said uneasily.

"No? Didn't you hear he was responsible for getting the traitor Ehlberg released? I don't know what the Vienna courts are thinking about. I'd have had the two of them strung up on the same gallows, side by side. What did Ehlberg pay you with, Lázár? Pieces of silver? Thirty perhaps?"

"Brotherly love," Lajos said blandly. "You should acquire a little some time — it might make you less angry." I closed my eyes. I hoped Lajos could talk himself out of trouble too.

"What? Does the peasant now advise the lord?" Acsády said sardonically, after a pregnant pause. "Oh, forgive me, I forgot. You are no longer a peasant, but a gentleman of Pest, a writer of learned articles, a lawyer of dubious repute!"

That raised another laugh, but with even greater alarm I recognized an ugly note behind Acsády's mockery. The man meant worse than mischief; for some reason, his hatred seemed to be more spiteful even than István's. He leaned down a little from the saddle, as if to speak confidentially to Lajos, though he made sure his voice could be heard all round the yard.

"Well, since you are now such a fine gentleman, I'll make you a gentlemanly wager." He paused and dismounted, all aristocratic grace, waiting no doubt for Lajos to enquire the nature of the bet. Lajos, however, merely stood looking at him. I couldn't see the expression on his face. "I'll wager ten forints — I'm sure a lawyer's pay will stretch that far — against your jumping Count István's horse over that wall."

He indicated the outside wall of the stable yard, which must have been at least six feet high with God knew what on the other side of it. István's horse, I should add, was an excitable, spirited brute of a stallion, very little loved by the grooms, and quite a challenge even to an experienced horseman. The boy who had just taken the beast's saddle off looked round with a hunted expression.

I found I was holding my breath in dread of Lajos accepting; so was the rest of the company, including the grooms and stable lads, for Acsády was as good as inviting Lajos to kill himself — to say nothing of István's horse. At the very least he was ridiculing him for his lack of gentlemanly accomplishments.

Lajos glanced at the wall, at the horse, and back to Acsády. "Sorry," he said coolly, and I felt my body relax with relief. "I leave pointless wagers to the bored aristocrats who have nothing better to do. Cheer up. It'll save you ten forints, which I'm sure you'll be grateful for when feudal servitude is gone. Good evening, gentlemen. Ladies."

And he flourished a bow to the company, at once mocking and supremely elegant. I felt a surge of pride in him, for there was no doubt that he had come off best on all fronts, and was about to make an equally impressive exit.

However, as he turned away, I clearly saw István's foot go out to trip him. Outraged, I opened my mouth as if to call a warning that was already too late.

The next instant, he sprawled full length on the hard, cobbled ground, to the delighted laughter of the noble watchers. That would have been bad enough, but István had chosen his position well, and it was into the particularly large pile of fresh manure just deposited by Acsády's horse, that Lajos fell.

For a second he lay quite still, and I was appalled as much by his possible injury as by his obvious humiliation. Instinctively, I started out of the tack room with the intention of going to help him whatever the cost, but again Mark was there. "No," he said softly, catching my arm and pushing me back. "Leave him. He'll cope."

Helplessly, I watched as he got slowly to his feet and turned back to face his tormentors. My heart went out to him, for the manure was everywhere, in his hair, on his face, all down his shirt and the front of his trousers, which caused a fresh outburst of shrill laughter. The loudest, I noticed again, was Teréz Meleki: not only was she failing to defend her lover, she was deliberately — or perhaps just carelessly — adding to his indignity. Well, I suppose it would have been funny, except for the deliberate malice with which it was done. Briefly, I caught sight of Katalin's distressed face, and had time to be pleased with her before my attention was all held by Lajos.

He stood facing Acsády and István, thoughtfully wiping one filthy hand on the back of his trousers, revealing no trace of the mortification I knew he must have felt. A man of the soil, he was hardly over fastidious about dirt, but to be deliberately flung into it so that it dripped from him for the sole purpose of debasing him in front of those he claimed as his equals — that was different.

There was a faint, unpleasant smile of triumph on István's lips which angered me even more. It struck me that he had waited a long time to so publicly shame Lajos; it must have been a bonus to have been able to do so before his mistress.

"Very well," Lajos said unexpectedly. "Since you insist, I accept your silly wager." And before Acsády could even guess his intentions, he had seized the Baron's hand in his own filthy one to shake on the bet. "Ten forints it is," he said blandly, as I heard a few smothered sniggers from the stable lads, and Acsády wrenched his hand free with an expression of strong revulsion.

"I beg your pardon," said Lajos gently. "It's only shit."

From somewhere came a shocked, feminine giggle. And only from that one unnecessarily foul word could I see his anger. Deliberately, he shook the dirt from his other hand, splattering it in front of him. István quickly stepped back, but even from some distance away I could see the stains on his coat. There was even a spot on his chin which gave me some satisfaction, but before he could react, Lajos suddenly sprinted under everyone's astonished gaze to where István's ill-tempered horse stood, saddleless and restless in the hands of the open-mouthed boy.

In a trice, Lajos had seized the animal round the neck and hauled himself onto its bare back. I had a glimpse of István's startled face, and then my attention was all on Lajos.

"Here, Gábor!" he called to the lad, seizing the reins and clinging determinedly to its back as the horse plunged and reared with an angry whinny that sounded more like a scream of rage.

"My God," I whispered with horror, "He's not going to do it? Not like that...?"

It seemed he was. A moment later the horse was careering wildly towards the wall, scattering people to left and right as it went. On its back, I had a glimpse of Lajos, his hair flying out behind him, his expression showing only supreme concentration.

I couldn't watch any more. I closed my eyes, listening in terror to the buzz of amazement in the yard and my own thundering heart. I heard someone's nervous laugh, then a collective gasp as the clatter of hooves abruptly stopped.

"My God, he did it!" yelled Mattias, and I opened my eyes again, relief flooding through me like a pain.

"Is he all right?" Katalin asked urgently, "István, look and see..."

"The wall is too high," István said indifferently, and I could have hit him. I had no idea what was on the other side of that wall, but I was very afraid it was a steep slope. The horse made no sound that I could hear, so I could only pray they had not come to grief...

"Look out!" called a voice from beyond the yard, and a second later Lajos, still astride the angry horse, came flying back over the wall. My heart leapt back into my mouth. I heard the hooves catch against the stone, saw the horse stumble as it landed, but somehow it kept its balance and came to a shuddering halt just in front of István and Acsády, blowing furiously and rolling its eyes while Lajos held it firmly in check.

It seemed he was not the novice horseman everyone had assumed him to be: somewhere, since leaving Szelényi, he had learned to ride, and ride well. Lifting one leg across the beast's back, he slid lightly to the ground; then, with a gesture somehow insolent, he held the reins out to the Baron.

"Care to try?"

The reins, as well as the horse itself, were covered in manure from Lajos. Acsády regarded the animal distastefully. "Not on that. I'll ride my own horse."

"Oh no," said Lajos. "That wouldn't be fair. The bet was on *this* horse. Play or pay."

"He's got you," said Mattias, and I could understand his delight.

"Give him his money, for God's sake," István said impatiently. "I can't abide the smell of him."

"Then you should keep your noble feet flat on the ground," Lajos said evenly, and into the sudden silence which followed came the sound of slow, mocking applause.

It was the old Count himself, standing by the door I had used only half an hour before, a faint, sardonic smile on his thin lips. I wondered how much he had seen, how much worse his presence would make things for Lajos.

"Bravo!" he called, still mocking, as he moved towards the little group. At the sound of his voice, Lajos turned quickly, as if he couldn't help himself, and suddenly, in spite of everything, I was intensely curious to see these two men together. Though the Count had paid for his education, it had not been willingly; there could have been little love lost between them even without Lajos's politics.

Their eyes met briefly. Lajos did not bow, or tug his forelock like the grooms; instead, he nodded, much as he did to everyone, and oddly, the Count didn't seem to mind. I presumed he had got used to it.

"Do you know," said the Count conversationally, "you are only the second man ever to have made that particular jump?"

"No, I didn't know; but I'm sure you were the first." It sounded automatic, and indeed his attention had already returned to Acsády.

"I was," the Count admitted modestly. "A long time ago... But I didn't know you had learned to ride, Lajos."

"I've learned a lot you don't know about." There was no smile on his lips or in his voice. More than anything else, this distressed me, but again the Count seemed to see nothing unusual in his manner.

"I'm sure," he said drily, turning to the others. "What is this all about?"

Now, to my surprise, I saw that István was looking uncomfortable. It was Lajos who answered.

"M. Acsády had the urge to redistribute his wealth."

A breath of laughter trembled in my throat and was still, for the Count stepped away from Lajos, wrinkling his nose in disgust.

"Good God, boy, must you come up here looking — and smelling! — like that? Don't tell me there's no water in the village!"

Again, Teréz Meleki led the laughter at his expense, but this time I didn't care. I was triumphant, for I knew from István's face that for some reason the old Count would not condone his behaviour. It was not "suitable". The tables were thus neatly turned, and István's own father would be Lajos's weapon against his tormentors.

But Lajos never even glanced at István.

"I haven't had time," he said briefly, and I almost shouted at him in frustration. István lifted his eyes from his whip to Lajos. I saw his lips twist slightly — whether with contempt or anger or simple amusement, I didn't know — but he said nothing.

Of course. They had grown up together. Lajos would not "tell" now, any more than he would have done when they were boys.

"*Make* time!" the Count barked, beginning to stump away. "Get out of my sight till you do!"

"I'm waiting for my money," Lajos said evenly. "Ten forints."

But Acsády only laughed. "For a peasant? One is enough." And he carelessly tossed a coin on to the ground. Lajos looked at it, then at the Baron, who laughed again. Neither moved.

But the old Count had turned back.

"In my day," he said fiercely, "we did not make wagers with peasants." The smile began to die on Acsády's lips. "If we had done, I imagine we would have paid our debts."

Acsády's face was flushed as he dug into his pockets and held a little pile of coins out at some distance from himself. For a moment, I thought Lajos wouldn't take them: the Count had obtained them for him in the end, and had done so with a reminder of the difference between their stations in life. It must all have added to his humiliation. I felt as if I couldn't bear much more.

At last, Lajos lifted his hand, but instead of letting the coins drop into his palm as the Baron clearly intended, he deliberately took them from Acsády's hold, making sure their fingers touched.

"Thank you. It seems you'll have nothing after all when your serfs are free. I have to thank you for a splendid evening's entertainment. Good-bye."

And he dropped the reins at last and strolled off, filthy and dishevelled.

"Insolent puppy!" the old Count shouted angrily after him, but his step never faltered. I watched his erect back, his casual gait until he was out of the yard. He looked as if he didn't care, but I knew that he did. He wouldn't have spoken as he had, done what he had done, if he had not felt pain at what Acsády and István had deliberately inflicted on him, solely for daring to stand up to them, for refusing to be bested by those who regarded themselves as his social superiors.

Weakly, I sat down on a rough bench, listening to their voices disappear. "...in the dirt where he belongs," I heard István say viciously.

"Yes, but he had the last laugh." That was Mattias, with a grain of satisfaction in his voice. "Who'd have thought he could ride like that?"

And Colonel von Avenheim, reasonable as ever: "There was no need to rile him at all. Given enough rope, the boy will hang himself without your aid."

Again I felt that lurch of fear. Then, as a shadow filled the door, I glanced up. It was Mark. "I told you he'd cope," said the groom comfortably, coming into the room.

I looked at him. "Does he have to put up with this sort of thing regularly?"

"Oh, not now. When he was a boy it was worse. He used to come to the castle for lessons, and believe me, young István and his cronies made his life very hard indeed. The Acsády boy was the biggest bully of all. I think it maddened him that no matter how often Lajos was beaten, he never lay down... The village lads picked on him too — special treatment, you see — but Lajos got round them in the end, so now there's not one of them wouldn't do anything he asked." He grinned. "He was always a persuasive young devil! But he never got round Count István. Oh no."

Fascinated in spite of myself, and in spite of the pity welling up in me for the abused, lonely boy I was beginning to imagine from Mark's words, I asked, "Did he fight?"

Mark shrugged. "Lajos? Only when he had to — cunning little bruiser he was, mind. He had to fight with his brain, because he didn't have the height or the weight to deal with the bigger lads. Talk of the devil," he added, as another figure appeared in the doorway.

I glanced up to see Lajos standing there. His hair and his shirt were wet, but there were still stains on his trousers. Mark was regarding him warily.

Lajos said, "I thought I'd better come and wash down that damned horse. I'm afraid I got as much filth on him as I possibly could."

Mark grinned. "Good thing too. Put the little..."

"Yes, well, where is the brute?" Lajos interrupted.

"Forget it, he's clean already. The lads would do it twenty times over for a trick like that."

"More fool them. I could have broken the beast's neck." There was a trace of bitterness in his voice now. His arm lifted, holding out the coins Acsády had paid him. "Here, give the lads these — it's all right — I washed them in the stream, though not to get rid of the manure..." Mark hesitated, looking at him, then took the coins wordlessly and went out.

Lajos shivered. "I washed myself in the stream too," he said to me, pulling his wet shirt away from his skin and looking for the first time quite touchingly like a little boy. I had never seen him as vulnerable before. It was as if memories of the hurts inflicted in childhood were haunting him again, making today's unpleasant little episode somehow harder for him to bear. He wasn't shaking, as I was, but he was shaken. And István's behaviour must have been hardest of all, for though I knew he didn't need István's friendship now, I thought he had once, quite badly, all those years ago... With the new understanding, my heart began to ache for him.

He shivered again. "You'll catch your death," I said, low. "You should go home and change." He nodded, looking down at me a little dreamily. "I'll come with you," I offered, and at last his lips curved into a genuine smile.

For a moment he gazed at me silently, then his freshly washed hand came up and gently touched my cheek. "Your sympathy is very sweet," he said, and I felt my face begin to burn under his fingers. "But don't waste it on me. I deserve everything I get; I work damned hard for it."

CHAPTER TEN

"Acsády?" Father Ránoczy repeated, without pausing from his soup to look. "I hold him up as an example to my flock when they complain about conditions at Szelényi."

Slightly taken aback, I lowered my voice. "Do they complain a lot?"

"Of course they do. So would you. They live as slaves, in abject poverty, completely at the mercy of the lord to whom they lose more than half their working week through robot. And robot — forced, unpaid labour in the lord's fields, to the inevitable neglect of their own — is not the only feudal due, just the most hated."

"I didn't realize you were so... " I broke off, a little confused.

The priest smiled. "Radical?" he suggested. "Oh I'm not. I merely dislike suffering. If it's real radicalism you wish to hear, you could do worse than listen to our local celeb..." Without warning, he broke off, and I realized with resignation that he was listening to the conversation at the head of the table, which, naturally, was all about the afternoon's incident with Lajos.

Seeing the priest's unexpected frown of distress, I said quickly, "Don't worry. He really came off best, you know."

He glanced at me in surprise. "You know about this already?"

"I *saw* it," I answered unguardedly, but he was already saying urgently, "Is Lajos all right?"

"In body, yes."

The priest relaxed, smiling faintly. "Don't waste your anxiety on his spirit, " he advised. "He will come about. I think you'll find he has already realized that this incident is quite unimportant in the grand scheme of things."

I met his sardonic gaze. "And is it?"

Father Ránoczy hesitated, then he laid down his spoon. "Perhaps," he said slowly, "it shows that Lajos has gone too far: the landowners are rattled."

"He'll like that," I murmured, amused in spite of myself.

"But will anyone else? Does anyone — even Lajos — really want the sort of slaughter which occurred in Galicia last year when the peasants rose up?"

I stared. "But surely such a thing could never happen here?"

He shrugged. "I pray it will not. For all our sakes."

It was a beautiful evening, with the light and the warmth of day just beginning to fade, and the mingling scents of wild flowers and new-mown hay hanging in the air. I needed no other excuse to be wandering outdoors, away from the castle grounds, down the hill towards Szelényi. The village was really just one long, muddy street with a church, a tavern which called itself an inn and a scattering of peasants' cottages, one or two of which were reasonable looking places with tidy gardens and an air of cleanliness. I found myself hoping uneasily that the Lázárs lived in one of these, for the alternative seemed to be one-roomed hovels of varying squalor.

I watched a few exhausted men returning from the fields, some scrawny children playing in the little square that had been formed between the tavern and the church, and a tiny woman in a brightly embroidered dress scolding two sheepish lads who towered over her. The children quietened as I passed, until I smiled, and then they grinned back and carried on with their game.

I found him quite easily in the end. Coming to what seemed to be the largest house in the village, I glanced over its wooden gate and saw him alone in the little porch which led up to the door. Instinctively, I opened the gate and went towards him. He didn't see me at first. Gently swinging himself in an old rocking chair, one knee was drawn up under his chin so that his foot rested on the seat. He had changed his clothes for some cleaner if shabbier ones, and he was gazing expressionlessly at nothing.

I nearly left him then, for I was suddenly afraid of simply irritating him by my unasked for and unwanted presence. I was even turning away when his eyes moved unexpectedly and saw me. Undecided, I paused, motionless like a mesmerized rabbit, until he smiled.

"Katie," he said, and he didn't sound irritated at all. With one fluid movement he unwound himself from the rocking chair and stood up. "Come and sit down."

I obeyed, silently since I couldn't think of anything to say. It was a hard chair, but the gentle motion was soothing. I watched as Lajos pulled a stool up close to me, and for a time we sat there, saying nothing. Oddly enough, I found it rather peaceful.

At last he turned his head to look at me, and when I glanced up, I saw the glimmer of a smile on his lips. "What a very restful person you are," he observed. "I think you're the only woman I've met who appreciates silence as much as talk."

It sounded like a compliment, so I blushed, dropping my gaze and saying tartly, "You've already told me how strange I am."

"Have I? Well, if it is strange to sit quietly exuding comfort..."

"Do you feel the need of comfort?" I interrupted a little desperately, simply to cover my own *dis*comfort at his words. Then I wished I had stayed silent, for I saw the smile die away from his eyes.

"Don't we all?" he said lightly. "Even you."

"Perhaps."

He leaned back on the stool, his head resting against the wall of the house as he examined me thoughtfully. "You're not quite so staid and capable as you pretend, are you, Katie Kettles?"

It was unfair of him to surprise me like that, but I managed to retort, "I believe I am not *in*capable. As for staid, that is a requirement for governesses!"

"But what actually goes on behind that cool mask you hold on to so efficiently?" he asked, his voice lazy though his eyes were as keen as ever, holding mine without effort and seeing far too much for my own ease of mind.

"I don't know what you mean." I resorted to stolidity, but relentlessly, he pursued his point.

"Yes, you do. You observe us all quietly, sardonically even, but your real feelings you keep safely locked up and out of sight."

"Perhaps because they are no one else's concern," I said sharply.

He leaned forward. "Then why are you so concerned for me, if I may not be concerned for you?"

My eyes fell. "I do not, at the moment, need your concern."

"Or my prying?" he suggested, and provoked from me a reluctant laugh.

"Am I being rude?" I asked ruefully.

"Just — prickly!"

"I'm sorry. The simple truth about me is that I just don't feel passionately about things."

"Nonsense," he said at once. "Everyone does, about something or someone. Haven't you ever been in love, for instance?"

I blinked. "Once," I found myself answering. "When I was too young to know better."

His lip quirked. "I gather from your cynicism that it was not a happy experience."

"Not particularly."

"What happened?"

"Nothing. We discovered in time that we did not suit."

His eyebrows lifted. "He must have been a fool to let you slip through his fingers."

I felt a silly surge of pleasure to hear him say so, but honesty compelled me to confess, "I didn't slip. I was pushed."

He looked startled at that, which made me smile. "He was employed at the Foreign Office," I explained. "And in truth, I would have made a quite dreadful diplomat's wife. I was always saying the wrong thing, forgetting the right faces. Part of it was due to my eyesight, I suppose — you've no idea what a blessing spectacles are."

He met my humorous gaze, but his own, too-clever eyes were not laughing. For a moment I wondered in panic if he could see the hurt I had felt all those years ago, if it was somehow seeping out of me like blood from a wound. But I was fairly sure he could not, for ever since that time I had worked very hard to hide my feelings.

He said quietly, "You'll have to trust someone else in the end, you know."

Shaken, I could only stare at him. My mask had definitely slipped.

But now excited voices in the street had grown suddenly louder in my ears, and three men were coming through the gate, all talking at once. Two of them were young and burly with black curly hair; the other was old but vigorous, and frowning so ferociously that I was reminded unpleasantly of the old Count.

"My father and my brothers," Lajos observed, and then the trio had caught sight of us.

"Lajos!" cried the youngest man, his face splitting into an open grin of delight. "Is it true what Gábor says—? Oh." Realizing my presence, he broke off in confusion. I didn't blame him. I was confused myself. Though intensely curious to meet the parents who had spawned so remarkable a child as Lajos, I had been conscious for some time of a *fear* of doing so, of seeing him with rough, vulgar people, as if it would somehow diminish him. And now these three men looked so little like him that it was hard to believe they were his family.

However, instinctive manners made me stand up to meet his father.

"This is Miss Katie from Scotland," Lajos said calmly. "The new governess at the castle. Katie, my father, Lázár Lázár."

An economic name, I reflected, if an unimaginative one. I smiled, inclining my head, wondering a little wildly if I should shake hands with the fierce old man. However, he solved the problem for me. He gave me a bow that may not have been elegant by drawing-room standards, but still held its own, rough dignity.

"Pleased to meet you," he said, adding sardonically, as if he couldn't help it, "But if you hope to keep your job, I wouldn't make a friend of my son!" He swung round on Lajos. "Where have you been, anyway? I'm just telling your brothers they've no excuse to slacken off just because *you* deign to turn up!"

"Quite right," said Lajos amiably, though I was shocked by the unexpected bitterness in the old man's voice. "These are my idle brothers," he added wryly to me. "Zoltán and Károly."

Károly, the younger one who had spoken so impetuously as he came up the path, bobbed a half-respectful, half-nervous bow; Zoltán merely nodded, much as Lajos did. He looked very like Károly, but his brow was lower, his mouth discontented and unfriendly, and he was obviously impatient to speak to Lajos.

However, old Lázár had things to say himself, and he would not be deterred even by my presence. As I sat down again, he demanded, "What's this you've been up to now? Gábor has been telling us some unlikely tale of heroics...!"

"There were no heroes," Lajos said lazily, dropping back on to his stool, "unless you count the horse."

"It sounds pretty brave to me!" Károly said indignantly.

"Pretty stupid," Lajos corrected. "Why don't you bring out a jug of that wine..."

"Don't change the subject," barked Lázár. "Did you do what Gábor is saying?"

Lajos sighed. "Yes, I did it, but it's not important..."

"Why?" interrupted his father. "Just for a bet? What in God's name were you trying to prove?"

I could feel the discomfort, the tension, in Lajos as if they were my own feelings. He shifted impatiently on the stool. "Nothing. I was proving nothing. I didn't do it for the bet, I did it in a fit of temper, purely and unforgivably because I dislike being made to look a fool by a pair of dandified nincompoops with little but gold-plated sawdust between their ears! Of course, I made an even bigger fool of myself, but that's my privilege — I have to live with it."

"What, did you fall off?" Zoltán demanded, sounding disappointed, almost outraged.

"No, I didn't fall off," said Lajos tiredly, but his father had latched on to the salient point.

"How were you made a fool of?" he asked distinctly.

"What, was Gábor sparing my reputation? Didn't he tell you about me being tripped into a good, fresh pile of horse-manure?"

Lázár stared, his lips thinning. "Who? Who did that?"

Lajos shrugged. "István, if it matters."

"Oh Lajos, couldn't you have let it go?" To my surprise, there was a touch of bewildered pleading in the old man's voice. He understood. "Let him have his petty satisfaction?"

"I could have," Lajos admitted. "And I could have hit him — I thought about that too."

"Christ, Lajos, you're a *peasant*! You don't need to be so fastidious about dirt!" Lázár's anger was back.

"It wasn't the dirt," Lajos said frankly, "it was the deliberate attempt to humiliate. I didn't see — I have never seen — why they should be allowed to do that to us."

"Oh God." Lázár cast his eyes to heaven. "Who in *hell* taught you to fight over every little wrong? To risk your neck against every petty injustice?"

In the face of his father's anger, I suddenly saw Lajos's face soften. His lips quirked upwards. "You did," he said simply.

For a moment, Lázár stared at him, bereft of words, and I began to understand. The clever, restless, *different* boy who had wanted so much more from life than Szelényi could give, had nevertheless begun his crusade for his own family, his own village. It was only later, I thought, that it had grown with his knowledge of the world...

A calm voice behind me said, "What are you all doing out here? Quarrelling again?" And I turned to find a neat, fresh-looking woman in the doorway. She wore the colourful dress of the peasant women of the district, but I barely noticed that at the time, for here at last I could see a resemblance to Lajos. She had his unusual colouring, the dark blond hair, though now tinged with grey, and the direct, dark brown eyes. There was something too in the smile on her faded lips, and the whole shape of her tired, once beautiful face.

Involuntarily, I smiled at her, and this time it seemed quite natural to hold out my hand and to introduce myself without waiting for Lajos.

"She's governess at the castle," old Lázár added by way of explanation, for there was an odd, puzzled expression on his wife's face as she looked at me, and at some point — surely it was when I had spoken my name? — her grip on my hand had tightened. Her eyes widened and now she was definitely staring at me.

My heart jolted. I stepped back from her in silly panic, for here at last was what I had looked for since I had first entered that hotel room in London and met István Szelényi. It was recognition.

She knew who I was.

CHAPTER ELEVEN

I was aware that the family held a private service in the castle chapel, but when I found my way there like some clumsy wraith, only a little after dawn, it was silent, deserted. My misplaced contentment of the last two days had utterly vanished, squashed under a much more substantial dollop of reality; my head was full of yesterday's events and the significance of Eszter Lázár's recognition.

Somehow I had gone through the motions with the Lázárs, making conversation, smiling politely while I waited for her revelation. It hadn't come. She had watched me. She had watched me a lot, with puzzlement and doubt, but she had said nothing, and as soon as I civilly could, I had left.

The chapel was surprisingly beautiful, a little dark perhaps, but the antique stained glass and woodcarvings were wonderful. I sat for a time in the front pew, letting the silence enfold me while my eyes fixed on the cross before me and I thought of my father's strong, simple faith.

For once, I let the tears roll unchecked down my face. What in God's name was I doing here? This pilgrimage of mine was not for them, my parents. It changed nothing for them. It was only hurting me. And I was wronging too many people who might in other circumstances have been friends...

I didn't hear him come in. It was only gradually I became aware of that feeling of being observed, and even then, I only looked up to reassure myself. It was something of a shock to see Lajos Lázár standing still among the shadows by the door. Gasping, I brushed my hand quickly across my eyes, and was almost surprised when the image did not disappear. How long had he been there? My fingers crept to my throat. I swallowed.

"Are you quite at liberty to wander the castle as you choose?" I enquired at last, with something closely resembling my usual sardonic manner.

He moved out of the shadows towards me. "I don't believe I have ever been forbidden."

"Merely an oversight on the Count's part, I'm sure," I said sweetly.

"Possibly." He was beside me now, gazing gravely down at me. "Katie Kettles," he said softly. "What exactly do you imagine you are doing here?"

My heart lurched, but I did not pretend to misunderstand him. My eyes fell from his. I said quietly, "If you want the truth, I don't know any more." I glanced up at him again. "How did she recognize me?" I asked simply.

He shrugged. "She was Sofia Szelényi's maid."

I felt my eyes widen. A memory stirred. "Eszter," I murmured. "She talked of an Eszter when I was a child..."

"What I want to know is why none of the Szelényis have recognized you." He paused. "Or have they?"

I shook my head. "No. Most of them never laid eyes on my mother, after all."

"I don't know how much like your mother you are...?"

"Not very," I said regretfully. "And of course the Szelényis look on me only as a servant — a superior servant, I would be the first to admit, but even so, they don't actually *see* me. The old Count doesn't like my name — which means he has noticed me, but I'm sure he couldn't ever imagine seeing me here in *this* guise. To his mind, Sofia's daughter is only likely to come to him declaring herself an equal — no doubt in a suitably vulgar voice — and demanding her inheritance, preferably with threats!"

"And is that why you are here?" he asked quietly.

I felt the blood rise into my face. "It is not," I said bitterly. "I would not take a penny from the old man which I had not earned."

"So why *have* you come? As the governess, of all things."

My flush of anger became one of shame. I dropped my gaze, then bravely met his once more. "I didn't lie about that. I *had* decided to become a governess, for the reasons I told you. When I saw the Szelényis' advertisement, I only answered it out of curiosity, to see who they were and how they were related — and yes, I wanted the opportunity to tell them just what I thought of their treatment of my mother... I knew at once that though István was too young to have known her, he was still tarred with the same arrogant, callous brush as his father. It made me — angry again. I meant to wait until he offered me the post — and I knew he would when I spoke Hungarian — and then throw it back in his face with a pithy denunciation of his family's history, habits and morals."

"It sounds like a good plan," Lajos said gravely. "What went wrong?"

74

I gave a funny, unnatural laugh. "*I* did. I suddenly realized that if I actually accepted the post, I could come here, meet the old man himself. I thought I could cause more — damage."

For a moment he was silent. I looked at my hands. I could almost see him revising his opinion of me, acknowledging the bitter, twisted, vengeful woman I had revealed myself to be.

"You must hate him very much." Amazingly, his voice held no repulsion, just a kind of puzzled compassion. It was the last thing I needed. I felt the tears prickle against my eyelids. Furiously, I tried to blink them away. "Why?" Lajos asked softly. "Why so much hate for a man you had never seen?"

I told him. It didn't take many words, and I all but spat those at him as if it were all his fault instead of my grandfather's. And then, abruptly, I broke off, angrily dashing my hand across my face. It was wet again.

"Oh God," I said desperately, and then I felt his hands on my shoulders, drawing me wordlessly to my feet, and I was held in his arms, my face buried in his shoulder. Curiously, it seemed the most natural place to be in my grief, so just for a moment I allowed the comfort, feeling the strong, steady beat of his heart against me.

He took off my spectacles, drying my eyes with a large, white handkerchief. Somehow I had not expected him to possess such a thing, and the thought almost made me smile.

"I'm sorry," I managed to say, taking the handkerchief from him and drawing myself out of his hold. I felt curiously forlorn again, but I blew my nose vigorously, almost blasphemously in that place, before drying my spectacles and replacing them firmly on my face. Resolutely, I held the crumpled handkerchief out to him. He eyed it without enthusiasm.

"You keep it," he said drily, "As a souvenir." I hiccoughed on a laugh, letting my hand fall back to my side. I waited expectantly to feel the shame and embarrassment of displaying such emotion to him, but oddly enough, they didn't come. After a moment, he said, "Why don't you tell them now? Get it over."

"Not yet," I said quickly. Please, not yet: it was too soon to lose everything, to go away...

"Your grandfather's not a fool, you know, however much he may behave like one."

"I can't think why my mother *wanted* his forgiveness," I said contemptuously. "He is a thoroughly unpleasant old man. You should hear the way he speaks to Margit."

"I have heard. She's afraid of him, and he can't abide that."

I looked at him without kindness. "That's no excuse."

"But she allows it."

"What else can she do? She is dependant on him!"

"No one is dependant. She could have left years ago."

"If she was as strong as you!"

"Or you," he said quietly. I stared at him, but before I could retort, the chapel door swung suddenly open again and Father Ránoczy came in, halting in surprise at the sight of us. I whisked myself away from Lajos, muttering, "I have to go...!"

"Wait." He caught my wrist. "Will you go and see my mother?"

For a second I hesitated, then, realizing I owed her at least that much, I simply nodded and fled from him, brushing past the curious priest with an incoherent apology.

As the summer days sweltered on and I still kept the secret which had become such an unexpected embarrassment to me, talk in the castle became fixed upon dancing. Apparently there was to be a grand ball — to which, naturally, every noble family in the district was invited — while the servants were looking forward to their own dance in the village, held every year to celebrate bringing in the harvest, however poor.

Katalin in particular grew increasingly excited about the ball, and I soon discovered why. Captain Zarescu had arrived at Szelényi, inspiring her with quite impractical hopes.

"If only Papa could *meet* him," she exclaimed to me in the school room, when the children had been dragged away by Zsuzsa. "Then he would realize what a fine man Alex is, and *surely* not oppose us?"

"I don't think character is the problem, do you?" I said quietly.

Occasionally, when my duties permitted it, I went to visit Eszter Lázár, and began to see more clearly why my mother had missed her. In her own, much quieter way, she was as remarkable as Lajos. She had his intelligence, his enquiring mind, without, perhaps, his drive, his will to make things happen.

"I should tell you," she said once, a little hesitantly, "that it was I who helped her to elope. I've often wondered if I did the right thing, and if she was happy..."

"It was only the Szelényis who made her unhappy," I said quietly.

Eszter shrugged. "The Count was devastated when she left, but as usual he looked around for someone to blame for his pain — and since it couldn't be himself, it had to be your parents."

This was a new way of looking at it for me, but I still could not forgive. There was no excuse for such selfish, stony-hearted silence. "But what of Margit?" I asked. "Surely such a — a *kind* woman would have made *some* contact with her own sister?"

Eszter hesitated. For a moment, she looked away, then, "She missed her sister dreadfully, I know that, and I know she read all the letters your mother sent."

My eyes widened. "I thought he — the Count — would have burned them!"

She smiled slightly, suddenly so like Lajos that it took my breath away. "No, he never burned them. He kept them locked in his desk — probably still does. But Margit had the keys even then."

I said wistfully, "Did she not try to write?"

"She was forbidden by the Count. Everyone was. I see you think that a feeble reason, but in fairness, the Count's anger *is* a thing to be feared. Then, Margit was a funny child — only fifteen when the lady Sofia left — obedient to a fault, and in quite *terrible* awe of her father."

Slowly, I shook my head. "She should have got away from him."

"She never had much chance. She took on all the duties of a chatelaine, making herself too indispensable to the old Count's comfort. When he married again she should have taken the chance to marry herself; there was someone, I believe, but when the new Countess died too, they say lady Margit turned her suitor away in order to care for her father... again..."

Towards the end of this speech, I realized that her attention was wandering, and rather impatiently I stood up, following her gaze to the window. In the garden I could see old Lázár, his face red and furious as he gesticulated and shouted. We could not hear the words, but they were certainly aimed at Lajos who crouched before him, his fingers pulling mechanically at some weeds while he looked up at his father. Behind him stood Károly, miserably twisting his hat between his hands as Lázár verbally belaboured his brother. And Lajos did not retaliate. His face was carefully expressionless.

"Oh God, not again," Eszter whispered despairingly. And then Lajos stood up. Spreading his hands as if accepting guilt, he turned away from his father. Lázár took a hasty step nearer, and then Károly stood between them. Lajos paused, glancing back at his father, not angry, I saw, but not smiling either. I saw his lips move as he spoke. And Lázár, with a last gesture of scorn, turned and stamped off.

Károly looked anxiously at his brother. With an effort, Lajos managed to smile at him, saying something light as he walked away.

"One day," Eszter said, her voice low and intense, as if she could not prevent the words, "one day he will go too far and Lajos will not come back. And I shall never forgive him for that. Never."

Then, much as Lajos had done a moment before, she tried to smile. I felt a rush of pity, for all of them. "I'm sorry. It's always like this when he first comes home. The boys don't know how to treat him... And Lázár is so fearfully proud of him, yet he doesn't understand him. In truth, he wants him here all the time and is hurt by his absence. He can't see that Lajos has outgrown Szelényi."

"Perhaps he can," I said quietly. "He is afraid Lajos has outgrown *you*."

I suppose it was impertinent, but Eszter only said sadly, "Perhaps he has. *I* never know what goes on in his head any more."

"Schemes and plans and revolutions," I said lightly, and she smiled tiredly.

I hesitated, unsure of my place, then added, "I know it's not only duty which brings him home."

She met my gaze and her face softened. "I believe you're right..." Her look became speculative. "Do you know what he gets up to in Pest and Vienna?"

"No," I said apologetically, "not really. I know he works for a lawyer, teaches..."

"Does he break the law?" she interrupted.

I shifted uncomfortably, remembering the police outside the Pilvax. "I'm not sure exactly what your laws are. To be frank, I think he sails very close to the wind, but he is very sure of his ground, very *calculating* about what he can get away with."

She took that in and I wondered if I had said too much. For a moment, I thought she was going to ask me something else — I wondered in panic if the rumours about Baroness Meleki had reached her. But she said only, "We seem to have wandered from your problem to mine, my lady. Have you decided what to do?"

"I'll have to tell them, I suppose," I said ruefully. "But to be honest, I'm too comfortable to wish to be sent away in a hurry."

"Perhaps that won't happen," she suggested, but I could see that neither of us believed it.

Of Lajos himself, I saw very little. From Father Ránoczy, I knew he was conducting a legal battle with the steward over common ownership of some of the Count's land. And of course, he was busy in the fields — we saw him at work there once or twice, stripped to the waist like his companions, the sweat glistening warmly on his brown, naked back, but he only raised his hand to us and carried on working. I was glad, because these encounters made me oddly uncomfortable. For the first time I was made aware of the hard strength in his deceptively slight body, and the knowledge confused me; I wanted to look away, offended by this invasion of his privacy, and yet I found I couldn't, for there was a strange, new, almost frightening pleasure in watching him so.

In fact, I had the lowering suspicion that Teréz Meleki was taking up all his free time — a suspicion which was soon reinforced in a very odd manner.

Late one afternoon, after Zsuzsa had taken the children away and I was tidying up the schoolroom, I became aware that I was being watched. I looked round quickly, but if I had hoped to find Lajos again, I was disappointed. It was Baroness Meleki. She was standing in the doorway, dressed for dinner, elegant, richly gowned, beautiful, her eyes full of mockery which I couldn't recall earning.

"Madame?" I said at once. "Can I help you?"

"Oh I doubt it," she said in her languid, amused voice as she strolled into the schoolroom. "You seem to be a very respectable person, Miss...?"

"Kettles. Thank you for your notice."

"I've certainly never noticed you before," she said frankly, "but it seems other people have."

"What other people?" I asked without much interest, laying my pile of books down on the desk.

"Oh, servants, mere peasants, but word spreads, my dear — and mud sticks. I should know." I frowned. I hadn't the faintest idea what she was talking about and told her so, not bothering to hide my impatience. "Why, haven't you heard what's being said about you?" she asked, mocking concern in her eyes. "They're saying that you are Lajos Lázár's latest mistress."

She had my attention now. I stared at her while the angry colour flooded into my face. "They're saying *what*? *Who* is saying such a thing?"

"Who knows where rumours start? I didn't enquire. I just thought I'd come and take a look at you, and see if I believed it."

I flushed at her insulting tone. "You don't need to look, only listen," I said flatly. "I am not and never have been Lajos Lázár's mistress, and you do neither of us any service by repeating such a thing."

She sat down at Anna's desk, stretching out one slim foot. "You seem rather flustered," she observed.

"If I am, it's because I am unused to back-stairs gossip," I retorted.

For a second, I saw an angry flash in her eyes, quickly veiled. Then she said in her usual manner, "Myself, I am more concerned with why, not where, this rumour started."

"I see no reason for you to be concerned at all."

"Oh but I am," she said softly. "Don't misunderstand me, dear — I could see the truth of your denial before you ever made it, just by looking at you. A man such as Lajos could never be interested in you. It's laughable."

She was only saying what I already knew. Yet it was unutterably painful, not to say humiliating, to hear it from her callous lips. I am not easily crushed, but at that moment I came very close to it. I looked down at my hands resting on the books before me, waiting for her next onslaught. It wasn't slow in coming.

"On the other hand," she drawled, "*he* has all the attractions of a strong man of the soil, all the thrills, if you like, without any of the inconvenient rough edges — again, I should know. A man with ideals, and a desire to change the world into one where *your* life, for instance, might just be a little better."

"And yours a little worse," I said sweetly. I refused to be crushed for long, not by her.

She stood abruptly, forgetting her habitual languor. "But make no mistake, little governess," she almost spat, "he is not doing it for you."

"I never imagined he was." I was pleased to hear that I sounded amused. I even drawled, much in her own manner. Her eyes narrowed; I had the satisfaction of seeing that I had confused her. I did not conform to her idea of a poor, love-sick governess. Which was just as well. One has one's pride.

"Good," she said, with commendable lightness. "For I came as one woman to another, to warn you not to misunderstand him. You are a stranger, a foreigner, friendless — perhaps liable through loneliness to read the wrong message from a man's kindness."

She was wrong there. I had never misunderstood Lajos's friendship, but her words were nevertheless insulting, not least because she was right about the loneliness. She came close up to me, confident, sophisticated, undeniably attractive, and, smiling faintly, she said, "I know you will find it shocking, but the truth is that Lajos is mine. He has been mine since we first met, and he will remain mine for as long as I choose to have him. So you see, in different ways, both our reputations are suffering from this silly rumour!"

She gave a tinkling laugh, and brushed past me. I wanted her away from me, so that I could sort out the jumble of pain and humiliation and conjecture which she had so kindly brought me. But I was not to be spared yet. Half way to the door, she paused, and I could have screamed with vexation.

"By the way," she said languidly. "Have you ever been to a coffee-house in Pest called the Pilvax?"

My breath caught. With thoughts chasing wildly through my head, I kept my face calm and expressionless — I am good at that: in my teens I had practised in front of a looking glass.

"I don't believe," I said gently, "that my movements are any of your business."

Her eyes narrowed again, this time with anger. "Perhaps not, but your insolence is, if I choose to make it so! One word from me, girl, and you'll be out on the street without a character."

With which threat, she swept out of the room in an impressive rustle of silk. When I was sure she had gone, I let myself sink into the nearest chair, trying to calm my hammering heart. I thought I had handled the situation quite creditably, but the truth is that I hate such confrontations. They leave my nerves jangling for hours afterwards, and in this case I had the added complication of Lajos to think about. I felt as if my friendship with him had been invaded, soiled. And now, more than ever and simply for his own sake, I wished that his affair with the Baroness was over.

Then, this rumour she had talked of... If it was simply servants' gossip, I could probably rely on the Szelényis to ignore it — or even not to hear it in the first place! But her parting question about the Pilvax bothered me. And yet, why was I so worried? My time here was running out for quite other reasons.

Later on, it struck me that Zsuzsa, who had her own peculiar ideas about my friendship with Lajos, might well be the unwitting source of the Baroness's rumours. However, pride would not let me mention it to her, though I never prevented her from keeping me informed about Lajos's activities. I found I was still worried about his stormy relationship with his family, though Zsuzsa soon gave me cause to believe that things there had eased a little — the unlikely reason being an evening spent at the Szelényi tavern.

The Lázár men had apparently led the entire village in a riotous drinking session — apparently not an infrequent occurrence — which involved, inevitably, Lajos riding around the tavern on his brothers' shoulders, making a hilarious speech about the stupidity of land owners. No doubt it was dangerously similar to the one which had so offended Baron Acsády; certainly it had had the villagers roaring out their approval when they could stop laughing for long enough. Later they had progressed to the house of the Szelényi estate steward, where Lajos and Zoltán, balanced precariously on the backs of fellow inebriates, had nailed up all the doors and windows while the poor steward snored oblivious; and Lázár himself had sat helplessly at the side of the road, howling with such glee that he had had to wipe the tears from his face.

Half-laughing, half-appalled, I said, "Oh no, surely not! He *must* have heard them!"

"Not him," said Zsuzsa contemptuously. "Too drunk on the Count's wine."

The next day she told me that Lajos had gone away for a few days. I wondered ruefully if it was with his father's blessing, or if it would set off the trouble between them all over again.

By then, of course, the Captain's presence in Szelényi had been discovered. Countess Elisabeth resorted to shock tactics.

At dinner one evening she suddenly said, "By the way, Katalin, I saw that young Romanian officer in the village this afternoon. Did you know he was here?"

To my distress, I saw that Katalin was very still. At last she looked up from her plate, meeting her sister-in-law's gaze squarely. "Why, yes, I did. He is staying at the tavern, I believe, which can't be much fun for him. I don't know why he doesn't stay with Lajos as he used to for at least Eszter's sheets would be clean! Actually," she added casually, "I thought I might invite him to the ball."

Elisabeth's eyes narrowed in recognition of the challenge. I saw Mattias looking closely and not too kindly at his sister, but then the Count, who had been paying scant attention up until then, sat up, staring at his youngest daughter. "You want to invite a friend of Lázár's to the ball?" he said incredulously, and as Katalin struggled for a reply, help came from an unexpected quarter.

"He may be a friend of Lajos's," Mattias said wryly, "but he is still an officer and a gentleman! Some of us are, you know."

"Oh? You count yourself a friend of his too, do you?"

"Yes, I do, as a matter of fact."

"Ha!" said the Count derisively.

"So, should I ask him?" Katalin persisted.

Maria opened her mouth to pronounce, but before she could, the Count said, "Yes, yes, I suppose so, if he's presentable. We have few enough young people in these parts."

"I hope," said István sardonically, "that it is the officer you are encouraging her to invite, and not Lajos?"

The Count gave a crack of laughter and finished his wine, crashing his glass back down on the table to draw the attention of the servants to its state of emptiness. Elisabeth was still looking at Katalin who, however, was holding a determined conversation with Baron Mirányi. It was not until the end of the meal that the two women spoke, and then it was only because Elisabeth held her back physically as they left the dining room, until the rest of the family were past.

As I slipped by them, I heard Elisabeth say, "I hope you know what you're doing, Katalin."

"Yes, I think I do," said the younger girl quietly.

I had almost squeezed past, but Elisabeth's eye caught me. "Did *you* know she was going to do this?"

"Yes, I knew."

The Countess looked form one to the other of us, suddenly not quite so languid. "I just hope you're not making matters worse."

"That's the whole point, Elisabeth," said Katalin wearily. "Matters couldn't be any worse." Elisabeth shook her head and stepped away, but then she paused and turned back to face me.

"What a good idea," she said lazily. "Miss Kettles, you shall go to the ball."

I blinked. She appeared to mean it, so I roused myself to point out, "In this garb I should hardly be an ornament to your party."

But she waved that aside. "Oh, you may borrow something of Katalin's."

"I'd need to borrow scissors as well."

"Stop making difficulties," Katalin commanded. "I think it's an excellent idea!"

I cast her a look which clearly said traitor and which she totally ignored. But I still had one card to play. "It would not," I said, "be suitable. The Count would not approve."

Elisabeth regarded me with amused tolerance. "I can see why you like her," she observed to Katalin, "but she would drive me mad in an hour. The Count will be perfectly happy, for I don't mean you to be there as a guest but as my aide."

Katalin gazed at her. "And as my chaperone?"

"I can see some of Miss Kettles's cleverness is rubbing off on you," said the Countess blandly.

Katalin shrugged philosophically. "I don't mind Katie, but if you set Maria on me, Elisabeth, I *swear* I'll do something outrageous!" she said and swung my hand into the air. "Oh, this is going to be fun, Katie! We must introduce you to someone dashing and rich, get you a husband to take you away from all this drudgery with us!"

"Thank you," I said politely, "but I do not wish for a husband."

"Nonsense," said Katalin firmly. "Everyone does."

CHAPTER TWELVE

By the day of the ball, the castle was in a positive fever of activity. An army of servants was charging from one end of the castle to the other, feverishly fetching, carrying and cleaning, hastily preparing rooms for guests staying the night — though in fact very few were, most preferring to make even journeys of several hours duration after the festivities. Considering the treacherous state of the local roads, I hoped the coachmen concerned would remain at least partially sober.

As soon as the children became Zsuzsa's responsibility again, I was swept into service by Elisabeth, to oversee the arrangement of various small matters such as cloak-rooms, flowers, buffet tables, card tables and so on; and it was in fact while carrying out these duties that I realized the main problem of the poor servants — too many people giving conflicting orders. Margit, Maria and Elisabeth all felt some claim to be hostess for the evening, but the servants, used to regarding the gentle Margit in this role, resented having her orders upset by more forceful — not to say imperious — members of the family. As a result, I spent a great deal of time trying to smooth things over and sort out the chaos while running between the Szelényi ladies to achieve a compromise.

When I had dressed myself for the evening in my old cream silk evening gown, which Ilse, Katalin's capable maid, had miraculously transformed simply by sewing two dark red bows on to the skirts, and one trailing ribbon rather tastefully on the left shoulder, I sallied forth to the fray once more. Elisabeth, István and Katalin were discovered in the ballroom — which was decked out for the occasion in what looked like miles of primrose silk — critically giving it a final inspection. In the gallery, the orchestra from Kolozsvár were tuning up.

"Why, Katie, you look lovely!" Katalin exclaimed, and I felt my cheeks begin to burn as the other two also turned and stared at me.

I had eventually given in to Zsuzsa's pleading to be allowed to dress my hair, which was a happy piece of generosity on my part for she turned out to have quite a talent in that respect, lifting my hair higher than normal and adding a cunning twist. When I had put my spectacles back on, I found my reflection in the glass almost pretty. "Thank you," I had said, with a surprised sincerity which had made her laugh.

Elisabeth, after examining me casually from head to toe, simply nodded. "What do you think?" she asked, waving her hand round the empty but luxurious ballroom.

"Beautiful," I said dutifully.

"If you see it becoming otherwise, rouse the servants," she ordered, bustling off to greet her first guests.

From then on, I was assailed by an endless string of petty tasks, but to be truthful, since I had to be there at all, I was glad to have something to do. I loathe such huge social gatherings. I always have, no doubt because in the dark days before my spectacles, everyone present in such a crowd looked exactly the same. The horror still clung.

It was Maria who imperiously commanded me to the kitchen half way through the evening, and there, the first person my eyes fell on was Lajos Lázár, standing only feet away by the big table, talking seriously to two maids and a man-servant. I blinked away the shock, deliberately steadying my heart beat after the jolt it always seemed to give on coming upon him unexpectedly. He saw me at once, and his lips curved upwards.

"What the devil are you doing here?" I demanded.

"Visiting," said Lajos blandly.

I looked him up and down. "You're not dressed for it."

"You, on the other hand, quite obviously are — and looking particularly beautiful."

"I wish I could say the same to you," I retorted, although I felt the colour rise to my cheeks. His eyes smiled, as though delighted by a compliment.

"I suppose you won't even dance with me until I'm in evening clothes?"

"Not even then," I said flatly, becoming aware of the grinning servants listening in with interest to this exchange. "Why don't you go home, Lajos?"

"I'm having too much fun here."

"I'm glad someone is! Gavrilla, may I tell Baroness Mirányi that supper will still be on time, and that the fish is dressed according to her wishes?"

"No," said Gavrilla crossly, lumbering over to me and clouting two idle servants back to work as she went. "You may tell the lady Margit!"

"I'll tell them both," I said pacifically. "Thank you." I turned away, deliberately without looking again at Lajos, but he had moved to the door and now I found him holding it open for me. When I glanced up to thank him, I realized he was following me out.

"What *are* you doing here?" I demanded severely as we walked together along the passage.

"I'm meeting someone."

Of course he was. My eyes fell, but I couldn't lose my last image of Teréz Meleki, more stunning than ever in a bold, sophisticated crimson gown, smiling with devastating if languid charm as she had waltzed past me in some nobleman's arms.

"The Baroness was dancing when I saw her last," I said woodenly.

"Which Baroness?" He actually sounded surprised.

"Meleki," I said drily, and risked a glance at him. For a moment, his eyes searched mine; then I saw a smile begin to grow in them.

"Why, Katie," he said softly. "Have you been listening to gossip?" I flushed, busily examining some flaking paint on the wall. After a moment he stopped and I was forced to do the same, for his fingers had taken hold of my chin, gently but firmly turning my face up to his. I was aware of his eyes smiling down into mine in a way that was making me curiously breathless and quite unable to focus any longer on either Teréz or the décor.

And then abruptly the kitchen door crashed open again behind us, releasing a babble of voices and activity. With a tiny gasp, I whisked myself free of him, and was already fleeing towards the ballroom before I remembered that I still didn't know what he was doing here, who it was he had really come to meet.

Entering the ballroom rather thoughtfully, I discovered Captain Zarescu propping up a pillar by the dance floor, watching with his great, sad eyes as Katalin waltzed past in the arms of another man. I could understand his misery, for she was positively radiant, but in truth her happiness was all to do with his presence here, and her hopes of it.

I said casually, "Did you know Lajos Lázár is here?"

"Yes; we walked up the hill together."

"He's not — up to anything, is he?" I asked apologetically.

The Captain looked amused. "What in the world could he be up to?"

"I don't know," I said frankly, wrestling with the perverse part of me that wished he was trouble-making in some way rather than lurking here in the hope of catching a glimpse of Teréz Meleki. Though I could hardly imagine a glimpse being enough for Lajos. I wondered if he had ever just gazed at his lady love on a dance floor as his friend was doing now. Deliberately, I avoided looking for her.

The dance came to an end, and I watched with amused interest how Katalin cleverly steered her cavalier to where we were standing. When I glanced at Zarescu again, his expression had relaxed. Katalin performed brief introductions before rather imperiously sending her partner for champagne. The poor boy was delighted to go: I felt almost sorry for him.

"I saved this one for you," Katalin said, smiling mistily up at Alex. They didn't even notice me as they waltzed off together. I moved my position quickly, before the unfortunate young man came back with her champagne, going to wait near enough Elisabeth to obey her commands.

A little later, I caught sight of Katalin on Zarescu's arm, making a beeline for her father. Craven instinct warned me to make haste to the opposite end of the room, but even as I changed direction, Katalin's eye caught mine with such a look of pleading even I could not ignore it. I went and sat down near to where the Count was standing, though what Earthly good Katalin imagined I could possibly be was beyond me. She drew her father away from the group he was with, leading him and Alex even closer to me. I felt distinctly uncomfortable.

"Papa," she said with commendable calm, "this is Captain Zarescu."

"Yes, I know. We met as he arrived. Delighted you could come."

"Thank you. It was kind of you to invite me." I had the impression they had said much the same things before.

"Not at all. I like to see young faces at these affairs. Old folk make 'em wretchedly dull! So, you're in the army, eh?"

"Yes, sir."

"Cavalry?"

"Infantry."

"Never mind," said the Count encouragingly. "I expect there are good promotion prospects."

"Yes, sir, I believe so."

"Good, good."

"Captain Zarescu knows Mattias," Katalin said a little desperately as the conversation seemed about to dry up.

"Do you? Wastrel," pronounced the proud father.

"He's young," Zarescu excused.

"He's a wastrel," the Count repeated firmly. "Where did you meet him?"

"Why, here in Szelényi, when we were boys, and then again at the Pilvax coffee-house in Pest," Alexandru said easily. Then I could almost see him kicking himself, but any hope he might have cherished of the Count not recognizing the name was quickly dashed.

"Pilvax, eh?" said the old man, looking at Zarescu a little more closely, and adding derisively, "Young Hungary!"

Katalin cast me an uneasy glance. I shrugged philosophically. The Count went on, "But *you*'re not a member of Young Hungary, are you?"

The Captain smiled. "Not formally; I would call myself rather a *friend* of the movement."

"You surprise me," the Count said casually. "I wouldn't have thought you'd be interested."

Zarescu's smile died. "Why not?"

"You're Romanian, aren't you? Not Hungarian."

"I was born here in Transylvania, under the Crown of St. Stephen," Alexandru said quietly. "And I now live in Buda-Pest. I have no reason not to support Young Hungary."

Katalin's gaze had become agonized, pleading. I mouthed urgently, "Change the subject!" But before she could even try, the Count surprised us all by emitting a crack of laughter.

"Well, you're not afraid to speak your mind, are you? Even to a reactionary old devil like me! Do you play cards, boy?"

"Why, yes, sir..."

"Good, good." And the Count took his arm and led him away towards the anteroom where card tables had been set up for the addicted. I closed my mouth deliberately.

Katalin all but collapsed into the chair beside me. "Do you know," she said weakly, "I think it is going well?"

"Better than I had dared to hope," I said frankly. Some distance away, Elisabeth caught my eye. I sighed.

"She wants you," Katalin pointed out, "and I want some more champagne!"

The Countess was, as usual, the centre of an admiring group of people, though I noticed she still contrived to keep an eye and an ear on her husband's conversation with the young Acsády girl. Stepping a little away from her companions to meet me, she murmured, "Well? What happened?"

"Nothing. They've gone off to play cards together."

She looked startled. "*Cards?*"

"Cards."

Her breath seemed to catch as she turned away, but I had already glimpsed the humorous response in her eyes. There were times, I thought, when she was almost human.

I didn't get the chance to speak to Alex until much later in the evening, for I was kept busy trailing from one end of the castle to the other with few noticeable results; but eventually, during a bid to avoid Maria's imperious gaze, I all but bumped into him. "There you are!" I exclaimed. My restless eyes had discovered Katalin with István on the other side of the room. Both looked rather heated. "How was your game?"

"I lost — I thought it prudent! But he's not half as bad as Katalin makes out, you know."

"I think you'll find he is," I said vaguely, watching uneasily as István all but stormed away from his sister. Though I prayed it wouldn't, his cold, angry gaze fell eventually on us, and at once he changed direction towards us. I glanced at Zarescu. "But at the moment, I'm afraid, your problem is István. I think the cat is out of the bag."

Cravenly, I moved away from him, meaning to find out from Katalin what had happened. I was privileged to hear István bark out, "Sir, a word, if you please." And Alexandru's calm reply of "Certainly."

Katalin, when I found her, proved to be inaccessible. She was the centre of a happy group of young people, looking as beautiful as she ever had, but there was a feverish glitter in her eyes, a slightly hectic flush to her cheeks that worried me. I suspected she had imbibed a little too much champagne for discretion.

"Miss Kettles," said Elisabeth's voice behind me. "Where is Captain What's-his-name?"

"Your husband is speaking to him."

"Ah." She lowered her voice. "I was obliged to explain to him the nature of Katalin's friendship — he saw them gazing stupidly into each other's eyes when they were dancing together. It might be a good idea if the Captain went home."

I didn't bother to hide the anger I felt at that. "Is that what your husband is telling him?"

"Go and see there is no — er — disruption, will you?"

I stared at her. "How," I asked patiently, "would you like me to do that?"

"I was told you were clever," she said lazily, waving her fan and moving away.

Once, I had been smug enough to consider my post an easy one. How in the world had it progressed to this? I threaded my way through the guests, who were about to go into the supper room, but I came upon Zarescu on his own, heading towards Katalin. He didn't even see me till I touched his sleeve.

"Captain," I said, and he turned to look at me. I was shocked. His normally good-natured face was livid, his lips tight with anger, and his great, sad eyes almost tragic. Impulsively, I took his arm, uncaring who saw, and we moved together through the throng until we had a space out of ear-shot. "What happened?" I demanded. "What did he say to you?"

Zarescu laughed mirthlessly. "He was pleased to accuse me of *importuning* his sister! Naturally, I denied it, after which he invited me to leave and to keep my filthy Romanian person away from his family in the future."

I blanched. "He said that?"

"He was angry," Alexandru allowed, fair to the last, dragging his hand through his black hair.

"What did you say?"

The Captain smiled faintly. "I said I was here at his father's invitation, and until the Count withdrew it I was perfectly happy to stay."

I couldn't resist saying roundly, "Good for you." But a second later, sense prevailed. "It wasn't very wise though, was it? You don't want to make a worse enemy of István. Perhaps you *should* leave before he speaks to his father...?"

"No," said Alexandru with unexpected firmness. "I am going for supper." And I watched helplessly as he marched up to Katalin and spoke to her. From the circle of her friends, she looked up at him in surprise. I saw her flush grow deeper and fade again. He offered her his arm; she smiled tremulously and took it, holding her head high as they walked across the ballroom towards the supper room.

I couldn't help admiring them then, their beauty as well as their courage. But it looked as if there would be fireworks now.

"Have the position of these chairs fixed," Maria's voice said suddenly in my ear, making me jump. I realized I was not to be allowed supper — it was not the lot of the governess. I expected I was not allowed champagne either, but catching sight of a full, deserted glass, I picked it up and took a sizeable gulp. I needed it.

Unfortunately, though I had thought no one was watching, Colonel von Avenheim happened to glance back over his shoulder and was accorded an excellent view. I saw his eyes crinkle with laughter before he turned back to his chattering partner. I liked the Colonel.

The dancing was beginning again after supper before I next caught sight of István. For some, who had a long way to go home, this would be the last dance of the evening. I had told myself, without much hope, that István would calm down, at least to the extent of waiting until after the ball to expose his sister's iniquities to the old Count, but now I saw him glowering at the spectacle of Katalin and Alex dancing together yet again. A moment later, I saw Maria say something sharp and surprisingly sensible in his ear — no doubt about drawing unwelcome attention to their sister by his behaviour — which caused him to turn away rather abruptly. A little after that I realized that he was dancing too, and made the mistake of breathing a somewhat premature sigh of relief.

CHAPTER THIRTEEN

It was as this dance ended that Katalin and Alexandru took their chance. Before I could guess what they were about, Zarescu had crossed the floor and was approaching the Count. I felt a stab of unease. I saw the Count shrug, then wave his arm a little exaggeratedly to the Captain to precede him.

"What is he doing?" I asked slowly, as Katalin came to stand beside me.

"He is asking for my hand," Katalin said softly.

I closed my eyes. "And you think your father will say yes, just because he beat Alex at cards?"

She stared at me. Clearly, she had drunk far too much champagne. "Don't you think it's a good idea?"

"No," I said faintly, "I don't. Katalin, your father will *explode,* and what he says so publicly, he could never reverse! If I were you, I would stop Alex now, before it's too late..."

Her eyes were enormous. I saw her teeth grip her lower lip. Then suddenly, she seized me by the hand. "Come on then," she muttered, and as fast as we dared, we moved towards the door. As it was, I intercepted a few curious glances as we sped by.

"Where have they gone?" I demanded.

"In here," said Katalin, indicating a poorly lit room opposite.

"Go on then, quickly," I urged. She drew a breath and went in, dragging me with her.

I saw at once that we were too late. They were standing in the middle of that dim room, face to face. The Count was staring at Zarescu in stark disbelief. "You *what?*" he uttered.

The Captain's eyes flickered to us. Impulsively, Katalin went forward. "Do you know what this fellow has just asked me?" her father demanded.

Katalin nodded, swallowing audibly. "Yes, oh yes, Papa, please say yes..."

"Say yes? Are you as mad as he is? Am I likely to give my daughter to a penniless Romanian nobody?"

"I am not penniless," Alexandru said firmly. "And my Romanian race is, in fact, a matter of pride to me."

"Young Hungary," mocked the Count.

Zarescu lifted his head. "Sir, I have asked you what Katalin and I consider to be a reasonable question. May I not have an answer?"

I felt pity well up in me, but I could do nothing now. The old man glared at him. "Yes, damn you, I'll give you an answer! You may *not* marry my daughter! You may not *speak* to my daughter! You may not even *look* at my daughter! Your presumption is so unbelievable, that were it not for the fact that the foolish chit has obviously put you up to it, I would have you whipped out of the village! Do you understand me?"

"Perfectly," said Alexandru, low-voiced and deathly white.

"Papa, how *can* you?" Katalin cried, seizing her father's arm. "How can you speak to him so? I love him!"

"You don't know the meaning of the word!" said the Count contemptuously, shaking her off. "What in God's name is the matter with the women of this family? You're as bad as your sister!"

Katalin paused, frowning, for now he had surprised her. He had surprised me too. "I thought we were not to speak of Sofia," she said abruptly.

"*You* are not to speak of Sofia! I shall speak of whoever I wish!"

"Then so shall I! I *will* marry Alexandru, whatever you say! And if you won't consent, then I shall run away, *just* like Sofia!"

The old man was white now too. I thought he was shaking. But he could still sneer. "Not you. You haven't got Sofia's guts! Possessions meant nothing to her! But where would you be without your allowance, your fancy clothes and jewels, every luxury at your command? For make no mistake, girl, *I* won't be paying for them!" He uttered a harsh, contemptuous laugh. "But it won't arise, will it? You'll never see him again, do you hear? And as for you, sirrah, I took you for a sensible man. I expected you to know better. Now, get out of my sight, both of you!"

Katalin was in tears, but she brushed past me to the door, pausing only to say brokenly, "Alexandru..." and reach out a blind hand to him. Despite the

Count's glowering presence, he took her hand and they left together. I was pleased about that, at least.

The Count strode after them, his choleric eye finally registering my presence and causing him to pause. "What the Devil are you here for?" he barked.

"Moral support," I said bitterly. "But I was of no use."

"Then mind your own damned business!" said the Count rudely, and swung out of the room.

Slowly, I followed him back to the ballroom. From the dance-floor, Elisabeth saw me come in, so I was not at all surprised when she sought me out only moments later. "My father-in-law is in the filthiest mood I have seen all year," she observed. "Katalin is not here, and neither is Captain What's-his-name. What, Miss Kettles, is going on?"

I told her, briefly and succinctly. She closed her eyes for a moment. "Is he still alive?" she enquired. "I would have expected my father-in-law to kill him. At the very least."

"I think he might just as well have done so," I said tiredly, and she shrugged her bare, elegant shoulders. Her eyes were already bored again, looking around while I waited impatiently to be dismissed, or sent about some business.

"What is all that about?" she said slowly, and I followed her gaze to the ballroom door. Through it, amazingly, I could see the steward almost wrestling with two footmen. "Go and sort it out, will you?" said the Countess casually, and strolled away.

I went, trailing my feet a little. I was depressed and angry and had a lot more to think about than a drunken steward behaving like a character in a bad farce. By the time I emerged, the footmen had manhandled him out of sight of the ballroom, but he was still struggling furiously.

"What is going on?" I asked resignedly, and, in truth, without much interest, but at the sound of my voice, the steward burst from his captors with a new lease of life, and skidded to a halt before me.

"Mademoiselle, you must listen to me!" he pleaded, as the footmen grabbed him again. "The peasants are massing at the gate! You must tell the Count!"

I stared stupidly. "*What?*"

"Peasants! Hundreds of them!" said the steward, as he was dragged backwards. Fear was clamping round my heart like a pain.

"Let him go," I said sharply, and, rather to my surprise, they reluctantly released him. "Go on."

"Some of the guests who were trying to leave are waiting at the gate. They're frightened to go on because of the mob — the carriages are lining up..."

I tried to force my brain to think. Lajos. It had to be Lajos, but what in God's name had he done? "Very well," I said to the steward. "I'll tell the Count at once." I glanced at one of the footmen, who was now contriving to look both innocent and wooden. "Where is Lajos Lázár?" I asked him.

"I couldn't say, Madame."

"Did you know about this?"

"No, Madame."

My eyes narrowed. "I hope you're telling the truth," I said flatly, "because if not, any blood shed tonight will be on your hands too!"

Perhaps it was unkind, but it made me feel better. I went quickly into the ballroom, where more and more people were taking their leave. István was hovering around his father, no doubt to discuss Katalin. I went to them at once. "Sir," I said to the Count, "may I have a word?"

"You again," he glowered. "Wait. I'm busy."

"It can't wait," I said firmly. "It concerns your guests as well as you."

The guests beside him looked surprised. The Count's eyes flickered, then he muttered something and stepped back. "What is it?" he demanded.

I told him exactly what the steward had said. And István, listening in, said at once, "Lajos Lázár!"

"Who else?" his father growled, and then suddenly roared out, "Peter! My carriage!"

The guests all looked startled, some worried, some amused. Even the orchestra faltered, but in the end struggled on manfully. "What will you do?" István asked.

"Go down there and sort it out. You stay here as host, and try not to let anyone else leave till I get back."

"May I be of assistance, sir?" It was Colonel von Avenheim.

The Count regarded him with surprise, as if he had quite forgotten his presence here. "Just the man!" he said, sounding pleased. "Come with me!"

The Colonel still looked a little baffled, so István quickly told his friend what I had said.

"Let me send to the garrison at Vanora," Avenheim said at once.

"No," I said without thinking, and they all looked at me in amazement. I blinked uncomfortably, for in truth I had spoken from instinct, remembering only the bloodshed inflicted by soldiers at that "little" demonstration in Glasgow. "It would take too long," I said quickly. "Besides, shouldn't you find out first what is going on? Perhaps they have just come to watch the guests in all their finery..."

"*Hundreds* of them?" said István drily. "I know the wretched steward drinks, but even *one* hundred is still far too many!"

"The lady is right, though," Avenheim said. "Let's go and have a look, and then decide what is best."

"It might be too late then," István warned.

"Let's hope not."

Still too anxious to be relieved by this decision, I found myself following the Count and Avenheim. In the hall, they collected the steward and we all trooped out into the courtyard. I remember feeling vaguely surprised by the light which gleamed down on the waiting carriage. The moon was bright that night and the castle grounds were all well illuminated for the ball, as far as the gates themselves.

"Where do you think you're going?" the Count demanded as I began to climb into the carriage ahead of the steward.

"I thought I might come with you, be useful," I said unconvincingly.

"For God's sake, what *use* is a governess likely to be against a mob of peasants!"

"I've been negotiating truces between your family and your servants all day," I retorted, stung. "What difference is there now?"

The old man barked out a laugh. "She's got guts, the governess!" Since no one then forbade me, I climbed into the coach and sat beside Avenheim. I was aware of his eyes on me, curious. I didn't blame him. I was curious myself as to why I was so determined to go, except that I *knew* Lajos was involved.

The coach bounded forward towards the main path, and down to the castle gates. Here there was indeed a queue of carriages. The Count stuck his head out of the window, saying a few reassuring words to the distinctly nervous-looking guests waiting there. As our coach edged its way to the front, I peered out of the other window, and felt my stomach churn with fear.

All the way down the hill from the castle gates, as far as my eye could see, the road was lined on either side with peasant men and women. Some held torches, and their grim, unsmiling faces were rather terrifyingly illuminated in the night. The coach halted. I listened to absolute silence. None of the peasants moved; none of them spoke; no one even coughed. It had the eerie quality of a dream.

I felt my throat dry with anxiety. Was this really the uprising Lajos had told me he did not want? What had he done?

"What in the world are they doing?" Avenheim murmured at last, looking out over the Count's shoulder. I noticed that his voice was puzzled rather than afraid, which calmed me a little.

"Nothing," the Count said slowly. "Absolutely nothing." He sat back, tugging at his lower lip and frowning ferociously.

Avenheim looked at him. "Do you want the soldiers?" he asked, and my breath caught again.

"What do you think?"

"I think it might be safest."

"But too late," said the Count after a pause. "I can't let this go on. The longer they stay there... Damn it, they're *my* people!" He rapped his stick sharply on the roof of the coach, and slowly, it went forward.

That was the weirdest journey of my life. With excruciating deliberation, we passed through the lines of silent peasants, three or four people deep in some places. As I had known I would, I caught a glimpse of Lajos standing at the beginning of the line, as stern and resolute as the others around him, more forbidding than I had ever seen him. As we passed, the torch-light played over his distinctive, angular face, leaving an impression of grim, immovable power. Only his eyes moved: they saw me, and they saw the Count, but his expression never wavered, which, on that normally mobile countenance, was more frightening than all the rest.

We drove slowly on, through an uncanny nightmare of solemn, hard faces, the only sounds the clip of the horses' hooves and the creaking of the coach wheels. The people did nothing, just watched. Some of them were strangers to me, some were Romanians, but others I recognized easily: one of Lajos's brothers, his parents, Zsuzsa's mother, the man who was László's brother, someone who had held the gate open once for the children to ride through...

The Count swore under his breath. Again, he thumped on the roof with his stick, and the coach stopped. "Turn it!" he yelled out of the window, and with agonizing sluggishness, the coachman performed the difficult task of turning his vehicle on the narrow road. The peasants watched with the same sullen interest.

The coach moved forward again in the direction of the castle. It was as if the peasants' silence was catching, for we said nothing either. When we were still some yards from the gates, the Count rapped on the roof again, and when the coach stopped, he moved to get out. Instinctively, Colonel von Avenheim reached out to stop him, but the old man smiled sardonically. "They're not going to hurt me," he said confidently, and got down without help.

Almost mesmerized, I watched him stand examining the peasants like a general at a parade. "Lázár!" he barked out suddenly, and I jumped. Lajos's father stepped forward in front of the Count, inclining his head with civility, but absolutely no servility. Eszter, I saw, was holding her head high.

Beside me, Avenheim moved. Something caught my eye, and I glanced at him to see that he was taking a pistol from under his coat. My eyes flew to his in dumb panic. "Just a precaution," he murmured easily, and I tore my eyes away, back to the confrontation outside.

"What are you doing here, Lázár?" the Count demanded, his voice not unfriendly.

"Minding my own business," said Lázár unexpectedly.

The Count peered at him, waving his stick up and down the lines. "And what are all these other people doing here?" he enquired.

"You should ask them."

"I'm asking you."

Lázár appeared to consider. "I should say they're minding their own business too."

"Bah!" exclaimed the Count impatiently. "Where's that boy of yours? Lajos! Lajos Lázár! Come here, if you dare!"

My palms were sweating. In the silence, the wild thumping of my heart seemed to fill my ears. I watched breathlessly as Lajos detached himself from the line and wandered casually down the road towards us. Lázár stepped back into his place beside Eszter, and Lajos inclined his head to the Count in much the same way as his father had. His light hair glinted in the torch light.

"I asked your father what you all think you're doing here," said the Count loudly. "He tells me you are *all* minding your own business."

Lajos nodded. "Yes, that's about it."

"You are impeding the business of my guests!" the Count growled. "So, move!"

"We are impeding no one. Your guests are welcome to pass."

Frustrated, the old man tried to stare down the young, but for all his ferocity, he could not intimidate Lajos. I had never seen anyone who could.

"These people," said the Count abruptly. "They are not all from Szelényi."

"No," Lajos agreed.

"But they are also minding their own business? In someone else's village?"

"Yes," said Lajos, adding helpfully, "Some of your guests may recognize them. They will certainly recognize your guests."

The Count turned away angrily. Then I saw his eyes narrow as he swung back again. "What is it all about, Lajos? What are you trying to do?"

Lajos considered. "Be seen," he said at last.

"*What?*" The Count stared.

"We are — making our presence felt. We, the people." For the first time, his lip quirked upwards in the characteristic half-smile. "Look at the people. Do you feel like Lord of all you survey?"

CHAPTER FOURTEEN

The Count took a hasty step nearer him, lifting his stick as if to strike him. I gasped; the peasants seemed to sway forward as one, threatening, but Lajos himself never flinched. "No," he said. "You and I hitting each other changes nothing. They—" he flung his arm out towards the lines of peasants "—will still be there. Recognize it. Change must come from you, but we, the people, we can force it."

Slowly, the Count's arm fell to his side. "Insolent ingrate!" he hissed. "You dare to *threaten* me?"

Lajos shook his head. "No. Just listen — believe me, I am returning a favour." Their eyes were locked together, the Count's full of half-bewildered rage, Lajos's registering only a sort of fearless tolerance which he seemed to be trying to communicate to the old man.

"I know it's your doing, boy. *You* brought them here," said the Count, more quietly now. Lajos said nothing, and the Count leaned forward. "Send them away again. Now!"

"We are doing no harm. We are just — there."

"Move them," the Count said again, his voice dangerously calm.

Beside me, I felt Avenheim stir, sliding into the seat opposite me, quietly levelling his pistol. My breath, which I seemed to have been holding up till then, escaped me now in a rush. "What are you doing?" I whispered with dread.

"Nothing yet," said Avenheim calmly.

"You don't need that!"

"Probably not."

My gaze dragged itself away from the weapon and back to the protagonists outside. Wildly, I thought of calling out to Lajos that the Colonel had a gun, but would that not spark off the riot we all feared? I saw Lajos's eyes flicker briefly towards the coach, and back to the Count. I prayed he had seen the pistol, and that it would make him disband these people, so terrifying in their stolid, immovable silence.

Slowly, Lajos was shaking his head, the faintest half-smile touching his lips. "No," he said simply.

Appalled, if not really surprised, I closed my eyes, but a slight clicking sound caused them to fly open again immediately. The Colonel had cocked the pistol and was aiming steadily. It raced through my fearful head that he was just making sure that Lajos could see the gun, to force his submission to the Count, and in truth, I couldn't imagine the kind Colonel *assassinating* anyone. But what was Lajos to him except a rebel, a danger to the establishment, to the state, to stability? I knew suddenly that this was *not* an empty threat. Desperately, I imagined hurling myself upon the Colonel to stop him firing, yet in such a situation of hair-trigger tension, what damage might I do? Unbearable panic rose up inside me.

Outside, the Count was saying, "The soldiers will come."

"Not for a while. But there is no need of soldiers. We are harming no one."

"You are threatening!"

"I guarantee your guests may pass with perfect safety," said Lajos. "The people are staying."

Abruptly, because I could stand it no longer, I leaned forward and placed my hand heavily on the barrel of the gun. It was cold against my sweating skin. "Don't," I said hoarsely. I saw that my hand was shaking. The Colonel saw it too, and lifted his gaze to mine.

"It's the best way to diffuse the situation." He looked puzzled rather than angry at having to explain his actions to a mere governess. "Remove the leader, and the rest, without a spokesman, will disperse."

"*Remove!*"

"I shan't kill him," he said almost casually.

"How can you be sure?" I whispered. "Oh, Colonel, this is not the way! Don't you see?" I was speaking urgently now, desperately pulling reasons from my mind to justify my plea. "Shooting Lajos will not disperse these people — it will enrage them! Look at them, Colonel — they have nothing now, no rights, no protection, no wealth, very little health even, hardly enough food to keep body and soul together, and worse than all that, they have *no hope* for a better life. Except in him." I stared at Avenheim, willing him to see it. "*Lajos* is their only hope, and if you take that away, their anger will erupt."

The Colonel looked at me thoughtfully, then back outside again. I felt as if the pounding beats of my heart were shaking me. Slowly, he lowered the pistol, and the relief which flooded through my trembling body was almost worse to bear than the fear. "Perhaps you are right," he said. "We cannot risk a blood bath here, but where will it end, Mademoiselle, if we constantly give in to this sort of threat? Where will it end?"

I shook my head dumbly, still shivering with reaction to the tragedy so narrowly averted, forcing myself to look out of the window again. Lajos was turning away from the Count, beginning to walk back to his original place. I caught sight of old Lázár's face, and it held a fierce sort of pride in his son which tugged at my heart.

The Count was climbing back into the coach, helped by Avenheim and the steward who had sat slumped with perfect terror in the corner throughout the entire proceedings. The coach moved forward. "Well?" asked Avenheim.

"We could all stay here till morning, let the soldiers sort it out," the Count ground out. "But I will not be held to ransom! They won't disperse for hours, I know it!"

I cleared my throat. "I don't believe they'll hurt anyone."

His erratic gaze fell on me. "And what do you know, Miss?" he said contemptuously.

"I know they are making a point," I said, refusing to be intimidated. "They won't risk arrest, death, by harming any of your guests."

"They are discontented peasants! Serfs! Not *reasoning* men!"

"Lajos Lázár is a reasoning man," I said, feeling a new terror at just speaking his name in this company, in this situation. "None more so. And they do as he tells them. You said yourself that he arranged this. And he won't risk his own arrest now in such a minor confrontation, not with the elections so close."

The Count stared at me open-mouthed, though whether at my temerity or my wisdom, I could not tell. Avenheim uttered a soft laugh. "The lady has prudence, Count. She has already prevented me from shooting young Lázár."

Startled, the Count turned his gaze on Avenheim. "Well thank heaven for that! If you'd shot him, they'd have torn us all limb from limb! They've made him into a — a *god* in these parts. They think he'll make them all kings. Hah!" He tugged at his lip again, looking at me. "Very well," he said abruptly. "We'll take the chance."

I slumped back in my corner, drained. But I could not relax yet. Once through the castle gates again, we stopped and got out, and the Count and Avenheim went to speak to the anxiously waiting guests.

Shivering in the suddenly cold night air, I watched the first coach beginning its journey at a fast trot. When it had passed, I glimpsed Lajos, still standing resolutely in the line opposite us. I had to give him credit: despite the fear it had whipped up — or perhaps because of it — it was a very effective demonstration. Without a trace of violence, it showed the masters of the land what the power of the people could be. It showed too that those masters already lived in terror of a peasant uprising.

But another figure had caught my eye now. Pushing past the next coach on the side away from us, his uniform shining brightly in the torchlight, his hat held firmly in his hand, was Alexandru Zarescu, on foot. Head held high, he walked through the gates ahead of the coach, without a trace of fear. But instead of walking on, he swung abruptly to the left and came to a halt beside Lajos, where he stood as still and silent as the others while the carriages passed through the lines. My heart went out to him, for now, surely, by so publicly taking his stand with Lajos — and through sheer anger, I was sure — he had lost all hope of the Count relenting. But then, he had never had any real chance of that. I could feel tears catching the back of my throat, tried to swallow them back.

For what seemed ages, the guests in all their finery left the castle through that interminable, silent line of poor, simple peasants. I could see their fear, their distaste, the nervousness of their drivers, whose sympathies I could only guess at. What a strange end to the Szelényi ball... I thought it would be a long time before any of these aristocrats visited each other's estates again in the hours of darkness.

"Katie?" It was Katalin, shivering beside me. "Oh, Katie, is that Alexandru with them? How could he do this now?"

"He's angry," I said, squeezing her hand. "It makes no difference, you know..."

She slumped against me. The whole disastrous evening, on which she had built all her unreasoning hopes, had finally defeated her. I saw the tears pouring unchecked down her beautiful face, and it was nearly too much for me to bear on top of all the rest.

"Come inside," I said gently, putting my arm around her and drawing us both away from the scene. "Don't cry, Katalin. It will be all right tomorrow, you'll see..."

When, eventually, I fell exhausted into bed that night, I slept badly. My dreams were full of unknown dangers and hard, expressionless faces, and behind them all, somewhere, was the figure of Lajos Lázár, hovering between the tragic and the terrifying.

I woke early, unrefreshed, but since I was unable to fall into sleep again, I rose and pottered around my bed-chamber, going over and over the events of last night in my mind. But I kept returning to Lajos and his "demonstration", his confrontation with the Count, and the dreadful risk which he and all the people involved had taken by staging such a gathering. I should have known, I thought, when I had come upon him earlier in the castle, that he had been planning something, for had his manner not been just a little odd? There had even been a time when he was almost *flirting* with me...

When the Count's summons came, I was not surprised: he had every reason to suspect I had encouraged Katalin and Zarescu in last night's folly. I confess I trailed my feet a little on the way to the library, but once there I took a deep breath, knocked briskly, and went in with a quiet confidence I was far from feeling.

The Count was alone, standing in front of a closed bureau. With a shock, I realized that it could be the very desk in which he kept all my mother's unanswered letters. He turned and looked at me. "Sit down, Mademoiselle." He could never bring himself to utter my name.

Demurely, I sat where he indicated, waiting almost resignedly for the axe to fall. The Count stood holding on to the back of the chair opposite, looking down at me with an expression both puzzled and thoughtful.

"I don't know why you should interest yourself in my affairs," he said suddenly, "but I have cause to be grateful."

I frowned. "I don't know what you mean, sir."

"I mean," said the old man impatiently, "the fiasco by the castle gates. I believe it ended as best it could, and for that I have largely to thank you."

I felt the colour seep into my face. "Hardly, sir!"

"You stopped Karl von Avenheim from shooting Lajos Lázár," the Count said drily, "and that alone probably saved all our lives — however much I might wish the wretched boy out of my hair!"

My eyes fell. I hadn't been trying to save their lives. I had been trying to save Lajos.

"You talked like a sensible woman, and we brushed through it without any riots, without any soldiers. Yours is sound advice, Mademoiselle."

I shifted uncomfortably. "Thank you," I muttered.

"You've got guts," he said, nodding. "I admire that. I *value* that, and I wanted to tell you, I'm glad to have you with us."

Almost without knowing what I was about, I stood up again. "Thank you," I said hastily, "but really, there is no need. It was all curiosity and common sense. If that is all, sir, may I go now and see to the children?"

I saw amusement glisten in his fierce, old eyes. "Yes, off you go, child. Take with you my thanks, all our thanks."

This was unbearable. I almost bolted to the door, and as I opened it, I had a sudden urge to turn back, to blurt out the truth about myself and watch him take back his kind, unexpectedly generous words until I could retrieve my anger against him. But, of course, I didn't. I fled to the nursery to find the children.

That Sunday felt like the longest day in my life. Tired and overwrought, I contrived to keep the children amused, or at least busy, while I worried about Katalin and Lajos and myself. Then, restlessly, I went back to my own chamber, where the cheerful laughter of the stable boys below was filtering through the open window. The servants had been full of suppressed glee all day, in sharp contrast to the family's nervousness and depression. Last night's events had been a shock to everyone, but at least, I thought, they had lessened the impact of Katalin's defiance...

A sharp crack on the window made me jump out of this reverie. Investigating, I could see nothing to have caused such a noise, until I looked down into the yard and saw Lajos standing directly below, gazing up at me. My heart jolted with sudden fear for him.

He lifted one hand, quickly signalling for me to come down. Terrified that he would be discovered by one of the family, I did not even pause to collect my bonnet, but ran down to the yard by the dark stairs and corridors I had discovered on my first evening, emerging into the warm sunlight more than a little breathless. Still alone, Lajos came to meet me. I could hear the muffled voices of grooms coming from various outbuildings.

"Are you mad coming here today?" I whispered urgently.

He took my arm. "Come for a walk, away from here. I need to talk to you."

As I let myself be led quickly out of the yard to the lesser village path, I could not prevent the silly surge of pleasure his words gave me. He didn't speak until we were some distance away from the castle. Then he led me off the path, around the hill a bit, to where a large, leafy tree provided some shade from the burning sun. "I've nothing for you to sit on," he said, making me smile at this lack of forethought, so unusual in him.

"It doesn't matter," I said, lowering myself to the ground. "The grass is quite dry."

He dropped down beside me, saying nothing for a few moments. His fingers began to pull distractedly at the grass while he looked at me with a steady, disconcerting gaze.

"You saved my life," he said suddenly.

My eyes flew to his, surprised, searching. "You flatter yourself," I said lightly, at last.

He shrugged. "I don't ask your reasons. It was best for everyone that the Colonel did not shoot me, but I'm sure you'll agree that I have especial cause to be grateful."

I flushed. "What makes you think I could have prevented the Colonel from shooting you?"

His lip quirked. "I heard you," he said simply.

Of course. I remembered the grim, uncanny silence, broken only by the occasional exchanges between Lajos and the Count, and by my desperate plea to Avenheim. I had been in far too great a panic to care about anything so trivial as the loudness of my voice, but it had never entered my head that anyone else — let alone Lajos himself — would hear me. The Count had not, but then he was old and angry.

My gaze fell. "I didn't know if you had seen the gun," I said, low-voiced.

"I saw it."

I looked at him again, with considerable indignation now. "Then why on Earth didn't you just disband the people?" I demanded.

"I couldn't. That is, I wouldn't. I had to trust that the Colonel was bluffing."

"I don't think he was. He is normally a kind man, but that sort of defiance is anathema to him. Why do you take such risks, Lajos?"

"I only take *calculated* risks."

"Did you calculate on an Austrian officer trying to shoot you, or on my being present — and willing! — to stop him?" I asked sarcastically.

He smiled faintly, but said only, "Something of the sort."

Frustrated, I tugged a handful of grass out by the roots and hurled it from me, watching the blades float and fall in the breeze. "I wish I knew exactly what you were trying to prove."

He shrugged again. "Just what I said at the time. We made our presence felt quite successfully, I thought!" For a moment he looked away into the distance, before confessing, "And I suppose I was testing the water."

I frowned. "What do you mean?"

"I mean, you don't need violence to make a revolution." He met my gaze, an almost triumphant smile in his dark eyes as he added softly, "Only the *threat* of it."

Shaken by such astoundingly deliberate premeditation, it took me a moment to understand. He hadn't just been making a stand for Szelényi last night. *He had been rehearsing the revolution.*

CHAPTER FIFTEEN

On Tuesday evening, Zsuzsa, looking particularly pretty in her colourful new dress, dragged me with her to the village festivities which, in a moment of weakness or inattention I had apparently agreed to attend.

Weirdly, things were almost back to normal at the castle. Katalin, partially restored by a letter from Alex, had risen in time for dinner on Sunday which had made me dread a blazing row with the Count. However, by tacit agreement neither of them had referred to Zarescu, each treating the other with chilly but faultless civility. István had looked at her askance once or twice, but took his lead from his father.

I felt so grateful for the fragile peace that I declined to break it just yet by revealing my own secret.

I could hear the music long before we came to the village. The musicians were gypsies — the price of this being the presence of their noisy, dirty children, who hung around the fringes of the village looking for trouble — "or purses", Zsuzsa said cynically. The hub of events was the village square which echoed to the sound of laughter and gypsy music and the sloshing of local wine out of a barrel. The moon shone brilliantly down upon the villagers, aided by the torches placed strategically round the square.

As we arrived there, I saw a group of people dancing — including Károly Lázár — while others stood around clapping and calling out encouraging or ribald remarks. It was a delightfully colourful scene, happy, rustic, yet, to me, exotic enough to be fascinating.

Zsuzsa introduced me to her mother, a jolly, wrinkled little woman with tired eyes who babbled away delightedly while she found me a cup of wine. I took it gratefully, watching with amusement as Zsuzsa went off on the arm of a dewy-eyed young peasant lad. Her mother shrugged resignedly, and laughed when I toasted her before moving around to get a better taste of the festivities.

In the centre of a rapt circle, a middle-aged couple were singing a duet which was obviously their party-piece. Everyone watching seemed to know the words, but it was performed with such exaggerated gestures and eyelash flutterings that the audience still laughed uproariously with each verse. I paused to listen, watching with amusement as the man twirled his moustaches, declaring:

"*I love you, my dove,*
As well as new bread,
I sigh for you
A hundred thousand times a day."
And his beloved, simpering to the delight of her audience, confessed:
"*I love you, I love you,*
But tell it to none,
Till on the church stones
We are sworn to be one."

I smiled at their antics, but then I got distracted from the rest of the intriguing song by Lajos's parents, who were both flatteringly pleased to see me.

"More wine!" came a cry from the other side of the square.

"Here it comes!" someone answered, and when I followed the direction of the general attention, I saw three men running up the street towards us, each rolling a barrel in front of him. I recognized two of the men as Lajos and his brother Zoltán. It seemed to be a race, and a somewhat hilarious one at that, for several of the villagers had spread out down the street to call encouragement to one or other of the men, who did not disdain such foul play as aiming wild kicks or shoving at each other as they came on. In the end it was Zoltán who won. I saw Lajos laughingly clap his brother on the back and stand aside for the winner to be presented with the first cup from the new barrel. Eszter was shaking her head, smiling.

"What boys we have, Lázár," she said, taking her husband's arm affectionately. "What boys we have." And Lázár only nodded, without a word of criticism.

I watched Károly, still with his pretty partner, join his brothers by the wine barrels; and then Lajos threw his arm round Károly's girl and ran with her to join the next group of dancers. Like the others, he was in festive dress tonight, his shirt brightly embroidered, a red kerchief knotted around his throat. Where now was the lawyer, the intellectual of the Pilvax...?

I lost sight of him after that because of the crowd, and instead accepted a piece of deliciously warm bread from a small, serious child with an overloaded plate. Wandering among the colourful company, I felt dull in my workaday dress; I had contemplated changing it for my one more festive garment, but the prospect of explaining myself to any castle people I might have encountered had eventually decided me against it. And now I even felt somehow constrained in my dashing bonnet, no longer so new or so dear to me.

I think it had something to do with the wild, insidious music the gypsies played. I had never heard anything quite like it before; the very tones and combinations of notes, the weird, hypnotic, ever-changing rhythms — it was all new, exciting and strange to me.

And then I saw Lajos and his partner emerge laughing through a wall of gaily dressed people in front of me.

"Katie!" he said at once. "Meet Maria." We exchanged smiles, hers a little wary, and then she excused herself and ran off.

"I hope I didn't frighten her away," I said wryly, as we began to stroll among the throng.

"Oh, she's off in search of more fun! Or Károly, which amounts to the same thing in her eyes. I'm glad you've come."

We were passing the wine barrels by then, so he refilled my cup for me and took one for himself, toasting me briefly, smilingly, before drinking. I had never seen him so relaxed. It struck me that for the first time in my acquaintance with him, he was set only on enjoyment, with no part of him involved in plans, work, duty or his wretched cause. The thought was somehow intoxicating, his attitude catching.

"I had a letter from Petöfi," he said once.

"Oh yes? How is the revolution?" I asked cynically.

Lajos's lip twitched. "He doesn't know. For once he's more full of love than politics — he just got married."

I smiled, genuinely pleased. "You must congratulate him for me!"

"Do it yourself. He'll be back in Pest soon enough."

"I won't be."

He looked at me. "You haven't told them yet."

"Tomorrow," I said quickly.

"You said that on Sunday."

"I know, but everyone's still a bit on edge," I excused myself. He took my hand.

"Worry about it later," he advised. "Let's watch the dance."

One or two couples were already waiting for the dance to begin, encouraging their friends to join them while the gypsies amused everyone by making their fiddles laugh and talk to each other. Lajos called something to them in a language I did not know, and one of them answered briefly with a grin on his dark, saturnine face. Lajos turned to me.

"In this sort of company I don't need evening dress," he observed. I looked at him warily.

"In this sort of company," I said lightly, "it is I who am not dressed to dance."

"Would you like to?"

I laughed. "How could I? I don't know the steps!"

"Look, there's Zsuzsa with another victim. Follow her, and I'll help you with the rest."

"No, really," I protested. "I have two left feet!"

"It's only fun," he said, reaching up suddenly and pulling the strings of my bonnet.

"Lajos..." I began in panic, but then Eszter was there, and Lajos had taken off my hat and handed it to her.

"Good! You're going to dance!" she said delightedly.

"I can't!"

"It's easy to learn — just enjoy it!" Eszter laughed, and her mirth was somehow infectious. I found myself smiling, submitting to having a pretty, colourful sash tied around my waist — which brightened up my drab dress beyond belief — and being led on to the "floor" by Lajos. I remember his mocking, flourishing bow, and my equally exaggerated reply — I think the strong village wine had already gone to my head, as well as the laughing cheers of the villagers.

Zsuzsa squeezed my arm in delight. The fiddlers struck up and I took the same stance as Zsuzsa opposite Lajos. I felt somehow free and exhilarated, ready to enjoy this new experience. Half-laughing, I followed Zsuzsa's example. It began slowly, the steps simple, the gestures modest. Zsuzsa grinned encouragingly and I smiled back, dividing my attention between her and Lajos. As the men danced towards us, we retreated, and gradually the music grew faster, the steps harder to follow. The men circled us, advanced; we retired again. The tempo increased, and I found I was enjoying it, not only the *feel* of it, but also the pleasure of watching Lajos, his slight, lithe body naturally graceful as he danced.

I don't know when it dawned on me that it was a courtship dance — perhaps when Lajos next advanced, and instead of allowing me to retreat, seized me round the waist. Smiling at him with surprise and sheer high spirits, I felt not the remotest embarrassment as he whirled me round in his arms and let me go again.

Dizzily following Zsuzsa, I danced even faster, revelling in the music, the freedom of movement, in a way I never had before, and this time when Lajos caught and held me, I welcomed him, laughing as we span round and round together, enjoying the hard, sinewy strength of his body against mine, the feel of his arms so tight and secure around me. The dance parted us again, leaving me suddenly bereft, almost aching to be back in his arms, while the music grew ever louder and faster.

His dark, oddly beautiful eyes were holding mine now. I had forgotten Zsuzsa completely; there was only Lajos and me and the wonderful music. Breathless as I was, I gasped when he reached for me again, emitting a tiny, almost moaning sound as my body fitted perfectly against his.

Round and round we span while the music climbed wildly towards its crescendo. I could see the smile on Lajos's lips, feel his quickened heart beat against my body, and starting somewhere near my stomach I felt a strange, wonderful, tingling ache begin to spread through me like wildfire. I had never in my life before been this close to a man. Moulded together, our bodies had no secrets from each other, and if it was shocking me, I loved it even more.

I clung to him desperately, glorying in his every movement against me as we span, until I thought I would die of exhaustion or joy or both, and then the music came to its final, shattering close and I was left gasping and exultantly happy.

But the experience was not over yet, for as I smiled up at him trustfully, his own smile began to die on his lips; and then his mouth came down on mine and it was the most natural thing in the world to receive his kiss. The ache in my body caught fire, and I was lost.

Yet soon, much too soon, he raised his head again, and I stared up at him mutely with, I'm sure, my wild new desire plain in my eyes for him to read. I could see it in his too, a warm, misty glow that was almost as exciting as the dance. His arms tightened for a moment, then relaxed, and his lips curved upwards again.

"More wine, I think," he said, and his voice was not quite steady. I felt confused, disorientated as we moved away with the other dancers. One couple was still locked together in a passionate embrace. I looked away, normal sense slowly returning to me. I was breathless and trembling slightly, shocked yet still happy with Lajos's arm supporting me. I was vaguely aware of Zsuzsa laughing beside me, of someone giving me more wine. I drank it, meeting Lajos's gaze over the rim of the cup. He began to speak, and then his attention was seized by the old woman and the girl beside him.

Yet I couldn't stop watching him. It was as if I was seeing him for the first time, and slowly, invincibly, a new, terrifying idea was forming in my mind and taking hold, a simple, obvious, blinding idea of such importance that I couldn't take it in all at once.

I drank some more wine, wonderingly, letting the idea take shape. Lajos turned back to me and smiled, and then I knew without doubt, with such certainty that my breath caught in my throat. I smiled back into his eyes, for I knew now what I should always have known. I loved him.

*

Lajos moved, and with my newfound awareness, I felt the touch of his hand burning into my arm.

"Lajos! Lajos!" someone called from across the square. I thought at first he would ignore it, but a man beside us nudged him to direct his attention. He sighed with the merest hint if impatience. His fingers slid down my arm to my hand, making me shiver involuntarily.

"I'll be back in a moment," he said softly. "Don't go away..." And he strode off across the square. I looked a little blindly into my cup, absently touching my lips with my fingertips. Never had I experienced so devastating a kiss...

The music, the people, the dancing, all of which I had found so fascinating only moments ago, were an irritant to me now. Inside me was a fierce, new joy which I needed to be alone to savour. Quietly, I laid down my cup and slipped away.

As I reached the end of the village, I began to run, as if I could bear the intensity of my feelings more easily by using up all my physical energy, and when I finally slowed down, the revelry was no more than a faint, happy echo. I moved off the path and sat down on the grass to think and to draw breath where no stray passer-by could see me. I was smiling. "I love him," I whispered to the full, harvest moon, and felt awed by my own daring. "I love him."

It seemed now that I had always loved him, ever since he had caught and held my attention in Vienna months ago now. That was why I had manipulated Katalin into going to the Pilvax, why I had tried so *desperately* to prevent the Colonel from shooting him, why I was jealous of the love he gave Teréz.

Of course, I had long recognized my unusual feeling for him, but being me, I had thought myself now too hard, too cynical to fall in love again. I had called it infatuation, as if it was a silly, half-formed schoolgirl crush which I could talk myself out of quite easily when I grew tired of it. Yet what I felt now made my previous, youthful taste of love pale into nothing.

I lay back in the grass and gazed up at the moon. Somewhere in the distance a dog was howling, a weird, pitiful sound that I barely noticed. It's the wine, I told myself; it's that mad dance. Between them they have stirred up feelings that simply won't be there in the sober light of morning.

I smiled at the moon, for I didn't believe my sane, sensible voice any more. I was in love with Lajos Lázár, and what in the world was remotely sane or sensible about that?

"Nothing," I whispered aloud. "Nothing at all." I sat up again, feeling the unfamiliar sash around my waist. Slowly, I untied it. In my mind, I looked at myself: Katie Kettles, twenty-seven years old, staid, dowdy spinster whose only saving graces were humour and a certain quickness of wit. I knew from experience that men thought little of such traits in women, less in prospective wives. If Lajos liked me, and I thought he did, it was not love. I was a friend, like Alex or Petöfi. He was kind to me, looked after me, but I knew as surely as I now knew my own heart that he did not, could not, love me.

But he kissed me, wailed a voice in my mind. Yes, and every girl in the dance was kissed by her partner. I thought longingly of the desire I had clearly read in his eyes as the dance ended. But desire in such a situation was no more love than friendship was. It was the movement, the closeness of the dance that had affected him; it was my femininity, not me, which he had desired.

I felt the tears prickle under my eyelids. I was alone; there was no need to keep them back, so I let them flow. I wept for what I could not have, but also for joy because behind it all there was still a poignant happiness in loving him. After a time, I dried my eyes on my skirt, and put my spectacles back on. In the dance, I had forgotten I was wearing them. I folded the sash carefully as I stood up and made my way slowly back to the path.

I had left my bonnet in the village. I thought of going back for it, but I was afraid to see Lajos again tonight. With growing unease, I wondered how much of my feelings I had given away during and after the dance, how much he had noticed, for dragging myself back to the real world, I knew I could only live with this new knowledge if no one, least of all Lajos himself, shared it.

I love you, I love you
But tell it to none...
It was just something else to hide. I was good at that.

The next morning, I was brought a letter from Aunt Edith with my morning coffee. I tried to read it, but in truth I couldn't concentrate on her scolding — her letters are always at least half-scold, even when I am positively angelic — for despite the rising feeling in me that life in Hungary was proving too much for me to cope with, a feeling that almost amounted to homesickness, I could think of nothing but last night's dance, of no one but Lajos.

With the vague idea of reading it later, when I was more settled, I carried the letter with me to the schoolroom, where Miklós asked me to admire a huge spider which he had trapped in a box. It was certainly an ugly monster, but I barely glanced at it, saying merely, "Most ill-favoured," as I laid down my books. He was obviously disappointed by this tame reaction, for he then released the insect, which scuttled in circles round the floor for at least five minutes, to the joyous squeals of the Enemy, before disappearing into some crack in the wall. After which, I had to exert all my fading energy to get the children settled down again and put to work on their daily arithmetic exercise.

While they toiled, I sat down at my desk and tried again to read Aunt Edith's letter. I haven't mentioned before her attitude to my working for the Szelényis, but naturally it was disapproving. She was appalled, first of all, that my pride permitted me to undertake any occupation in their household, and, secondly, that I was deceiving them as to my identity, a crime which she considered almost as despicable as theirs.

By the time of this most recent letter, she was becoming definitely agitated about the length of time I was prepared to keep up the masquerade. "I cannot bear the thought," she wrote, "of Count Szelényi discovering such deceit in a Kettles. Your behaviour in this is entirely repugnant to me. I am now convinced that by far your best course is to give notice to Count István and come home at once without revealing to anyone that you are Sofia's daughter. If only the money you have can take you as far as Vienna, your uncle will arrange for more to reach you there. Truly, it has gone on too long, when it is something which should never have begun..."

I sighed and let the letter drop from my fingers. More lowering than anything else was the fact that Aunt Edith was right, and in the light of that I considered her most recent advice. I thought of my likely life, somewhere in Scotland, or maybe England, teaching children who were not Miklós or Anna, far away from anyone who had ever heard of Lajos Lázár. I would never even know if he were free or in prison...

Yet what was my alternative? To seek another post in Hungary? The Szelényis would hardly give me a reference if they knew who I was — and if I kept my identity to myself as Aunt Edith now suggested, well, *I* couldn't bear to do that. No, I was going to have to confess; and after that, I would just have to learn to live without any communication, without any news of Lajos. Perhaps it would even be easier than seeing him...

Here, misery threatened to overwhelm me, so it was as well that Miklós announced he was finished. I went to mark his work, and it was while I was doing so that István came in, as he occasionally did to review his children's progress. I straightened at once, but he said, "No, no, carry on. There is no hurry."

So I left him to wander while I corrected Miklós's arithmetic and then Anna's. And only as I was explaining an error to her did I suddenly become aware of my own mistake. For István was standing idly by my desk, and Aunt Edith's letter was lying there.

For a moment, I felt frozen. Surely István would not lower himself to read a letter addressed to someone else? No, but what if his own name, so liberally

108

scattered across the sheets, just caught his eye? He would have to be inhuman not to let himself read on. Surreptitiously, I glanced at the desk, praying that the letter was folded, but of course it wasn't. It lay where I had dropped it, spread out at the page which even mentioned my mother's name. And István was looking at it.

What a silly way to be discovered, I thought, almost irritated and wishing violently that I had screwed up my courage earlier. But I knew now why I hadn't: that too had been all mixed up with Lajos.

I was holding my breath. Slowly, he lifted his eyes and met mine over Anna's head. It was plain to see at once that he knew. It's over, I thought stupidly. It's over.

Revolution

November 1847 — March 1848

CHAPTER SIXTEEN

On a cool November day, I found myself again on the Danube steam-ship, going back the way I had come only six months ago. The wonder of the river scenery had not changed since then — except in its glorious autumn colours — but I rather thought *I* had.

I stood alone by the ship's rail, letting the wind blow the ribbons of my bonnet across my cheek, poignantly remembering that other journey in the spring when I had struggled to control Miklós and Anna and secretly conversed for the first time with Lajos Lázár. Today there were no children dangling from my skirts, and I knew for a fact that Lajos was not on board — he was already in Pressburg, waiting for the opening of the Diet. He would be in his element: agitating, inciting, heckling, no doubt holding illegal street meetings to stir up support for the Opposition.

I smiled to myself. So much was hoped for from this Diet that I didn't see how it could ever live up to expectations, not just Lajos's, but *everyone's* — Zarescu's, Father Ránoczy, Count Batthyány's, Kossuth's, the Szelényis'...

Of course, between them, the Szelényis represented the whole range of public opinion, from the reactionary old Count to the mildly radical Mattias — with István somewhere in the moderate middle. Well, for all his arrogance and temper, István was a moderate man, as I had cause to know. He hadn't even been angry with me when he had read Aunt Edith's letter, or at least not after the first shock. He had been more — suspicious.

Katalin's reaction had been harder to bear. Tripping gaily into the schoolroom in the midst of our confrontation, she had been brought up short by our serious faces.

"What is it?" she had asked in alarm, and István had answered harshly, "Don't you know? Let me introduce you to your niece."

"My *niece*? Stop being ridiculous!"

"Sofia's daughter. I wondered if you were in on the secret, since you spend so much time here — and since you seem to imagine you have something in common with Sofia."

Katalin was looking bewildered. "What is he saying?" she asked me, a trace of impatience visible through her puzzlement. I forced myself to meet her gaze.

"He's saying that I am Sofia's daughter."

"But you can't be!" She looked from me to István and back again, then sank slowly into the chair by the desk.

"You stay with her," said István abruptly. "I'm going to speak to Father." And he moved away, peremptorily gathering the children as he went, as if I could now contaminate them by my mere presence. Katalin was still staring at me.

"I don't understand," she said, just as István had. "Why have you never said? Why are you the *governess*, for God's sake?"

I looked at her. "Can't you work it out? Sofia is dead. I took the opportunity of this post to satisfy my curiosity, to seek a little revenge!" Her eyes widened. She took it in slowly, and the understanding in her eyes was almost unbearable.

"I see," she said. "I see. So that is why you agreed to help Alex and me. You hoped to cause trouble through us."

"At first," I said, looking down at the desk. "Partly."

"Well, congratulations," she said bitterly. "You succeeded!"

"No," I protested, stung by the injustice of that. "Katalin, I never wished you any harm..."

"Didn't you?" She looked at me, hurt standing out in her beautiful eyes, like a puppy who has been kicked for no good reason. "I trusted you. I thought you were my friend."

"I was," I said, low. "I am."

"No," she said simply, and I turned away to hide my own feelings.

I had always known she would be hurt by this revelation, but if I had imagined I would not, I had been fooling myself. Wayward and selfish as I knew her to be, she was also warm and kind and my closest companion over the last few months. I would have been terribly lonely without her. But I could not tell her all this, then. She wouldn't have believed me, and that too was my fault.

Unhappily, I watched her stand up and leave. After a moment, I went too, going back to my bedchamber and drearily laying out my few possessions. However, I hadn't got very far before a servant appeared to inform me that the Count had summoned me to the library. I went at once, trying to tell myself that this was the confrontation I had sought since May; but things were no longer the same, no longer so black and white. I understood the old man a little now, his courage and his pain as well as his absolute stubbornness. And my own behaviour was hardly above reproach. Besides all of which, I remembered miserably that I hated confrontation...

Only days ago I had received his thanks in this room. He was alone, his back to the great, stone fireplace. I closed the door and advanced a few steps, then paused and waited. For several seconds he examined me in silence.

"So," he said eventually, his lip curling unpleasantly. "You are John Kettles's daughter, and quite as deceitful as he ever was!"

"My father never deceived anyone," I said at once.

"No? He deceived me into believing him to be a man of principle! But I don't wish to discuss him. It's you who interest me now. My son tells me you don't want money."

"No," I said shortly, lifting my chin.

"Good. Because I'm not prepared to give you any. What *do* you want?"

I looked at him, allowing all his contempt to wash over me. It was true that I was not blameless, but how dared this fierce old man accuse me of extortion or whatever it was he imagined I was here for?

"From you?" I said softly. "I want nothing. Not even an apology, for neither my mother nor my father is here to receive it."

The old man's brows flew together. "They'd get no apology from me!" he barked. "*I* did not wrong John Kettles! *He* wronged me!"

"A little, perhaps," I allowed. I found triumphantly that I was quite unafraid of him. He could not hurt me. "But you wronged them twice, first by denying them the right to marry, and then by refusing to recognize them when they did marry!"

"Don't you preach to me, girl!" he growled, and now my anger really flared.

"Why not? It's time someone did! You're a brutal, selfish, heartless old man, totally lacking in any generosity of spirit or human affection...!"

He took a hasty step towards me, his face growing livid with anger. "What do you know of affection, you *silly* little girl?" he ground out. "*Or* generosity, you who took a position and money from my son under false pretences!"

"I earned every penny of my salary," I returned at once. "And at least I was acting out of love for my parents, which is more than you ever did!"

"I *owed* them no love! Your mother disobeyed me and *chose* to leave!"

I stared at him. "So you cut your love off, just like that? Unspeakably shallow…!"

"You know nothing!"

"I know you were immune to the last pleas of your dying daughter!" I flashed, and abruptly he turned his back on me. But I could not leave it there: this anger had been building up for too long. "Could you not have forgiven her even then, on her deathbed? What sort of monster are you?"

"No," he said in a half-strangled voice, so quietly that I had to take a step forward to hear him. "I *couldn't* forgive her, even then."

In the face of such obvious pain, I felt my anger begin to drain away. Baffled, almost frustrated, I gazed at his rigid back.

"Why not?" I said helplessly. "For God's sake, why not?"

"She didn't ask," he murmured, so softly now that I was straining to catch the word. He half-turned towards me again. "She never admitted she had done wrong, so she never needed my forgiveness."

"So," I said slowly. "All it would have taken was for her to admit she was wrong in marrying my father?"

He met my gaze again. The ferocity had gone from his eyes, but so had the pain. "I can't change, any more than she could." And before I had the chance to dispute, he continued, "So, now you have said your piece. You have said what I presume you came all the way from Scotland to say. What do you want to do now?"

A little disoriented by this change of tactic, I took a few moments to answer.

"I'll go to the village for tonight," I said at last, "and in the morning I'll leave for Buda-Pest — and home, I suppose."

"It's a long way to travel alone in a foreign land," he remarked, almost idly.

"I shan't be alone," I lied at once. "I shall travel with Captain Zarescu *and* Lajos Lázár."

I waited calmly for his explosion of anger, rejoicing in my immunity to it; but frustratingly I saw an unexpected gleam of amusement in his hard eyes.

"You are trying to rile me," he observed. He looked at me, tugging his lower lip in a characteristic gesture of indecision. His expression was unreadable. Then, "Don't go until we speak again," he said abruptly. "I want to talk to my family, and I would rather you stayed at least until I have done so."

"Why?" I asked suspiciously.

"Do you question everything?" he responded, pulling the bell rope beside him. "I presume you have no objection to Margit's company? She at least will have none to yours."

Poor Margit. She slid into the library, a little at a time. At first, only her fingers appeared around the door, then her nose, and finally her whole head peeped round, looking expectantly, I think, for the bodies.

"Hurry up and come in!" the Count snapped impatiently. "I presume I don't need to introduce you to your niece."

"Oh dear," said Margit vaguely, purposelessly. "Oh dear..."

"You'll be happy to look after her while I talk to the others, won't you?" he added, his voice a little unkind again. "You pined enough when your sister left; take her child with you for an hour."

"You need take me nowhere," I said to Margit, casting an angry glance at her father. "The Count is..."

"Oh dear, tush tush," Margit interrupted, seizing my hand and squeezing it compulsively. "Come with me, now..." And somehow I was silenced and bundled out of the room.

She chattered about nothing all the way upstairs to what seemed to be her private sitting room, a surprisingly ordered, tidy chamber, full of books and pleasant, modern furniture. I looked at Margit with new eyes, and found her gaze devouring me.

"You knew," I blurted. " You always knew."

She nodded several times, like a bird. "Well, I knew your name, you see, and you are like her, a little, in expression perhaps more than feature..."

"Why didn't you say?"

"You had your reasons to keep silent," she said simply. "I could only wait for you to tell me."

She stopped, staring silently at me until I said, "My mother missed you. Very much." And then a huge tear squeezed out of her watery eye and rolled down her faded cheek. "Oh, Margit," I said, and went to her. She fell into my arms, her frail, bird-like hands clutching me to her.

For the first time that day, I had felt my own tears close to the surface, and was obliged to fight them back.

In the end it had been nearly two hours before we were summoned back to the library, and by then I had felt quite unequal to the family's joint disapprobation, their contempt. I wasn't even sure why I was making myself go through with it, except perhaps that I owed it to them.

Margit had all but pushed me into the room in front of her, much as I have seen bitches nudge their pups, and once there I forced myself to look calmly around the company. As before, the Count was standing with his back to the fireplace, his expression unreadable. On the sofa to his left sat Maria and Baron Mirányi, the former tight-lipped and obviously displeased. István, in a chair by himself, was looking at me thoughtfully with his cool, grey gaze.

Elisabeth and Katalin were seated on the other sofa. Elisabeth's eyes were, if anything, amused, but Katalin had turned her head away as if she didn't want to see me. I didn't really blame her. Mattias was leaning over the back of the sofa, between them. His handsome, young face expressed curiosity as he regarded me, but no hatred. I supposed we had had too little contact for him to feel anything very much about me.

"Come and sit down," said the Count, not unkindly.

"Thank you," I said. "I prefer to stand." I resisted Margit's pressure, letting her sit while I stood beside her and waited to find out why I had been brought to face this tribunal.

"We have been talking," the Count began, more blandly than was his wont, "and the children have convinced me that I do owe you something. You have already said that you don't want money from me, but nevertheless, I propose that I make you a reasonable allowance — I'm sure we could agree on a sum?"

Unreasonably, unspecifically disappointed, I gazed at him, and didn't prevent my lip from curling.

"I doubt it," I said contemptuously. "If you have nothing further to say, I'll bid you all good-bye."

Mortified, I turned on my heel, but Margit's fingers closed with surprising strength on my wrist, and behind me, I heard the Count say triumphantly, "I told you she wouldn't take it!"

Slowly, I turned back to face him, met his fierce yet pleased eyes. "*You* were testing *me*?"

"No," Maria said. "*I* was. I doubt your motives, if not your identity — who can blame me in the face of what we do know about you?"

"No one, I'm sure. My motives were strictly uncharitable — in fact totally reprehensible. For what it is worth to any of you, I'm sorry. I misjudged many things."

From the corner of my eye, I saw Katalin turn her head at last and look at me. Deliberately, I met her gaze.

"I'm sorry," I repeated. And since I had to get the apologies off my chest, I shifted my gaze to Elisabeth, saying jerkily, "I did teach the children to the best of my ability. I apologise for the lies. They seemed at the time to be necessary."

"Don't apologise to me," said Elisabeth lazily. "I think it's the best joke I've heard in a year."

István, of course, did not. But he managed to make me feel even worse by saying reasonably, "However we may deplore them, your actions are understandable in the light of the treatment which your mother received from this family..."

"The point is," the Count interrupted, "that I have a proposition to put before you."

"Another test?" I enquired politely, and Mattias laughed.

"No," said the Count with surprising patience. "A genuine proposition. That we let bygones be bygones. That you join our family, which is your family, and live with us accordingly, naturally with an allowance appropriate to our station."

I blinked at him. I thought of asking him to repeat it, but I could see from the faces of the others that I had indeed heard him aright.

"You want *me* to live with *you?*" I said stupidly. "After what I have done?"

"You didn't *do* anything," the Count said. "Except shout at me. I reserve the right to shout back when I choose."

Of course, it was not possible; and once I had picked my jaw up off the floor, I strove to explain this to them. Even at the time I had the weird feeling I was fighting myself as much as them, and in any case Katalin soon put a stop to it by exclaiming, "Katie, do stop being so *wretchedly* noble! We *want* you to live with us! At least the three of us, and Papa, do, and Mattias thinks it might be amusing, which is just about his level, so why don't you stop *atoning*, and stay?"

I gazed at her, almost more surprised by this than by all the rest. For the first time, I allowed myself to consider the possibility of remaining, of "joining" the family. I had many reasons for staying, none at all for going, except my foolish pride and dislike of accepting charity. Another idea was born. Thoughtfully, I looked at István.

"I have a slightly different proposition," I said, "if you will listen."

"*Now* we get to it," Maria muttered audibly. I ignored her.

István nodded. "Go on."

I took a deep breath. "I propose that I continue to teach Miklós and Anna, at least until you decide to send them away to school, or find a more advanced tutor for Miklós."

István looked startled, but I could see the idea did not displease him. He glanced across to his wife. So did I. She was regarding me with fixed fascination.

"Do you *like* being a governess?" she enquired.

I almost smiled. "More than I thought I would," I confessed. "But truthfully, I have grown fond of the children, and they are used to me now."

"We're all used to you, that's the trouble, and I admit my soul sighs with weariness at the prospect of finding a new governess. But how then am I to introduce you to Society — oh yes, that *is* part of the plan — if you spend all day in the schoolroom?"

My sense of humour was returning. "It caused you no qualms before," I recalled.

"True." Her gaze had grown highly speculative.

"I would drive you mad in an hour," I reminded her.

"I shouldn't put up with your company for any longer," Elisabeth retorted.

And late that night, bemused and curiously relieved, I had settled down to reply to Aunt Edith. "My Dear Aunt," I had begun, "Many thanks for your last letter, which has had *considerable* influence on the Szelényi household..."

CHAPTER SEVENTEEN

Despite István's impatience, we had not returned to Buda-Pest until the day of the elections themselves. This was partly due to the old Count's reluctance to part with us: though he refused to leave Szelényi, neither did he wish to be alone again, with only Margit and the servants for company.

I wondered briefly if he was afraid after the peasants' strange, silent demonstration, but he showed no other signs of that, and the peasants themselves seemed to have reverted to sullenly ignoring their lord and complaining about the poor yield of this year's harvest. Most of them showed no interest whatever in my 'return', the exceptions, of course, being Lajos's parents, who were touchingly pleased about my happy reunion with my family. Of Lajos's reaction, I knew nothing; he had gone back to Buda-Pest the day after my discovery, leaving me oddly small and lost in my new splendour. It was his mother who had discreetly returned my bonnet.

Yet curiously enough, although I sensed the resentment of the castle servants — even Zsuzsa's manner was restrained — I seemed to settle into the family with remarkable ease. If I was not yet the most trusted member, I was undeniably accepted and, I saw with something approaching surprise, liked.

And when we did finally part, the Count said to me abruptly, "Will you write?"

"If you bother to reply," I said unkindly. He looked at me, a small, twisted smile dawning on his thin lips.

"You see? It's not so easy to forgive."

My eyes fell before his. "No," I said quietly, "it's not easy." But like the others, I kissed his hand and his cheek when we parted, and resolved to try harder.

We eventually arrived in Pest in the middle of an election procession. It seemed to be the custom for voters to march to the polls in massed, triumphant throngs, and this one, clearly supporting the liberal opposition, was certainly huge.

Unable to pass for the cheering crowds, we pulled into the side of the road to let the procession go by, and I was astonished. It was led by the same Count Batthyány I had seen at Teréz Meleki's house in July, only now he and the other nobles behind him wore national dress, a sort of rich, idealized peasant costume, with huge red, green and white feathers in their hats to proclaim their allegiance. Mounted on a beautiful, thoroughbred horse, Batthyány still looked magnificent, graciously doffing his hat to the crowd as he rode by.

As the procession passed in a blaze of colour and splendour, I could clearly see the different social ranks of the voters. Following Batthyány and the great men came those on less expensive mounts, then those with no horse at all.

"Are they the Honoratiores?" I asked Mattias about this last group, remembering Lajos's explanation of the honorary nobles.

"Lord no, just poor nobles — sandaled nobles, we call them because they can't afford boots. Magnates like Batthyány — and my brother here — buy their votes with banquets and patronage."

István regarded him with dislike.

"I have never bought anyone's votes," he said repressively.

"Ha!" said Mattias derisively, then, "There, Katie, these look more like the Honoratiores. Do you see? Clerks and teachers and lawyers..."

"Who have no right to vote anyway," István interrupted.

"They do in Pest."

"That," said István, "is constitutionally doubtful. My God! Is that Lajos Lázár? He has no business voting here or anywhere else!"

While Mattias disputed this with him, I searched the procession with something approaching desperation, but in the end, he was easily found. Marching along in the midst of the swaggering group of young men at the end of the line, he was holding one end of a banner bearing the colours of the Opposition.

Mattias abruptly left off his argument and leaned out of the window beside me to yell encouragement. Some of the faces turned towards us, Lajos's among them. I thought he laughed. Certainly he dipped the banner as if saluting us, and then raised it even higher so that I could clearly see the words embroidered across it: *Liberté, Egalité, Fraternité*.

I didn't know whether to be amused or frightened by this boldness. I wondered if the respectable Count Batthyány knew that they or their deliberately provocative banner were behind him. One or two of the young men were waving to Mattias, signalling him to join them until, with a laugh, he began to push open the carriage door.

"What the devil are you doing?" István demanded.

"I'm going to cheer the vote," Mattias said gleefully. He was too young to vote himself.

"Not with that hoard of rabble-rousers and peasants! If you must march with the Opposition, for God's sake go with men of your own rank...!" But it was too late; Mattias had gone, running into the centre of the group to be greeted by his friends. When he finally disappeared from view he was arm-in-arm with a disreputable looking student on one side, and on the other a flamboyant young man who might have been an actor.

I glanced at István. He was tight-lipped and angry. "Fool of a boy!" he said furiously.

"I gather *you* won't be voting that way," I said, with an attempt at lightness.

"No!" He looked at me and relaxed slightly. "Forgive me. To be honest, my inclinations are with the Opposition, but men like Kossuth I cannot abide!"

"But why do you so dislike him?" I asked curiously, as the procession receded and the crowds began to part.

"The man is a trouble-maker. A landless upstart with delusions of grandeur. A pompous, lawless..."

"Surely not lawless," I interrupted in the spirit of justice.

"He has already been in prison once for sedition."

As our coach moved forward again, I regarded István just a little provokingly. "Very well, but in what way is he an upstart? I thought he was noble."

"Oh he is — of the minor nobility. But his family have no land and he has to work for his living."

"That is certainly very bad," I said gravely. István looked at me suspiciously, and I added hastily, "I am interested in Kossuth. Everyone seems to regard him as the man of the moment, whether or not they approve of him."

"He is certainly becoming difficult to ignore," István allowed ruefully. "But *this* sort of following surely condemns him!" He waved his hand speakingly after the disappearing radical Honoratiores and their blatantly revolutionary banner, adding bitterly, "If anything else were needed to prove the dangers of Kossuth's policies, surely that rabble is it — damned Jacobins!"

*

Everything was different for me now. Though I held out determinedly against my family's desire to foist a personal maid on me, I had still been moved to a more suitable bedchamber. Naturally, the servants had been informed of my changed state, so for the first couple of days I was the subject of many furtive glances and whispers. On the other hand, the morning after our arrival, when I went to collect the children from the nursery, I was secretly touched to hear Zsuzsa giving a furious lecture to a couple of lowlier maids and a footman who had apparently been criticizing me.

Though with difficulty, I did make a point of going to see both Ferenc and Frau Schmidt to offer some kind of explanation. After all, they had been kind to me well beyond necessity and as the friendship between us had grown, they had even uttered indiscreet remarks about the family in my presence. Not unnaturally, they were a little stiff. Philosophically, I waited for things to settle down.

And of course, on the very first day back, my spacious new bedchamber was invaded by Elisabeth and Katalin, for once in unholy alliance to take me shopping.

"I will not look at that drab garment one day longer," Elisabeth announced. "It's more than I should be asked to bear."

Somewhat uneasily, I gave in. I had occasionally been granted a terrifying glimpse of the prices the fashionable were prepared to pay to cover their nakedness, and though I was happy to accept the hospitality of my family, running up huge bills at their expense was not part of my plan. István had already given me an unnecessarily large purse with the mind-boggling rider that he would keep the rest until I needed it. I couldn't imagine ever needing it. In a dazed whirl, I was dragged through umpteen fashionable couturiers in Vaci Street, and returned to the palace some hours later totally exhausted and the proud owner of what seemed to me a complete new wardrobe.

"That will do to start with," said Elisabeth with satisfaction, leaving me, for once, speechless.

And this was the pattern of my new life. In the mornings at least, I taught the children — who seemed just as pleased with Cousin Katie as with Miss Katie the governess. On most afternoons I was extracted from the schoolroom by my relatives and taken either shopping or visiting. On the occasions of the latter, I amused myself by searching for recognition in the faces of my hosts, who never seemed to see a connection between the Szelényis' new, fashionably dressed relation and their old, dowdy governess. Yet I was sure the news must have filtered through the city via the servants if no one else. I could only conclude that it would have been bad manners to recognize me as the governess now, just as, apparently, it had been good manners to ignore me when I *was* the governess. Polite Society has always been a mystery to me.

My evenings were generally full of frivolity. Of course, Buda-Pest being now obsessed with politics and patriotism, no aristocratic ball was complete without at least one czardas — a rather more restrained version of the dance I had learned with Lajos — and national costume was becoming accepted fashion. Fascinated, I enjoyed the colour and the novelty of it all, especially when I was engaged for every single dance at the Esterházys' ball. This was a felicity quite unknown to me before: whether it was due to the Szelényis' rank and influence or to my own oddity in being Scottish, bespectacled, and a female acquiring an undeserved reputation as a wit, I had no idea. I simply savoured the experience and treasured up amusing incidents with which to entertain Lajos at our next meeting. If we ever met again.

On one memorable evening, I finally encountered the great Kossuth himself. This was, apparently, quite a coup achieved by Baroness Meleki, for Kossuth was generally too hard at work and too austere by nature to attend social functions, especially now that he had been elected to the Diet — by a huge majority, needless to say. However, Teréz had somehow contrived to acquire a reputation for political seriousness, as well as discreet adultery, so the great man was persuaded to attend her dinner party whose guest list, admittedly, read more like a political rally.

I was rather surprised to have been invited, because although Teréz had treated me with perfect civility since learning my identity, it was quite obvious that she liked me as little as I did her. I imagine she believed I might tell her friend Elisabeth how she had once threatened to have me dismissed, a memory which I was treasuring rather maliciously now, but which I was, at least for the moment, keeping to myself.

When we arrived in her fashionable drawing-room, it was to discover just about every prominent liberal politician already present, including Count Batthyány and the sad, cynical Count Széchenyi, who had accepted the invitation before he realized his arch rival would also be there. István felt much the same about Kossuth, and with amusement I watched him and Széchenyi gravitate towards each other. Only Kossuth himself was lacking. I admit to an unworthy glee at the prospect that he might have let her down at the last moment, but since I was, in fact, extremely curious to meet him, I managed to squash my spurt of ill-nature quite easily.

And Kossuth did indeed arrive in the end. Watching him, unexpectedly handsome and graceful with a fine, round beard, a proud carriage and an air of importance, I suspected he liked to make entrances. Yet I was immediately aware of his distinctive *presence*. His eyes were grave, direct and brimful of extraordinary energy.

I came to his notice only because I was seated beside Elisabeth, who was being courted at the time by Batthyány — for political rather than amorous ends, I should add — and Kossuth could hardly ignore the man who was to so large a degree his patron. Batthyány was obliged to introduce us both to Kossuth. During the performance of this ceremony, I noticed with amusement that Mattias — who had done us the unprecedented honour of accompanying us solely in the hope of exchanging a word with his hero — was making his way determinedly towards us. It came as quite a shock, when I pulled my attention back to my companions, to discover that Kossuth's clear eyes were not on my beautiful aunt, but on me.

"So, you are from Great Britain?" he said, in careful English. "I am a great admirer of your political system." I murmured something gratifying. "In Scotland," he pursued, "you have your own law, within the British monarchy, is it not so?"

"Yes..."

"I find that admirable. An example to us in the Empire, perhaps."

"We don't have our own Parliament in Scotland," I pointed out, "which, I suppose, puts Hungary rather ahead of us!"

He smiled slightly. "No Parliament? But how does that come about?"

"We voted it away."

"For good reasons, I hope?"

"For greed," I said cynically. "You speak English very well, Mr Kossuth."

"Thank you! I learned by reading Shakespeare when I was in prison." He was shockingly blasé about something as shameful as incarceration, but since he had in fact emerged from his experience both a martyr and a hero to the people, I felt my eyes begin to smile in response to the twinkle in his. There was something very charming about Kossuth. He was a little pompous and terribly arrogant, but I confess I liked him.

*

Now, on the Danube steam-ship two weeks later, finally en route to Pressburg and the opening of the Diet, Kossuth was the name on everybody's lips.

But I remembered Lajos and the deadly serious young men in the Pilvax. I found myself praying quite hard that their hopes would be at least partially fulfilled. If they weren't, I didn't want to think of the consequences.

CHAPTER EIGHTEEN

A week later, I returned to Buda-Pest quite disgusted.

I had seen the King-Emperor, poor, gentle Ferdinand, open the Diet amid wild optimism and infectious enthusiasm. And then I watched it all collapse in a welter of furious heckling by the young men in the public gallery — led, inevitably, by Lajos and his friends — and in endless fights between the Upper and Lower Houses, between supporters of the Government and the Opposition, between Magyars and Croats and Serbs...

I gave up.

By the time Lajos returned to Pest, winter had closed in. The Danube had frozen over, the hills above Buda had turned white, and Pest sparkled with bright, cold frost. I loved the new beauty of the cities, especially in the early dusk — which was why I chose to walk home from an afternoon spent in Buda with some amusing new friends. And it was then, dawdling along the Pest side of the river, that I finally came face to face with Lajos.

He was with a group of perhaps eight working men, all standing talking by the light of a lamp-post, right in my path. My heart lurched uncomfortably; my step faltered; then I forced myself to go on, drawing my guard around me like a wrap. Despite everything, despite my new life, my new feelings, I needed his friendship very badly...

Already I could hear him saying seriously, "That's why they keep it from us, so that we feel isolated — but we're not. All over Europe, ordinary people are organising their discontent, and all over Europe, things are changing. The French are forcing it, with their great political banquets for the people, uniting them against their government..."

"But where will that lead?" some one asked with a terrifying cough. "What will it do for us?"

"For them, for us, I hope it will lead to revolution," Lajos said frankly, and I didn't know whether to laugh or cry. Then, unexpectedly, he looked up and saw me; and the smile which lit his eyes was quite spontaneous. Relief flooded through me like a tide. I returned his smile with uncomplicated gladness, because we were still friends. And then I was squeezing past his companions, passing on.

"The revolution will free all the peoples of Europe, Hungarians included..."
Inevitably, I was fighting a sense of anti-climax. We had met at last, but just as in Pressburg, he was busy with politics. And of course, Teréz was in Buda-Pest...

In my misery, I was hardly aware of the light, running footsteps until they came along side me. Lajos said, "I didn't realize they still let you out alone."

I recovered quickly. "They consider me too eccentric to cross."

Risking a glance at him, I saw his lips quirk in the half-smile I had so missed, and then he said casually, "You look well."

Inevitably, his eyes had strayed to my new sartorial elegance. I met his gaze defiantly. "You should see my ball gown," I said challengingly, and saw amusement glimmer in his dark eyes.

"I should love to," he said promptly. I regarded him with hostility.

"Do you know, even if my family had authorized it, I wouldn't have given the money to the poor. I wanted a new dress. *Several* new dresses."

"I wasn't criticizing," he said mildly. "How could I? I spend my pay on wine and books and the production of pamphlets that make policemen's hair curl."

I eyed him suspiciously. "Don't you think it's a waste of money?"

"The books are, perhaps, but not the wine."

"Lajos, I'm serious! I mean, I was sure you would disapprove of wasting money on such fripperies!"

"Come, I'm not a Presbyterian!" He drew my hand through his arm and I let it lie there, peaceful and content. His eyes were laughing at me. "As for the poor, it's not charity they need; it's work, better wages, cheaper food and more respect. Here endeth the first lesson."

*

"Shall we go and visit Petöfi?" Lajos said.

We were still strolling by the glassy river, companionably eating hot chestnuts which Lajos had bought from a street vendor. I had forgotten I was expected at the palace. Under that clear, darkening sky, walking so comfortably by his side, watching our breath hang in the cold air around us, I felt a fragile contentment steal over me. I found myself pretending that he loved me, that we were just such a couple as I could see hand-in-hand in front of us.

I looked up at him. "At the Pilvax?" I asked, a little dubiously.

"Petöfi's a married man now," Lajos said wryly. "He can't fritter away *all* his evenings in a café. But we could go to his house."

I confess that the prospect of meeting the charismatic poet and his new wife in their own domain intrigued me. I glanced at Lajos. He was shivering slightly, his only protection against the icy winds blowing in off the Great Plain being an old and inevitably shabby top-coat. Ruthlessly quashing my anxiety for him, I said only, "Would Madame Petöfi not mind?"

"No; she is remarkably tolerant of all his friends, however disreputable."

"Even you?" I mocked.

His lips curved a little ruefully. "Well, she puts up with me for Petöfi's sake, but to be honest, I don't think she cares for me a great deal."

I was surprised by that. I thought of several witty responses, but in the end I simply asked, "Why not?"

"I suspect Petöfi told her that I tried to dissuade him from marrying her."

I blinked. "Why did you do that? You'd never even met her!"

Lajos shrugged. "I know. It just seemed wrong for him — shouting about liberty with every second breath — to leg-shackle himself for life to some female he scarcely knew. But the feeling went deeper with him than I guessed."

"But she hasn't forgiven you?"

"Not yet," said Lajos, "I'm working on it."

We walked on while I ate the last chestnut without compunction. After a little, unable to resist, I asked lightly, "Have you never had the urge to be — er — leg-shackled, yourself?"

"I don't believe I'm a marrying man," he answered in the same vein. I knew I should hold my tongue, but I couldn't.

"Wouldn't you like to marry — Teréz, for example? If it were possible."

At that, he turned his direct gaze upon me. I met it innocently enough, veiling my true interest in his answer. There was a definite pause before he said briefly, "No."

I had time to feel a quick upsurge of gladness before, unexpectedly, his hand came up, gently pushing an escaped lock of my hair back under my hood, and that lightest caress of his finger tips on my cheek made me catch my breath. I brushed his hand away with a quick laugh that sounded nervous to my own ears.

I couldn't bear his touch. I felt all my self-control dissolve, leaving me as vulnerable as if I were naked. I gazed blindly across the glittering river to Buda's magnificent skyline, keeping my face averted from his penetrating eyes in case they read the abject longing in mine.

I was relieved, even glad, when we came to Petöfi's abode, which he shared with his fellow radical, the writer Mór Jókai. Jókai was not at home, but Petöfi and his wife made us very welcome; and if Madame Petöfi's manner was a little reserved, particularly towards Lajos, she betrayed no trace of discomfort or dislike, fetching food and wine and treating us to the friendliest hospitality.

While Lajos and Petöfi lapsed into the half-political, half-bantering conversation peculiar to them when they were together, Madame Petöfi and I began the preliminary civilities of two rather reticent women meeting for the first time but prepared to like each other.

Once I glanced at the men and found Petöfi's eyes on me with undisguised speculation. For the first time I wondered how he and his wife regarded this visit of mine in Lajos's company, and I flushed, both with irritation at not having considered this before — Lajos's casual manners were too *lulling* — and with sheer embarrassment.

Petöfi smiled at me. "My friend tells me you are not a governess after all, but an aristo of the first order!"

"Sándor!" Julia protested.

"Only on my mother's side," I said meekly. "And I am not yet so used to living in a palace that I should object *very* strongly to being turfed out of it — come your revolution."

Petöfi laughed. "That's the spirit! Would you like to see my engravings?"

Since these were rather good portraits of the French revolutionaries of 1789, including Robespierre and St. Just, I said promptly, "I saw them when I came in. Very proper for a man of your principles."

Lajos smiled. "You won't get the better of her, Petöfi."

"I shan't try any more. I *still* like Miss Katie!"

"Look gratified," Lajos recommended. "It's meant to be an honour." Petöfi threw a newspaper at him.

The Szelényi new year ball was the biggest social event of the winter, but it stands out in my mind for quite another reason, namely my discovery that I had a most distinguished admirer. Colonel von Avenheim came all the way from Transylvania in appallingly treacherous weather conditions, apparently just to be at the ball; and once there he chose to dance only with me.

After our second waltz, tired but exhilarated, I accepted his escort to a seat — which turned out to be situated in a curtained alcove.

"Your warnings were quite unnecessary, Miss Katie," he said, smiling, letting the curtain fall back behind him and sitting on the sofa beside me. "For you dance delightfully."

I regarded him with scepticism, but returned the compliment sincerely. "Why, so do you, Colonel. Believe me, it was only your skill which kept me off your toes!"

He laughed, and to my surprise I thought I detected a new, deeper warmth in his normally cool blue eyes. "Then I may hope for another dance this evening?"

I looked at him quizzically. "I shall be accused of monopolizing you," I said at last, lightly.

"I should like very much," he said softly, "to be monopolized by you..."

Unexpectedly, he bent his head towards mine as if he meant to kiss me; involuntarily, I turned my face away and stood up, but it wasn't primness or repulsion which compelled me — how could one be repelled by a gentleman as attractive as the Colonel? It was simply that there was only one man whose kisses I wanted, and he was not here.

"I think," I said firmly, "I would like some more champagne." He rose also, and took my hands, smiling down at me.

"Forgive me," he said simply, lifting my fingers to his lips.

"Perhaps," I said lightly, "but I insist on the champagne." And I drew my hands out of his hold. He raised the curtain for me to pass through, and I found I was consumed with a nervous desire to laugh.

Katalin was, as usual, enjoying herself with her multitude of admirers, despite Captain Zarescu's absence, but she still found time to twit me about the Colonel's attentions.

"*I* saw you disappearing into the alcove with him," she said teasingly, taking my arm and urging me to walk with her. It was, in fact, the custom for ladies to go about in pairs at such parties, a form of discreet chaperonage which we had both been avoiding until now. "But seriously, I have never seen the Colonel behave so, and we've known him forever. Do you like him?"

"Of course I do," I said coolly.

"Oh Katie, wouldn't it be wonderful if..."

"Very wonderful," I interrupted drily. "In fact, incredible."

All the same, it did appear that I had engaged the Colonel's interest. He stayed in Buda-Pest only a few days, and seeing my distaste for secret dalliance at the ball, he behaved afterwards like the perfect gentleman I knew him to be. Yet he sought me out on many occasions, walked with me in the snow, played with the children, sat near me and showed me such charming attentions that I began to wish I could fall in love with him.

When Katalin, Mattias and I arrived at the Pilvax that evening early in March, I was plagued by the dread that Petöfi or one of the others might betray too great an acquaintance with me by over-friendly greetings. However, I need have had no fear of that, for they never even noticed my entrance.

We were there largely because István had just bolted to Vienna to try and reassure the Imperial Government after Kossuth's latest incendiary speech — *"The dynasty must choose between its own welfare and the preservation of a rotten system..."* — and because Elisabeth, having watched him go broodingly, as if she had suspected him of taking another woman with him in her place, had suddenly revived to the extent of attending some select party at Teréz Meleki's house.

On sudden impulse, Katalin had used this rare opportunity to harass Mattias into taking her to the Pilvax in the hope of meeting Alex there. I was necessarily included in her project, though naturally I made a show of reluctance — not least because of the unwisdom of meeting her lover under Mattias's nose.

I saw them at once, at their favourite long table: Lajos and Petöfi and Vasvári and Mór Jókai and several other familiar looking young men. There was wine on the table, but the flagon was still half-full and the men themselves were in the middle of a heated debate which involved much gesticulating and scribbling on pieces of paper.

Of course the news from France must have electrified them: just as Lajos had foretold, the French had risen in revolution, overthrowing the government and forcing the King himself to abdicate. And already the Pest radicals had turned wild with joy and anticipation, whipping up increasingly large and noisy street meetings — which caused respectable people to voice genuine alarm about the dangerous influence of such agitators as Lajos Lázár; while Petőfi himself, according to Mattias, had rushed back to Pest from holiday, in abject terror lest the Hungarian revolution start without him!

Now, in a moment of relative quiet, their voices drifted clearly across to me. "I don't care," Lajos was saying flatly. "Universal suffrage is fundamental." "'Responsible government' would cover it," Petőfi argued. "We can interpret it later to suit ourselves."

Someone else spoke then, but I didn't hear it, for in the disconcerting way he had, Lajos suddenly looked up and straight into my eyes. His fleeting half-smile dawned and then the man next to him was beating the table in front of him to gain his attention. I could almost have believed that he returned to the debate with reluctance; but then I was becoming more and more given to these fantasies.

"He's not here," Katalin said tragically in my ear as we followed the waiter to a vacant table. Stupidly, I had opened my mouth to say of course he was, before I realized who it was that she meant. It was becoming very easy to betray myself. I squeezed her hand.

"Perhaps he'll come later," I breathed. "Did you expect him?"

She shook her head. "I suppose he is on duty... Is that Lajos over there? Does he *live* here, Mattias?"

"More or less," said Mattias vaguely, while I kicked Katalin under the table. If she was not meant to have been here before, it would hardly do to recognize the regular patrons! She immediately looked guilty, but fortunately Mattias was too concerned with the discussion at Lajos's table.

"I wonder what that's all about?" he murmured. "Do you suppose something's happening at last?"

He was obviously dying to find out — so was I — but civility compelled him to order our wine and cakes and to wait at least for their arrival. While I looked around me, drinking in the almost feverish excitement evident in the café that night — Lajos's group was certainly not the only one engrossed in spirited discussion — I gradually became aware that Katalin's beautiful mouth was beginning to droop with a misery I could understand only too well. The unhappiness of her romance was made all the sharper by fear that Alex would soon be sent to Italy to put down the rebellions which had broken out there since the new year.

I coughed to attract her attention, casting a quick glance at Mattias. His eyes were unusually serious and, more worryingly, they were fixed on his sister's tragic face. Even as I looked at him, he put out one hand and lightly touched hers.

"Are you thinking of Zarescu?" he asked bluntly. "Do you actually *love* him, Katalin?"

She met his gaze and didn't even think of lying.

"Yes," she said simply.

Mattias drew in his breath. "Oh the devil, what a coil! Couldn't you have chosen more wisely?"

Katalin shook her head. "No."

Just then the waiter appeared and began unloading things from his tray. Mattias sat back, but his eyes were still on Katalin.

"Cheer up," he said lightly at last. "Something will turn up, you know. It always does."

She looked back at him, an arrested expression in her eyes. Mattias poured the wine and politely passed the plate of cakes. By that time, Petöfi was rising to his feet, which seemed to be a signal for the break-up of his party. Mattias followed my gaze and promptly stood up too.

"Back in two minutes," he promised, and hastened towards the other table.

"Do you know," Katalin said slowly, "that is the first kind thing he has ever said to me about Alex?"

Behind her, I saw Petöfi with his coat and hat on, making for the door while still talking animatedly over his shoulder to his friends who were all sitting or standing around the same table. I heard one of the young men saying in reply, "All right, all right! We'll have a National Guard! Good night!"

And Petöfi laughed and waved and was gone. Lajos was standing by the table, listening to Mattias. I saw him smile and reach across the table for the wine, pouring it out as he answered him. He drank half the glass in one draught, clapped Mattias on the shoulder and went past him, pushing Vasvári towards him instead. The next moment he was strolling in our direction.

"Good evening," he said easily. "May I join you?"

I indicated Mattias's chair. "On condition that you tell us what you've been plotting."

He sat down, laying his glass on the table. "You'll find out soon enough. The Opposition have asked us to draw up a petition and collect signatures to send to the King."

My eyes widened. This was recognition, success indeed.

"They asked *you*?" Katalin uttered, tactlessly amazed. Lajos's lip twitched.

He said gravely, "Not me personally. My friends and me. Young Hungary if you like."

"Well, I hope you won't petition His Majesty for my head," Katalin said with an attempt at lightness, though there was a glint of suspicion in her eyes.

"It's a belief of mine that heads and bodies should remain firmly attached wherever possible. Alex will be sorry to have missed you," he added casually. "He is on duty tonight."

"Yes, I thought he must be," Katalin said with commendable calmness.

"So, when will it be ready, this petition?" I asked, to distract his too penetrating gaze from Katalin. "Or will you be just like the Diet, unable to come to an agreement?"

"Oh no. It will be ready by Saturday." I regarded him sceptically until his lips quirked in the fascinating half-smile that always left me weak. "Don't you believe me? I'm always right about such things, you know."

I rallied. "Such as Kossuth's speech, which still waits upon the Lords' pleasure?"

"No it doesn't." He had wanted me to bring that up. "The Lower House is sending it to the King anyway, without the Lords' approval."

I blinked. Katalin said with certainty, "They can't do that. It's illegal."

"They'll do it all the same. The Lords are not elected: they have no right to speak for the people."

Katalin shivered. "Are you *trying* to cause chaos in the country?" It was a silly question, with only one answer.

"Yes," he said, smiling. Katalin, it seemed, was taken back to her childhood.

"I hate you when you're like this," she said, frowning, but at this point I became distracted by Vasvári who had appeared beside us with Mattias.

"Has Lajos told you what we are doing?" he said as soon as I met his glittering gaze.

Pál Vasvári was a grave, clever youth, unfailingly polite and passionately intent upon his goals. He taught history at one of Pest's more progressive schools and, like Lajos, he was astonishingly well-read for a man of his age; yet there was something rather unworldly behind his air of practicality. He seemed to regard me now almost as one of them; I didn't know whether to be flattered or appalled.

"Yes," I said easily. "You have acquired a large responsibility!"

"One we have long sought," Vasvári said gravely. "The chance to speak for the people."

Something almost fanatical in his youthful eyes made me say, "Be sure that you do." Vasvári looked slightly taken aback, but when I glanced at Lajos, I saw his eyes alight with laughter. I could only guess that Vasvári in his excitement had needed taking down a peg, and I had been the thoughtless and unwitting instrument. Ignoring Katalin's expression of boredom, I said hastily, "What are you going to ask for in this petition?"

Pulling a crumpled piece of paper from his pocket, Vasvári waved it in front of me, saying, "This is our first draft. It begins: *What does the Hungarian nation wish?* And underneath we list twelve demands — we're still debating the precise order and wording — ending with *Liberty! Equality! Fraternity!*"

I drew in my breath, quickly sweeping my eyes over the document. "It goes rather further than the Opposition's Declaration," I observed. I glanced at Lajos. "I suspect it also goes a great deal further than the Opposition Circle asked of you."

Lajos smiled. "What did you expect?"

"Will they use it?"

"We won't ask them," Vasvári said carelessly.

"Then they'll repudiate it!"

"No; we have the people on our side, and that makes us far stronger."

"How can you know that?"

Vasvári glanced at Lajos, then shrugged and said, "We're going to organise a banquet in the French style, for the nineteenth of March when the peasants flock into Pest for the fair at Rákos." His eyes gleamed. "We'll unite all 40,000 of them at the banquet! Believe me, the Opposition will repudiate nothing."

Even in this persuasive company, that was too much for me. I stared at Vasvári, feeling the blood drain out of my face. "My God, you would stir up 40,000 peasants to violence in Buda-Pest?"

"We won't need to," he said simply.

And I understood. Slowly, I turned my head and looked at Lajos, but I was seeing him not as he was now, relaxed, smiling, idly twisting his wine glass between his fingers, but as he had been on the night of the Szelényi Castle ball, the torch-light flickering over his grim face and his worn, peasant clothes as he stood at the head of that indescribably threatening line of people.

"*You don't need violence to make a revolution*," he had said the next day. "*Only the threat of it.*"

He met my gaze and saw that I had understood. He raised his glass in another silent toast.

I said, "I hope to God your calculations are correct."

His lip twitched. "My dear, God will have nothing whatever to do with it."

CHAPTER NINETEEN

The week passed on a wave of continuing excitement in the city, so that by Sunday, when nothing had happened, I began to think once more that nothing would. It seemed to me that the fear of revolution had grown stale.

Then, around noon on Tuesday, a servant gave me a message from Elisabeth asking me to bring the children downstairs for luncheon. This was a rare enough event to produce squeals of delight from Miklós and Anna, though I, having seen Baroness Meleki arrive earlier that morning, was rather less joyful.

However, when we entered the room, I was immediately alarmed by Elisabeth's manner. There was a tinge of fear in her normally languid eyes, and she hugged the children to her almost compulsively. I paused, my hand still on the door knob, looking slowly from this maternal vignette to Teréz, whose whole demeanour shrieked of suppressed excitement. That alone was enough to frighten me.

"What is it?" I asked with sinking dread. "What has happened?"

Elisabeth looked at me over Anna's fair head. "Vienna is in the hands of the mob," she said unsteadily. Something lurched inside me. Italian revolts, French revolutions, they were somehow distantly exciting, but Vienna — Vienna was too close, and its significance extended far beyond Austria. If it was truly in the hands of a mob, no wonder Elisabeth was frightened. I found I had crossed the room and sat down at the table beside her. Thank God István had come home yesterday...

"Oh, come." Teréz was amused. "It's hardly as bad as that."

Somewhat relieved, I met her gaze and demanded, "What exactly *has* happened?"

She began to help herself to cold meats. "Apparently, the Vienna students have been stirring up the people for days, mainly by reading them Kossuth's speech. Then, yesterday morning, a group of them invaded the Estates' meeting and forced it to send a mass delegation to the Emperor with a reform petition."

I swallowed. "That doesn't sound so very bad."

"No, but at the same time the workers rose and indulged in an orgy of machine-breaking and arson. There were huge demonstrations which, inevitably, clashed with the soldiers."

She chose her vegetables with care. Watching her, I asked slowly, "How many were hurt?" I knew what happened when soldiers met demonstrators.

"Forty or fifty, I think," she said without much interest.

"Badly?"

She looked surprised. "Dead."

I felt a chill spread through my bones. Was the cause of reform really worth fifty deaths? Was any cause? You didn't need violence to make a revolution, according to Lajos, but it seemed it was always the result.

Teréz picked up her knife and fork, a note of triumph in her voice as she said, "But you haven't heard the best of it yet. The Archdukes have dismissed old Metternich, that prop of the Ancien Régime himself! And of course, Kossuth is *bound* to take advantage — if he doesn't push through *all* the liberal reforms now, he's not half the man I know him to be!"

I dropped my gaze from Teréz, giving in at last to Anna's insistent tugging on my arm. I helped her to some food, thinking as I did so how odd it was to be carrying on with such mundane little tasks when all over Europe the world we knew — an unjust, even a rotten world, I was prepared to admit — was crumbling around us with a speed I could never have guessed at when we celebrated the new year so blithely barely two months ago.

* * *

The next day, the fifteenth of March, was a grey, wet Wednesday, a dull, miserable day to look out on, yet it was destined to turn the whole country upside down.

It even began unusually, with Mattias leaving punctually for the university, voicing the gloomy opinion that he might as well since nothing more exciting seemed likely to happen. And then Katalin, looking distressed, begged my company on a quick, early-morning visit to her favourite hat shop. After one glance at her woeful countenance, I abandoned the children to Zsuzsa for an extra hour, and went with her to the shop.

The bonnet on which she had so earnestly desired my opinion was certainly a charming confection, and I had no hesitation in recommending her to buy it. However, it struck me that she was showing remarkably little interest in it, considering the importance she was according the decision, so I was not altogether surprised when, back in the carriage again, she confessed that Alex had failed to meet her as arranged yesterday, and that the hat shop was merely an excuse, for we could easily return home via the city hall, and just possibly catch sight of Alex going either in or out of the coffee-house nearby.

I only blinked at that, and she hastened to assure me that Alex often went there in the mornings when he was free.

"Lajos is usually there then, and they can talk in peace when the café is quiet," she said, peering out of the carriage window. "Drat this rain! I can't see a thing..."

But as we turned into the boulevard, the rain was no longer blown against the left-hand window, and we were thus able to see quite clearly the large knot of people gathered outside the Pilvax, and the men who were running to join them from all directions.

"Oh, Katie," Katalin breathed. I said nothing. The relief I had felt on the previous evening when no disturbances had occurred in the city, and even Mattias had given up hope of them, now vanished with a jolt. "Something's happening..."

Something was. In the time it took us to drive the length of the street to the café, the knot had swelled to a crowd, and it was still growing. I could see Petőfi and Jókai climbing on to chairs to be seen, both holding pieces of paper before them like weapons.

Impulsively, I knocked on the carriage roof with my umbrella, and László obligingly pulled his horses in directly opposite the Pilvax.

"What are they doing?" Katalin asked fearfully.

"I don't know." I pulled down the window, and the hum of noise outside seemed to explode into an excited, passionate shout. My hand to my throat, I searched the crowd for Lajos — but I could see neither him nor Alex.

My stomach was tight with dread, and with something else that might have been anticipation. There had been street-meetings in the city before — noisy but harmless: I had no reason to suspect that this one was any different, yet I *knew* it was. This one was serious. This time they were starting something I was terribly afraid would go out of control.

"Look, there's Lajos," Katalin said, staring to the left. "Trust him to be in the thick of such a thing!"

My eyes flew after hers, and saw that she was right. He was running towards the crowd, at the head of a group of workmen, and the huge banner he waved above his head was not the colours of the liberal Opposition, but the bright red of revolution.

He was shouting something, but I couldn't make out the words. Petöfi and Jókai were applauding their arrival, and as they joined the ever-increasing crowd, Lajos gave his flag one last flourish, and the people cheered loudly in response. Joining in the shout, Lajos passed the banner back to the man behind him, and pushed through to the front, calling something to Petöfi and Jókai.

The noise of the agitated crowd was deafening; no one seemed to notice the drizzling rain or pay the least attention to our stationary carriage. Vaguely, I wondered if László felt vulnerable up there on the driver's box, or if he was secretly cheering with the crowd. He too had been born in Szelényi, I reminded myself; he would have known Lajos all his life.

"Katie, let's go," Katalin said quickly.

"Wait a moment..."

Petöfi had held up his hand for silence, and amazingly all the noise died away. "I have written a Song!" he cried. "A Song for Hungary, for all Hungarians!"

The demand to hear it was overwhelming. Into the renewed silence, Petöfi spoke again, his voice vibrant now with emotion, feelings which could not but be infectious. They were passed on in his words, rousing, simple, unquestionably moving.

"*Arise, Hungarians! Your country calls...*"

"Oh no," said Katalin. "Oh no, they can't do this, not here..."

"Hush," I said, with barely understood impatience. "Listen."

"*Are we to live as slaves, or be free?*" Petöfi was demanding. "*This is the question. Choose!*" He paused for effect, then answered himself intensely, passionately, "*We swear by the God of Hungarians, we swear we shall be slaves no more!*"

That answer was his refrain. By the end of the poem, the people were shouting it with him; and the crowd was still growing, almost stretching across to our carriage now. The final cheer was strangely terrifying in its enthusiasm. There was no doubt that these people at least were behind Petöfi, that they were no longer prepared to be slaves of poverty or feudalism or any other injustice.

I felt my breath catch in my throat. I was afraid; but I was moved too, and I had to stay just a little longer.

Into the noise, Petőfi was shouting, "We have written Twelve Demands to end slavery in this land! Jókai will read them to you!"

I knew the contents of this. While Jókai read them out and the crowd cheered each point wildly, my eyes were fixed on Lajos. Half-hidden from me by the crowd, I could still sense the tense stillness of his body. But his eyes were busy, searching the crowd, gauging their reactions. I saw him nod at something Vasvári said to him. I saw his eyes meet Petőfi's, and I saw the communication pass between them, a flash of understanding and triumph.

I was shut out. Suddenly I knew that I could not even have his full friendship, for the affinity between us stopped short of what he shared with Petőfi. Helpless, pointless jealousy surged through me, leaving me weak and unable to give László the order I knew I should.

Only Jókai's final call for "Equality, Liberty, Fraternity!" and the deafening roar of the crowd's approval, jerked me back to reality.

"These are what we demand of the King!" Jókai shouted.

"So what are we waiting for?" someone cried. My heart lurched, for it was Lajos. "Let's go and print them!"

That drew another cheer, but into it someone shouted uneasily, "What about the censor?"

"To hell with him!" Lajos said promptly. "Don't the people want a free press?"

Clearly, the people did.

"To the printing shop!" Petőfi cried into the uproar. "But first, let us march to the university and get the students to join us!" He leapt off his chair, pushing his way to the front of the cheering crowd, linking arms with Lajos and Vasvári as he went.

I found my voice at last. "László," I said through the open window. "Drive on, please." I was shaking, but I couldn't take my eyes off the crowd as we pulled away from it. Somehow it had changed from a seething, shapeless mass into a marching column with the young radicals at its head and the bright red flag, soaked by the rain, still waving bravely in their midst.

"Thank God Alex is not with them," Katalin whispered.

I didn't point out that Alex was more likely to be with the soldiers who would inevitably confront this mob. Lajos and his friends had deliberately roused the people, like a sleeping tiger, and I didn't see how they could possibly control the consequences. Blood would be spilled, as it had already been spilled in Vienna and Paris and Italy.

CHAPTER TWENTY

My hands had stopped shaking by the time I retrieved the children from a wide-eyed Zsuzsa — news of the demonstration outside the Pilvax had reached the palace already — but it was very difficult to concentrate on the task of teaching when my mind was full of anxiety and a desperation to know what was happening. Neither István nor Mattias came home all morning. There was no sign of Elisabeth, but Katalin, as restless as I, soon came to the schoolroom and stood beside me at the window, watching the rain roll down the glass in great, fat drops. The weather was getting worse: I could only hope it would damp revolutionary ardour.

"Do you think Alex will be at the Museum this afternoon?" Katalin murmured.

I stared at her. "Did he arrange to be?" If I had known that, I would not have gone with her this morning and I would have been spared this agony of worry. On the other hand, I could not be sorry that I had seen it. Wildly, I hoped it would not prove to be the last time I saw Lajos.

"Yes," Katalin was saying, "but how can I know..." She broke off as a door slammed somewhere in the house.

The sound of Mattias's voice, excited and laughing, came nearer. Katalin and I exchanged glances. As one, we moved to the door to intercept him, but we had barely taken two steps before the schoolroom door burst open and Mattias himself came striding in. He was soaked through and dishevelled, his face flushed as if with exertion, his eyes positively shining with enthusiasm.

"This is wonderful!" he cried, hardly even noticing the children, but coming straight to us. "I came to tell István, but Ferenc says he's in Buda..."

"Tell him what?" I interrupted. "What's happened?"

"The revolution has begun, and we've abolished censorship!" he cried, seizing Katalin's hands and dancing her round in circles, to the great and vocal joy of the children.

"You can't have!" Katalin gasped, pulling her hands free. "What are you talking about, Mattias? I can't bear this..."

"It's begun," he said triumphantly. This was getting us nowhere. Desperately, I caught him by the shoulders. I could feel my stomach churning with dread all over again.

"Mattias, what has begun?" I demanded urgently. "What exactly has happened?"

He perched himself on my desk, grinning at us in sheer high spirits. Still, he could hardly contain himself.

"I don't know where to start. I was at the university, listening — or at least yawning through the most tedious lecture you can imagine on the — well, it doesn't matter what it was on, for we were suddenly interrupted by a great crowd of people outside, who'd marched up from the Pilvax! Petöfi had written a song — here it is..."

He delved into his coat pocket and produced a crumpled piece of paper which he held out triumphantly. I took it without looking at it.

"We know about Petöfi's *Song*," I said quickly. "Go on."

"Do you?" Mattias sounded interested. "Well, it's a great poem, and it has *inspired* people as you'd never believe. Anyway, they had decided to print it, along with Young Hungary's Twelve Demands, and came to the university to gather the students as support."

I glanced down at the piece of paper in my hand. It was printed. My breath caught. They had printed it without the censor's approval, which meant that now they had broken the law, publicly and irrevocably. Lajos would be imprisoned at last, hanged...

"Go on," Katalin was saying impatiently. "I suppose you joined them?"

"Of course! We all did, and just when I had given up hope too! The old Prof tried to stop us, crying out, 'Gentlemen, in the name of the law...', but we never heard any more than that, for the crowd swallowed up the rest of his words in a great roar and he took to his heels in fear for his life! Vidacs told us that we were forbidden to go on pain of expulsion from the university, but we went anyway. And you needn't look so disapproving, Katalin, for your Zarescu was there too — not in uniform, fortunately, but I saw him as clearly as I see you now. Anyway, with all the students joining the demonstration, it was a huge crowd of us who marched off to Landerer's printing shop — it was the nearest to us, as well as the biggest in town — and we elected a committee to go inside and get the thing printed. So Petöfi and Irinyi and Lázár and some others went inside, and while we waited Vasvári and Jókai made some rousing speeches."

"In this rain?" I couldn't help saying sceptically.

"Oh yes. We were all huddled together under umbrellas — we must have been a funny sight. Jókai warned us that in an hour it might be bullets instead of rain falling on us." I couldn't control the shiver than jerked through my body, but my eyes were fixed on Mattias's youthful, wondering face. "Do you know," he went on, "that as one man, everyone closed their umbrellas, and we just got wet."

I swallowed the sudden lump in my throat. There was something oddly serious, even brave, in the symbolism of that act.

"Go on, go on," Katalin urged again.

"Well, the next moment, Lajos appeared at the door of the shop, holding up a sheet of printed paper. 'Here it is,' he cried, 'the first child of the free press!' And a huge cheer went up, deafening me! But I was shouting so loudly myself that my voice cracked."

"But how did they do it?" I asked abruptly. "Did they print it themselves under Mr Landerer's nose? Did they threaten him or his workers? *Hurt them?*"

Mattias grinned. "Lord, no. According to Petöfi, they just politely asked Landerer to print the two manuscripts. Naturally, Landerer said it was impossible without the censor's permission. He was so calm about it that even Petöfi was temporarily baffled, and then while they dithered, and the shop workers stood around gaping, Lajos realized that Landerer was hissing at them, 'Seize one of the presses!' So he nudged Irinyi who — being nearest — promptly laid his hands on the biggest machine and cried, 'We seize this printing press in the name of the people!' At which Landerer, good man, looked terribly sad and said, 'I cannot resist force.' Apparently the print workers then broke into cries of 'Long live the people!' After all they have more cause than most to hate the censorship laws!

"And that," he added, smiling happily from his sister to me, "was how we abolished censorship."

"For one day," I said, but mechanically, for my head was spinning with fears and speculations. "So what happens now?"

"There's another meeting called for three o'clock this afternoon, outside the Museum."

"Oh no," Katalin uttered, truly dismayed now. The fates were not kind to her and Alex these days. Surprised, her brother cast her an interrogative glance.

"We were going to take the children to the Museum this afternoon," I said quickly.

"Take them somewhere else," Mattias advised, dropping down from the desk and heading for the door. "They'll have more fun that way!" And he swung out of the room, pausing only to ruffle the head of either child on his way past.

I met Katalin's gaze for a long moment.

"It's happening here too," she said at last. Her voice was small and lost and frightened.

Distractedly, I regarded the children as they squabbled over some toy they shouldn't even have brought into the room. They were going to be impossible now.

"Never mind," Katalin said airily, recovering. "We'll take them out this afternoon."

I stared at her. "We can't, Katalin. Didn't you hear Mattias? The revolutionaries have called a meeting before the museum!"

"Perhaps no one will turn up. After all, it's pouring with rain."

"It didn't stop them this morning, and according to Mattias the crowd was huge by the time they reached the printers' shop."

"Mattias always exaggerates."

"I don't think so, not this time. And anyway, I doubt Alex will have time for you if he's involved in these events."

"Of course he will!" Katalin said indignantly.

"It doesn't matter," I said hastily. "We can't risk taking the children into an angry mob." I put it harshly quite deliberately, for in her single-mindedness, she was quite capable of endangering the children for the sake of one meeting with Alex.

She was silent for a moment, looking indecisively at the children, who were now crawling under their desks. "We'll take the carriage," she said abruptly, "as we did this morning. We'll just go and look. And at the first hint of trouble — or even a crowd like this morning — we'll turn back."

I still could not like the idea, but in the end I gave in, partly to avoid confrontation which I did not feel able to cope with, and partly, I confess, to satisfy my own curiosity. I needed to know what was happening. So we duly set off in the carriage. Ferenc saw us go, and warned us of the afternoon's planned demonstration. I promised we would be careful and gave László explicit instructions as to how vigilant he was to be.

I kept telling myself that no one had been hurt in the morning's adventure, but the soldiers had not been there then. This time they had plenty of warning, and the people would be flushed with the morning's victory, prepared to be both rash and brave. But perhaps the threat of military intervention would be enough to call off the meeting.

I didn't really believe that, but it kept me sane on the brief drive to the museum. I was so lost in thought that it was left to Katalin to scold the children for fighting and shouting at each other. I barely heard them. And as we drew nearer to the museum, despite the driving rain, I saw the numbers of people in the streets increasing. The roads on to the square itself were filled with crowds pouring in the same direction.

Mindful of his orders, László brought the carriage to a halt. I drew in my breath.

"We have to go back, Katalin," I said, and she nodded miserably, dumbly waiting for me to give László the order. Yet now it was I who hesitated. I couldn't just go home, when yards away *this* was happening...

In the end, I moved so suddenly that even the children were startled. I had the door open in a trice and was already half out of the carriage when I turned and said quickly over my shoulder, "You take them home — I'll see what's happening and take a fiacre back."

I had the briefest glimpse of Katalin's bemused face before I closed the door on it. Then I gave László his instruction and hurried after the crowd in the direction of the square. I think Katalin called after me, but I didn't stop.

As I melted into the throng, I couldn't help thinking of that other meeting I had walked into in Vienna a lifetime ago; I even imagined it was the same voice I could hear now speaking so passionately over the approving roar of what I realized must be a very large audience. Even so, I was certainly not prepared for the sight that met me as I moved into the square.

I came in to the right of the museum itself, so I saw at once that the revolutionaries were using the building's steps and landing as a stage. I saw too the shocking size of the crowd: there must have been ten thousand people there, sheltering under a colourful sea of umbrellas as the relentless rain battered down on them. I felt dwarfed, instinctively afraid of so huge a mass of bodies, far larger than any I had ever seen in my life before; and yet I could not even try to leave.

Though the streaming water on my spectacles was blinding me, I still knew the man speaking to this multitude simply by his distinctive stance on the steps, at once poised and casual, as much at his ease as if he were addressing his friends at the Pilvax. I had been right to recognize the voice earlier. As I paused to wipe my glasses, standing firm against the jostling people around me, I was not really aware of his words, just of his familiar, persuasive voice, a little less lazy, a little more impassioned than I was used to.

I crammed my dry glasses back onto my face. I could see Petőfi standing to one side of him; I saw Vasvári and Jókai and several other young radicals from the Pilvax all around the lower steps, listening to Lajos and watching the intent, excited crowd. Just as I had in Vienna, I moved nearer.

The rain was already obscuring my vision again, but as I wiped impatiently at the glass, a large, kind man held his umbrella over me. I glanced up to smile my thanks, and received an unexpectedly huge beam of good will in reply, and despite the emotionally charged atmosphere all around me, I felt soothed. I stood still among the monstrous crowd, able to listen at last to Lajos's confident words.

He was urging everyone to stand fast in defence of what they had done that morning, and what they would do in the days to come, asking for the same unity I had only half-understood him to be advocating in Vienna, of all races and all classes, to make the people's demands legally as well as morally right. He said there was nothing they could not achieve with this union; it was invincible. There would be no more serfs, no more nobles as we understood it, only one people.

A ripple of approval, of *longing,* seemed to pass through the crowd as he spoke.

"One people!" he repeated, raising his suddenly vibrant voice. "And then no power on this Earth could possibly hurt us — because the power will be *ours!*" His arms went out exultantly to encompass the whole square, the whole country. "My friends, the power *is* ours! Let us use it!"

The applause was tumultuous. I felt a lump rise in my throat, for I dared to think he was right: so many people here, of all walks of life, and all united behind his dream of a free and just Hungary. And suddenly I wanted very badly to be up there beside him, because I believed in him...

I swallowed, watching as his eyes searched the wildly cheering crowd. There was a smile playing on his lips, a new fire in his eyes born of today's success; and yet there was an element of calculation too, as there always was in him — how far to push the crowd and still carry it with him, how much to say to frighten his opponents just enough without inciting actual violence. For I could see now that this was not the sort of revolution which was tearing Vienna — or not yet; it was still under control. If only the soldiers did not come...

And I knew too, that even if I stood right next to him, tugging at his coat tails, he wouldn't notice me, for now he was in his true element at last. This was what he had lived for and worked towards, for so long. And he was loving it.

At last, he held up his hand, and obediently, the roars around me subsided. I found myself glorying in his mastery, even while I acknowledged its danger. He was walking a tightrope, and if he fell, the consequences could be disastrous.

"This morning, we printed our Twelve Demands. We also printed a song of freedom, a *National Song;* I call on the author of that *Song,* the poet of our revolution — Sándor Petöfi!"

And then, in the renewed cheers, Petöfi strode up to him, embraced him from sheer high-spirits, and I saw their lips move as they exchanged a few quick words. Released, Lajos jumped down a few steps and half-turned so that he could see both Petöfi and the crowd in the square who were chanting now for the *National Song.* Clearly delighted, Petöfi bowed to their wishes.

They were silent now, and he quite serious, as he began to recite the poem that had so inspired this revolution — if such it proved to be. And it was Lajos who led everyone to roar along with the refrain, "*We swear by the God of Hungarians, we swear we shall be slaves no more!*"

I felt the might of these words, the strength of the united voice ringing out across the city, and I wanted to weep. My eyes were held by Lajos, his arm raised high to the crowd, his voice lifted to heaven. He was like some shabby, untidy angel fighting for his people, risking his very life for them; and yet was there not something just a little demonic about someone so able and so willing to manipulate those same people, in whatever cause...?

And he hadn't noticed me in the multitude. I knew he wouldn't. Not today. I had seen enough. I turned and began to push a little blindly through the crowd.

"Katie! Katie!" A voice was shouting over the cheers, making me pause. It was Alex in civilian dress, reaching his way through to me. For the first time I was glad of the rain on my spectacles, hiding my eyes.

"My God, Katie, isn't this wonderful? Are you by yourself?"

"Yes; Katalin went home with the children, but I wanted to find out... Alex, you will be careful?"

"Of course! It's all under control. Tell Katalin I'm sorry about this afternoon, and yesterday, and do you think you could manage to bring her to the Pilvax tonight? Tonight, I couldn't be anywhere else, but I long to see her — will she come?"

"I don't know," I said truthfully. "I'll pass on your message."

"Wait, have you no umbrella? Here, I'll come with you..."

"No," I said quickly. "No, I'm fine. Good-bye!"

And I almost bolted through the crowd away from him. I wanted desperately to be missed, as Alex missed Katalin.

Dinner at the Szelényi palace that evening was, as you might imagine, somewhat fraught. Not surprisingly either, István arrived late and angry. I thought I might have to wait for the departure of the servants, who were themselves tense with suppressed excitement, to find out what he knew of the day's events, but István had the aristocrat's complete disregard of menials — they were, in fact, furniture to him. So, when Mattias excitedly demanded to know if he had heard about the demonstrations, he began speaking at once.

"*Heard* about them?" he exploded. His brow was thunderous. "I've had the wretched rabble bellowing in my ears all afternoon!"

Mattias grinned unsympathetically. "You *were* at the Vice-Regal Council then?"

"I wish to God I hadn't been! I suppose you were one of the dogs baying under the windows?"

"Woof," said Mattias provokingly. His brother glared at him.

"What are you both talking about?" Elisabeth asked, her voice only slightly less bored than normal, though there was a frightened glint in her eyes. She took a dainty forkful of vegetables and waited to be informed.

"I told you about this morning," Mattias said.

"Printing your silly leaflets? Yes, you told me."

"It's not silly, and you know it. Well, we had another, even bigger demonstration this afternoon, outside the museum, and we decided to go from there to get the Pest City Council to endorse our Twelve Demands."

"And did they?"

"With fifteen thousand people yelling in the street below them?" said István contemptuously. "Of course they did!"

"So did you," Mattias said, "so you needn't sneer at them."

István threw down his knife. I was so interested in the conversation, I hadn't yet picked mine up.

"What happened?" I asked.

"Well, I think the City Council were sympathetic anyway. Rottenbiller, the Deputy Mayor, even suggested we form a revolutionary Committee of Public Safety to maintain order — naturally with himself as chairman!"

"But who else is on it?"

"Oh, those you'd expect: Petöfi, Vasvári, Irinyi, Lázár, a couple of liberal nobles called Klauzál and Nyári, and some Council members, I think. Anyway, they decided we should present the Twelve Demands to the Vice-Regal Council. So we all marched across to Buda."

"Why the *Devil* couldn't you have waited, collected signatures and passed it on to the King, as even *Kossuth* wanted?" István demanded.

"It would have taken for ever. This way, it's done. What happened in there anyway? Petöfi was fuming, raging that Klauzál was so humble before you that he sounded like a schoolboy before his master."

"He could afford to be humble with the threat of an angry mob behind him!" István retorted bitterly. "He was pleased to lay before us three requests: that censorship be abolished in law; that we release the political prisoner Táncsics; and that we order the army not to interfere."

I felt my whole body sag in relief at that. But Elisabeth, her fork poised half-way between her plate and her mouth, said, "Oh dear. Did you give in even to that?"

"Damn it, we had to! Though I must admit I would have reserved my right to call on the army to restore order. But some of the Council were so petrified by the mob that they would have voted themselves into prison rather than risk offending it! And it didn't help that Lajos Lázár chose to drape himself across the window, with an utter lack of respect — like some sort of thug — as if he was about to call on the crowd below to invade the chamber at any time! It made a nonsense of Klauzál's humility, of so-called requests!"

I looked at my plate, but I wasn't seeing my food; I was seeing the threatening picture of Lajos which István had painted.

Elisabeth frowned. "He's getting a little above himself, is he not?"

"Lajos? Oh no," said István sarcastically. "He even thanked us for our time, after we had given in to everything!"

"Poor István. You've had an awful day."

"We all have," Katalin murmured.

"I haven't," Mattias protested. "I've had a wonderful day!"

"I think you'll find your wonderful day has landed us *all* in the basket!" said his brother. "Oh, don't look so worried, Elisabeth, we shall come about. We're still in control. We may even shake off some of Vienna's interference, which would be an excellent thing, provided it is no more than that."

Some hope, I thought. *It is already more than that.*

Katalin directly refused to go to the Pilvax that night. The day's events had shaken her, and she couldn't help seeing the young revolutionaries as anti-aristocratic Jacobins. For the first time, I think Alexandru's involvement with them actually bothered her. She had a few things to come to terms with, so after dinner I left her to herself.

On the stairs, I met Mattias, leaping down two at a time.

"Where are you off to in such a hurry?" I asked, amused by his unrelenting energy.

"The Pilvax, of course, and then the National Theatre!"

All at once, my breath caught. As he moved to go on, I laid my hand on his arm to stay him.

"Mattias, may I come with you?" I asked abruptly.

He blinked, then grinned. "Why not? Get your finery on quickly though, for I'll not wait forever!"

CHAPTER TWENTY-ONE

The festivities at the Pilvax that night had a carnival air about them; Petőfi and the other leaders of the day's demonstrations were being fêted as heroes, and they were exultant.

I noticed two things at once: Lajos was not there; and Alexandru was, sitting a little apart and looking thoughtful. His face lit up as soon as he saw us — and clouded when he realized Katalin was not with us. I knew I was going to have to speak to him immediately, whatever Mattias might think, but to my surprise it was Mattias himself who, taking my arm in a firm grip, said, "Let's go over here — I want a word with Zarescu."

I rather hoped he didn't also want to fight. Alex stood up a little stiffly as we approached him, but Mattias immediately startled him — and me — by holding out his hand with obvious friendship.

"Well met, Zarescu! You know my cousin, Katie, don't you? Dash it, she's not my cousin, she's my *niece*, but I can't get used to that!"

Alexandru looked amused, but carefully greeted me more formally than usual, holding a chair for me to sit down. When we had all duly sat, Mattias said directly, "I've been wanting a word with you, Zarescu. About my sister."

"Indeed?" The air had turned frosty again.

"Yes. I want to apologise for being so — *stuffy* about you and her. After all, it doesn't make sense. You're the best of good fellows, Zarescu, and if you still want her, you have my blessing for what it's worth — which isn't much. It's my father you have to get round. But I wanted you to know I'll stand your friend in this, as in the cause."

If Alexandru was half as stunned as I at this handsome apology, he covered it well. He was certainly silent for a moment, but then his face broke into a delighted grin, and he reached across the table to shake Mattias's hand again.

"Thank you," he said simply. "Katalin is everything to me. I'd give her the world if I could." He glanced at me. "Er — where is she?"

"Sulking," said Mattias, surprising me for the second time that evening. "Because you were at the meeting *outside* the Museum this afternoon, instead of lurking *inside* waiting for her — even if she couldn't come anyway! Women!"

"How do you know that?" I demanded, appalled that he knew so much. He grinned. "She told me. Don't worry — her sulks don't last..." He broke off. "Hallo, here's Lajos!"

My eyes flew to the door, and sure enough there he was, striding into the room with an unusually purposeful gait. As one of the day's great heroes, he was greeted by a standing ovation, which brought him to a surprised halt. Just for a second, I thought he looked confused, as if his mind had been somewhere quite different; then the half-smile appeared. He flourished his arm, giving an exaggerated bow to the company.

"Speech, Lázár! Speech!" yelled one of the young men.

"*Another* speech?" Lajos groaned. "My throat is raw!"

"Get up there, you weakling," Petöfi ordered, and together with Vasvári, he hoisted Lázár up on to a table, to the half-bantering applause of his friends.

He surveyed his audience a little resignedly, before eloquently shrugging his shoulders. "I don't know what else I can say, except that today we have begun it, and that is a great thing. But it *is* only the beginning. We've won the first skirmish, yet there's a whole war waiting to engulf us if we weaken. More than ever we must work to unite the people, to unite *ourselves,* put aside our petty prejudices of race and class, stand as one with our Romanian and German brothers, so that *no one* can take from us what we have won today. So that we can bring the revolution to its only, rightful conclusion. My friends, I give you a toast..." He reached down and plucked Jókai's glass from his hand, raising it high. "To the Revolution! Long live the people!"

He threw the contents of the glass down his throat as everyone else, including Mattias and Alexandru beside me, fervently echoed his toast. And while they drank, I saw his eyes quickly scan the room. For a second I thought he saw me, and I couldn't stop the foolish leap of my heart, but then his gaze passed on and I knew I had been mistaken.

"Thank you," he said abruptly, and jumped down from the table to the sound of more applause. I watched him give the empty glass back to the grinning Jókai, and then, amazingly, he was making his way towards us, carelessly acknowledging greetings and shrugging off such adulation as he met with en route. I forced myself to breathe normally.

"How does it feel to be a hero?" Alex enquired sardonically.

"Ask one," Lajos recommended, seizing the chair beside me and sitting on it back to front with his arms resting across its back. He was smiling at me. "Katie Kettles. I never even hoped to see you tonight."

It was so totally unexpected after his single-minded pursuit of revolution, that I was taken unawares. I felt my cheeks burn. I could think of nothing to say. And then, like a gentleman, he turned to the others.

"So you two are friends again? I hope it was something I said."

"Hola, Lajos!" Petöfi called from across the room. "Come here and listen to this!"

Lajos sighed and met Alexandru's amused gaze.

"You could always say 'come here and *tell* me this'," the Captain suggested.

"I could," said Lajos, "but then he would. Excuse me."

And he swung his leg round the chair and stood up. Trying not to watch him, my eyes fell instead on Julia Petöfi, sitting alone and a little aloof in the corner. After a moment, she caught my gaze and smiled her recognition. I excused myself to my not very interested companions and went to speak to her.

"You must be very proud," I said, after the greetings were over.

"Very proud, and very nervous," she said frankly. "Of course, I am behind him in this as in all else, but sometimes I think they are in another world, my Sándor, your Lajos and the others..."

I flushed, saying hastily, "He's not *my* Lajos."

"No? Sándor believes he is." She regarded me directly. "I suppose it's as well if you are right. He doesn't believe in God, or in marriage, you know."

I laughed with genuine amusement. "I'm not surprised, somehow! But tell me, were you at the meeting this afternoon?"

We exchanged idle chat for a little, until I saw Petöfi, clearly remembering his husbandly duties, returning to the table. I stood up to go, stopping only to congratulate the poet on his *National Song*.

"I only wrote it two days ago, for the peasants' banquet in fact," he confessed with a boyish grin, and I began to make my way back towards Mattias.

"Katie. Just the person," said a familiar voice. I paused, turning my head to see Lajos leaning against the pillar beside me, another empty glass in his hand. I wondered whose it was this time.

"Just the person for what?" I enquired, pleased to hear the steadiness in my own voice. He smiled slightly, easing his lithe body away from the pillar and laying the glass down on a nearby table.

"For running away with," he said unpredictably. "Shall we?"

"Where to?" I asked in the same spirit, answering the smile in his oddly restless eyes.

"Anywhere. Away from people, all this..."

"You love all this."

"So I do, but tonight I'm tired of it. Come, Katie, let's run away from it all, you and I!"

There was an amused, half-mocking challenge in his eyes that would have been mischievous in anyone else. I found myself responding to it. After today, recklessness was in the air. But then, after today, what on earth was reckless about leaving a coffee-house with a friend?

I laughed. "All right; but I'll have to tell Mattias..."

"No, Nico will tell him," Lajos said, stopping a frantically overworked waiter and giving him a quick request, together with a nod in the direction of Mattias and Alex, after which I found my arm taken in a strong grip and my person almost hustled to the door. We only paused once on the way, to collect my cloak, and then we were outside.

Fortunately the rain had gone off by then, but we still had to negotiate the large group of people who had gathered outside the cafe to cheer their heroes. Discreetly, I drew my hood well forward, while Lajos, firmly holding on to my arm, exchanged a few encouraging and humorous words with the crowd. At last we were past them and walking freely down the road, but at the first turning we came to, Lajos steered me round it to the right, and then suddenly seized my hand and began to run.

I gasped, half-laughing as I was dragged along, then gave in and ran with him. He pulled me down empty side streets and alleys, avoiding people, which, looking back, was just as well. It would have done neither my own nor the Szelényis' reputation any good if I had been seen scampering along the street hand-in-hand with Lajos Lázár. Or with anyone else for that matter.

At last I managed to ask breathlessly, "Where are we going?"

"I don't know — to the river, I think."

I gave a choke of laughter. "Lajos, you're quite mad! Oh, slow down, I'll die!"

"You have no stamina, you aristos," he said provokingly, but he did stop, allowing me to catch my breath for a moment, watching me with that distinctive half-smile I had come to love and fear. I tried to draw my hand free, but his fingers tightened and I submitted.

I met his gaze. There was an odd, feverish glitter in his eyes, reflecting the light from nearby windows, and suddenly, belatedly, I realized the cause of his subtle strangeness this evening.

"Lajos, are you *drunk?*" I asked straightly.

He swung my hand into the air and began to walk again. "I believe I am intoxicated," he admitted, "but I don't think it's the wine. Shall we go to the Erzsébet Island? It's a pleasant spot."

I felt the laughter bubble up in me again. "How do we get there?"

"By boat, of course. A friend of mine by the harbour will lend us his..."

I confess I doubted him, but he did indeed borrow a small boat from a tolerant old man who lived near the harbour, and even rowed us quite expertly down the river. It seemed he was right: whatever was making him so — exhilarated — it wasn't solely alcohol.

I sat back, trailing my hand in the cold, dark water. The river was deserted; everyone was either hiding indoors or celebrating the day's events elsewhere. I gazed up at the harsh castle of Buda, wondering with a sudden return of dread what plans were being laid there, despite the Vice Regal Council's promise of no military intervention.

"The soldiers faced us as we marched up to the fortress this afternoon,"

Lajos said. "They stood by their guns with burning fuses in their hands while we came on shouting for liberty and equality. And they did nothing."

"Perhaps they won't always do nothing."

"They might join us," said Lajos. "After all, they're only people — like Alex."

I regarded him across the darkness. "You must be very pleased with yourself."

"I'm very pleased," he said, after consideration. "Are you?"

Was I pleased? Certainly, I was *aroused* by this united action of the people; I prayed it would bring them a better future; but still I was terrified that in reality it would lead only to violence, greater suppression, more bloodshed.

At last I said, "I don't know. I'm afraid."

A ghost of a laugh came from him. "So am I."

I stared at him, but I couldn't see his expression in the gloom. It was so easy to forget that he was only twenty-five years old, little more than a boy, yet with a large share of the responsibility for a national revolution pressing on his shoulders. He had wanted it so much that I had never imagined he could have doubts too.

I felt the ache in my heart grow stronger. I closed my eyes for a moment, listening to the rhythmic splash of the oars, yearning to give him comfort and strength, but not knowing how. And then, without any warning, without even interrupting his strokes, he began to talk. The words fell from him as if he could no longer keep them in, pouring out his elation at the day's success, his pride in this bloodless revolution he had begun, his desperate, straining hopes for its future.

I listened, as I always listen, and gradually a quiet gladness began to seep through me. For the first time in our enigmatic relationship I felt he needed me, and though it was so much less than I secretly craved, I found my own contentment in the fact that it was me he wished to tell all this to, not Alex, or Petőfi, or Teréz Meleki. And as he spoke, the strange, restless tension I had sensed in him all night began to drain away, until his voice at last faded and died, leaving behind only the tranquil shadow of his triumph.

For a time we were both silent. Then he said in the old lazy, humorous voice I knew best, "Have I bored you, or terrified you?"

"No," I said economically. I hesitated, then added slowly, "You're working as hard as you can for what you believe is right. I can only admire that."

Now he was silent again, and I had the impression he was surprised. "Thank you," he said quietly, making me smile into the distance. And suddenly I was aware that Erzsébet Island was looming out of the darkness only yards away. Seeing my alarm, Lajos glanced over his shoulder.

"Shall we go ashore?" he suggested calmly.

The island was a popular place for summer picnics; exactly what he wanted to do there on a wet March evening in the pitch darkness, I couldn't tell, but it was a delightfully *pointless* expedition, and just for tonight I think he needed that. He rowed us into the island as far as he could, then stood up and leapt into the shallow water to pull the boat ashore.

"You'll catch pneumonia," I warned.

"Nonsense," he said, straightening his back and reaching for me. I tried to give him my hands, but instead I found myself taken by the waist and lifted clean out of the boat. He swung me round and then let me slip slowly to my feet.

He was holding me so close that I could smell the wine on his breath, and that nearness, the touch of his body against mine, was beginning to make me dizzy. I tried to ignore the surge of desire that shot through me, yet I wanted this closeness; I wanted it more than anything in the world...

Despite the dark, I could tell he was smiling; hazily, I thought it must mean that he too was having second thoughts about this mad start, so I smiled back at him.

"Lajos, what are we doing here?" I asked.

I heard his breath catch. "This," he said, and bent and kissed my lips as if he would never stop.

Shocked, I gasped into his mouth, instinctively dragging up my hands to push him away, but his arms went round me, drawing me inexorably even closer, and then it was quite another, much stronger instinct which made me hang there so weakly, and my traitorous hands were not pushing, but clutching at his coat while I let him kiss me and prayed it would go on forever.

He wasn't smiling any more when he lifted his head. His eyes were warm and serious. Helplessly, I tried to gather my wits, but all I could manage, in a tiny, shaken voice, was, "Let me go, Lajos — you mustn't..."

"Mustn't I?" he said softly. "Come, Katie, don't you think its time there was some honesty between us?"

"What do you mean?" Slowly, an amazed, exultant hope was creeping over me and I was afraid I was wrong. Afraid I was right — yet how could I be?

"I mean I want you," he said candidly. His finger was lightly tracing the line of my jaw and making me shiver. "I've always wanted you, ever since I first saw you in Vienna, and you looked at me so sweetly, with your eyes so ready to smile even while your mouth tried to disapprove. I still want you, more than ever, more than I had thought possible."

I stared up at him dumbly, disbelieving, yet fearful that I would wake too soon from the dream.

"But — you can't," I blurted, and now his eyes were laughing. His fingers stroked my cheek, lingered on my lips.

"Why can't I?" he enquired as I caught his hand.

"I'm too old," I floundered, "too *dull* for you..."

"That's rubbish, and you know it."

"No, Lajos," I said painfully, "I don't know."

He paused then, searching my face in the darkness, and I stood there in the circle of his arm, waiting to be hurt, vulnerable as I had never been in my life before. At last, he said softly, "Then I'll have to show you," and his mouth came down on mine again.

There was no point in pretending. I don't think I could have if I'd tried. I melted. I felt his arms tighten and lift me off my feet; he walked forward, carrying me as easily as a baby. I felt leaves brush against my hair, saw the dense blackness of trees all around me, and then I was laid gently on the spongy ground and he was beside me, leaning over me.

"It's quite dry," he murmured, deftly loosening my cloak, "The trees shelter it here..."

I caught agitatedly at his hands. He let me, and began to kiss my fingers one by one, with infinite tenderness. Wonderingly, I watched him. How was it possible that *he* could feel this for me? Slowly, I reached out with one uncertain hand, touching his hair. It was unexpectedly soft, which made me smile. He smiled back, then gently, sweetly, he kissed my mouth again, and everything in me leapt to meet him. I clung to him. For a brief, exciting moment I felt the weight of his body and gloried in it, then he was lying beside me, holding me, caressing me till I burned.

I was lost in sensation. It seemed his lips, his hands — those clever, unbearably sensitive hands — were everywhere, brushing aside clothing, kissing and stroking every part of me, arousing me to an impossible fever of longing.

At some point in the wild, shatteringly sensual onslaught, I had a moment of lucidity. I remember whispering, "Lajos, I can't — I can't..."

"Can't what?" he murmured, but I didn't answer, and it didn't actually matter, for as it turned out I could, and I did, and I thoroughly enjoyed every breath-taking, joyous moment of it. And as the ultimate waves of ecstasy began, I held on to him in bewildered wonder and gasped into his mouth, "I love you, Lajos. I love you."

CHAPTER TWENTY-TWO

Afterwards, I must have fallen into a brief sleep, for I remember waking to absolute silence and darkness. I was wrapped in my cloak and his coat, and held against his breast like a child. He was in his shirt-sleeves, sitting with his back against a tree, and I could feel his rhythmic, wakeful breathing and the warm, naked skin of his chest under my cheek. For a second, I let the memory of what we had just done engulf me. I knew I should be ashamed, but I wasn't. Not in the slightest.

I knew too, because my mother had told me at the start of my brief, youthful engagement, that most women found their first experience of physical love a little shocking, if not downright distasteful. I had felt none of that, only pleasure and a delight that quite obliterated the pain. Of course, I wasn't married. It seemed I was shameless on two counts.

I knew he was watching me, but for a moment I just lay in his arms, loving the magical warmth and closeness, until at last he stirred, whispering in my ear that we must go before we really did contract pneumonia. I smiled into his shoulder, and felt his arms tighten around me. Tenderly, he turned my face up to his, searching my eyes in the darkness.

"Are you happy, Katie?" he asked unexpectedly, and now for some reason I was shy again.

"Yes," I whispered. I saw him smile.

"Don't let anyone make you feel otherwise about tonight, whatever they say about 'decency', or about me. Promise."

I smiled. I didn't see how anyone or anything could make me regret this. "I promise."

The night sky was a little clearer as we wandered back to the boat, his arm still comfortably around my shoulders. For a little, we paused on the beach, gazing down the river in the direction of Buda-Pest. In some strange way, I felt that what had just happened here was connected with the earlier events in the city — I suppose because Lajos had managed both of them. Slowly, I turned within his arm to look up into his strong, calm face.

"Lajos?"

"Yes?"

"Did you plan this?" I asked curiously. I heard rather than saw him smile.

"No. I only wanted to be away, alone with you, to talk to you. The rest just — happened." He looked down at me, his fingers caressing my shoulder as he added, "Not that I haven't wished it to happen for months."

I shook my head wonderingly, then laid it tenderly against his shoulder. I felt his arm tighten, and gloried in its strength.

"It never entered my head," I said with difficulty, "that you could think of me — in that way."

His hand turned my face back up to his. "How the devil did you imagine I thought of you?"

"As a friend, I hoped."

He dropped a gentle kiss on my head, saying tenderly, "What a little fool you are after all." I smiled, sliding both arms a little shyly round his waist. I wondered how it was possible to feel so much happiness.

"Men have never been in the habit of declaring undying love to me," I observed, with just a touch of my customary dryness.

"I expect you daunted them," he said, urging me towards the boat. I climbed in and he pushed it off, splashing again through the water to join me. With a kind of languid content, I admired his quick, efficient movements as he collected the oars and began to row. At last, I lifted my eyes to his face again.

"Why didn't I daunt you?" I asked in a small voice, which I almost hoped he wouldn't hear above the splash of the oars. But he did. He gave another of his soft, infectious laughs.

"You did daunt me, quite considerably!" he said wryly. "But fortunately, I am endowed with patience and persistence. At times, I was sure you cared for me — especially when we danced at Szelényi."

Even after the greater closeness we had just known, the memory of the village dance made me flush warmly in the darkness.

"Why did you run away from me then?" he asked softly. I swallowed.

"I was afraid. I needed to think. You see, it was only then that I realized I loved you. Before, I had thought it just some silly, childish infatuation, induced mainly by your utter unsuitability!"

"Thank you." He sounded amused. His eyes were still watching me through the gloom as he rowed. "But I don't see why you then held me at an even greater distance."

"I didn't!"

"Yes, you did. If I so much as touched your hand, you jumped a mile. I didn't know whether you were perhaps ashamed of your feelings, or afraid, or whether I had been a coxcomb ever to imagine you cared in the first place. Once or twice I thought you were actually jealous of Teréz — you do know that is over? — yet still, when I made even the slightest movement towards you, you drew back."

"I had to," I said quietly. "I could only live with my feelings if no one knew — least of all you."

For a moment he was silent, then: "What a lot of time we wasted, Katie. Until now..." He laughed aloud. "My God, what a day it's been!"

We walked back through the streets a little more decorously than before, my hand tucked comfortably in his arm, still talking fitfully of small, important things. Despite the cold night air, I felt marvellously warm and close to him.

He said, "There's a meeting tonight of the Committee of Public Safety. I should go."

"Yes," I agreed, feeling no neglect, only a suddenly fierce pride in him. "You should."

"We could go first to the National Theatre," he suggested casually, "for the victory celebrations."

I looked at him uncertainly. Part of me longed to stay with him, and I confess I no longer cared two hoots who saw us together — in fact I would have been proud to stand with him before the whole world. But this was his day, and I would have died rather than hold him back now. I would let him enjoy his triumph without the burden of gossip my presence would cause. And I, I would go home to bed, to hug this amazing new happiness to myself till morning...

He was still waiting for my answer. I shook my head, smiling.

"No; I should go home. *I* need sleep, if you don't!"

"Whatever you wish," he said easily. "Shall we hail that fiacre?"

I nodded, perversely sad now that the magical night was to end, even though it was I who had decreed it.

It was a winter carriage, closed and cosy. As we bounded through the streets, Lajos put his arms around me and I nestled comfortably against his chest, eagerly returning his sweet, exciting kisses, so that I was slightly bemused as well as disappointed when the fiacre came to a halt. Reluctantly, Lajos let me go.

He got down and helped me out. "I'll come to you," he said seriously, pressing a warm, brief kiss into my palm. "Very soon."

I nodded. It was enough. I touched his cheek fleetingly, and turned and ran into the square.

The palace was in darkness save for the light that always burned in the hall. Letting myself in, I discovered Gyorgy the porter mercifully asleep at his post, encouraged, I suspected, by the contents of the empty flask which lay accusingly on his lap. As I crept past him up the staircase and along the black passage to my bed-chamber, I reflected that it was as well my eyes had become accustomed to the dark in the warm, passionate hours before. It didn't seem important then that never in all that time had Lajos mentioned love.

*

Not unnaturally, I slept later than normal the next morning. And even when I did wake, I spent some time just stretching luxuriously and smiling at the ceiling. The constant ache of trying to suppress my love for Lajos had finally vanished. I was *allowed* to love him. It wasn't impossible after all. It wasn't impossible at all.

"I'll come to you," he had said. "Very soon."

Until then, I would have to hide my new happiness. The first test was in the breakfast room that morning, where I met Mattias gulping down a cup of coffee and looking distinctly the worse for wear.

"*There* you are!" he exclaimed, somewhere between relief and accusation.

"Apparently." Calmly, I poured myself some coffee and sat down opposite him.

"I was worried about you," he said indignantly. "I got some garbled message that Lajos Lázár was taking you home. Naturally I didn't believe that, but I couldn't find you anywhere in the Pilvax — where the devil were you?"

"On my way home, with Lajos Lázár."

He put down his cup and looked at me, a slightly harassed expression on his boyish face. He dragged his hand through his hair, eventually saying, "Katie, *I'm* aware Lajos wouldn't harm you, but you know, it isn't quite the thing to let a fellow like that escort you home. Damn it, *Lajos* isn't quite the thing!"

"Why, Mattias," I mocked. "What principles were you marching for yesterday?"

He flushed. "Dash it, I'm not referring to his birth," he said uncomfortably. "He hasn't got the purest reputation, you know. It's not so long ago that people were saying that Meleki woman was his mistress — it's my belief she still is." I smiled into my cup. "The point is, Katie, such odd starts won't do *your* reputation any good. And besides, István will kick up such a rumpus that life won't be worth living."

"He can kick all he likes," I said frankly. "I have no intention of choosing my friends to suit his tastes."

"Well no," he agreed reasonably. "But if you'll take my advice, you'll be a little more circumspect about how and when you associate with them."

I smiled. "I believe you have become almost — responsible!"

He grinned. "You needn't mock. It's damnably hard to be responsible with a head like this."

"Rough night?" I asked sympathetically.

"Shocking," he confessed. "And I've a feeling we shouldn't be having this conversation either!"

I drifted through the day with remarkable normality. I even taught the children quite efficiently, and was polite to the point of friendliness with both Maria Mirányi *and* Baroness Meleki when they came respectively to bemoan and rejoice over the revolution.

I found myself watching Teréz with a new fascination. She was still everything I wasn't: beautiful, sophisticated, experienced, and she positively exuded that tantalizing kind of languid sensuality that must surely have drawn men to her like bees to honey. How could a man like Lajos come from her to me? For a moment, I panicked as I recognized how much more than I she could give him, but then the memory of Erzsébet Island flooded warmly through me and I knew that however peculiar it might be, he *had* chosen me.

So, patiently and with quiet confidence, I waited for Lajos to come. Looking back, I'm not quite sure what I expected of our next meeting, except that it would somehow resolve and confirm our relationship. I had really begun to believe that after all the years of loneliness, there could be some sort of happy ending for me.

Outside, in the city, peaceful demonstrations were continuing. Enthusiasts began to sign up to a newly formed National Guard to protect both the revolution and public order. And the Pilvax Café, where it had all begun, was renamed the Hall of Liberty.

I didn't see any of this, for I was afraid to leave the house in case Lajos came; but I heard it all from Mattias who, I think, found me the only sympathetic listener in the family. István, meanwhile, hurried back to Pressburg, for news had come that the Diet, spurred on by the Buda-Pest demonstrations, had sent a delegation to Vienna to demand a separate Hungarian ministry with Count Batthyány as Prime Minister.

But Lajos did not come to me that day. It was the following afternoon when Zsuzsa, as once before, appeared in my bed-chamber with the message that Lajos was in the Little Room waiting for me.

I don't know what I said to her. I don't remember even leaving her, but by the time I reached the Little Room I know my heart was hammering wildly in my breast, and my hand grasping the door knob was not quite steady. I took a deep breath and went in, closing the door behind me, and leaning against it for support.

This time he wasn't reading, but standing by the window as if he had been looking out onto the back yards. He met my suddenly fearful gaze, and smiled. The spell broke. I went quickly to meet him, impulsively holding out both hands which he took in his and immediately placed around his neck. I melted into his embrace, loving the feel of his rough, warm cheek against mine. I closed my eyes.

He moved and kissed me, a tender, overtly sensual kiss.

"I missed you," he whispered against my lips.

I swallowed. "Good." I heard his soft laughter.

Then, loosening his hold a little, he said, "I've come to tell you I'm going to Transylvania tonight, to see what I can do there."

The disappointment was like a blow. I lowered my eyes, let my hands slip down from his shoulders.

"Then you've come to say good-bye," I managed to say with forced lightness, moving out of his arms. I could feel him still watching me.

"Not if I can help it. I would rather you came with me."

My eyes flew back to his face, searching. The thrilling, warm look was still there, but as so often, his eyes were shielded and secretive. I took a breath.

"How can I do that, Lajos?" I asked. I thought I knew the answer. It wasn't, after all, so great a miracle as the one which had already taken place on Wednesday night. His lip quirked upwards.

"Put a few things in a bag, say good-bye to your family and come on the stage coach with me."

"They might not accept me back in those *precise* circumstances!"

"You don't need to go back," he said softy. "Ever." He took my hands again, drawing me back towards him. "Come with me. Stay with me."

Involuntarily, my eyes closed again. I lifted his hand to my cheek, holding it there. I found I was smiling.

"Are you proposing marriage to me, Lajos?"

His eyes smiled back. "We don't need the permission of a priest to be together."

For a moment I was paralysed. I went on holding his hand, letting the true meaning of his proposal wash over me, staring at the same point on his coat, while my bright, new happiness drained away to nothing and the world came crashing round my ears. I remember knowing, even then, that this was only the beginning of a pain worse than any I had ever known, one that would go on and on and on.

It was only when he spoke again that I was able to move. "Will you come with me, Katie?" he said in that low, persuasive voice that had swayed so many, myself included.

I dropped his hand as if I'd been stung, jerking away from him to the window. "No," I said, and my voice sounded very peculiar to my own ears - harsh, stiff and a little too high. "I will not come with you. I will not go as far as the door with you. Ever."

He was silent. I could sense his shock, but I felt no triumph in that, only a misery that was increasing unbearably with every second. At last he followed me, touched my shoulder. I flinched, and his hand fell away.

"I've shocked you. I'm sorry. Forget I said anything so stupid; it doesn't matter."

"Oh yes, it does matter. It matters a lot. I won't be despised, Lajos."

This then was why young ladies were so discouraged from granting pre-marital favours. I had heard Aunt Edith say it, that such girls lost the respect of the men who had used them. I hadn't paid that much attention, preferring to believe that the real reason for chastity was the possibility of untimely babies, but it wasn't, or not completely.

What hurt more than anything was that he was prepared to so humiliate and disdain me after allI had given him of myself, of my trust. And he had the excuse ready. I should have listened more seriously to Julia Petőfi when she told me Lajos did not believe in marriage.

"Good-bye," I said loudly, somehow keeping the desperation out of my voice. "I would be grateful if you didn't come here again."

"Katie, don't do this," he said, an urgent note of warning in his tone, and something else that might have been alarm or a kind of pain. "If I misunderstood, I'm sorry, but you can't believe I despise you — how could I? Can't you see this doesn't change how I feel? Nothing has changed since Wednesday..."

"For you perhaps," I said contemptuously. I turned abruptly and pushed past him, making for the door. It was only a tattered and fast-dissolving pride that was holding me together, that forced me to keep my dignity by walking rather than running away. But I had forgotten how fast he could move when he chose.

Even as my fingers closed on the door-knob, his hand was before me, holding the door shut as he slid round in front of me. I held my head down, staring hazily at his boots.

"Please," I whispered achingly, "let me go..."

But instead, I felt his finger under my chin, insistent, forcing my head up. I thought I would die. I wished to die. Somewhere, I knew surprise at the expression in his eyes — it was helplessness.

Slowly, his hand came up and with one curiously gentle finger he touched the escaped tear which was rolling traitorously down my cheek.

"Oh Katie, don't," he murmured. I thought his voice cracked, but I couldn't think about that then, only about preserving what was left of my self-control.

"Let me go," I whispered again.

For a second, I thought he wouldn't; then, with awful deliberation, he moved and opened the door. I didn't look at him as I all but ran out. I couldn't.

Recovery

April — September 1848

CHAPTER TWENTY-THREE

It was more from inertia than anything else that I allowed myself to be driven out to Rákos to see the bonfires being lit in celebration of Hungary's latest triumph. I sat drearily in the carriage with Elisabeth, Katalin and Teréz Meleki, while Mattias rode dutifully beside us. I knew he would disappear into more congenial company just as soon as he found it, but I didn't care about that. I didn't really care about anything.

Impassively, I gazed out on to the darkening streets, changed these days beyond recognition — nearly every house was decorated in Hungary's new colours — while the people filling them wore cockades of red, white and green, and the radicals added huge red feathers in their hats. More worryingly, all the young men now wore swords — Petőfi's was so large that his friends had christened it his guillotine, and even Mattias, who had grinned when he told me this, had taken to wearing his sword to lectures, though what he planned to do with it against his revered and ageing professors was beyond me.

We arrived upon a scene of ecstatic jubilation at Rákos. Bonfires were lit all over the field; wine and food were being passed around the happy citizens. Speeches of triumph were being made by enthusiastic young men, and prayers of thanks offered up by the pious. A few noble parties like our own had come out to watch; some even joined in, though it seemed to me this was really the celebration of the townspeople, of the ordinary folk who had discovered with surprise that they had the power to influence kings and governments.

Almost immediately, I saw Jókai and Petöfi laughing with a crowd of students. Anxious to avoid them, and all the other familiar faces surrounding us, I kept close to my family.

It already seemed a lifetime ago, though in fact in was little more than two weeks, since I had left Lajos in the Little Room, and gone straight to my bedchamber. I remember lying face down on my bed, staring blindly at the counterpane, which was wet although I don't recall crying then. The awful thoughts churning in my head were like a pain, and they went on and on until there *was* only the pain.

When someone knocked on the door, I moved and realized I felt sick. The door itself was heaving alarmingly, and almost surprised, I became aware that the dreadful pain in my head was physical. For the first time in my life I welcomed that pain, fiercely, relievedly, because I knew I could not think through it, because only the agony of a migraine stood a chance of drowning the greater pain.

I collapsed again on to the bed, giving myself up completely to the nightmare. I was vaguely aware of Katalin fussing around me, of a maid drawing the curtains, their anxious voices slicing through my aching head like an axe. I welcomed that too. I remember muttering, "It's only a migraine — I've had it before. Just leave me alone until it goes away."

Of course, they were incapable of doing that, but I was equally oblivious to the doctors and the servants and the potions they made me drink. I knew from experience that there was no cure but time — and I was more than happy to give up a couple of days to it, days which I had no idea how to live through anyway. So I existed in a miserable heat of pain and sickness, my eyes closed against the moving walls and the searing daylight which pierced the curtains from time to time.

I lost two whole days in this way.

I don't remember falling asleep, but I recall waking eventually to darkness and dull, hopeless misery. The pain in my head was gone, leaving only a feeling of extreme delicacy. I felt neither sick nor hungry, though I was a little thirsty. There was a glass of water by my bed, but I ignored it. Now that I was free of the migraine's agony, I needed other discomforts to distract me from the one important ache. None of them, I knew, would work, but at least they would serve as punishment: for stupidity, for trusting unwisely, for falling in love against my own judgement, for loose behaviour — the list was endless and pointless, but I went on lashing myself with it until I fell asleep again.

When I woke this time, it was to the sound of the bedroom door opening. If I had been properly awake, I might have had the forethought to pretend sleep, but as it was I sat up without thinking, and saw Katalin bearing a tray of the doctor's evil potions.

"Oh, Katie, are you better?" she asked in a hushed voice.

I tried to smile. "Yes; the pain has quite gone."

"You won't want this then," she said dismissively, all but dropping the tray on to the first table she passed. She came and sat on the side of my bed, searching my face with eyes that were comfortingly anxious as well as curious. At least Katalin cares for me, I thought with monstrous self-pity.

"I've never seen anyone so prostrated by a headache before," she observed.

"Not all headaches prostrate me," I said vaguely. "Only *that* one."

"Do you suffer them often?" she asked uneasily.

"Hardly ever now. When I was younger they were more frequent, but actually it's years since I had one like this... Once or twice, when we were travelling on those awful roads, I was afraid it would happen, but it didn't..."

"Are you really well, now?" she asked dubiously. "You still sound very — odd."

"I'm a little weak, that's all," I excused myself.

"Of course, you've had no food since Friday's lunch!"

I looked up from my fruitless contemplation of the counterpane. "What day is it?"

"Monday," she said in surprise. "Monday, the twentieth of March."

"What has happened to the revolution?" I heard my voice crack, and wondered if I would weep in front of her. If she noticed, she must have put it down to my general weakness.

"It seems Hungary is victorious," she said brightly. "Kossuth and the delegation from the Diet won the King's consent to everything, including a separate cabinet. Count Batthyány is Prime Minister; István thinks Count Széchenyi will be minister for public works, and Kossuth minister of finance. Feudal dues have been abolished — with compensation to be paid later, which is just as well since in addition to having to pay labourers now, we shall also have to pay taxes. Yes, the Diet passed that too."

A shadow of interest slipped through my torpor. "So much so quickly?" I said. "Is it actually law?"

She shrugged. "The King has still to pass the bills, but he promised to agree to all laws the new cabinet suggests."

I smiled mirthlessly. "He must have been terrified."

"It's as if the whole Empire is falling apart."

"You don't seem unduly put out by it," I observed, unconsciously reaching for the glass by my bed and sipping the water.

"Oh well," she said carelessly. "Even István seems to think it will make Hungary strong, so it can't be all bad. Do you know, he even spoke a word of *admiration* for Kossuth? Of course, it helps that there has been no blood shed in the disturbances here."

Something else from my memory made me frown. "Monday the twentieth?" I repeated. "What happened at the banquet, and the peasant fair at Rákos?"

She actually laughed. "Nothing. The peasants were only interested in buying and selling! And even the radicals had given up the idea of a banquet; after the fifteenth, they didn't need the peasants."

He had been right after all. You really didn't need violence to make a revolution, not if the fear of it was strong enough...

When Katalin had gone, and the maid was pottering about me, I sat lethargically in front of the glass, gazing bleakly at my own reflection. My spectacles seemed suddenly too large for my face, which had grown paler and thinner since I had last looked at it. My eyes appeared huge and tired, and the shadows beneath them were almost black.

"Well," I murmured at this vision. "Can you really blame him?"

Yes; I could, and I did. I wished to God he had left me alone with my unrequited love — it had been hard, but I had been able to live with it because I had still had my pride. Now, I had given everything, confessed the fullest depths of my feelings in return for a few short hours of passion that had lifted me up to dizzying heights of joy and hope. And then I had been cast down again like a stone when he had revealed the precise nature of *his* feeling. Oh yes, liking, a little, desire, a little, but it was all shallow; there was no respect, no real love, not for me...

My image grew hazy and I realized I was weeping. For that one mistake, his and mine, I now had nothing. No friend, no love, no pride. He shouldn't have done it, I thought, not when it meant so little, not when he *knew*...

*

But that had been two weeks ago. I was stronger now: I could despise the weakness of those early days, for I had learned to concentrate on Lajos's iniquities rather than on his kindness or his humour or his all-embracing compassion. I had told myself that he only cared for people in the abstract; that far from being out of my reach, he was not worthy of me. Deliberately, I had sown the seeds of hatred; and slowly, painfully, I had rebuilt my mask until I flattered myself that no one could see behind it the hurt, frightened woman who had fallen from grace and lost all her self-respect.

Of course, it helped that Lajos was out of the way in Kolozsvár, even sending back articles to the new radical newspaper — *March the Fifteenth*, naturally — describing how he had marched there, arm in arm with Hungarians, Romanians and Germans, all united in their support of the Hungarian revolution and their desire to share in its new liberties.

As usual, it was vivid, powerful writing. But I was not moved. I hadn't been moved by anything that had happened in the last two weeks, even when the King had broken his promise and refused to grant separate ministries, or to accept the Diet's reforms. Everyone else was outraged by this betrayal, of course, even István, home on one of his brief visits from Pressburg.

"You'll never leave it at that?" Mattias had demanded.

"Of course not," István said impatiently. "The King will be — persuaded."

"How? By more threats?" Elisabeth enquired.

István smiled reluctantly. "Well, already Kossuth is making fiery speeches warning of further revolution if the laws are not passed. I believe he has even urged the Committee of Public Safety to 'risk everything for the Fatherland!' Which, it seems to me, is a direct invitation to riot."

I regarded him curiously. "You don't seem very upset by the prospect," I observed.

"I'm not," he admitted. "I think Kossuth can control the hotheads in Pest, and through the *threat* of them, control the King too."

And it seemed he was right, for after this new and even more turbulent upsurge of revolution, the King had given in to all the Hungarian demands — which was why the people had come out here to Rákos to celebrate.

I was already wondering how soon we would leave when my attention was caught by an outburst of shouting and laughter from the National Guardsmen who were policing the scene. Turning idly in their direction, I saw they were boisterously welcoming someone. Someone I was not ready to meet.

Even as my stomach gave a sickening lurch, I saw the revellers begin to acknowledge him with delighted greetings and back-slappings. Vaguely, I was aware of Teréz saying, almost involuntarily, "So he's back." And then Petöfi's voice yelled with joy, "Lajos, you deserter! About time too!"

Abruptly, I cringed back behind Elisabeth, but even so, he almost brushed against me as he made his swift way towards his friends. I only had an impression of his strong, distinctive face, of his travel-stained clothes, which implied he had only just arrived in the city. My heart was thundering so that I could scarcely breathe. There was a roaring in my ears, a sudden weakening in my legs. It was the unexpectedness of seeing him, I told myself. No one had expected him back so soon. I didn't love him any more — how could I after what he had done? It was simple hatred now that made me react so...

Yet I couldn't look away. Petöfi had leapt forward to greet his friend. I saw their embrace, and his warm handshake with the nearby Vasvári. I saw his arm raised to acknowledge Jókai and the others behind who were grinning at him, and all the while he listened intently to Petöfi who was no doubt bringing him up to date with events in the capital.

And then I saw him bend to examine Petöfi's huge sword, holding it between finger and thumb as he looked quizzically up at its wearer. And Petöfi laughed. I felt my hatred burn brighter. Everything was just the same for him...

I swallowed the nameless emotions that were threatening to choke me, turning abruptly away from the unbearable scene, only to find Teréz's eyes upon me, speculative, enigmatic.

"Satisfy my curiosity," she drawled in a low voice that the others were unable to hear. "Did you heed my words concerning him at Szelényi Castle?"

And because I was angry at my own emotion, at feeling anything at all, I said gently, "Come, Madame. Do you really imagine I valued my post as highly as all that?"

And thus ended the doubtful truce between us.

Yet only moments later, my eyes strayed again to where Petöfi and Lajos were watching the cheering only yards from us.

Without warning, Lajos turned his head. He saw Katalin first, standing a little apart from me, but even before I could move further away, his eyes found me too, and I was paralysed. For a second that seemed an eternity, the rest of the world receded. Stricken, I met his steady, unsmiling gaze. Neither of us stirred. And then Petöfi took his arm, drawing him on with a sardonic word I could not hear, and the spell was broken; my eyes were free.

I drew in a shuddering breath. I had done it. The next time would be easier. It would have to be.

Though the Diet was rushing to get through the last of its work before the King was due to close it on the tenth of April, the most stunning event of the month was undoubtedly the publication of Petöfi's new poem, *To the Kings*. Even Mattias was shocked by its disrespect for the Monarchy, its openly republican sentiment; while Elisabeth, when she had read aloud its refrain, "No matter what impudent flatterers say, there is no *beloved* King any more," simply dropped it on the floor saying, "I won't have that in the house, and if you don't care for my views, I advise you to be rid of it before your brother comes home."

For once subdued, Mattias stuffed the poem in his pocket. I seemed to be the only one not shocked by it: in fact I rather admired *Petöfi's* impudence! It was like him, though I suspected it would in the end win him more enemies than friends. Despite the revolution, Hungary had a very royalist tradition.

I did not see Lajos again until the Cabinet arrived to take up its residence in Buda-Pest. Like most of the city, the Szelényis and I went en masse to the quay to greet them. But it was Vasvári, looking at once absurdly youthful and gravely dignified, who spoke the official words of welcome on behalf of the Committee of Public Safety, which he said would now dissolve, leaving the capital and the power of the revolution in the government's safe hands.

Almost wonderingly, I heard him say, "We have prepared the way. Our revolutionary movement lasted exactly one month; and tomorrow the people will return to private life…"

I could not believe it was really over, though Vasvári himself was saying so. There was so much that had *not* been achieved, so much that I knew Lajos at least still wanted. Involuntarily, my eyes sought him out among the Committee of Public Safety. He wasn't smiling; I couldn't read the expression on his face, but somehow I knew just from his stance that for him the revolution was far from over.

CHAPTER TWENTY-FOUR

The hardest part of my recovery was going back to the Pilvax. It would have been an easy punishment to avoid, yet when Mattias unexpectedly suggested it — purely as an excuse to avoid his lectures — I didn't even try. Instead, lashing myself, I accepted.

I never really doubted that he would be there, and of course he was, at the same long table with a familiar group of revolutionaries, including Vasvári and Jókai. Somehow, I had known too that he would look up immediately and see me. Prepared this time, I inclined my head distantly. Gravely, but with just a hint of irony, he returned the gesture, and then I looked beyond him to Vasvári, who had glanced up too and smiled. I even smiled back, moving forward with Mattias to our own table.

It was a little nearer to Lajos than I would have liked, but I could hardly have made a fuss without incurring the sort of attention I dreaded, so I sank into my chair, relieved and quite proud of the dignity with which I had handled myself.

While Mattias and I talked in a desultory way about various things, and the waiter brought us coffee and cakes, I found myself thinking that Lajos was looking more tired than ever. In the brief glimpse I had allowed myself, the lines around his eyes and mouth had seemed far more deeply etched than I remembered; and there had been a permanent-looking frown on his brow that I had never noticed before. I wondered if it was weariness, or disappointment at the revolution's tame — if peaceful — outcome which had changed him. Then, abruptly, I put a stop to that line of thought, which was dangerously close to the sympathy I had no intention of feeling.

"I thought you liked these," Mattias said suddenly, and I realized I was still toying with a very appetizing cake.

"I do," I said at once, eating a piece with difficulty, for in truth I had never really recovered my appetite after the migraine. With relief, I turned back to my coffee, and looked casually around me.

A group of three young working men were standing awkwardly by the door, obviously arguing with a waiter. One actually raised his voice, and I heard him say aggressively, "No! We've come to see Pál Vasvári!"

At the sound of his name, Vasvári looked up. Seeing the three men, he looked surprised, but signalled the waiter to bring them over. Significantly, though, he did not stand up to meet them, merely made space for them to sit down beside him. I heard him say that he was Vasvári, and ask politely what he could do for them.

"I know who you are," one of the working men said, a little too loudly. "I recognize you. We know you to be a man who believes in equality, who is unafraid of taking practical action."

Vasvári bowed, a little ironically. The man took a breath, and at a nudge from one of his companions, continued in a lower voice which I had to strain shamelessly to catch. I was not alone. Mattias too was blatantly curious.

"We represent four thousand journeymen who are opposed to the tyrannical guild laws. The laws hold us back, stop us becoming independent craftsmen because we can't afford the ruinous entrance fees to the guilds. So we are stuck here as we are, on pitiful wages, with no hope of improvement until we are old!"

Vasvári nodded sympathetically. My eyes flickered to Lajos, who lay back casually in his chair, his fingers playing idly with the handle of his cup; but his eyes were fixed on the artisans — men of about his own age — and there was no doubt that he was paying attention.

"Your case is hard," Vasvári agreed. "But I don't see how I can help you."

The spokesman leaned forward. "Lead us," he said intensely. "Lead us in a march to capture the guilds' chests by force, and burn the unjust laws which are kept there."

Mattias's mouth formed a silent whistle. I was impressed too, both by the workmen's seriousness and by this proof of the reputation which the young radicals obviously now enjoyed with the people. Here was a new cause for them — perhaps it lacked the highly political idealism of their previous struggles, but it was still an injustice which was clearly strongly felt.

But into the amazed pause which followed the workman's plea, Vasvári said, "Oh I don't think we could do that." To my surprise, he even sounded *amused*. "It smacks of looting."

The journeyman frowned, but he still nodded eagerly. "Very well. We're uneducated men; we don't know the best way to go about things — but you do. You showed that on March the fifteenth. How *should* we get rid of the guild laws?"

"I don't think you quite understand," Vasvári said gently. "I cannot help you."

There was silence. I saw consternation on the artisans' faces. Lajos was not looking at them now but at Vasvári.

"Why not?" asked the spokesman at last. He was astounded, bewildered. "We're only asking for the equality in the Twelve Demands."

Vasvári shrugged. "I sympathise, and I truly admire your spirit. But this is not a cause in which I can interfere — it's for your guilds to sort out, and failing them, the government."

Stark disbelief now crossed the journeymen's faces. I felt something of it myself.

"The *government?*" said the spokesman bitterly. "The government will not listen to the likes of us! If we are to have any hope, *you* must help us!"

"I've told you," Vasvári said with a touch of impatience, "I cannot help you. Now, you must excuse me — my friends and I are busy."

The spokesman rose to his feet so abruptly that his chair fell with a clatter. His companions joined him. Their plain, thin faces wore an almost frightening expression of anger mixed with disbelief, and extraordinary bitterness.

"So this is the equality you say you believe in!" one of them burst out. "This is what all your talk of *the people* is worth! Nothing!"

"Leave it, Dániel," said the spokesman tiredly. "The *gentlemen* obviously have more important things to think about." And with a last contemptuous look, he turned on his heel and stalked out, the others following with their heads held high. Looking from them back to Vasvári, I saw that his eyes were locked now with Lajos's.

Lajos said quietly, "That was not very well done, was it?"

Vasvári shifted in his seat uncomfortably. "Perhaps I was tactless, but I had the sudden idea, listening to their talk of force, that we can keep them in reserve for the next phase..."

"Do you imagine that they — or their friends — would lift one finger in any cause of yours now?" Lajos interrupted, and Vasvári flushed under the contempt in his voice.

"Don't preach at me! You said yourself we can't provoke mass action again now!"

"It didn't need to be *mass*, Vasvári, and you know it."

Uncomfortably, Jókai stepped into the breach. "Perhaps he was insensitive, Lajos, but what has he — what have we? — to do with the guilds?"

Lajos pushed his cup away from him, standing up and looking around his friends. I had never seen such scorn on his face before; it was startling, almost frightening.

"I think," he said shortly, "that you've forgotten who it is we're fighting for." Then, without waiting for a reply, he strode out of the café without a backward glance. I dropped my gaze from the disconcerted revolutionaries to my half-eaten cake. I didn't want to recognize the nobility of his gesture.

"Phew!" said Mattias, impressed. "Strife in the radical camp! The trouble with Lajos is, he doesn't recognize his own limitations — or anyone else's!"

"He's just seeking greater glory," I said contemptuously, "through criticizing the others."

Mattias's eyebrows lifted in surprise. "Do you think so? I thought you quite approved of old Lajos."

"No," I said simply. I pushed another piece of cake into my mouth. The whole scene had left a nasty taste and a jumble of feelings I wanted to squash rather than sort out. I finished my coffee. "Shall we go?" I suggested.

Mattias was willing enough, since none of his particular friends were there. I felt only relief as we departed, but then, outside the door, we ran unexpectedly into Lajos and my stomach gave one of its more unpleasant lurches.

He was with the journeymen who had sought Vasvári's help, and as I came out he was passing a scrap of paper to them. Their spokesman was nodding, a slightly more hopeful glint in his eyes.

"Any time tomorrow," Lajos said, moving aside to let us pass. The men thanked him a little doubtfully and went on their way, exchanging low-voiced arguments as they went. Lajos glanced at us a little impatiently, as if wondering why we didn't go past — I couldn't, for Mattias now stood in my way — but when he saw us, his face cleared. At once, I looked beyond him, as if searching for a fiacre.

"Hallo," Mattias said in surprise. "Are *you* going to help them then?"

Lajos shrugged. "If I can."

"I must say you don't look very revolutionary!" Mattias complained. "Where's your sword?"

"I think Petöfi's guillotine is big enough for both of us, don't you?" Lajos said drily, and I risked a glance at him while Mattias laughed. Unfortunately, his eyes were on me, and he wasn't smiling. Forcing myself to meet that steady gaze, I wished the nerves in my stomach would settle before I felt sick.

"How are you?" he asked quietly. I almost believed he was interested.

"Very well, thank you," I replied, woodenly polite, and then, after a pause, because it sounded better, I added, "And you?"

His mouth curled into a smile of unexpected bitterness. "Oh, I couldn't be better!"

"You shouldn't quarrel with your friends," Mattias said severely. "I think you offended Vasvári."

"I meant to," Lajos said briefly. "Go and find a fiacre, Mattias."

Mattias took this rejection of his wisdom in good part, shrugging philosophically. He moved to the front of the pavement, looking up and down the road. In panic, I tried to follow him, but Lajos suddenly laid his hand on my arm.

"Wait. Are you really well?" he said urgently.

"Perfectly," I said with commendable calm, looking significantly at his detaining hand.

He ignored that, saying steadily, "Katie, I need to know if there are consequences after Erzsébet Island."

"*Consequences?*" I repeated stupidly.

"We made love, Katie," he said deliberately. "I presume you understand the possible consequences of that?"

I jerked my arm free, blushing a fiery red under his bluntness. Anger and embarrassment and sheer outrage flooded through me with a strength of feeling I had not known in a month. Of course, it was not *my* good which concerned him, it was his own reputation!

In that moment I hated him quite as fiercely as I had ever loved him. With contemptuous loathing, I said, "You may rest easy. There are no consequences of that night. None whatsoever!"

$* * *$

Two days later, the first blood of the revolution was spilled on the streets of Pest.

Having selfishly deserted Katalin and the children outside the Museum, where we had spent a rare morning with Captain Zarescu, I made my own way to my favourite bookshop, a tiny store run by a learned, elderly Jew called Aaron Klein, whose chief charm lay in not only recognizing his regular customers but remembering the last conversation he had had with each.

Almost the only sign of homesickness which I had found in myself was the desire to read novels in English — there is a special sort of relaxation in escaping into a fantasy world described in one's own language. Now, more than ever, I needed that escape, but as I sped a little desperately along the streets to Klein's shop, I found it difficult to banish Alexandru's face from my mind. I was shocked by the change in him. His huge dark eyes were sadder than ever; there was a sick, almost hunted look about his face, but I knew from Katalin that his illness was not physical. Quite simply, he was in agony over the conflicting loyalties pulling him in three directions.

On one side, he was a conscientious officer who had sworn allegiance to the King-Emperor; but his friends as well as his spiritual inclinations were on the side of the revolution, and he lived in constant dread of being ordered to arrest, or even kill, his closest acquaintances. For some reason, this had not bothered him in the intoxicating days of March, but now that he had time to think, to brood on the consequences of Hungary's defiance, he was deeply disturbed. And then there was his loyalty to his race, the downtrodden Romanians who no one, even the revolutionaries, seemed very keen to help.

According to Katalin, he hardly ever went to the Pilvax now; he found it too painful, and he had, besides, quarrelled with several of the radicals over the rights of minority races. Katalin, though more relieved than anything else by his break with the radicals, was still anxious about the strain on his nerves. She had almost resigned herself to his being sent to Italy, where, I think, she imagined he would distinguish himself by such conspicuous gallantry that even her proud father would be glad to welcome him as a son-in-law. And, in truth, I think it would have been something of a relief to Alex himself to leave Hungary just now. In many ways it would have been better for him if he had...

I recall being aware, as I walked down the narrow street to the bookshop, of the sound of shouting in the distance. But since rowdy demonstrations had become a common occurrence in Buda-Pest in the last weeks, I paid no special attention to it. Instead, I went into the bookshop and smiled brightly at Mr Klein.

"Miss Kettles!" he beamed. "How delighted I am to see you — and how desolate." He spread his arms deprecatingly. "I have no new books for you!"

"None at all?" I was disappointed.

"Not in English. Some German, some French — George Sand perhaps?"

"I'll look around," I said, and squeezed past the shop's only other patron to the French novels. I scrutinized them all, but was satisfied with none. Discontented, I moved towards the Hungarian literature.

It was then I realized that the noise outside had grown louder and nearer — and what was more worrying, I could hear breaking glass and unfamiliar crashing noises too. Alarmed, I looked at my fellow patron, a middle-aged professional man with a nervous tick at the corner of his mouth and a positively frightened gleam in his eye. I asked him politely if he knew what was happening outside.

"No, I don't," he said quickly. "But if I were you, I wouldn't go out again until it stops!"

Aaron Klein had opened the door and was looking up the street in the direction of the noise. There was another crash of breaking glass and a clear, definitely human, scream of pain which did more than anything else to frighten me. Someone ran past the door, calling urgently to the bookseller in a language I did not know. Slowly, Aaron Klein came back inside, and his black eyes were no longer twinkling.

"What is it?" I demanded. "What's happening?"

He smiled with an obvious effort. "Nothing that you need worry about. I think, though, that perhaps you should go home now. And if you, sir, would be so good as to report the trouble in the proper quarters..."

The customer looked outraged. "You do not expect us to go outside with a *mob* rampaging at the end of the street?"

"If you're outside, they won't touch you," the bookseller said simply, and something in the inflexion of his tone made my breath catch.

"No? I notice *you're* not going out!"

"Please; I believe you will be safer away from here..."

"Why the devil should I be?"

"Because," I said sharply, "*You* are not a Jew." In the sudden silence, I faced Aaron Klein. "That *is* it, isn't it? This is against your people?"

He nodded slowly. "It's been coming for some time. In Pressburg, it already has. Even in revolution, people look askance if we begin to have the same rights as everyone else."

I had paid so little attention recently to public events. With an effort, I vaguely remembered debates on the rights of Jews; the Diet forbidding Jews to join the National Guard, and the Committee of Public Safety in reply merely organizing special Jewish units of Guards. But that was some time ago. Here, it seemed, was the violence we had escaped, even at the height of revolutionary fervour. Now it was erupting in an anti-Jewish pogrom, as ancient and as reactionary as the Old Testament itself.

"What can we do?" I asked quickly.

"Go."

166

"Will you come with us?"

"They will destroy my shop."

"Won't they do that anyway?" I asked brutally. "Sir, you *must* come."

"I won't run away this time," he said wearily. "I'm tired of running."

I swallowed, touched both by pity and admiration. "I won't go if you don't," I threatened at last.

Aaron Klein smiled again, genuinely this time. "You are a sweet child, but I don't expect to come to much harm. Sir, will you take her away before they come any nearer?"

The man with the tick looked undecided, but at that moment the decision was taken out of his hands. A group of men ran past the door, yelling. One of them was laughing. I heard the chant of, "Kill the Jews! Death to the parasites!"

"Lock the door," I said urgently, but Mr Klein only shrugged philosophically. "They'll only break it down."

The chant had come nearer. Now it ended in a roar, and the door of the shop burst open to reveal a large, burly labourer who stood, hand on hips, surveying the premises. Pushed from behind, he moved further forward and four other men piled in after him. The burly man grinned ferociously at the bookseller, stupidity and blood lust shining out of his little eyes in almost equal measure.

"Kill the Jews!" he shouted. "Death to the parasites!"

His companions took up the awful chant until I felt like covering my ears. Aaron Klein waited placidly before them, while the man with the tick and I stood, ignored, at the back of the shop. Appalled, I watched one of the men pick up a weighty volume, swinging it in his hand until it caught the Jew's attention. Then he hurled it quite deliberately through the window; but at least the crash of the breaking glass had the effect of ending the unbearable chant.

The burly man laughed and took another step towards Mr Klein, almost casually pushing over a case of books as he went. The others, mob-like, crushed after him — at which the man with the tick took his chance and bolted, scuttling out of the shop so fast that the invaders actually looked startled, and for the first time noticed me.

"Who was that? Another God-forsaken Jew?" said the thin, ugly one at the back. "What about you, Jew? Want to run away too?"

Aaron Klein shook his head slowly. "I ask you to leave," he said quietly. Undecided, I stood poised for flight. If I could find help...

"Well, that's a pity," said the burly man, "because *we're* telling *you* to leave! Leave the city! Leave Hungary, you filthy parasite!"

He ended on a thunderous roar as another bookcase went crashing down, knocking against Aaron Klein's shoulder and sending the old man sprawling. Instinctively, I pushed past his laughing tormentors, abandoning my half-formed plan to flee.

"Stand aside!" I said sharply, falling to my knees beside the bookseller's prone body. "Sir, are you hurt?" I asked anxiously.

He stirred. "Only winded."

I took his arm to help him to rise, ignoring the burly man's stare as he said in a voice of mock amazement, "Now what have we here? A Jewess, or a Jew-lover?"

"A Magyar lady," said Aaron Klein quickly, "so you had better leave her alone!"

But I was angry at the stupid, pointless brutality now, and refused to shelter behind the tiniest untruth.

"I am neither Magyar nor Jew," I raged, "but if you know what's good for you, you'll get out of here right now!"

They laughed their derision in hoots and howls. I hadn't really expected anything else — I have never been a commanding figure — but I had never felt so helpless as I did now, watching the ugly man throw book after book through the window, each time trying to choose a part of the pane which was not already shattered. His friend, a youngish man with blond whiskers, improved on this by throwing books at Aaron Klein. One hit him in the chest, another caught him on the side of his forehead, making him stagger.

"Stop it!" I cried desperately, standing in front of the old man, though he tried to push me away. I saw the cruel smile die on the burly man's face. With one hand he reached out and plucked me aside. With the other, he quite casually hit Aaron Klein in the face. The old man went crashing backwards under the dreadful force, falling heavily into the table behind him. I saw the agony on his face as it dug into him.

The other men advanced as my captor dragged me out of the way, saying sneeringly, "So, a little Jew-lover, eh? Can't you do any better than that old fool? You're not so bad-looking without these things." And he wrenched off my spectacles, tossing them carelessly over his shoulder.

Now my unaccustomed blindness added to the terror of the situation, but I didn't need my spectacles to see the other men repeatedly punching Aaron Klein. For a moment I felt utter despair at man's inhumanity; but then sheer anger as well as fear lent me strength. Viciously, I kicked my captor in the shins, tearing free and launching myself on the old man's attackers, screaming, "Leave him! Leave him alone, you'll kill him! For God's sake, leave him alone!"

But of course, they didn't leave him. I was flung back into the arms of the burly man, just as I heard the sound of the shop door opening, pushing against broken glass and fallen books.

"Had enough, Jew?" the blond-whiskered man was jeering breathlessly.

I found I had closed my eyes in prayer. *Please, God, let whoever has come in be a good man. Let him fetch the soldiers, and oh please God, quickly...*

CHAPTER TWENTY-FIVE

A voice of searing-white anger cracked through the commotion like a gunshot.

"What the *hell* do you think you're doing? Release these people *now!*"

Open-mouthed, the men dropped Aaron Klein. My own captor's hold grew slack as they all turned to stare at the newcomer. That one man should stay to speak so to these brutes was wonderful enough, but it was the voice itself which paralysed me. Unaccustomedly harsh as it was, it undoubtedly belonged to Lajos Lázár.

Through my myopic haze, I saw him stride the length of the shop towards me.

"I said, release her!"

The burly man obeyed, pushing me aside, but only to square up sneeringly to Lajos who was, after all, the smaller and lighter man.

"Why should I?" he jeered.

For answer, Lajos swung back his arm with extraordinary speed, and quite unexpectedly crashed his fist full into the burly man's face. He fell like a stone. I remember being amazed, for I had never seen Lajos use physical violence against anyone. I remember too the fierce, almost frightening satisfaction it gave me to see his victim go down. In a flash, Lajos had his foot on the man's neck.

"That," he said gently, "is why."

"Lajos," I said hoarsely, for the others were advancing behind him. This was worse than anything...

Almost casually, he glanced over his shoulder. "Come a step nearer and I'll break his useless neck."

The thin, ugly man uttered a vicious obscenity and kept coming, but to my surprise, the blond-whiskered man held him back, saying uneasily, "No wait, don't you know him?"

But he was shaken off. "I don't care if he's Kossuth himself."

"He's Lázár! Lajos Lázár!!"

There was a pause. I could hear it. Something intangible had snapped.

Lajos took his foot off the burly man's neck. I moved and knelt, trembling now, beside Aaron Klein's fallen, bleeding body.

"Is he badly hurt?" Lajos asked, his voice still clipped and watchful.

In fact, I thought that the old man was dead, but to my unspeakable relief, his lips stretched into a smile. His eyes opened. "I'm fine," he said shakily, with a patent lack of truth, but it reassured both Lajos and me. I helped him to sit up, and then began to search blindly for my spectacles.

By now, the burly man was back on his feet, shaking his head like a dog, as if to clear his fuddled wits. He stared at Lajos, fists clenched. With clumsy hands, I pushed my recovered glasses on to my nose. Lajos, I saw clearly now, was staring back with utter, withering contempt.

"No. I don't think so," he said scornfully. "Your friends won't back you now, for I'm not a defenceless old man, or a girl. I'll fight you if you like, but I warn you, I know more dirty tricks than you ever will."

He had needed to, I thought irrelevantly, to hold his own against the older boys in the village and against István and his aristocratic friends...

"Who is this little turd?" the burly man demanded, but his bravado was forced now, I saw, and desperate, designed only to get the others back on his side.

"Didn't you hear?" said the blond man impatiently. "It's Lázár."

"At your service," Lajos said ironically. "And what do you men imagine you are doing here?"

Weirdly, the situation had completely reversed. Lajos was in charge, now. The five brutes were at his mercy, preparing to answer to their better. Lajos let his eye wander round the wrecked shop, the broken glass, the carnage, coming to rest at last on Aaron Klein's battered figure.

"He's a Jew!" said the ugly man by way of an excuse.

"I know. So what? This lady is Scottish. I happen to be a Magyar. You, if I don't mistake, are German by origin. What is that to say to anything?"

"*You* should understand!" said the burly man, blustering. "It's for Hungary! We're ridding the Fatherland of foreign oppression!"

I thought Lajos whitened at this, but without pause he lashed back, "Rubbish! You're stirring up hatred of the Jews to justify your own petty, cowardly desire for violence! Don't you *dare* pretend this is for Hungary, for the revolution! What is remotely great or glorious about five grown men beating up a solitary old man and a girl?"

I think it was his presence — the same presence which had spellbound thousands — rather than the words themselves which had the effect. But the men actually began to look almost sheepish. They shifted from one foot to another like monstrous, naughty schoolboys, and started to mutter.

"Exactly," said Lajos contemptuously. "Nothing. Nothing at all. It's pathetic, paltry, cruel, a crime against humanity *and* against the revolution itself. Do you really think we risked our necks on the fifteenth of March, and every day since, so that *you* can choose to beat old men whenever the fancy takes you? No, that's not what we meant by liberty."

He pushed casually past the burly man and rested his hips against the table as he looked from one man to the next. He even put his hands in his pockets. But though he appeared so much at his ease, I could sense the desperate tension in him — after all, I knew him very well.

"Before you leave," he said conversationally, "let me also give you a short lesson in equality — the second principle of the revolution. Equality means that Aaron Klein is no better and no worse than you — at least when you were all born. But now, your action has placed him immeasurably above you — not because he is better now than before but because *you* have sunk to depths lower than animals."

That penetrated. Trembling uncontrollably now, I was terrified that he had gone too far. The ugly man certainly took a hasty step nearer him, but Lajos held him back with one look.

"I haven't finished. I hope you feel proud, gentlemen, because you have spilled the first blood, brought the first shame on the revolution, and that is how you will be preserved in the history books. Hungarian children will revile you. I certainly do. Now, get out — I hope the soldiers catch you."

He was so completely in command that despite his deliberate insults — or perhaps because of them — the brutes could not even meet his gaze as slowly, silently, they shuffled out of the wreckage of the shop. Like the whipped curs they were, I thought with loathing.

I sat back on my heels, resting my head on my arm from sheer relief. Vaguely, I was aware of Lajos moving towards us. As I lifted my head again, he dropped to one knee on the other side of Aaron Klein, gripping the old man's shoulder with one strong hand. But oddly enough, it was at me he was looking, for the first time since he had entered the shop. The tension in him was still taut as a bow, his eyes heavily veiled, almost opaque.

"Are you hurt?" he asked quietly.

I shook my head. "No," I said unsteadily. "I'm just in a fiendish quake."

"Not you!" the old man said with surprising strength. "Brave as a lioness, Lajos!"

"I know." His gaze fell to the bookseller. "And you, sir? How bad are you?"

Despite everything he had just done, he still gave the natural respect of youth to age. Of course, they seemed to know each other... Somewhere beneath my daze, I was surprised to see that his hand, resting on the old man's shoulder, was shaking. Its knuckles were cut, sluggishly bleeding.

Aaron Klein shrugged and winced. "As you see, I have a bloody nose and a few cuts and bruises. I have a sore back and a pain in my chest. And I fear I may be sick if my stomach doesn't stop hurting soon."

Lajos looked around him. "There's nothing here... come, I'll take you to my place and you can clean up and rest."

"I can't leave the shop — not like this!"

Lajos blinked. "Why the devil not? Do you imagine you'll get customers?"

The old man choked on a laugh, and winced painfully. "Drat you, boy, don't do that."

Lajos's hand almost clenched on the thin shoulder. "Christ, Aaron, I'm sorry..."

"For what? You probably saved my life and what's left of my shop."

"Sorry that anything I ever said might have led them to believe that they could do this."

"Forget it," Aaron Klein said kindly. "It happens. Governments, revolutions, come and go, but persecution of my race is eternal! Still, it must be said in favour of my people — and yours — that we are still here."

"Then I'm sorry I didn't come sooner..."

"I don't know what fate brought you here at all."

"Neither do I, but he had a nervous tick. Can you stand?"

"I expect so..."

I didn't hear the rest of the conversation, for my breath had caught on unexpected laughter and then, quite suddenly, the subdued emotion of weeks erupted inside me, not with violence or hate, but with clear, devastating self-knowledge.

Stricken by the truth, that I couldn't turn love into hate simply by manufacturing disapproval, I turned away from them, stumbling blindly through the carnage towards the door. Of course I loved him. I would always love him, because anything else was impossible for me now. But it was equally true that while he may not have been the villain my fever of hurt had tried to make him, he still did not love me. Otherwise, he could not have made the sort of proposal he had. Oh, he cared; I knew that now, and before the fifteenth of March that might have been enough for me. But for two whole days I had dreamed of being everything to him, and now nothing less would do. I could not stand beside Teréz and his other women, past, present and future. I could not bear his casual, priestless, temporary 'marriage'.

Behind me, I heard his voice speak my name, but I would not stop. I fled, oblivious to the mobs which could still be rampaging through these streets, and quite careless of the appearance I must have presented, running away from Aaron Klein's shop with the tears pouring down my cheeks.

It was shortly after this that Baron Acsády appeared in the capital. It must be said that the news was not greeted with undiluted pleasure. Katalin's nose wrinkled with distaste, and Elisabeth's eyes positively flashed with venom — aimed, I was sure, at the sister whom she suspected, on no grounds that I ever discovered, of having designs upon her husband.

"I wonder what brings them here?" István said thoughtfully. Katalin looked at him.

"I thought you had," she admitted. "I was all set to tell you that nothing in the world would induce me to marry him."

"Acquit me." István smiled faintly. "I'll not deny I once thought it would be a good idea, if you could like him, but to be frank, I believe that now is not the best time to be allying yourself with a man whose views are quite so — reactionary."

I smiled into my wine glass, watching Katalin's eyes widen with shock and quickly recover.

"So I must still make my marriage to suit your interests?" she said indignantly.

"No," István said quietly. "To suit yours."

She met his gaze squarely. "You know where my interests lie."

He sighed. "I know where you think they do."

I wiped my mouth delicately with my napkin and ventured, "You must allow her to be constant in her affections." I was gratified to see the slightly arrested look in his eyes as they met mine. Slowly, he moved his gaze back to Katalin.

"Do you think of him still? That Romanian?"

"Captain Zarescu. He has a name!" Katalin said fiercely.

"It's a Romanian name," Mattias observed casually, "but for all that he's a good fellow. His family have land, you know, east of Kolozsvár. He *is* a gentleman."

He won a huge smile from his sister for this accolade, but István was beginning to look harassed, much to my amusement. "Are you all against me now in this? It's not *my* consent she needs!"

"But a word from you would help," Katalin said, a certain wheedling note creeping into her voice. István regarded her for a long moment, thoughtful but far from happy.

"I cannot like it, Katalin," he said at last.

"I know that, but in time you will grow used to it. And truly, István, he is the only man I shall ever love."

"Oh, rot!" said her brother, driven back to impatience by this unwarranted sentimentality. Katalin opened her mouth to join battle, but I pressed my foot heavily down on hers and she glared at me instead.

"Leave it," I murmured under my breath, and after a second, her face cleared. She had scored a point with István and should not now risk setting his back up again, but wait and see the result.

For me, the other welcome outcome of the Acsádys' visit was that it prompted our early return to Szelényi. For, apart from his constant carping against Kossuth and the revolution, the Baron brought with him rather frightening reports of trouble in Transylvania. Though I couldn't actually imagine my grandfather in any danger, I did know relief at the prospect of leaving Pest and Lajos behind me. I would not have to avoid him, or suffer the pain of seeing him and knowing I could not be with him. At times, I woke in the night, the pillow wet under my cheek, my body aching for his touch, and my heart telling me just to go to him, to forget his lack of love for me. He wanted me, and in the hot, restless nights, I longed for that to be enough. Perhaps in Szelényi, I too would find a little peace.

Before that could happen, however, I found several new anxieties to deal with. The first was when Katalin and I stumbled upon a public meeting outside the Museum. These gatherings were no longer so frequent as in the heady days of March, and this one rather took us by surprise. However, like everyone else in the city, we had grown blasé about organized mobs, so we stayed for a while to listen. At this time, Katalin was making a concerted effort to understand Alexandru's conflicts of loyalty, so she was almost eager to hear what his radical friends had to say.

Unfortunately, we had chosen a bad meeting. Amongst other familiar faces, Vasvári and Petöfi were there, and the radical noble, Nyári. So was Lajos, but I noticed that he was a little apart from the others and that he sat rather than stood on the steps, as if he was not going to speak.

The speeches were on the suffrage law, mainly demanding a much lower property qualification than the Diet had set. The mixed crowd were, in the main, quite in favour of this, and lustily cheered each speaker in turn. But I couldn't help watching Lajos who, sitting so casually on the steps, bore a closer resemblance to a street-urchin than a lawyer. I was reminded unbearably of the first time I had seen him in Vienna. As then, his eyes were on the crowd, but suddenly he turned and looked over his shoulder at Petöfi, who was coming to the end of his speech. In the applause which followed, he stood up, not moving to join the speakers further up, but staying apart as he was. Nevertheless, the crowd quietened expectantly.

"Why," he began abruptly, "do we need a property qualification at all?" The crowd was divided on this, but the cheers were still loudest.

Someone at the front threw a square of red cloth towards him, shouting, "Equality, Lajos! You tell them!" Lajos smiled, deftly catching the red kerchief and threading it through his buttonhole where it waved like a brave flag of defiance in his otherwise plain dress.

"My friend Táncsics has already told you it is a crime against nature to deprive a man of his voting rights, just for his of lack of property!" He lowered his voice thoughtfully, almost confidingly. "Property, you see, is the problem. Some of us have none; others have more than they can cope with, let alone *use*. Now: it seems to me we could avoid this whole quagmire simply by redistributing the lot, so that we all have, if not equal shares, then at least a fair amount to live on."

My breath caught. He had gone too far. I saw Petöfi start towards him as if involuntarily, then hold back. There was a shocked silence in the crowd, while Lajos stood still, letting the idea sink home.

Then someone shouted triumphantly, "*That* would be justice! That would be equality!"

"It would!" Lajos agreed, raising his voice again to an intense plea. "It would be the *ultimate* justice! A world in which there is no more poverty, no more envy, no more waste! It is the right of every man, woman and child to have *enough*. And we can do it — now is the time for change! Don't let the revolution end here! Let us push towards this greatest goal: deprive the bloated lord of a little wealth, in order to give every peasant land to live on! Take away from the fat and useless, and feed the poor!"

There was uproar in the crowd, panic among the obviously propertied burghers, though I could also see a gleam of hope or of thoughtfulness in other faces. Lajos sat down again on his step. There was a faint smile on his lips as the conflict raged around him.

I felt a surge of emotion rise in my throat: he was still shaking people up, still pushing one step closer to his dream. It really didn't matter who was in power. He would always be against them...

"He's mad," Katalin whispered wonderingly in my ear. "Lajos has finally gone raving mad."

"Not he," I said unsteadily.

Already, Pal Nyári the radical noble, was holding up his hands for peace. "No, that is not justice!" he began, and under cover of his refuting speech, I watched Petöfi slip down the steps till he stood a couple below Lajos, speaking urgently and angrily to him. Still sitting, Lajos looked up at him, his lips curving further. He reached out and took the scabbard of Petöfi's huge sword in his fingers, placing it significantly on his own neck.

An icy, prophetic shiver ran through me. Petöfi was staring at him. For a second, neither moved, then the poet abruptly wrenched the sword from Lajos's hold and leapt back up the steps to stand beside Vasvári. Lajos gazed after him for a moment, then turned back to the crowd.

CHAPTER TWENTY-SIX

For perhaps two days after this meeting, there was panic in the city, but when it became apparent that no one, even Petöfi, seriously intended redistributing property, it died away, leaving only an uneasy memory in many minds — and a severe rift in the radical camp. According to Mattias, Petöfi had grown distinctly cool towards Lajos, while Vasvári wouldn't so much as speak to him. Even then I thought it a bad omen for the revolution. But then real disaster struck.

Coming downstairs for breakfast one morning, I found György the porter endeavouring to prevent an early morning caller from gaining admittance. Since I was sure György knew his job better than I did, I at first paid no attention to the incident, merely casting a cursory glance as I crossed the hall. However, that one glance made me pause, for the caller was an army officer swathed in a military cloak, and I knew his face very well. His foot was in the door, but since György was quite capable of dealing with that, I moved swiftly to intervene.

"Is there a problem?" I asked innocently, then appeared to recognize the caller with surprise. "Why, Captain, how unexpected! Come in at once — it's all right, György, I am up and about as you see, and willing to receive!"

As I babbled, I registered shock at the sight of Alex, for he looked dreadful: it was no wonder György had refused to let him in. His face was unshaven and pale, his hair dishevelled, and his eyes red with sleeplessness and full now not only of tragedy but of utter despair.

I led him quickly into the nearest room.

"Don't worry," I said low. "No one uses this room so early in the day. Alex, what is it? What is the matter?"

He sank into a chair without a word or regard to courtesy, passing his hand wearily yet somehow vaguely across his eyes.

"I've deserted," he said flatly.

I blinked, but he added nothing, so I murmured inadequately, "Oh dear," and sat down opposite him. After a few moments, he spoke again, with an obvious effort.

"I just came to see Katalin before I leave the city. I have to escape, you see."

"You had better tell me," I said quietly, then: "Better, still, I'll go and fetch Katalin first."

This I duly did. Coming back into the room with her, I was made even more anxious by the fact that Alex was still sitting just where I had left him. He hadn't moved at all, but he did raise his head when we came in, and at sight of Katalin he jumped to his feet, took one stride to meet her running figure, and crushed her in a convulsive embrace.

"Oh Alex," she whispered. "What have you done? What have you done?"

"You must hate me now; I am dishonoured..."

"Never," she said vehemently. I thought it time to intervene.

"We must decide what to do," I said, deliberately matter-of-fact. "Katalin, sit down. Alex, tell us what happened."

They sat very close together on the sofa. I disposed myself on the foot-stool nearby, facing them, and Alexandru told his tale.

"Last night," he began, "we knew a group of students and other youths planned to create a disturbance outside Baron Lederer's house." Baron Lederer, Austrian commander of the Buda garrison, reviled as an enemy of the revolution ever since he had lied to the Committee of Public Safety about having no weapons in store... "You know the sort of thing, the 'katzenmusik' at which the Viennese excel!" A faint, painful smile passed over his face and died. "Lederer planned a surprise for them. He filled his house with infantry and had the cavalry standing by."

"And you refused to go?" I suggested.

"No. I went. How could I object to defending my commanding officer from a mob?" He shrugged. "I admit I thought he was over-reacting a little, but I suppose these katzenmusik concerts are rather frightening for those on the receiving end."

"And did the mob come?" Katalin demanded.

"Oh yes, it came. A large crowd of youths armed with nothing more offensive than their own powerful lungs, some drums and anything else they could find that would make a noise. And they certainly made a horrendous din. In any case, as soon as they had formed up outside the house, Lederer gave the signal for the lights to be put out. But then he — he — actually ordered us to attack."

"To *attack?*" I was startled. "With *weapons?*"

"With drawn swords. From the other side, the cavalry rode them down."

I drew in my breath. That was senseless, unforgivable...

Katalin was staring at Alex. "But you didn't? Couldn't you have pretended?"

"No," he said simply. He didn't even smile at her naiveté. "I found I could not. They were young, defenceless, only angry at what they saw as injustice." He lifted his huge, tortured eyes to hers. "Katalin, I *knew* some of them! One of them was a student called Isaak Klein whose father was beaten in the anti Jewish riots... How could I kill my unarmed friends? And for nothing!"

"What did you do?" I asked slowly.

"Nothing. When the others charged out of the house, I stood still. I didn't command my men; they simply charged with the others. I stood like a stone. Lederer saw me. He just stared with infinite contempt, and I knew I could expect no mercy either. I didn't really care then, with the awful thing being done outside. I remember feeling *relief* at having finally made one decision. I walked out of the house as the crowd dispersed. I even stepped over injured bodies and just kept walking, all night... I think it was probably hours later before I realized that just by staying away I had also technically deserted. I should go back and be shot, but I find I don't want to die."

Katalin was pressing his hand over and over, her eyes full of terror for him.

"And the people at Lederer's house?" I asked him fearfully. "Were they killed?"

"I don't know. I don't imagine the soldiers had much stomach for killing unarmed civilians, but some were certainly hurt. You can't charge a crowd of people from two sides and not have casualties. There was blood..."

"There will be more over this," I said with prophetic dread. "Listen, Alex, Lederer *must* be in the wrong to have ordered such an attack. You will surely be treated with leniency because of that?"

"I doubt they'll wait to ask questions. You can't have soldiers who are liable to disobey orders as they see fit. I would be dead before an enquiry could begin — if one was ever going to."

"Oh there will be an enquiry," I assured him. "Lajos for one won't rest..." I paused. "Have you seen Lajos?"

He shook his head. "They would look for me there: they know he is a friend of mine — I've even been warned against intimacy with him! No, I only came to say good-bye to Katalin..."

"No," she cried, casting herself into his arms again. "Where will you go? Oh Alex...!"

"I'm not sure. To Transylvania, I hope. There must be something I can do there for my people..."

While this exchange had been taking place, I had been listening with only half an ear, for one certainty was forming in my mind. "We must speak to Lajos," I said firmly. "He will know what best to do." Katalin nodded slowly, but now I was frowning: two women arriving unattended at the Pilvax to see Lajos would cause just the sort of curiosity we had to avoid... "We must get Mattias to help," I said abruptly.

And ten minutes later, leaving a morose and slightly dazed Alexandru behind us, hidden in the Little Room with Katalin's maid, the faithful Ilse, guarding him, we departed for the Pilvax, properly escorted by Mattias who was hotly indignant on Zarescu's behalf.

By the time we entered the coffee-house, my heart was beating uncomfortably, and it had little to do with Alexandru's problem. I had not spoken to Lajos since the day of the anti-Jewish riots. I had not even exchanged glances with him, let alone thanked him...

"He isn't here," Katalin said flatly. "The only time...!"

"Just wait," Mattias recommended, pushing her in front of him. When we were seated and the waiter had gone off to fetch coffee, he added, "Petöfi and Jókai are here and Vasvári has just come in. He'll be here soon."

To make sure, he went over to speak to Petöfi, and came back with the news that Lajos was indeed expected and would be informed immediately that Mattias wanted him. In the end, we had to wait nearly half an hour, and then he strode in looking as disreputable as ever, throwing a casual word of greeting to the waiter and heading straight towards Petöfi's table. However, his watchful eyes found us as he moved, and just for a second, I thought his step faltered.

"Lajos!" came Petöfi's indignant voice. "Have you heard about last night's outrage?"

"Petöfi won't remember to tell him," Katalin said in an agonized voice, as Lajos sat down with his friends and immediately entered into the discussion. "Mattias, you must bring him over..."

"Hold on, for pity's sake!" said her harassed brother, and sure enough, after about ten tense minutes, Lajos stood up and came towards us. He walked quickly and he was frowning and serious. I wanted to run away. I wanted to take his desperately tired face in my hands and kiss away the heavy lines.

"Good morning," he said civilly, his eyes resting equally briefly on both Katalin and me before turning on Mattias.

"Lajos, you have to help us," Katalin said impulsively and his gaze swung back to her in surprise.

"Of course," he said, taking the chair which Mattias pulled towards him, and sitting down beside me. His elbow almost touched mine, but his steady, dark eyes were on Katalin. "What can I do?"

She took an unsteady breath. "It's Alex," she said tragically, and Lajos's frown quickly deepened.

"What about him?"

Swiftly, and with commendable if surprising conciseness, she told him. Lajos's breath caught. "Who knows he is at the palace?"

"Just us."

"None of your servants?"

"Only Ilse, my maid, who is *quite* loyal. Oh and György the porter, but Katie bribed him."

For the first time since he had sat down, his eyes came to rest on me, and it was almost a shock to see the amusement in them. "How practical of her," he observed.

"Can you help him?" I asked bluntly, and he began to drum his fingers thoughtfully on the table. However, before he could speak, there was an interruption. Someone burst, rather than walked, into the café, crying, "There are soldiers in the street! I think they're coming here!"

Babble broke out, mostly defiant, but Lajos stood up, breaking through it. "How many?"

"About six."

"Well," said Lajos reasonably. "You can't close down the Hall of Liberty with just six men, can you?"

Petöfi laughed. "Nor with six hundred! Sit down, man and have some coffee."

Lajos turned back to us briefly. "I expect they're looking for Alex, so it would be as well if they didn't see us together. I'll come to the palace later." And then he was gone, back to his friends.

He had barely sat down again before the soldiers entered. Silence fell in the café. All heads turned to face them as they stood still, examining the room unhurriedly. There were four of them. Presumably two were outside, guarding the entrance. A waiter bustled up to them.

"Gentlemen, how may we help you? A table?"

"No. We seek one Lajos Lázár." My stomach lurched unpleasantly. It was my fear coming true, that Lajos would inevitably be arrested one day... By his accent, the soldier was German; however, it was not his nationality but the name he spoke which caused the threatening rumble within the café.

Lajos rose to his feet quite casually.

"I'm Lázár," he said carelessly. And at once Petöfi and Vasvári stood with him — it seemed all quarrels among them were over. Then everyone at their table stood too, and then every man in the coffee-house, including Mattias. Lajos's lip twitched, but he said with perfect gravity, "What can I do for you?"

And the officer, looking rather taken aback by this unanimous display of solidarity — which would certainly have made it impossible to arrest Lajos without bloodshed — said in a blustering way, "You will tell me, if you please, if you are acquainted with one Captain Alexander Zarescu?" Stupidly, I couldn't help being relieved.

"Alex?" said Lajos with well-feigned surprise. "Yes, of course."

"Do you happen to know where he can be found?"

"No," said Lajos gently. "You should ask at the castle."

"We have *come* from the castle!"

"Ah. Then I'm afraid I cannot help you. I haven't seen him for several days." The officer took a step nearer him. Instantly, there was a movement from those at Lajos's table. The officer's eyes flickered to them and back to Lajos. "Are you quite sure of that?" he said.

"I believe I said so," Lajos responded with just a touch of hauteur.

"It would be better for Captain Zarescu if he were found now," the officer said quietly.

"Be assured, I shall tell him so, if I see him."

The officer stared at him for a long moment, then cast another penetrating glance around the room before turning on his heel. He barked out an order to the soldiers and they departed as smartly as they had entered. Lajos watched them until they had gone; then he turned and made a flourishing bow to the café's patrons.

"Gentlemen, I thank you for your support!" They gave a rousing cheer, overcome by the ease of their victory over the soldiers whose true purpose none of them had fully understood. Only Petőfi, as the cheers died away, said curiously, "What has Zarescu done?"

"Nothing dishonourable — you may be sure of that," Lajos said curtly, resuming his seat.

Mattias stood up. "Come on," he said decisively. "Let's go home and wait for Lajos."

It was after five o'clock before any news reached us. Without warning, the door of the Little Room quietly opened and Lajos sauntered in, casually pushing it shut behind him again. Despite the undramatic, almost careless nature of his entrance, we all gaped at him speechlessly for several seconds. He paused, amusement registering in his dark eyes as he regarded us. It was Alex who spoke first.

"You know, if I were a Szelényi, I would worry about the ease with which you go in and out of my house."

We had been sitting on the floor like children, but now Katalin sprang to her feet, going quickly to Lajos. "Lajos, what has happened? Is he safe?"

Lajos took the hands which she impulsively held out to him, saying at once, "Yes, he is safe."

"Oh thank God!" she cried, relief causing her to press his hands with something approaching rapture. Beside me, I felt Alex sag, and I laid my hand encouragingly on his arm.

"Save your gratitude," Lajos warned. "I said he is safe, for now, but there can be no pardon before an enquiry."

"What do you mean?" Katalin frowned. Lajos led her across to where the rest of us sat, and squatted down beside us, meeting Alexandru's half-hopeful, half-anxious gaze. Alex swallowed.

"What happened?" he asked, then: "The Devil, where are my manners? Whatever happened, thank you for what you have done!"

Lajos took his outstretched hand, briefly gripping it, then said, "I presume you heard about this afternoon's meeting? The people were furious, more enraged than I have seen them — and of course, Petöfi was magnificent, denouncing Lederer and the Cabinet with a glorious lack of discrimination! 'I would not trust my *dog*, let alone my country to such a Cabinet!' he bellowed. Anyhow," he added, catching sight of Katalin's impatient face, "it was easy to get the crowd on your side, and to get myself on the delegation which went to the Cabinet to make the people's wishes plain.

"They were meeting in Batthyány's house at the time, but they must have known of the demonstrations, for they received us at once. Petöfi told them that we wanted immediate elections, an enquiry into last night's atrocity and the punishment of those responsible. Batthyány agreed at once. I think they had expected us and agreed in advance what they were prepared to grant. So, whatever else comes out of last night, we have been promised an Assembly within two months."

"Well, that is good news!" Alex said, distracted in spite of himself. Mattias grinned approval while Katalin stared at the men indignantly.

"They have trouble with priorities," I told her kindly.

"They have trouble keeping to the point!" Katalin exclaimed.

"Don't be ungrateful," Alex scolded her gently.

"I'm not ungrateful! I have already thanked him, but I want to know what he has done for *you*, and how he did it!"

"Not unreasonable," Lajos conceded. "Well, when Batthyány had agreed to our first three demands, I told them that there had been an officer involved last night who had refused to obey the order to attack, and who was now to be charged."

"What did they say?" Katalin asked breathlessly.

"Batthyány said he would look into it," Lajos said wryly. "I said that was not good enough, that you, Alex, had done your best to protect the people — which was, in fact, the Cabinet's job — and that it was not fair that you should be the only soldier to suffer for the night's work. I said we, the people, wanted a pardon for you."

"That's it, Lajos!" cried Mattias, delighted. "Have at them!"

But Alex, looking at his friend, said sardonically, "I don't suppose Batthyány sat down and signed it though, did he?"

"No," Lajos admitted. "There followed a whole collection of excuses, such as it was the business of the war minister, currently unavailable; and how a soldier who disobeys any order is at fault, and so on. I said the people did not see it that way, and looked directly at Kossuth. I think he understood me. The people had dug him out more than once; now it was his turn to give, or pay the price. And then István — did I tell you he was there?"

"*István?* He's not in the Cabinet!" Mattias exclaimed.

"No, but as a member of the Vice-Regal Council he still has influence and knowledge which the Cabinet needs. He had been watching me with some suspicion since I had started to speak, but now he asked suddenly the name of the officer in question."

"Oh dear," I murmured. "Did you tell him?"

"I had to," said Lajos, glancing at me.

"I don't suppose you induced him to see Alex as a hero instead of a deserter?"

"You over-estimate my powers of persuasion. István will make up his own mind on that."

"We thought we were winning him over," Katalin said sadly.

"Who knows? He may be won. He certainly never mentioned the one thing he knew against Alex — that he had, in uniform, sided with our silent protest at Szelényi. I've no idea whether Kossuth would count that in his favour or not, but I have a feeling István was right not to bring it up."

"So did Kossuth support the pardon?" Mattias asked eagerly.

"Not exactly. He pointed out quite reasonably that Alex could not be pardoned until the results of the enquiry vindicated him. I accepted that and suggested that in the meantime he be granted leave of absence and a safe conduct to travel anywhere in Hungary or Transylvania until either the enquiry exonerated him, or a date was set for a hearing."

He smiled slightly. "I promised that if it was the latter, I would defend you, Alex, and assured them categorically that you would be acquitted."

"I have always admired your vanity," Alex observed, a laugh lurking in his huge eyes.

"So did Kossuth, and he knew I wasn't referring solely to my skills as a barrister: the people are on your side. Anyway, the Cabinet conferred for a few minutes, and then agreed. I more or less dictated the wording — here."

He produced a folded paper from his pocket and held it out to Zarescu. "I have a copy, and one has been sent to your commanding officer."

Slightly dazed, Alex took the paper from him, but continued to gaze at him. At last he said, "I can't believe that after all these years you are still bailing me out of trouble."

"Well, I've always done my best to get you into it in the first place," Lajos said, a touch ruefully. He rose to his feet. "I wouldn't go back to barracks just yet though. You can stay with me till you decide what to do."

"I have decided," Alex said, standing with him. "I shall go to Blaj — to the Romanian congress."

Lajos nodded, faintly smiling. "Good. Remind them that they must stay with the rest of Hungary if they are to gain anything, if any of us are!"

It seemed that the crisis was over. So, with the vague idea that I should now put as much distance as possible between myself and Lajos, I moved unobtrusively towards the door.

"You'd better check first that no one is around," Mattias said, carelessly ruining my plan. "Ilse had run out of reasons to be skulking down here."

I nodded, but as I laid my hand on the doorknob, I was aware of Lajos beside me.

"I have become adept," he said lightly, and I barely had time to whisk my hand away before his fingers closed over where it had lain. Yet for a moment he did not open the door, but just looked at me. My eyes fell instinctively, and then pride forced me to meet his gaze again — which was a mistake, for he was too close and I could not step back without admitting my weakness. As if he understood this, his lips quirked upwards in the oddly charming half-smile that had always been my undoing.

My already troubled heart seemed to leap into my throat. I had the sudden urge to cast sense and caution to the winds and go with him wherever he chose, in whatever role he desired me. There was nothing else in the world that I wanted, and in that moment I yearned for it with a strength that made me dizzy.

Through the argument and chatter of the others, he said quietly, "Thank you for coming to me with this."

I swallowed, but no words would come. I could only look up at him with dumb, helpless misery, and hope I was not as transparent as I felt. And suddenly he frowned; I heard him swear softly under his breath as he glanced quickly at the others.

"Katie, this is impossible," he said urgently. "I have to speak to you."

"No," I managed to return firmly. Somewhere, behind the blind emotion, my head and my sense of self-preservation were still functioning. "There is nothing to say."

And then, mercifully this time, Mattias was beside us, talking. A moment longer, Lajos hesitated, then he opened the door a crack and looked out. All was pronounced safe and I fled towards the stairs without waiting to say good-bye to either Alex or his saviour. It was as well everyone already considered me eccentric.

CHAPTER TWENTY-SEVEN

The power of the people, it seemed, was still paramount. Lederer was recalled to Vienna; an enquiry into the incident was opened, and the Cabinet announced a National Assembly to open on the second of July.

Mattias, naturally, was exuberant. At last an Assembly would exist which was truly representative of the people.

"Of the people with property," I corrected drily.

"Or education. It still enfranchises more people than are allowed to vote in Britain!" Mattias said triumphantly. "They're all to stand for election, you know — Petöfi, Arany, Irinyi, Irányi, old Táncsics."

I nodded thoughtfully. And Lajos — what a fine achievement it would be for him to sit in the National Assembly; no doubt it would be the beginning of a glittering political career, for I could not imagine that he would fail to shine in the Assembly, to stir it up and carry all before him...

By this time, we were ready to go to Transylvania, and I felt a sudden panic at leaving Buda-Pest. The elections, the Assembly, would happen without me; Lajos's life would go on without me.

The day before we left, I ran into Petöfi in Vaci Street, swaggering towards me with his wife proudly on his arm. He no longer wore the monstrous sword of March days, but it was still somehow incongruous to find him doing anything so mundane as shopping with his wife. His face lit up when he saw me, and Julia smiled welcomingly. Despite their connection with Lajos, I could not but be pleased at their friendliness, so I stopped to exchange greetings and news.

"How are you?" Petöfi demanded. "We never see you these days!"

"That's because you are too busy," I said lightly. "And soon to be more so, I hear. Where will you stand for election?"

"In my home town — I have a good chance."

"I'm sure no one has a better," I said genuinely, and won a smile from Julia. "Are your friends also standing?"

"Yes, except for Vasvári and Jókai, who are under twenty-four and therefore two young. And Lajos, of course." His gaze grew speculative, even as I frowned in quick surprise.

"Lajos is *not* standing?"

"He says not. I assumed you knew."

I flushed under his bright, penetrating gaze, but I managed to say calmly, "I have not spoken to him recently..."

"Perhaps you could persuade him?" Petöfi suggested, and when I opened my mouth for instant refusal, he added quickly, "I know you will say it is his choice, and you are right. But how can his choice *not* be to serve the people?"

It was what I was wondering myself. "What does he say?" I asked evasively. "That he can better serve the people by staying outside the establishment," Petöfi answered with a shade of ruefulness. "And yes, I see his point, but to deprive the Assembly, *the people*, of his not inconsiderable talents — you see?"

"Yes, I see."

"And then, it would be such a step forward in his career. I know Lajos cares nothing for that, but his friends do."

"Yes," I agreed sadly.

"Then you will speak to him?"

I smiled a little nervously. "I'm afraid you over-estimate my influence with him — I could not persuade him."

Petöfi smiled unbelievingly, and would have spoken further, but I quite distinctly saw Julia pinch his arm, and in the end he said only, "Oh well, if you see him, you might try."

"I'm leaving Buda-Pest tomorrow," I said quickly, "but I wish you, and your friends all success in the elections — good-bye!"

*

We reached Kolozsvár in time for István to take part in the Diet's crucial vote on union with Hungary. I wondered that Lajos was not here to add his weight to the cause, but it seemed the result was never really in doubt. The Diet voted for union, and the people of Kolozsvár celebrated in the streets, for the gains of the Hungarian revolution were now theirs too.

Katalin and I walked among them, as if both of us in our loneliness were feeding off their uncomplicated joy. But as we wandered around the crowded central square, trying to ignore the admiring stares of the grenadiers who were lounging outside the Guardhouse, I suddenly caught sight of a man standing in the shadows of the old cathedral, a tall, gaunt figure whose face expressed not jubilation, but doubt. I glanced at Katalin, but it seemed she had not yet seen him.

"Did you arrange this?" I asked suspiciously.

"Arrange what?"

I looked significantly towards the corner and she followed my gaze without much interest until it alighted on Captain Zarescu.

"Alex!" she cried in amazed delight, starting immediately in his direction. He seemed to hear her voice, as if his ears were specially attuned to it. His face lit up, and he strode to meet us. I wouldn't have been altogether surprised to see them fall into each other's arms, but fortunately discretion was not yet completely lost to them. Alex contented himself with passionately kissing her hand, before pressing a more chaste salute upon mine.

"How wonderful!" he exclaimed, drawing us away from the crowd, back towards his old, quiet position. "I hoped I would run into you here, but I didn't even know if you would stop."

"István wanted to attend the Diet — but we thought you were in Balasz-falva."

"I was."

"Was it an interesting meeting?" I asked politely.

"Most — I'm only sorry I arrived too late to take part!"

"Oh dear — so you had a wasted journey?" I said sympathetically, and he smiled.

"No, not at all. I met some very interesting people who *had* been at the congress. They made me realize how out of touch I have become with my own people, how remote Buda-Pest is — even radicals like Lajos and Petöfi — from truly understanding."

I frowned. "But I thought the Romanians supported the revolution. Lajos said Hungarians and Romanians marched together, arm-in-arm, rejoicing!"

"That was in March," Alex said ruefully. "Look around you — you won't see many Romanians here today celebrating the union."

"But why not?"

"Because it was negotiated without consulting the Romanians who make up the majority of the population; because its terms don't even acknowledge us as a nation, equal with the Magyar, Szekely and Saxon nations. The Romanians fear being *Magyarized*, instead of gaining the equality, the freedom, which at first they believed the revolution would bring."

"You should introduce them to Lajos," Katalin said sharply, indignant at so much time being wasted on politics, but Alex only smiled.

"Yes, I should," he agreed. "For a less racially prejudiced person I have yet to meet. Especially, I would like him to meet an impatient young man called Iancu..." He broke off with an apologetic look at his beloved.

Tactfully, I looked away, and tried to close my ears to the rest of the conversation, which quickly became softer and more personal without me. We walked together for a little, pretending to look at the shops around the base of the cathedral, and then parted reluctantly when it was time for Katalin and I to return to the inn.

Since we were due to leave Kolozsvár in the morning, the lovers made no definite assignation, but from Katalin's brittle excitement I knew that something was in the wind.

"I suppose he will come to Szelényi," I probed, "even without the excuse of Lajos's presence." Inevitably, of course, István would hear of it, but I had no way of judging how he would react. He had said nothing to Katalin about his knowledge of Alexandru's predicament, although she had provided him with several opportunities to do so.

Katalin was smiling so secretively now that I became positively alarmed, and demanded to know what she was up to.

"Why nothing — yet!" she laughed. "But later in the summer, when I suddenly choose to go away on a visit to an old friend, you must support me all the way."

"Why?" I asked suspiciously.

"Because I shan't be visiting her, of course; I shall be meeting Alex!"

I stared, endeavouring to retrieve my dropped jaw. "Never tell me you are going to run away with him at last?" Now that it seemed to be a serious possibility, I no longer knew what to think of it, but Katalin only laughed again.

"Not for ever. I only want to spend a little time with him, where no one knows us or judges us."

I could understand that, but duty compelled me to point out the impropriety of travelling with him in this way — if such was really her intention.

"Don't be so prim," she mocked. "Besides, you know there will be no impropriety."

"The world — your father — will not see it that way."

"My father need never know," she said blithely; but it still appeared to be a crazy sort of a scheme to me, and I could only hope it would founder on Alexandru's good sense if on nothing else.

When we finally came to Szelényi, I couldn't help comparing this arrival with my first last year. Then it had been dark and I had been the governess, ill and exhausted. The castle itself had seemed oppressive, overpowering. This time we arrived in daylight. Driving past fields alive with activity, the full beauty of the countryside assailed me in all its glory, and the castle looking down on us was magnificent, impressive rather than frightening.

Even the great eerie entrance hall was less daunting when I followed Elisabeth inside. The children were still quiet, clinging to my hands, but at least this time Zsuzsa and I did not have to carry them when we could barely stand ourselves.

Margit came flying down the huge staircase to meet us, and there was a flurry of embracing and chatter and laughter. The children and I were hugged as one. I felt an unexpected rush of affection and pity for her tired, vague, happy face.

The Count himself was located in one of the upstairs rooms, looking exactly as I remembered him, old and fierce, but there was a glimmer of benevolence in his hard eyes as he embraced his family. When it was my turn, he held me by the shoulders, a little away from him, saying quizzically, "So you came back?"

Genuinely startled by this greeting, I said, "Did you think I would not?"

"I didn't know," he said frankly. "Sometimes you are — an elusive creature."

This was too obscure for me. I stood aside to let the children be kissed, watching his craggy old face and wondering at how little importance I now placed on his crimes against my mother. It made me feel guilty, as if I were somehow betraying her, but so much had happened in the last year that the events of thirty years ago had faded inevitably into insignificance.

I wondered too exactly what I felt for him now. I had grown fond of his family and their odd quirks of behaviour, but of the old man himself, though he certainly aroused emotions of some kind, I was still unsure. I had forgotten the strength of his dominating, overpowering presence.

"So," the Count said loudly when we were all seated round the great dining table, "you voted for the union with Hungary — I suppose it's to the good!"

István smiled faintly. "I thought you were opposed to the April Laws."

The Count shrugged, picking up his knife. "It makes no difference. The peasants had more or less stopped performing their robot in any case! I've had precious little work out of them since March!"

"That must be making things rather — difficult."

"Difficult! Another year like this and I'll be forced to marry Katalin off to an English merchant to save the family fortunes!"

Katalin, making the most of her father's joviality, merely laughed.

István said, "We heard from Ferenc Acsády that there is unrest in the country."

"There certainly is in his," the Count said grimly. "I wouldn't have been surprised if his people had lynched him — it's no wonder he bolted to the city."

"It's true then? I admit I thought he was exaggerating! But what of Szelényi lands?"

The Count shrugged again. "The peasants grow bold, refuse their dues, make trouble for our steward, fight over the east field which they say is common ground but never has been in my day — of course, Lajos Lázár put them up to that last year! But no one has offered me violence. At least, not yet."

CHAPTER TWENTY-EIGHT

"He has come to see *you*," Katalin whispered in my ear with glee, while Colonel von Avenheim paused to confer with Mark on the care of his horse. We had come upon the Colonel's unexpected arrival just as we had been preparing to ride out ourselves, and had cheerfully turned back with him.

"István, more likely," I returned calmly, though it was not an unpleasing thought that I still had an admirer: it soothed my bruised vanity.

Everyone was delighted to see the Colonel. He seemed to have the lucky knack of being valued by all, from the crusty old Count to the children, without regard to nationality or politics. Silently, I wondered how he had managed to avoid the dreadful conflicts of loyalty which tormented Alex, but after dinner that evening, I discovered that even he was troubled.

It was another sunny evening, the coolness in the air just beginning to make itself felt. As we strolled in the formal garden, the Colonel carefully draped my shawl around my shoulders, his fingers lingering just long enough to be solicitous. We were talking of various things.

Once I asked, "Have your troops been involved in — in dealing with peasant unrest?"

"Occasionally."

I looked at him curiously. "It can't be very pleasant work."

"It's not; but the troops are there to keep the peace, and that is what we must do. At the moment." Some inflection in his pleasant voice made me frown.

"At the moment?" I repeated. "Are you expecting the situation to change?"

"I hope not," he said heavily. I continued to watch his averted face as we walked, and when he said nothing further, I felt again that prickle of alarm.

"You are thinking of war," I said bluntly.

At that, he turned his head and met my gaze rather gravely. "Believe me, I pray daily that it will not come to that."

My hand crept to my throat. "Then you are afraid it might. As the radicals are."

He stopped then, taking my hand reassuringly in his. "There is no fear of it at the moment." He hesitated, then went on almost reluctantly. "But sooner or later the Emperor will realize he has the military power to take back what he has lost."

My frown deepened. "Italy?" I suggested, without much hope.

"The Dynasty's right to absolute power," Avenheim said quietly. "In all its realms. And Hungary will have to bow to that, or fight."

The prickle in my heart became an unpleasant thud. "I don't see Hungary bowing now."

"Neither do I."

"Then war with Austria is inevitable?"

"I fear so. And it is a war which Hungary cannot win."

"Oh, I hope you're wrong," I said intensely. He was still holding my hand in a warm, firm clasp. Now he raised it to his lips and lightly kissed it.

"So do I," he said softly.

Primly, I withdrew my hand, but curiosity made me ask, "And you, Colonel? Where will you stand in all this, if there is war?"

"There is only one place I can stand. It is many years since I took my oath of allegiance to His Majesty, but I could not renege on it, even if I wanted to."

"Then you are prepared to fight a Hungarian army?" I think I meant to be cruel, as cruel as the men willing to spill each other's blood over opposing ideals, but his face did not change, and when he answered, it was still calmly, though with an edge of sadness in his voice.

"If I am commanded to do so, I will."

I stared at him. "And if Mattias, or even István, stood against you?"

He looked away, and now here was a tightness around his mouth. "I would not wish to know. I could only do my duty, to my Emperor and to my country — and that would be the tragedy, for the Hungarians would believe they were doing the same. It would be old comrades of the one, Imperial army, split into two and killing each other without conviction. If there is a war, it will be the hardest any of us have ever fought."

Those first weeks at Szelényi were an interlude of peace, a period of healing for me. I drifted through the days almost in a vacuum: I taught the children, played with them, took them on expeditions in the summer sunshine; I spent hours talking with Margit or quarrelling with my grandfather who seemed to take a perverse delight in hearing me abuse him; I visited the Lázárs occasionally too, but not so often that they would notice my neglect if Lajos came home.

Then, one late afternoon in July, I sat in the library pouring over the *Radical Democrat* — organ of the newly formed Society for Equality — avidly reading the text of a speech Lajos had made. I felt foolishly guilty when Colonel von Avenheim strolled into the room and looked over my shoulder. I should say that he had reappeared for odd days throughout the last few weeks, but on this occasion he had taken a whole week's leave of absence.

"What are you reading so devotedly?" he enquired, and I smiled quickly up at him to hide my unreasonable nervousness.

"Only an old newspaper which Mattias sent."

He bent more closely, so that his chin almost touched my hair. "Ah. The Society for Equality — I suppose the radicals had to join something after so few of them managed to get elected! What are they saying now?"

"Oh, debating the rights and wrongs of aiding the Emperor against the Italians." I folded the paper rather hastily and glanced at him again. His eyes, I noticed, were really very blue. "Would the Emperor really turn next upon the Hungarians, once the Italians are beaten?"

"He would certainly be in a stronger position to do so."

"So the Assembly would be mad to grant troops for such a purpose?"

"Not necessarily. As I understand it, it is to be — ah — quid pro quo. The Assembly will send troops to Italy if the King will deal with Baron Jelacic and his rebellious Croats, who are clamouring for autonomy in Hungary! But I didn't come to discuss war and politics. I have just been talking to your grandfather."

"Always a salutary experience," I murmured, and since he did not sit, I stood up and wandered towards the window: I didn't care to be loomed over. "What did you talk about?" I asked when he remained silent.

"You," he said, following me to the window. Surprised, I turned to find him smiling at me. "I hope you will forgive the impertinence, but I felt I should at least *begin* according to custom and propriety."

"Begin what?" I asked, bewildered but prepared to be amused.

"A formal proposal," he answered steadily. I blinked. My hand was taken in his while I continued to regard him doubtfully.

"I don't suppose you mean that as it sounds..." I began.

"I do. Since he is, at least informally, your guardian, I asked him if I might pay my addresses to you."

He spoke quite calmly in his usual, friendly way, which perhaps was why I did not feel in the least flustered. In spite of myself, I could not help asking curiously, "What did my grandfather say?"

"He was pleased to grant his permission," the Colonel said gravely, though his eyes had begun to smile down into mine.

"And if he hadn't?" I asked quizzically. If I had ever been taught the correct way to answer a gentleman's proposal of marriage, I had forgotten.

"I would still be here," Avenheim said softly. "Miss Kettles — Katie, you must know how I feel, that I love you... Will you do me the honour of becoming my wife?"

Instinctively, although I had known it was coming, I tried to pull my hand free. With sudden panic I wondered what to say, how to refuse such an offer civilly after I had all but encouraged him to make it. Not for the first time, I cursed my stupid tongue. But he held on to my hand, and as I parted my lips to speak, he pressed one finger to my mouth.

"No; don't answer yet," he said. "Not just yet..." I had a moment in which to avoid his kiss, and I did make one jerky, almost involuntary movement to be free, but then I was still, allowing the embrace.

It was gentle; a nice balance of passion and respect. It was even pleasant. But nothing moved inside me. I did not melt. I felt no desire to prolong it. And when he raised his head and looked down into my eyes, I could only think helplessly of another face clouded with desire, and other delicious, shattering kisses.

"Well?" he whispered. "Will you marry me?"

Would I? Suddenly I was being offered a tempting way out. He did not stir me. I did not love him. Not yet. But I liked him very much; I respected him; I knew I could be comfortable with him. In that moment I could almost imagine our pleasant, unexciting life together, free of pain and doubt. And surely, in time, his love would ignite mine, exorcising Lajos from my mind and heart...

My breath caught. Would I? *Could* I ever be content now with another man than Lajos? Yet surely I should *try* for this chance of happiness...?

His clear, blue eyes continued to gaze into mine — honest, honourable eyes. And abruptly I was ashamed. He deserved better than a woman who would try to pretend he was another man. My eyes fell from his.

Slowly, I shook my head. "Forgive me..."

"For what?" he said ruefully. "Something tells me that this does not bode well for my cause."

"I'm sorry, but I cannot marry you." I did not look at him. I was afraid of seeing my own pain reflected there.

For a moment he was silent, then: "May I know why?"

I shook my head, unable to speak.

He said gently, "I was coxcomb enough to think you loved me."

My eyes flew involuntarily to his, and I forced them to stay there. "I thought we were friends..." And yet was that strictly true? Had I not soaked up what I instinctively knew to be his admiration, as a balm to my own wounds? How unfair of me...

"Then don't say no so quickly. We have not, after all, known each other for so very long. In time..." He broke off as I shook my head.

"I never meant to give this pain to anyone," I said with difficulty, "let alone to you. But I can't give you false hopes either. I cannot love you, because... because I — I love someone else."

"Ah." At last my hand was released. His eyes dropped, then lifted again to mine. "So when may I wish you happy?" There was bitterness as well as pain in his voice; it made me feel even worse

I managed to say calmly, "If by that you mean when shall I announce my engagement, I shall not. My love is not returned. In any case, it is impossible."

His lips twisted. "Then we have something in common."

"I'm afraid we do."

"May I know who he is?"

I shook my head dumbly, afraid that now the tears would start again; yet even then, I was aware of unexpected grimness behind his calm exterior, a depth of passion I had not suspected in him.

"Is he married?" Avenheim asked bluntly, and at that a grain of saving humour passed through me, tugged at my unhappy lips.

"No. He is not married."

There was another pause. I could feel a desperate, silent fight going on within him, but then he said only, "Is it not possible that your affections will change?"

I shook my head. "No."

He was silent. I couldn't look at him any more. I couldn't bear to be inflicting on another the same pain that was in me. And yet I suppose part of me just couldn't imagine him feeling as I did.

I said, "For what it is worth, if I had not met him and loved him first, I believe I would have found in you everything I wanted."

"That does not," he said, with sudden harshness, "make me feel better."

My stupid tongue again. "No," I agreed, moving tiredly away from him, but he caught my shoulder, turning me gently back, and now there was pity as well as hurt in his eyes.

"Thank you," he said quietly. I shook my head, speechlessly. For a moment he hesitated, then bent and pressed his lips briefly to mine. The next instant he was gone.

I stood alone where he had left me, my eyes tightly closed, but the tears still squeezed out and rolled helplessly down my face. I didn't know if I was weeping for him, or for me, or for the lost chance of love between us.

CHAPTER TWENTY-NINE

I dreaded dinner that evening, and with cause. Colonel von Avenheim had gone. Almost as soon as we had sat down at the table, my grandfather fixed his fierce old eyes on me, and I prepared to weather the storm. It went on a long time.

He was furious. He had fully expected to see me respectably married, and took my failure as a personal affront. According to him, I was wayward, perverse and just like my mother. I thanked him for the compliments and went to my bed-chamber.

Here, I prepared slowly for bed. I was somewhat distractedly brushing out my hair when a knock at the door heralded Katalin. In the mirror, I met her gaze.

"Oh, Katie, why? I thought you liked him!"

"I do. But I don't wish to marry him."

She sat down on the bed, regarding me thoughtfully. "Why not? Is it...? Katie, you are not — *afraid* of marriage?"

I laid down my brush, looking at her uncomprehendingly. Her face flushed, and with sudden understanding, I laughed. "Why, Katalin," I mocked. "You never used to be so mealy-mouthed! No, I am not *afraid.*"

"Oh." She watched me stand up and climb on to the bed, and as I slid between the crisp sheets, she said a little wistfully, "Don't you love him?"

I shook my head.

She leaned forward eagerly. "But, Katie, that is no reason to turn him down! You are turned twenty-eight, after all: if you don't love anyone else, surely in time you will learn to...?"

I dropped my eyes quickly, but obviously not quickly enough, for Katalin had seen something there which made her break off in mid-sentence. "Katie?"

"I'm tired, Katalin. I would like to go to sleep now."

"You *do* love someone else! Oh, Katie, who is it?"

"No one. It doesn't matter."

"Of course it matters! Why haven't you told me before, you sly old thing!"

"Because I knew you would behave exactly like this! And because he doesn't love me. Now, will you go away?"

I heaved the sheet over my ears and flung myself down upon the pillow.

There was a pause. Then I felt her fingers gently drawing the covers down from my face. I closed my eyes tightly in a parody of sleep.

"I found that it made me feel much better," she said softly, "when I could speak about Alex to you."

At that, something touched a chord in me. It might have been just that I heard genuine sympathy as well as curiosity in her voice. I opened one eye and regarded her helplessly.

"Katalin, I'm not like you," I pleaded. "I can only live with this if no one knows!"

"Does he know?"

"Oh yes," I sighed. "He knows."

"But what makes you think he does not care? Has he ever kissed you?"

A wild hysteria sprang up at that, threatening to overcome me. I swallowed it back so that my faint "Yes" came out as a choke.

"Well, surely that is a good sign?" she said bracingly.

I sighed for her innocence and sat up. "You don't understand."

"No," she admitted, "but I'm trying. It would help if I knew who the devil he was. Am I acquainted with him?"

I hesitated. Then: "Yes, but don't press me any more, Katalin — truly, it's not kind."

Still, inevitably, I could see her mentally reviewing her many male acquaintances while she said thoughtfully, "Then it is someone we both know quite well?"

"Katalin!" I said exasperated.

"Oh, don't worry, I can't think of anyone!"

"Can't you?" I meant it to be dry, mocking even, but it came out just a little wistfully. Somehow there was pain too in everyone but me seeing our total incompatibility for what it was.

"No," she said, frowning. Then, abruptly, her eyes widened again. "That is, unless it is... no." I said nothing. I watched my fingers twisting the coverlet. "Katie, it's not — *Lajos?*" she said apologetically.

I closed my eyes, waiting for the world to fall in upon me now that someone else knew. But nothing happened. The pain was no better and no worse.

"It *is*." Katalin's voice was awed. I took a moment to order my expression, then opened my eyes again, feeling almost defiant. But Katalin was gazing past me, hazily, dreamily.

"*Now*, what is it?" I demanded impatiently, and with a jolt her eyes refocused on me.

"I was just wondering," she said apologetically, "what it would be like to be kissed by Lajos."

I regarded her with a fascinated eye. "I thought," I said severely, "that you were in love with Alex?"

"Oh I am," she assured me, "But one can *wonder*."

I suppose she had always considered him so far beneath her that she had never thought — perhaps had never allowed herself to think — of him in such a way before my shocking revelation. As I watched her uncertainly, her gaze grew speculative. For an awful moment I thought she was going to ask me for details, and wildly regretted letting her worm even this much out of me.

However, she pulled herself together, observing only, "It seems to be a failing among the women of our family — falling in love with unsuitable men. And he *is* unsuitable, Katie, much more so than your father or Alex, or just about anyone else I can think of!"

"It doesn't matter," I said simply, then with a little more of my usual spirit I added mockingly, "After all, I am only *half* Szelényi."

But her mind had already bounced past his unsuitability and back to the previous subject. "I still don't see how you can be so sure that he does not love you. I have noticed that he is — different with you. And Alex too once said..."

"Oh Katalin don't," I said in sudden anguish. "Of course he cares for me as a friend. He simply does not love me, as — as Alex loves you. Now, please, let us never speak of this again — I couldn't bear it to become a subject of girlish gossip. And Katalin, promise me you will never tell anyone about this — not Ilse, or Mattias, or even Alex."

At the last name, she looked mutinous and her eyes definitely flickered as she said reluctantly, "I promise."

"I mean it, Katalin," I said urgently. "I don't want you and Alex putting your heads together over this, because you will only make it worse!" I paused as she took that in and then, to clinch the matter, I added, "And if you ever doubt that, consider your own reservations — better still, consider István's! — about welcoming Lajos Lázár into the family!"

She was forced to concede the point, but somehow the victory did not make me happy.

*

I had not planned to visit the Lázárs that day. I was merely walking, making the most of the solitude I had gained by Elisabeth's rare desire to spend the afternoon with her children. In fact, I was skirting the village, deep in my own thoughts, when I ran into Eszter.

She had just taken some food up to her sons who were working in one of the top fields, and her face was pleasantly flushed from her exertions in the heat of the sun. I didn't mind giving up my solitude for Eszter, so I was quite happy to accept her invitation to go home with her. We sat on the little porch while she mended shirts and I let the peace and beauty of the day wash over me.

In a little, Lázár appeared, saying with some glee that he had worked hard enough for one day. I smiled, for only last summer he and his sons had laboured all the hours of daylight. But that was before the Revolution. Now they were no longer required to work four days a week on the Count's land, to the inevitable neglect of their own.

Lázár sat down, throwing his hat on the ground and smiling his welcome to me. Most of the time he forgot I was related to the Szelényis; only occasionally he seemed to remember my place in society with a shock. But they still called me Miss Katie, which I liked, although the castle servants had adopted a more respectful form of address.

Eszter had just stood up to fetch him a drink when we heard the excited cries of a child running at top speed through the length of the village. Amused, we all leaned out of the porch to see what it was all about. It was a peasant boy of perhaps ten years, waving his worn old hat in the air and joyfully shouting something that I eventually made out to be, "He's coming! He's coming!"

"Who's coming, boy?" Lázár asked severely, but for once the child was not intimidated.

"*Lajos* is coming! Your son!"

My hand crept to my throat, as if to still the sudden jumping of my heart. I wanted so very badly to see him; yet I was afraid to the point of panic. I wondered if I could escape before he arrived in the village...

"We saw him from Odon's west field," the boy was explaining, "and I was sent to tell you, and the others have run to the other fields..."

Lázár had reached out to grab the boy by the shirt. "Are you sure?" he demanded hoarsely. "Is it *definitely* my son?"

"Oh yes," the boy panted. "By himself, riding on a big black horse. He even shouted a greeting to us! It *is* him!"

Lázár looked at his wife, who was clasping her hands together with something approaching rapture. Almost as breathless as the boy, she said now, "Have you strength left, Dániel? Go on to the square where the other boys are playing, and tell them to run up to the top field to make sure Zoltán and Károly know their brother is home..."

Grinning, the child ran off again, his legs a little wobbly, but still willing. Eszter threw her arms around her husband, as the village women began to come out into the street, loudly congratulating the Lázárs on the return of their hero son. Amazed, I followed Eszter out of the garden, watching the uneven line of men streaming in from the fields.

Petöfi might have been ignominiously run out of his home town on election day, but no opposition in the world could make Szelényi act in a similar fashion to Lajos. The whole village was turning out to welcome him home! My heart swelled with pride in him, with gladness in the pleasure it must bring him. Only I was out of place here.

I touched Eszter's arm. "I shall go now."

She looked surprised. "Won't you stay to welcome Lajos?"

"I'm sure you wish to be private..."

She laughed. "With *this?*" she exclaimed, waving her hand around the busy street. And I saw that if I wished to avoid a fuss, I would have to stay. I didn't know whether or not I was glad of it.

By the time Lajos rode into the village, he had collected a rowdy escort of peasants who were striding along beside his horse, all laughing and talking at once. I couldn't see his face at that distance, but I would have known his figure anywhere — nonchalant yet graceful in the saddle as he held his tired horse to a walk with one hand, and bent his blond head to talk to his companions. One of them presumably directed his attention for suddenly he straightened and saw the welcoming crowd.

Spontaneously, the villagers surged forward to meet him with loud, almost hysterical cheers. Eszter and Lázár held back, waiting, but I saw the tears of joy glistening proudly on her lashes and I wished desperately for so uncomplicated a love.

Lajos was laughing, reaching down his hand to shake those of his old friends.

"This is ridiculous," I heard him say. "I feel like Jesus Christ!"

And then Zoltán and Károly came running to join us, breathless from their sprint down from the fields. I thought they had come too quickly to have been brought by Eszter's messengers: they must have seen Lajos coming from their vantage point on the hill. Károly laughed from pure high spirits and dashed at once into the crowd, pushing his way through to his brother, though Zoltán, I noticed, hung back.

"Here, let me off my donkey," Lajos was saying, continuing the Palm Sunday image, and I watched him slide easily to the ground and embrace Károly. He was smiling, at ease, apparently delighted with his welcome, yet refusing to take it seriously. And even this, calculated or not, added to his charm.

At the Lázárs' house, the procession stopped and the crowd parted respectfully for the hero to meet his family. Zoltán had moved forward almost instinctively, I thought, but it was left to Lajos to close the gap between them, which he did easily, coming to a halt in front of him.

"Well, little brother," he said carelessly, holding out his hand. A smile touched Zoltán's sulky lips.

"Well, dwarf," he retorted, taking the hand in a hard grip. Lajos cast an arm around his shoulders, and they went forward together.

And then Eszter was there, in his arms, hugging him unrestrainedly, and my throat was dry with longing and jealousy. I remembered so well the feel of that warm, rough cheek against *my* hair. The scene before me grew hazy. I had to exert every ounce of control to pull myself together, to blink away the tears, slowly, before they betrayed me.

Unobtrusively, I stepped away from Lázár, but I was hemmed in by the hedge and by the crowd; I could not escape entirely. I should have been stronger and forced myself to leave when the news first came.

It was a long moment before he released his mother. Smiling, wet-eyed, she led him by the hand to his father. Since I had returned to Szelényi, Lázár's attitude to his most difficult son had been so proud that I had imagined this meeting between them would be easy, however fraught their reunions of the past. But now I saw it wasn't easy at all.

Lázár was glowering, and though I was sure it was only to hide his excessive emotion, it was hardly a warm welcome. He made no movement towards his son, and I sensed a slight tension in Lajos, a sort of still watchfulness, as he met his father's fierce eyes. But all his life, Lajos had been having these encounters with Lázár and over the years, it seemed, he had learned how to cope.

"You're home early," he observed conversationally. "I expected you to be still in the fields."

"Why should I be?" said Lázár aggressively. Then, slowly, an almost mischievous smile dawned on his severe face. "No robot!"

Even as Lajos's lips curved in spontaneous response, a cheer went up at Lázár's words. Positively grinning now, Lázár embraced his son, and I had a glimpse of Lajos's face over his father's shoulder, his eyes closed as if in relief. He looked desperately tired suddenly, and I ached to soothe and comfort him to sleep...

For a moment his fingers showed white as they gripped Lázár's shoulders. Then Lajos's eyes opened. He was smiling again as he was released. I wished someone would stand between me and the Lázárs, but it was too late. Almost casually, Lajos's eyes met mine. I forced calmness into my face, praying that the result was not just wooden. His own face betrayed no surprise beyond a faint twitch of one eyebrow. Slowly, he inclined his head. I did the same.

We had exchanged this same, meaningless gesture in the Pilvax, the day Vasvári had sent the artisans away. Painfully, I remembered the times when he had smiled at the sight of me, that quick, spontaneous quirk of the lips that had seemed so personal.

For a second longer he held my gaze, and then, quite carelessly, he turned back to his family and friends; and I, released, lifted a trembling hand to my throat. With instinctive good manners, the villagers were dispersing, leaving the Lázárs alone, but with loud promises of festivities in the evening. I melted away with them. None of the Lázárs now would notice that I had gone.

On the day of Captain Zarescu's expected arrival in Szelényi, it rained. Katalin, who had risen early from pure excitement, was extremely irritated: there were less excuses for going outside in such weather. I sympathized, and said with perfect truth that I was sure she would find a way.

She burst into my room late that afternoon, as I was changing my dress for the evening. Her eyes were gleaming with such joy and mischief that my heart sank. I knew before she told me that she and Alex were proceeding with their highly questionable "holiday" together. The only thing which did surprise me was that she was prepared to go at all when Alexandru's reason for the journey was political — he was going to Nagyzseben to talk with the Romanian nationalists.

"You'll hate it," I said with conviction.

"No, I won't, for I shan't be at their wretched discussions."

"Then you'll be bored while he is away!"

"Well, that's where you fit in, dear niece."

I regarded her warily. "I?"

She smiled sunnily. "Of course. You were right in Kolozsvár — I can't travel alone; but it would be quite proper if you were with me."

"No," I said repressively, "it would not."

"*More* proper, then."

"Forget it, Katalin," I said with finality. "I have quarrelled often enough with your father. I'm not coming."

Undeterred by this steadfast utterance, she dragged me off that evening to speak to Alex himself. Though I confess I approached their rendezvous a little warily — more than half-expecting to find Lajos with him — it was a solitary figure who lurked in the wood, and he was quite clearly Captain Zarescu's shape. He greeted me like an old friend, and then, even more worryingly, thanked me for agreeing to help them.

"I have not," I said repressively, "agreed to help. And I won't. I had thought better of you, Alex."

"I mean nothing improper," he assured me, a little anxiously. "It's just that we never see each other. This last year has been hell for both of us, with Katalin so hemmed in for fear of her meeting me..."

"I know that," I interrupted, "and I'm sorry for it, but truly, this is not the way..."

"Once, I thought that too. I was very scrupulous over the sort of clandestine meetings I arranged. Given the circumstances, I think we have both behaved with honour."

I nodded wordlessly, and he went on, "But now I have come to believe that whatever Katalin and I want is the only right worth considering. So," He took a deep breath. "I want Katalin to come with me to Nagyzseben. We both need this time. And it would be so much better for her if you would come too. Please."

He took my hand. I looked up into his huge, velvet, sad eyes — and even I could not remain unmoved by their appeal. He must have read my acquiescence in my face, because his eyes lightened, and he raised my hand to his lips.

"I had a spaniel like you once," I said unkindly, gracelessly pulling my hand free. And Katalin, sensing her victory, laughed and hugged me in an excess of joy.

Bumping painfully over the hard, dried mud of the road leading south from Besztercze, I thought I must have been stark raving mad to agree to this extra, unnecessary journey. We were travelling in the oldest coach possessed by the Szelényis, since its crest was rubbed and faded into something pale and indistinguishable. Astonished that his sister should choose to visit in so unstylish a vehicle, István had remarked that he hoped it would bear the strain, to which Katalin had calmly replied that Mark had assured us it was quite safe, and that for her part, she would feel much more comfortable travelling in these days of revolution *without* the Szelényi arms emblazoned on the carriage for the world to see. That, at least, was true, though not for the reasons István was led to believe!

Mark drove the carriage, while Katalin and I sat inside with Ilse; and Mattias, refusing to be cooped up all day, rode on horseback beside us.

Poor Mattias, having only just arrived in Szelényi, had been harassed and cajoled against his better judgement — much as I had — into joining the expedition when the Count had refused point blank to allow us to travel anywhere without the escort of at least one male member of the family. Even Katalin's desperate excuse that Laure Kossary — whose family we were meant to be visiting — had only invited the two of us, failed to dissuade him in this, so we were forced to initiate Mattias into the secret. Though at first his eyes had shown an alarming tendency to pop, he had been gradually beaten down and persuaded to lend his reluctant countenance to the proceedings. On reflection, I thought it was a good thing, for if this ever came out, then at least Mattias's presence lent us respectability.

"There it is," said Katalin suddenly, holding on to her elegant hat as she poked her head out of the window. "Mark!" she shouted. "We'll stop here!"

And the coach swerved off the road and up to the dilapidated, one-storey inn where she had, apparently, arranged to meet Alex.

"Thank God we're not obliged to put up here," I murmured, eyeing the building with disfavour.

"Well, we can't stop anywhere we are known," Katalin said reasonably, and I sighed, looking forward to a series of such primitive accommodation, and followed her out of the carriage.

"There he is at the window!" Katalin exclaimed joyfully, and flew up to the house. I exchanged looks with Mattias, who grinned, lightly dismounting and handing the reins to a bemused looking individual I could only suppose was the ostler.

"I think," I said firmly, "I shall wait out here."

"Quite right," Mattias agreed. "That pair are enough to give you indigestion *before* you've eaten!" And he sauntered off after the ostler, presumably to make sure the man knew what to do. I didn't blame him.

While a boy brought water for the carriage horses, I left Ilse and Mark to supervise, and walked a little way back towards the road. A low wall round the inn yard provided me with a seat from which I could gaze around me at the flat fields and the distant hills. I decided I wasn't sorry to have come, despite the awful roads — though I might well change my mind if this ever came to my grandfather's ears...

A shadow fell across me, distracting me from my own thoughts, and I turned, already smiling to greet Alexandru. For a moment, the sun was in my eyes, blinding me, and then I saw that it glinted not on black hair but on blond, and my stomach tried to jump into my throat.

In panic, I stumbled to my feet.

"Lajos!" My voice was hoarse. I swallowed. "What are you doing here?"

He moved, and now I could see him clearly. He was looking surprised, though his eyes were as watchful as ever.

"I? I'm going to Nagyzseben, of course."

CHAPTER THIRTY

Oh no, I thought stupidly, this is not fair.... Beyond Lajos's shoulder, Katalin had appeared, nervously smiling. It was easy to see she had known all along. No wonder Mark had been so easily persuaded to accept our change of plan — like everyone in the village, he would do anything for Lajos.

Blindly, I pushed past them both, walking quickly back to the coach. I saw Alex wave cheerfully from the inn door, and could barely lift my hand to reply. I was shaking as I pulled myself into the carriage, as much with anger at Katalin as with the unexpectedness of coming upon him unprepared.

I have to get out of this, I thought wildly.

Almost timidly, Katalin was climbing in after me. "Katie? Please, don't be angry..."

"You should have told me," I ground out. "How dare you do this, Katalin? How dare you?"

Abruptly, I turned away from her frightened eyes, staring sightlessly out of the window instead.

She touched my arm. "I thought you would like it, if only you didn't have to admit it — Katie, I'm sorry, I didn't mean to upset you..."

"I told you not to interfere!" I said fiercely. "I suppose you have told Alex..."

"No, I swear I told him nothing. Lajos was always coming."

"Well, he had better have a horse because I will not travel..."

The sight of him just then, mounting a black horse in front of the inn door, finally closed my mouth. I tried to pull myself together, realizing at last that I was betraying altogether too much to Katalin and achieving nothing.

But only when the coach had rumbled and bumped through the village did I realize what I should have done. I should have left them there, pleaded illness and gone home. Instead, I had doomed myself to a week of this torture. It seemed I was incapable of staying away from him; but then, I always had been.

We stopped for the night at an inn remarkably similar to the one at which we had met Alex and Lajos. By then, I had myself better in hand, and although Katalin was still regarding me rather warily, I was able to behave in much my usual manner while we ate. Lajos and Mattias kept up a witty barrage of conversation, to which I was obliged to contribute only a few sardonic remarks. For the most part, I was thankful to have the attention off me, for I still felt my mask liable to crumble with the strain.

After the meal, I left them in the inn's so-called parlour. I said I was going to bed with a slight headache; but I didn't. I went outside into the last of the evening's sunshine, and walked until I could no longer see the inn.

I found a clear, bubbling stream where I cooled my burning cheeks, and then sat down by its side to try to find some way of dealing with the next week. I was still in the same position, chin in hand, gazing unseeingly into the water, when he found me.

"Katie?" He was on the bank behind me. I looked up at him, over my shoulder, not surprised, somehow, just wishing he would go away. "Are you all right?"

"Yes," I said distantly. I thought he hesitated, but then he moved forward, jumping down beside me. I turned away.

"I'm sorry," he said quietly. "I didn't mean to startle you. I assumed you knew I was coming."

I didn't bother denying the shock. It didn't seem worthwhile. Instead, I said rudely, "Do you really imagine I would be here if I had known?"

I wasn't looking at him, but still I knew the rueful, upward curve of his lips as he said, "I hoped you would."

This was unbearable. Abruptly, I got to my feet. "It doesn't matter," I muttered, walking away from him; but I hadn't taken more than a few steps before his voice stayed me as effectively as a chain.

"Katie."

I paused, not moving, but not turning back either. I heard the ground rustle under his feet, felt his fingers, light, unthreatening, on my arm. In the failing light, I allowed myself to face him and his hand fell away, though his eyes held me even more securely. I tried to summon the strength I knew I would need for these moments: I only hoped they would be brief.

He said gently, "Won't you stay and talk to me a little?"

I swallowed, shaking my head. "There is no more to say."

"But there is. I have many things to say, things which should have been said in March, if only you would have let me."

I knew I should turn and walk away, but I couldn't. I only stared mutely up into his eyes and waited for whatever was to come next.

"Oh Katie, there shouldn't be all this hurt and anger between us," he said ruefully. "Not through misunderstanding..."

I was almost relieved that I could be strong. I even felt a tinge of the old anger as I interrupted, "I didn't mistake you, Lajos."

"But you did," he said at once. "We both did, though I admit it was my fault. I was lost in my own dreams of perfection; oblivious, perhaps, to yours."

I dragged my gaze free. His eyes had always compelled belief, collusion. "I don't understand," I said flatly.

"When I asked you to come to me without marriage, it wasn't from contempt, Katie..."

At that, I rallied. I even looked at him again. "Of course not," I said politely. "It was, perhaps, a sign of respect?"

"Yes," he said seriously. "We were so close that night on the Erzsébet Island, that it never entered my head that you might not like to live exactly as I did."

"Your mistake, Lajos," I said quietly.

"Yes," he agreed. "And yours was in misunderstanding my motives."

"I don't think so," I said contemptuously, turning quickly away, but again I felt his fingers on my arm, drawing me back, and I waited, afraid to hear, yet knowing I had to.

"But yes," he said gently. "You know me, Katie. I always follow my beliefs to their logical conclusion — I can't stop just because they have grown too uncomfortable or too difficult. So political freedom must mean nothing less than total democracy; and personal freedom must mean no ties of church or state constraining people to stay together — only choice. I don't need a priest to tell me who I may live with. I don't believe in God; I don't need His blessing, still less that of the men who consider themselves His tools on Earth."

He paused, giving me time to absorb it, then continued quietly. "So, ever since I was old enough to think of girls in that way, it has been my dream to find a woman I cared for, who would stay with me freely, from choice, without these other ties or constraints."

My eyes fell away. I had thought that I had felt every hurt I could over Lajos, but for some reason the knowledge that I was so far from his dream made a new wound that seemed too sharp and painful to bear.

His relentless voice went on. "I didn't want someone who would stay from duty or convention or convenience, or even from self-interest." At that, I managed to cast him a look of mocking derision, but he only smiled. "You think that's vanity talking? But I assure you, in some circles I am considered quite a catch. For a peasant girl to marry a lawyer — however lowly his birth — is considered social promotion."

Oddly, I had never thought of that before. I wondered how many girls in Szelényi had set their caps at Lajos simply for the chance of going with him to the city, of mixing with his noble and semi-noble friends — and of being able to come home again and crow over their own former neighbours and pity them their ordinary husbands.

Just for a second, I thought it might have hurt as well as irritated him.

"I take your point," I said quickly, "but what sort of woman do you imagine would accept your kind of proposal?"

His lips moved. "I had hoped you would."

I felt my skin flush, but I forced myself to meet his gaze. "Whatever I may have led you to believe," I said quietly, "I am not a slut."

And suddenly his face broke into a smile so tender that in spite of myself, my heart reeled. "Oh Katie, I know what you are! You are a child of your time and your upbringing, and I was a fool not to consider that. I was thinking then in leaps and bounds, of too many things and with too much euphoria. But by all I hold dear, I never meant to insult you." His fingers, rough and warm, touched my hand, held it while he watched me intently. "Do you believe that?"

I swallowed. "Perhaps. But I cannot believe you are so impractical! Unless your taste runs to sluts, Lajos, I doubt you will ever find your dream."

A faint frown had appeared on his brow. "Why do you keep talking of sluts? Do you think of yourself like that because we made love on Erzsébet Island?"

From time to time, that was exactly what I had thought; but mostly I had only used it as a lash to take away the real pain, and now, I couldn't think it at all. There was no shame at what I had done, though it went against everything I had been taught, everything I had always known to be right. Wordlessly, I shook my head. For some reason I could feel tears very close, and I was appalled.

"Then why," said Lajos softly, "would you be a slut if we made love every night of our lives? Believe me, there is nothing I would like better."

With a gasp of outrage, I tore my hand free, stumbling away from him, but again he caught me, holding my trembling shoulders in his firm, gentle hands. This time I would not turn to face him, but I felt his mouth very close to the back of my head as he murmured soothingly behind me. "Katie, wait; there's no need to run away again. I'm only trying to explain to you that if you had come with me then, you would have been just as chaste as a wife — more so than many!"

Like a tamed animal, I felt my agitation fade under his calm voice, and as if he sensed that, his hold slackened a little. His voice was peculiarly grave as he added, "I'm sorry. I think I've made you very unhappy. I even heard you were ill while I was in Kolozsvár — I hope that was not my fault too."

Though he was unable to see my face, I closed my eyes tightly. "No," I lied flatly. There was a slight pause while I wondered wildly if he believed me. I couldn't bear the emotional strain of this conversation for much longer

Then he said, "If it's any consolation, I've been miserable too."

"You never appeared so." I meant it to be light, dry, but even to my own ears it only sounded wistful. His fingers gripped suddenly tighter.

"You, of all people, should understand my not wearing my heart on my sleeve. But I worked too feverishly on too many things, and became so ill-natured that I fell out with all my friends."

"I'm sure you got round them again," I retorted.

"What use is that?" he said quietly. "When I don't have you?"

For a second, it seemed my heart did not beat at all. Before I could control it, a tear spilled under my lashes and rolled down my cheek. Involuntarily, I had half-turned towards him, whispering brokenly, "I'm not your dream, Lajos — that much is obvious..."

"But you are," he said immediately. Too late, I tried now to avoid his gaze, but I was turned inexorably, forced to look up into his face. With terrible gentleness, he touched the tear on my cheek, brushing it away, reminding me unbearably of the time I had left him in the little room in Pest when I had first discovered the precise nature of his plans for me.

"Before you, the dream had no shape," he said softly, "no personality. I had no idea what this woman I thought I wanted would look like, or be like." He smiled deprecatingly. "Except, of course, that she would love me to distraction."

"How could she not?" I said sweetly, and saw his eyes crinkle in a rare, full smile.

"Exactly. But then I met you, and nothing else mattered." The smile was dying in his eyes, leaving them wonderfully tender, almost mesmerizing, as he added softly, "You know, you became an obsession with me, and only you could not see it..."

"Lajos, stop it," I whispered, longing and afraid to believe, just as before. His fingers caught my chin and held it, as if to prevent my escape.

"No, let me finish this time. I know — I always knew — the value of what you gave me that night on the island, because it was even more precious to me." His hand moved, caressing my cheek, my hair, and astonishingly, I felt its unsteadiness. "Katie, it's you I want; you as you are, not some meaningless dream. And I want you on any terms you will have me. I can't help being indifferent to religion, but if a priest is important to you, we'll have a priest. Only stay with me."

Vaguely, I knew the birds were singing their final song of the day in the trees above us. A small, shy creature scurried past my feet, but I never moved a muscle. At last, I swallowed.

"Lajos," I said carefully; though my voice was hoarse, spoiling the effect, I had to ask. After all, I had been wrong before. "Lajos, are you, after everything you have just told me about your dream, and freedom, asking me to marry you?"

His lips quirked. "Yes."

"But you don't wish to be married!"

"I want to be with you — that is enough." His head bent closer to mine; his thumb was on my lips, lightly exploring as he murmured, "And you, Katie? Do you not still care for me a little?" Feather-light, his lips brushed against mine, barely touching, yet causing everything in me to leap towards him.

"Lajos, this isn't fair," I whispered, and the tears were prickling again behind my lashes. To my surprise, he drew back a little.

"Don't you wish to marry me?" he asked gently.

"Oh, how can I? Once, in March, I would have given up everything, everyone, to marry you, and never have thought it the slightest sacrifice! But now, so much has happened..."

"Nothing that matters."

"I've taught myself to live without you, Lajos," I said seriously. "Without the hope of you. You can't do this to me again..."

"But are you happy?" he interrupted.

I looked away. "That's not the point."

"It's exactly the point." He took my face between his hands, gazing down at me in a way that melted my very bones. "I'll make you happy, Katie, I promise..." And his mouth took mine, as if sealing his word, while I hung from him and let the gladness flow through me, healing the long months of pain, filling my emptiness.

But still I could not give in like this, on a tide of emotion, without thought or reflection. Somewhere, I was still afraid of being carried away by feeling, as I had on Erzsébet Island. This time, I had to be sensible.

Carefully, I freed my mouth. "I need time, Lajos," I said huskily. "Time to think."

I felt his hands move on my back, caressingly. His eyes were warm, knowing. I think we were both aware that there was only one answer I could give, and that he could convince me to give it there and then if he chose; but he was always generous in triumph.

"Have your time, Katie," he said softly. "I'll still be here." He released me, but only to take my hand and kiss it. Now, suddenly, I was shy of him, flushing under his steady gaze.

"I should go back," I said breathlessly, and he smiled, drawing my hand through his arm.

"Come then; I'll walk with you."

The remainder of the journey was unexpectedly hilarious; largely, I suspect, because we were all conscious of doing wrong. An air of mischief, of daring, hung around us, infecting us with an excitement that was almost joyous. Before long, I even forgot to worry that Katalin or Mattias might see the change in me, for my own sudden happiness seemed to blend harmoniously into all the rest

As we came nearer to Nagyzseben, Lajos and Alex showed a tendency to lapse into a continuing debate about how best to approach the Romanians.

"Who exactly is it you are going to speak to?" I asked curiously over our meal, late the next afternoon.

"In the first place, a man called Avram Iancu," Alex said. "He is an apprentice lawyer and, like Lajos, a peasant's son. He has grown impatient with petitions and committees. In fact he has started recruiting a small army."

I stared at him, seriously alarmed. "For what purpose?"

"That is one of the things we need to talk about," Lajos said wryly. "He means to use it against the Hungarians, to win autonomy for the Romanian nation within Transylvania."

"But surely he could never win such a fight!" I exclaimed.

"Not alone," Lajos agreed, pushing his empty plate away from him. "But if they unite with the Austrians..."

"They wouldn't!"

"They would. They are already negotiating with General Puchner, believing the King will give them everything they want while the Hungarians only grind them under foot."

I took a deep breath. It seemed I had been so involved in myself over the last weeks that I hadn't even had an inkling of the danger threatening this country, just when things had begun to improve, when there was at last genuine hope for the future. Just like Katalin, just like me, the people were no longer satisfied with a little; they wanted *everything* to be right.

"What can you do?" I asked simply.

Lajos shrugged. "Persuade them that the Hungarians *will* listen."

I smiled. "You make it sound very simple, very easy."

"It will be anything but," Lajos said ruefully.

CHAPTER THIRTY-ONE

We arrived at the inn on the outskirts of Nagyzseben around noon. Stepping down from the carriage, I saw a young man come out of the inn and walk quickly up to Alex who, with Lajos and Mattias, had just dismounted.

By any standards, the newcomer was arresting. Dark, strong featured, grave, moving with decisiveness and swift economy, he seemed to be little older than Mattias, despite the stern expression on his handsome face. As Katalin and I approached the men, I saw his grimness vanish suddenly in a smile of genuine welcome.

"Zarescu!" he exclaimed, and then he was embracing Alex, speaking quickly in Romanian. Alex grinned, though he replied in Hungarian.

"It's good to see you too! But let me introduce my friends." He moved to allow the other men a better view of the stern youth. "Gentlemen, this is Avram Iancu. Iancu — Lajos Lázár."

Lajos went forward with his usual, casual grace and for a moment the two young men, so different in appearance and character, yet not so very far apart in either personal or political background, silently assessed each other. Then Iancu slowly held out his hand.

"I've heard of you," he said in Hungarian. Lajos took the hand, and for an instant I saw a flicker of surprise cross Iancu's face — perhaps because the hard roughness of Lajos's fingers could only come from manual labour. Lajos quickly introduced Mattias, and as Iancu moved to shake hands, he caught sight of Katalin and me. This time, his surprise was definite.

Iancu bowed slightly in our direction, saying, "And are these ladies your wives?"

I couldn't help it. I laughed. I have never been a great deal of use in diplomacy. However, Alex, who had just noticed our arrival upon the scene, was already saying, "Forgive my bad manners! No, this lady is Szelényi's sister," — his chin went up a little — "and my fiancée. And this is Miss Kettles, their niece from Scotland."

I could tell from Iancu's interested gaze that he knew something of Katalin already. However, he greeted us both with perfect politeness and ushered us into the inn, saying to Zarescu, "I have only reserved two rooms for you, but the house isn't busy — I'm sure there will be no difficulty..."

There was none, though again Katalin and I shared a chamber, where we combed our hair and freshened ourselves a little before rejoining the men in the coffee-room downstairs. I had no idea whether or not we would be welcome there, but I was extremely curious as to how Lajos would be received by Iancu and his friends and how he would win them over. For some reason, I never doubted that he would succeed.

"Are we *de trop?*" Katalin asked brightly — and just a little hopefully — as Alex came to meet us. He had been sitting at a corner table with Lajos, Mattias, Iancu and another two respectably dressed men, also young and serious. It reminded me a little of the Pilvax Café; though the surroundings were rougher, I was sure the debates would be similar.

"Not in the least," Alex answered, leading us across to the table. "This isn't a formal meeting; it's only introducing Lajos to Iancu and a couple of his friends. You will be very welcome."

The men certainly greeted us civilly when we were presented and sat down at the end of the table, beside Alex and opposite Iancu, who said, as he took his own seat, "Are you interested in our politics, ladies?"

"In these times, isn't everyone?" I answered lightly.

"Even a lady from so far away as Scotland?"

Beside me, Lajos turned and said lazily, "I think you will find Miss Katie a perceptive and impartial observer — half Magyar but wholly sensible."

I flushed slightly, though perhaps the staid compliments were hardly the ones a woman most wishes to hear from the man she loves. Everyone's eyes were upon me, which was not in the least what I had intended, and I thought Iancu was both scathing and challenging.

"So what does she think of the Romanian cause?" he said.

This, I thought, is quite unfair. I should not have been put in such a position — but then, I had chosen to insinuate my company. I took a deep breath.

"I think that you have long had just cause for complaint," I said truthfully. "That you have every right to expect equality with other nations. And that you should not fall out with your friends in pursuit of that equality."

"But who are our friends?" Iancu pounced. I didn't look at Lajos.

I said slowly, "I would say, those who at least profess to believe in equality."

Iancu's gaze turned on Lajos, who, I found, was looking at me, the faintest smile playing on his lips. His head moved unhurriedly to face Iancu.

"*I* believe in equality," he said quietly. "I believe wholeheartedly, and without exception."

"I know," Iancu said impatiently. "But you do not speak for all Hungarians."

Lajos shrugged. "I would be the first to admit that there are flaws in Hungarian friendship, but at least there is a *will* to believe in equality, even if it stumbles over tradition and prejudice. I'm sure you don't imagine that the King can even *allow* himself to think about such a thing — it would, after all, put him out of work."

That won an involuntary smile from Iancu, and from one of the other Romanians, but the other, who was addressed by his friends as Petru, uttered something in his own language. I don't know what he said, but I had the impression he was not complimenting Lajos. Lajos, however, replied to him at once, in fluent, unhesitating Romanian. Petru flushed under his steady gaze and was silent.

Alex said uneasily, "Perhaps for today, in consideration of the ladies and Szelényi, we could continue to speak in Hungarian? Tomorrow, of course, we shall use our own language. As you hear, my friend is quite proficient."

"It is unusual," Iancu remarked, "in a Hungarian."

Lajos shrugged. "I have friends of all races, and I pick up languages easily."

"Did Zarescu teach you?"

"No. I learned from people in the next village to mine, but certainly I learned more refinement from Alex." His lip quirked. "It seems to me that language should not be permitted to become a barrier between peoples. After all, it is the best means we have of communication."

Iancu regarded him with amusement. "You are very glib. You must be an excellent lawyer."

"I choose my cases with care."

"Are we to believe you choose to defend our language?" Petru asked sceptically, and Lajos turned on him with a look of unexpected haughtiness.

"I would have brought proof if I'd known it was required. But I have, in fact, written several articles to that effect."

"He means no disrespect," Iancu said quickly. "But there are few Hungarians who do not despise our language."

"I know many," Lajos said at once. "And I have read pieces in Hungarian journals praising the beauty of Romanian."

"Articles written by your friends."

Lajos acknowledged it, but said, "I have many friends."

Iancu shifted impatiently in his seat. "Radicals! The 'Pest youth!' But what power do they — do you — actually have?"

Lajos's lips curved. "Not long ago, I believe we changed the government of Hungary, won autonomy from Vienna, abolished censorship, serfdom..."

"The radicals alone did not do that," Iancu interrupted.

"No, but without us, it would never have happened at all. Kossuth — and even Batthyány — admit that, and they still acknowledge our influence. You see, we follow our ideas to their logical end — don't we, Katie?"

I knew precisely what he meant and was both outraged and amazed that he could think here about our private conversations. But he only cast a swift, mocking glance in my direction before returning to his point.

"Iancu, you are not so isolated as you think. Have you heard of the Society for Equality? Our aim is to eradicate the barriers of race as well as of class, because we acknowledge that the cause of freedom is common to all, and that we can only achieve it together. United."

When Lajos spoke like that, no one could doubt his sincerity; you were forced to believe him, and I could see his effect on the Romanians. At last, in the thoughtful silence that followed, they dragged their eyes from Lajos to exchange glances with each other.

Then Iancu said slowly, "Yet if the King offers us what we want, we would be foolish not to take it."

Lajos raised his brows. "I should be very wary what I accept from princes; they are notoriously untrustworthy."

Iancu smiled cynically. "I heard you were a republican."

"I am also a communist. But I'm not so foolish as to believe I can achieve everything overnight. I think you would find the King's equality among nations means us all struggling equally under the old systems of absolutism, serfdom, censorship and the rest. Vienna is courting Jelacic and the Croats to make trouble for Hungary; Puchner is trying to do the same here with you, because united, Hungary has the strength to win this struggle. Stay with us and you have hope — we all have. But if you and the other races turn against us, we all lose. For once Hungary is defeated, Vienna won't need you any more. We shall all be sinking in the same boat — all with nothing."

"You admit you need us," Iancu pressed eagerly.

"Freely. But you need Hungary too. Don't give up the revolution just because you haven't at once got everything you want. It's our only chance. And remember that the Romanian nation has friends and allies among the Hungarians."

Iancu was nodding slowly.

"There is sense in what he says," Petru allowed reluctantly. "We shouldn't break with Hungary, not without a great deal of thought." The other nodded emphatically, and Iancu looked from them to Lajos with a kind of rueful admiration.

"I'm not surprised Kossuth fears you! Will you speak to some of my colleagues tomorrow? Members of our Permanent Committee?"

"Gladly," said Lajos at once.

Iancu smiled and stood up. "Shall we eat?"

As we all rose and moved towards the private parlour which had been arranged for us, I found Lajos beside me.

"Quite a performance," I murmured cynically in English.

"That?" he said deprecatingly. "That was only the preliminary skirmish — but thank you for your opening volley."

"Don't mention it."

Conversation during dinner was conducted in a bewildering mixture of Romanian and Hungarian. As a result I only understood part of it, but the Romanian elements were not intended as rudeness to us, but simply as a necessity since the subject under discussion was Romanian literature — about which, naturally, Lajos knew as much as they.

Mattias, as much in the dark as Katalin or me, only grinned. "Ignorance is bliss," he remarked.

"But knowledge," I returned thoughtfully, my eyes on Lajos, "is power." For he was using his undoubted knowledge to impress Iancu and his friends, who were at first surprised that he was so aware of their heritage, and then, amazingly quickly, took it for granted. Earlier, he had won something of their trust. Now he was gaining their liking, and no one knew better than I how easy it was to like and trust him.

Food was passed down the table; wine flowed, and laughter, inevitably, followed. Under Lajos's beguiling leadership, ably assisted, of course, by Alex, the young Romanians relaxed, lapsing into banter instead of serious debate, applauding Lajos's clowning and eventually howling with glee at his wicked mimicry which spared no one.

At this point, I decided that Katalin and I should excuse ourselves so that the gentlemen could indulge their increasingly riotous humour uninhibited by female presence. Our hands soundly kissed, we retreated to our own chamber, from which we could still clearly hear a male voice raised in powerful tenor, singing an extremely questionable drinking song, and the roars of male laughter which greeted it.

Katalin was looking indignant. "That is Mattias!" she exclaimed, then suddenly giggled. "Do you think they will get any drunker?"

"Depend upon it," I said drily, climbing into bed. But I was all admiration for Lajos. He had planned it this way; it was how he won over his family and the villagers again after his long absences. And yet it was part of his charm that he did it with perfect sincerity — no one enjoyed these hilarious drinking sessions more than Lajos. Whatever else came out of them was only a bonus.

I lay awake for a long time, listening to Katalin's even breathing beside me, and thinking of Lajos. For the first time I allowed myself to dwell on what he had said to me the other night, using my brain instead of my heart, looking beyond the serenity and self-respect which he had given back to me.

I could not doubt the sincerity of his words, why should I? I couldn't believe he had made his offer purely from an attack of conscience. And yet, something in the whole situation did not ring true, causing a pang of unease to twist through my happiness. I loved Lajos. I could think of no greater joy than sharing my life with him. That he had asked me to be his wife, despite his dislike of the institution of marriage, surely proved that he loved me. Yet he hadn't ever said so.

I banished that last thought as foolish. If I was the fulfilment of his dream, however unlikely, then he loved me! There was no need to say it. I was loved. I was happy. Yet something was not right.

I thought of our future life together, of braving the Szelényi wrath, to say nothing of Aunt Edith's outrage; of living with Lajos as well as with his wretched cause — and it was then that I began to see the truth. If I married Lajos when he was so sincerely opposed to marriage, then I would have pushed him, entrapped him, as surely as if I had played some vulgar trick, like pretending I was with child, as Aunt Edith's maid had once done.

I tried to throw the thought away, to tell myself that none of that mattered, because he loved me. But it did matter. I would become the personification of the constraints of marriage which he so despised, until I too was held in contempt.

And I... Could I have any pride left if I married a man who did not want to marry me?

CHAPTER THIRTY-TWO

"I think you are very clever," I said truthfully the next morning, when Lajos asked my opinion. I took a sip of coffee. "But you can't get the whole Permanent Committee — which includes, I believe, two bishops — rollicking drunk."

Lajos's eyes were alight with sudden laughter; I didn't see how I could bear to give him up a second time.

Overhearing me, Alex was saying wryly, "Not on wine perhaps." And that gave me something else to focus on.

I regarded him curiously, "What will you do, Alex, if this fails? If your people break with Hungary, rebel...?"

His eyes flickered, but he said firmly, "We won't speak of failure, if you please!"

"No," Katalin agreed eagerly, but there was a new alarm in her eyes, as if she had never before contemplated this new obstacle to their happiness.

She was quiet and thoughtful all day. After Lajos and Alex had ridden off to meet Iancu, she and I, escorted by Mattias, strolled after them less hurriedly into Nagyzseben which was then a very neat, tidy town with wide, rather charming streets; though the very beauty of the valley surrounding it made it appear dull to me. Only once, Katalin interrupted our conversation to say abruptly, "Lajos *will* persuade them, will he not?"

"If anyone can, he will," Mattias agreed, looking at her in some surprise. "And even if he can't persuade all of them, at least he has your Zarescu safe for Hungary!"

I opened my mouth to dispute that, and then, unwilling to upset Katalin further, I closed it again. But I doubted very much if Lajos either would or could persuade Alex to stand against his own people.

It must have been an hour after I had retired when, still wakeful, I heard them come in. Alex was laughing. Then I heard Katalin's anxious voice, and her lover hushing her. All was well. The voices were cheerful. It seemed Lajos was successful.

When Katalin and I entered the parlour the following morning, we found Lajos and Mattias already there. In his shirt-sleeves and looking relaxed as he lounged in his seat against the wooden table, Lajos glanced up at us. "Thank God," he remarked flippantly. "I thought it was Alex with his sore head."

"Good morning to you too," I said affably. "Don't *you* have a sore head?"

"I never over-indulge," he said grandly. Mattias hooted derisively, but as I sat down, I reflected that I had only once ever seen him noticeably affected by drink. *"I believe I am intoxicated, but I don't think it's the wine..."*

Abruptly I shut off the memory, saying instead, "I presume you imbibed with Mr Iancu and his cronies?"

"Somewhat."

"Then you were celebrating? You were successful?"

"They listened," Lajos allowed. "All I have to do now is make Batthyány and Kossuth listen."

"It has never been a problem to you before," I said drily.

Just then Alex came in, a little woolly round the edges but still cheerful. Katalin regarded him indulgently and poured him a cup of coffee. However, he had barely lifted the cup to his lips when a sudden commotion outside was heard. A second later, a voice I recognized was raised impatiently in the house. We exchanged startled glances, and then the door burst open to reveal Avram Iancu. He was breathless and fierce, and his eyes seemed to be almost spitting with anger.

"So," he said bitterly, his wild gaze seeking and finding Lajos. "This is what your fine words and promises amount to!"

Slowly, Lajos got to his feet. "Tell me," he invited.

"Don't you know? Were you not sent to keep us off guard?"

"No one sent me." His eyes were wary now, as I had seen them before, and he uttered the denial mechanically, absently. "I don't know what you're talking about, Iancu, but you had better tell me before you burst."

Something in the calm humour of his voice seemed to soothe Iancu slightly. Abruptly, he came into the room, slamming the door behind him. Zarescu spoke sharply to him in Romanian, but he only shrugged irritably, still looking directly at Lajos.

"Baron Vay, your Commissioner for Transylvanian Affairs, has ordered the arrest of all members of the Permanent Committee. Is this the tolerance and equality you spoke of so eloquently?"

"Apparently not," Lajos said steadily. "So, are they all arrested?"

Iancu flung himself into the nearest vacant chair. I poured a cup of coffee and pushed it towards him. He drank it distractedly, almost without noticing.

"No," he said, laying down the cup. "They only found two at home — Laurien and Balasescu, but they are in prison, and that is bad enough!"

"Correct me if I am wrong," Lajos said slowly, "but Vay has no power to do that."

"Apparently he is acting on the specific instructions of your Minister of the Interior."

Lajos swore under his breath. I heard him though I could not understand the words. "Then he has no *right*," he said aloud. "And if I have learned one thing in the last year, it is that the power of the people is stronger than any one man."

Iancu frowned. "What do you mean?"

"I mean, go and get your friends out of prison. Raise as many people as you can quickly; fetch in the peasants — *and* the priests if they'll come."

Iancu stared. "You mean start the war now?"

My stomach lurched, but Lajos was saying, "Oh no, I don't think you need a war for a little matter like this." He sounded faintly amused, yet it struck me that he was angry.

"*Little* matter!"

"Yes, little. Fetch your crowd. Shout, demonstrate, threaten. I guarantee it works. I'll come with you, if you like — I'm very good at making noise."

Iancu swallowed, licking his dry lips convulsively and looking suddenly very young. "You would do this for us? Demonstrate against your own government?"

Lajos's lip twitched. "What do you think I have been doing all my life? In one cause or another."

In the first tiny inn of our return journey, while Katalin slept, I found myself gazing out on the night from our bed-chamber window, and thinking of Nagyzseben, of Lajos's purpose and his apparent success so stupidly marred by the arrests this morning.

Yet, as he had predicted so confidently, the demonstration, combined with threats of a general peasant uprising, had had its effect. The two Romanians were promptly released, and the peasants who had swelled the crowd were led home by their triumphant priests; so, surely that too had worked in Lajos's *personal* favour in the end, because he had been seen to be helping the Romanians against those who were regarded as his own people. Whatever the setbacks, he had it all in hand. He didn't need me...

Unhappily, I moved away from the window and lay down in the huge bed, but my mind was too active, too troubled to allow sleep. In the end, I decided to read, and had already relit the candle before I remembered that I had left my book in the coffee room. For a moment, I hesitated, then, taking up my shawl and the candle, I crept along the passage. I found my book with ease, but as I picked it up and straightened, I became aware of a silent, shadowy figure by the window. A single candle burned beside him and a book lay open on his knees, but he wasn't reading it. He was staring out into the night, much as I had done only minutes before. He hadn't even heard me come in.

For a moment, I hesitated, then, drawing my shawl more closely around me, I moved towards him. Still, he didn't turn.

"Lajos?" I said gently, touching his shoulder. He jerked quickly towards me, and I stepped back at once. "I'm sorry. I was afraid you were ill."

His impatient expression vanished. "Not at all. And don't apologise. Stay with me a while, if you are not tired."

In the dim light, I hesitated, then, calmly, I sat in the chair beside him and waited for him to speak.

"What did you think of Iancu?" he said at last, and I relaxed, for that seemed easy to answer.

"That he is very serious, and very young, and probably very dangerous." I thought he would laugh at the last description, but rather to my alarm, he only nodded.

"Yes. I thought so too."

"But you won him over," I pointed out.

He lifted one hand deprecatingly. "To some extent, perhaps." The candle-light flickered over his angular face, making his dark eyes appear very deep set and shadowed. "We achieved something. A little trust. A little understanding. Even a little friendship."

I looked at his averted, steady gaze, and felt rather bewildered.

"Then why are you so sad?" I asked gently. "Isn't that enough?"

His head turned to look at me, and what I saw in his eyes frightened me. "No, I don't think it is enough. I don't think it's nearly enough."

Instinctively, I stretched out and took his hand. And at last his lips moved into a semblance of the smile I loved. The hand I held turned and clasped mine. With the other, he reached out and touched my cheek caressingly.

"Katie," he said softly, "my sweet, my only comfort..."

Under his palm my skin burned. Now, I thought, now I should tell him my decision before I find it impossible to turn back. But his eyes, those dark, terrible eyes, kept me paralysed. He leaned forward, and my breath caught. I felt panic. I felt longing. And then his mouth softly kissed my forehead.

"Good night, Katie," he said quietly, and then he was on his feet, past me and gone before I could act on my crazy instinct to call him back.

When we resumed our journey in the morning, Lajos still seemed a little strange and preoccupied, but gradually, as we travelled through the beauty of the country, it seemed his spirits began to lift, and with him we all rose, though my own almost desperate happiness was hiding a deeper misery.

That night was the last of our stolen week. While we waited for supper to be cooked, I tactfully left Katalin and Alex alone together and went to my bed-chamber, where I did nothing but sit on the big, soft bed and think of how and when I could tell Lajos of my decision.

But that was taken out of my hands too. I heard a tap on the open door, and looked up quickly to see him strolling into the room. For a second I was paralysed. Then I found myself on my feet, starting towards him in panic.

"Lajos! What are you doing here? You can't...!"

"I wanted to see you."

"Not in my bed-chamber!" I said indignantly. But his eyes were laughing at me. "Lajos, I'm serious! It's — it's an invasion of my privacy!"

He was standing in front of me now, his dark eyes grown watchful.

"It's the sort of invasion I hope to do a lot more," he said quietly, and my gaze fell. I looked at my hands, twisting together before me until I stilled them deliberately. I could feel his eyes on me, as searching, as penetrating as ever, while he asked directly, "Have you had time to think, Katie?"

Defeated, I didn't even pretend to misunderstand him. I nodded.

"And?"

Slowly, I looked up at him again. I could see the texture of his skin, the deep, fine lines on his young face, his warm, steady dark eyes. Surely I should not have to do this....

"It — I — it is not possible," I said with difficulty, and as if he had expected some show of opposition, his lip quirked. Casually, he turned back and pushed the door closed with his foot, and then he came and took my hand; it jumped in his and was still.

"I think I can convince you that it is," he said softly.

"No," I said quickly, as he began to draw me into his arms. I was lost if he came too close. "You do not wish to be married."

He paused. "I told you. I wish to be with you — that is enough."

I shook my head. "Not for me. I couldn't live with you knowing I had *dragged* you to the alter. And I believe, in time, you would not be able to live with the woman who had made you abandon your principles and your freedom. I won't be your 'constraint', Lajos. I can't be."

He had gone very still. "That isn't how it would be."

"Yes," I said firmly. "It is."

"You're making this too complicated." There was an edge to his calm voice now, and I rejoiced in it, for part of me still longed to be beaten down, defeated, taken. But I smiled.

"Everything to do with you is complicated. I'm glad you told me what you did — I can't begin to tell you what a difference it makes to me. I think I can live with myself in peace now, but I couldn't live with you, Lajos, as your mistress or as your wife. Though I am honoured..."

"*Honoured?*"

He threw the word back at me with a revulsion that struck me like a blow. His face was suddenly white, his lips thin as I had never seen them, his whole bearing tense with an anger so fierce that it frightened me. "Do you think we're playing some silly, social game? I'm not one of your aristocratic puppies that can be turned off with any old piece of flattery — *so honoured by your proposal, kind sir!* — don't *ever* treat me that way!"

Appalled, trembling at the storm I had provoked, I was staring at him, at his unnaturally pale face, at his eyes which were hard and glittering with a tempestuous, dangerous passion. It was not the passion I had seen directed at me before — that had been warm, exciting; this was close to sheer fury.

"I didn't *mean* that," I said desperately. "I *truly* honour you — I always have. God knows I value every sign of affection you have ever given me, how much you will never know! But I cannot marry you, Lajos..."

He turned abruptly. My hand, which he almost flung away as if it burned him, fell uselessly back to my side as he strode towards the window. Miserably, anxiously, I watched his rigid back. I had never seen him like this before, never expected such a reaction. Listening to my own uneven breathing, I felt helpless, afraid.

At last, he turned to face me again. He was calmer, and the terrifying glitter had gone from his eyes, but it had been replaced by a contempt that pierced me through the heart.

"Don't give me that flummery, Katie," he said quietly. "The truth is, you are afraid of life, and make feeble excuses for not taking the chances which offer. You love me, but you would rather stay quietly where you are — bored, moping, miserable and *safe* — than risk anything for the sort of happiness you could have with me. And one day of that happiness is worth more than a lifetime of your tedious safety. But of course, you will never know that."

A small, mirthless smile tugged at his lips as he walked towards me. Shocked by his words, by the shattering, unacknowledged truths they contained, I backed away from him. But he came after me, still speaking, his words like so many slaps.

"One day you will have to risk something; you will *have* to reach out and grasp life with both hands before it passes you by. But it will have to be your decision, Katie — I'm damned if I'll make it for you, though we both know that I could."

For a moment, I was dragged into his arms. A brief, hard kiss was pressed on my gasping mouth, and then I was released. A second later he was gone, and I was alone.

Slowly, I turned and stared at the closed door. He was right. In his embrace, I would have agreed to anything and I hated myself for that weakness as well as for everything else. His words had stung me, shaken me, but I knew I was in the right. Besides, he had been hurt: *I* had hurt him, and some wicked, unamiable part of me rejoiced in that power to wound. But he had had no right to speak to me as he had, to say these things about me when I was only trying to look after us both.

I brushed my hand across my wet face, but it made no difference. The tears kept coming.

We parted at more or less the same spot as we had met more than a week ago. It was hardly a sad farewell, since Alex and Lajos would be in the village at least for the next few days, and I was not about to show anyone how I really felt about the ending of our adventure. My sardonic wit well to the fore, I bade a careless good-bye to our less reputable companions, and then Katalin and I were driven smartly into Beszterce, properly escorted by Mattias. We stopped briefly at a comfortable inn where the Szelényis were well known, and a little later drove on to the castle and the battlefield which awaited us.

CHAPTER THIRTY-THREE

The unthinkable had happened. We had been found out. The first we knew of it was when we stepped out of the carriage into the gathering dusk to see a footman hurrying down the steps towards us. Rather to my surprise, he hissed something to Mark on the box before bowing to us and remarking woodenly that the Count awaited us in the library.

It was the tone of his voice rather than the actual words which caused

Katalin and I to exchange glances of alarm. Being well brought up, we did not question him, but went on into the castle with sinking hearts. Mattias, however, had no such scruples. "Hopping mad, is he?" he asked ruefully behind us, and the footman answered in the affirmative, still perfectly wooden. Katalin looked at me again, her eyes dilating.

"Shall we go and change first?" she suggested anxiously. "In fact, if we go straight to bed, he might leave us alone till the morning."

I admit I was tempted, but in the end I said resignedly, "No, let's get it over with. Do you have any ear muffs?"

Katalin giggled nervously. "They wouldn't make any difference, not if he is really angry. I wonder how he found out?"

We discovered that almost immediately. Laure Kossary, Katalin's friend with whom we were supposed to be staying had, in fact, written asking to come and visit at Szelényi. The letter had arrived only yesterday, and the Count, torn between concern and curiosity, had finally opened it himself. As a result, though he had no idea where we were or whom we were with, he certainly knew where we were not.

The three of us stood before him like guilty school children while he waved the damning letter in our faces and, purple with anger, demanded to know where we had been. Mattias looked at the ceiling. Katalin shuffled her feet. I sighed.

"Nagyzseben," I said succinctly. The Count blinked.

"*Nagyzseben?*" he repeated blankly. "What the Devil is there in Nagyzseben? Apart from a parcel of Saxon and Romanian malcontents!"

I saw Katalin's eyes flicker to him and away. For a moment I hoped he might have missed her involuntary gesture — a tortuous and extremely plausible tale was already forming in my unprincipled brain — but he was still sharp-eyed. He stared at her.

"You wouldn't," he said unbelievingly, and I knew the game was over.

"Wouldn't what?" Katalin said defiantly.

"Did you go there to meet that Romanian nobody I sent about his business last year?"

"Captain Zarescu," I said helpfully.

"We know his name, Miss," my grandfather snapped. "I choose not to speak it!"

"Then you are being very foolish," I said calmly. "It was that same foolishness of yours that compelled us to act as we did. Since you will not permit Katalin to meet the man she loves in the respectable security of her home, she is driven to underhand methods. You must excuse Mattias, incidentally. He didn't know what we were about until too late, and then he felt obliged to stay with us to preserve — er — our reputations."

The Count's choleric eye turned on his son. "You should have brought them home immediately," he ground out.

"He couldn't," I said at once, "without causing a scene."

"So the pair of you cooked this whole thing up yourselves? Dragged you brother *and* the damned servants into it?"

"More or less," I said cautiously. "Ilse and Mark were in the same boat as Mattias — except, of course, that they are obliged to obey orders."

"Not when they are contrary to mine! I'll turn them off for this!"

"They didn't know," I said firmly, "that our orders were contrary to yours. I expect they thought we had just changed our minds."

"My God, this passes all bounds! Have you no shame? Either of you?"

"I have done nothing to be ashamed of, Papa," Katalin said valiantly. "Apart from lying to you, and it was *you* who forced us to those lengths. What is more, I should be obliged if you did not shout at Katie, for she was only trying to help me."

"*Help* you? I'll be surprised if she has not ruined you!" He swung suddenly on me with renewed venom. "Is this your revenge for my supposed slighting of Sofia?"

Anger stirred within me, but knowledge of my own guilt managed to quell it.

"No," I said calmly. "And I don't see how Katalin can be ruined when she had her brother, her maid *and* me with her for the entire journey."

The old man's face was draining of colour. I knew this to be a bad sign. From nowhere, I wondered if this time he really would fall down in an apoplexy and die.

"I suppose the whole scheme was yours?" the Count demanded.

"I suppose it was," I said thoughtfully.

"No," Katalin said at once, but I gave her a fierce, silencing look.

"Don't try to protect me," I said. "It's time to be honest now." I confess a slightly hysterical urge to laugh assailed me as I spoke those words, but my grandfather's reaction was far more overwhelming.

"*Honest?*" he exploded. "When have you ever been honest in your life? You *deceived* your way into my household, insinuated yourself into my family's affections, and now repay us with this disgusting, deceitful prank! But then, I should have known what to expect from the daughter of *your* parents!"

And suddenly, I couldn't help it. I was speaking before I even felt the resurgence of the old anger inside me. And I didn't just speak: I yelled like a fishwife, and quite as loudly as he; and everything came spilling out, all the pent-up resentment and rage of years, fed, I think, by all my suppressed emotions concerning Lajos. In any case, I lost control. I was only dimly aware of Katalin and Mattias standing open-mouthed on the edges of the scene while my grandfather and I abused each other at the pitch of our voices, sharing nothing except a white-hot fury.

I don't remember exactly what we said. I don't even remember leaving the room, but all at once I was standing in the hall, on the other side of the closed door, staring at it, shaking. My face felt both frozen and burning hot. My head was aching. Hazily, I wondered if I had gone mad.

When I rose in the morning I was still tired. My nerves still jangled from last night's outburst; but mingling with my shame for the truly awful things I had said was the odd remembrance that never in the entire fracas had my grandfather told me to go, and I had never once offered to. Perhaps, underneath everything, we did actually love each other...

At this point, a brief knock at the door heralded the arrival of Katalin.

"You're up early," I observed in surprise.

"Yes, I couldn't sleep. I came to say thank you."

"For what?" I asked distractedly, aiming the last hair pin with more hope than accuracy.

"For drawing his fire. Mattias and I were most impressed."

"Actually, I am not quite so selfless," I said ruefully, inserting the pin and dropping my arms to my side. "Do you think he will forgive me, if I apologise?"

"He likes apologies," Katalin said non-committally.

I looked at her directly. "Has he forgiven you?"

"I don't know. You rather took his mind off me. Mattias and the servants have been cleared of blame, though they still languish in the darkness of His Excellency's disapproval. I don't expect we shall be allowed over the door now without a chaperone, and that will no longer include each other."

"How sympathetic is Elisabeth?" I asked flippantly.

"Not very."

I sighed. It didn't seem worth mentioning Maria. "Come on. Let's face him again."

However, when we only encountered Mattias at the breakfast table, I couldn't help feeling relieved, for it never seemed to matter how contritely one began a scene with my grandfather, sparks always flew before the end of it.

It was as I left them to go to the nursery that I first became aware that something was not right. There were no servants around for one thing; but in addition, I was conscious of an inexplicable atmosphere of unease. I should not have been surprised, for my grandfather in a temper could cast a blight over the entire district; this just felt — different.

Passing the narrow staircase used by the servants, I paused, listening to the definite sounds of commotion drifting up to me. I knew it was trouble. I would have blamed it on Lajos, if he had not been with me over the past week.

A door slammed suddenly below, and the next instant a maid shot up the stairs towards me as if all the fiends in hell were after her. For a moment I thought they were. But it was only human beings who pursued her, fellow-servants, though from the sounds they made they were scarcely recognizable as such.

Before I could properly take it all in, the maid had crashed into me. Automatically, I caught her by the arms, but she leapt back with an animal cry of such terror that my hands fell back nervelessly to my sides. It was the timid maid who used to bring my coffee in the mornings; but even she had never looked so frightened before. She was trembling uncontrollably, her dark eyes hugely dilated in her white, wild face, as they stared into mine.

"What is it?" I said inadequately. "What in the world is going on?"

And at last, recognition dawned in her fearful face. Behind her, the other servants had come to a reluctant halt, jostling each other on the stairs so that I imagined my presence was only a temporary hindrance to their plans. Their faces were grim, angry, contorted out of all familiarity. Uncomprehendingly, I looked from them back to the timid maid.

"Help me, madam," she whispered. "Dear God, help me..."

"Of course I shall help you, if somebody will tell me what this is all about." I tried to speak calmly, but I think even then I knew in the pit of my stomach that this had gone beyond me.

"You can't protect her!" cried one of the footmen. "The murdering little..."

"*Murdering?*" I repeated involuntarily.

"I never," gasped the maid. "I never killed anyone! How could I?"

It was what I was wondering myself, but before I could voice doubt, the servants all burst out at once, "Your people did! It's the same thing! Your people are killing..."

Of course. The girl was a Romanian. Had I ever recognized the fact before? This was a racial fight.

"Oh for Heaven's sake!" I interrupted impatiently. "You can't blame her for atrocities committed anywhere—"

"Not anywhere," I was interrupted in my turn. "Here!"

That silenced me for at least five seconds. I counted the beats of my heart, staring at the speaker. I swallowed. "What has happened?"

They began to tell me, all at once, with anger and fear, while sheltering behind me the little Romanian maid shook like a leaf. I knew how she felt. Apparently, the Romanian minority in the village beyond Szelényi — still owned by the Count, of course — had turned on their Magyar neighbours only this morning, looting and burning and killing; and significantly, they were helped by other Romanians who had arrived in the village last night. They had, I inferred, been incited by the strangers, but now it sounded as if full scale war had broken out.

So it had come here at last, the race-violence which even Lajos feared, and just when he and Alex had done so much to try to build trust between their peoples.

"Does the Count know about this?" I said slowly.

Not only did he know, he had gone there.

"With soldiers?" I said in surprise. "Already?"

But apparently there were no soldiers with him, although he had sent to

Vanora for them. In fact, he had gone alone, with neither son nor servant to protect him. It crossed my mind, briefly, that he hadn't known all the facts. He didn't know what he was walking into...

"The soldiers will sort it out," I said calmly, "and punish those responsible." As if this would make everything all right again. "It is not for you to take it out on the one Romanian who is so obviously innocent. Now, go back to work."

I didn't wait to see if they would obey me. I was fairly sure they would not. Instead, I walked quickly away, pushing the timid maid in front of me.

"Will you be safe here?" I asked her abruptly.

"I want to go home," she whispered, by way of an answer.

I nodded. "Go then." God knew what she would find there, if the stories were only half-true, but my own mind was fixed only on my grandfather, on the danger he was walking into; and, for some reason, the fact that I hadn't apologised to him for my behaviour last night, though surely that was unimportant now...

In the stables, I learned that he was only ten minutes ahead of me.

"Saddle me the mare, then, quickly," I urged. "I can still catch him."

Mark stared at me. "You'll never turn him back. Not the Count..."

"Do it," I said fiercely.

He did it. And I, without waiting even to tell István or Mattias — after all I had no intention of letting either of us get into serious danger — galloped off in pursuit of my grandfather. I wasn't sure how I would do it, but I was determined to turn him back before he reached the fighting — it would come to Szelényi, and to the castle itself soon enough, unless the soldiers were extraordinarily quick.

I had never ridden so fast in Szelényi, nor so improperly dressed. I didn't even have a hat, but there was no one in the fields to be outraged. In fact, I saw no one at all, until I had ridden across the hill and finally reined in above the tiny village. This was where all the people were.

"Oh no," I said aloud. "Oh no." For now I could see fires in the fields as well as in the village. I could see groups of men fighting with fists and feet and farm tools, others running from place to place, shouting, enraged. And ahead of me, I could see my grandfather, ram-rod straight in the saddle, motionlessly watching his people do their best to exterminate each other; but even as I called to him, he spurred forward, unheeding. His deafness had never seemed so frustrating.

There was nothing I could do but follow him, and try to catch up. In the end, we were in the village itself before I could get near him; and that was like riding into a nightmare. Huddles of crying women and children, Magyar and Romanian, were crouched in the road just outside the village. I thought some of them were injured, even dead. Involuntarily, I stopped beside a woman who was weeping uncontrollably over a still child.

"What can I do?" I said with desperation. I didn't even know if there was a doctor in the district. Certainly I had never heard of one. But the woman turned on me such a look of fierce anger mingled with her awful grief, that I rode on. There was nothing I could do, not for them.

I saw Alex first. He stood helplessly on the edge of the square before the Orthodox Church, where most of the fighting seemed to be. His hands clutched at his hair in a gesture of helplessness that was almost a caricature; but as I watched, he dropped to his knees beside some wounded creature. Directly opposite him, on the church steps, stood the Orthodox priest, his arms raised in some sort of desperate prayer for people who didn't even hear him. And I knew some of these people: there was Gábor from the stables, in tears, dragging someone away from a burning cottage; and Zoltán Lázár in the thick of the fighting, using his fists with vicious energy.

And then I saw Lajos. Dressed just as the others, yet standing out from them, even in this carnage, he was snatching a blazing torch from a man's hand, throwing it on the ground under his feet. Shouting constantly, he pushed the man towards the priest; and then, recklessly, he threw himself into the middle of a vicious looking fight. I closed my eyes, sure he would be stabbed by the farm fork being wielded so furiously in the mêlée. When I opened them again he was no longer among these men — they had actually stopped fighting and were looking towards the priest; and Lajos was several yards away, pulling one man off another by his shirt, still shouting something at the top of his voice.

He's stopping it, I thought in wonder, in the beginnings of hope. Gradually, he is stopping it...

Belatedly, I remembered my grandfather, who had brought me here in the first place. Suddenly frightened for him again, I looked wildly around until I caught sight of him at the foot of the hill behind the church, beginning to move along the side of it towards the priest. Following quickly, I saw Lajos leap up the steps beside the priest, his shirt torn and patchy with dirt and blood; and now I could hear his voice above the others as he shouted. He had their attention; they were listening; and gradually as more and more people stopped to hear him, others paused to see why, and then they listened too. And yet, judging by the carnage of the village and its environs, it had taken him a long time to get even this far.

I could hear his words now, a jumble of Hungarian and Romanian, be-seeching peace.

"*We* are not enemies!" I heard him cry, his voice so hoarse that I knew it must be painful. "It is madness to turn on each other — that is what the *true* enemy wants of us, to weaken us! My God, how much weaker are we now, after this? We have made new wounds when we should be healing, growing strong enough to make our own future...!"

The noise was so much less now that I could hear the catcalls quite dis-tinctly; but it was the strangers who made them. People I recognized were shaking off the jeerers. The villagers knew Lajos: it was for him they had turned out at Szelényi Castle last year and stood side by side with their Magyar and Szekely neighbours, people whom they had just now been trying to destroy. And the Hungarians, in this case not the aggressors, began to lose the light of righteous battle which had been in all their faces, as it had been in the castle servants'. Some of the women even began to creep back into the village.

Riding quietly down the side of the church in my grandfather's wake, I finally came to a halt beside him. But he didn't even notice me. His eyes were fixed on Lajos's face, and I could see from the set of his shoulders that he was angry. Still and always angry...

"In the name of the revolution we all believe in, stop this," Lajos was saying, "before we have nothing left..."

"Romanians have nothing to start with!" someone shouted. One of the strangers. And Lajos turned on him at once, in his own language. It was working, I thought. God knew how long this damage would take to heal, but at least he was stopping it from getting any worse.

And then, into the pregnant, thoughtful silence which followed his speech, my grandfather said suddenly, "Well, Lajos? Satisfied?" And Lajos swung round so quickly that he had no time to guard his expression.

"Oh Jesus Christ, not you."

CHAPTER THIRTY-FOUR

There was a bleeding cut below his eye, where he had got too close to flailing fists. Involuntarily, he dragged his hand through his hair as if he couldn't deal with this; and with a sudden return of fear, I realized that *he* was afraid, afraid of what my grandfather would do to the situation.

The peasants too now saw the old Count for the first time — I could tell from the threatening rumble which rippled round the crowd.

My grandfather was speaking with barely controlled rage. "You think you can fix *this* with a few speeches? Go on, tell me how you can fix it!"

"*Fix* it? I can't. We all have to..."

But my grandfather would not let him speak. Already he was interrupting, his old voice louder now than Lajos's poor, worn out one. "No, of course you can't. But *you began it*, didn't you, Lajos? You roused the people, and this is the result. *It's your fault*."

At that, I made a noise of distress, as if to contradict him, and for a second, Lajos's eyes flickered to me. I saw pain in them, quickly veiled; and then he had turned back to the peasants.

"It's no *fault* of the people to be roused to the injustice of their lives," he declared. "We all know about injustice!"

"Except him!" someone shouted, pointing at my grandfather in loathing. "Except the great lord!"

"And the lord is a Magyar!" one of the Romanians said grimly.

"Aye, the worst Magyar of the lot!" said another, and turned and struck his Hungarian neighbour in the face, while the others, indescribably threatening, heaved forward as one towards us.

I was appalled. And then Lajos had stepped in front of us.

"*I* am a Magyar!" he cried in his new, hoarse voice, and reluctantly the mob was still again, though only just.

Someone shouted, "Yes, so what gives you the right to speak for us?"

"Shouldn't we all speak up for each other?" Lajos returned at once; but with despair, I saw that he had lost them. He had been loosing them since they had first seen my grandfather. There was just too much hatred bottled up in all of them against their tyrannical old lord. The only way Lajos could control them now was to unite them against their common foe, the Count, and this, I saw with mingled relief and distress, he would not do. He understood only too well the nature of the mobs he had brought into being.

Fights were breaking out again. I saw Alex pushing two women behind him, away from the violence. And then a stone landed with a thud only inches from my grandfather's horse, startling both our animals. Through their frightened whinnying — and my own — I heard Lajos saying, "But certainly, speak for yourselves! Here is your lord — *speak* to him!"

But they had done with speaking. Impatiently, almost furiously, I laid my hand on my grandfather's arm.

"Come away, Grandfather," I pleaded. "He can do nothing when you are here!"

But my grandfather did not move. I felt him tense under my fingers. His breathing was fast and ragged and, I realized with sudden new dread, painful.

"Grandfather?" I said, anxiously, and then Lajos was there, all but lifting him off his horse in front of my frightened eyes.

Lajos said something over his shoulder to the priest, then to me, "Help me get him inside. Open the door."

Wordlessly I obeyed, sliding to my feet and pushing open the church door for Lajos to carry my grandfather inside. The door closed on the noise, on the fights breaking out all over again.

Lajos was on his knees, easing my grandfather onto the hard, wooden floor. I couldn't speak for the fear clutching at my heart, but I found I was kneeling beside him, loosening his tie with hands that trembled, while he lay in his pain, staring not at me but at Lajos.

"It's your doing!" he panted. "Yours!"

Lajos's face never changed. Sitting back on his heels, he said only, "Perhaps." And I saw my grandfather's eyes search his, one to the other. When he spoke, his voice was stronger, but it still sounded strange to me.

"You agree with me? Now why does that worry me more than all the rest? Am I dying?"

I made a small, meaningless gesture of distress. For a moment, I could hear only my own heart, then Lajos said evenly, "I don't know. The priest is sending for the doctor."

But now, perversely, my grandfather gave a funny, rueful smile and said simply, "Too late."

"No," I whispered, and he turned and looked at me. There was no recognition in his eyes. Impatiently, he turned back to Lajos.

"You must be delighted," he ground out, his hands clutching involuntarily at the renewed pain in his heart. "At last..."

"Why should I be?" said Lajos. He sounded indifferent, and I saw that he was listening to the noise from outside; it was growing increasingly wild without him. And yet he didn't move. For some reason, he would not leave the dying old man who was his enemy.

"You hate me," my grandfather said conversationally, and then, when Lajos's eyes had come back to him, he added with sudden bitterness, "A hundred times more than those poor fools out there, you hate me!"

A groan of purely physical pain was wrenched from him. His eyes clenched shut, then slowly opened.

Lajos said, "I don't hate you. I never hated you. Only what you stand for."

At that, a terrifying, rattling laugh broke from my grandfather. "*Nothing personal*, is that it, Lajos?"

A pause, then, "Yes," said Lajos. "That's it."

"Liar," said my grandfather tiredly.

Lajos stirred. "No. I have no right to judge you. My own behaviour — to you — has not always been — exemplary."

The old man's eyes widened, then relaxed. "Oh. That," he said dismissively. "I was glad to give you the money in the end. I watched you, waited to see how far you could go before you fell, or before you abandoned your principles and chased power and wealth like everyone else. And every time you didn't, God help me, I was *proud* of you."

Lajos's gaze did not falter, but I saw his fingers twist suddenly together before he stilled them.

"You had the right to be," he said quietly. "I learned a lot from you."

I was not part of this. I felt as if I should not even be there. And then, into the strange peace which had sprung up between them, something crashed suddenly against the church door. I jumped, jerked unpleasantly back into reality. My grandfather gasped; his hand reached up, claw-like, grasping at Lajos.

"Don't let them in! Don't let them see me like this, Lajos — for God's sake leave me that much dignity..."

Lajos's hand turned, clasping the gnarled old fingers. "For any sake you like, I'll keep them away. I promise."

Satisfied, my grandfather fell back, eyes closed as if in sleep. He still held on to Lajos's hand, and Lajos let it lie there, unmoving. For a long time none of us stirred. I felt very cold, very alone, an onlooker at a scene charged with a tension I didn't understand. Yet the tension was not in my grandfather, not any more. I had never seen him as contented as he seemed in those few minutes when he lay quietly trusting in the protection of the young man who was his enemy, the enemy of everything he believed in.

Nothing personal. No. Something very personal. To each of them. I found myself wondering if this was yet another reason for István's hatred, this strange pride of the old man in his peasant protégé.

At last, when something else crashed against the church door, Lajos slid his hand free and stood up. He didn't look at me as he went quickly to the door, which was already opening. The noise grew briefly louder; I saw Lajos push somebody outside with him, and then the door closed again. My grandfather seemed to be sleeping, though his breath was so laboured I didn't see how. I heard Lajos's voice from the steps outside, quiet at first, then raised in anger. A moment later, the door reopened and he came back in alone, and stood there by the door, quite still.

But something had alerted my grandfather. He was staring up at me now. "Sofia? Is it Sofia, come back after all these years?"

Now, now I wanted to cry.

"No," I whispered, swallowing back the tears. "It's Katie."

"Katie," he repeated. "Katie." And I had no way of knowing if the name meant anything to him. I couldn't hear his breathing now. His eyes were staring into mine, but slowly, their dull light was fading.

"Grandfather, don't die!" I pleaded. I picked up his hand, squeezing it convulsively. "Please don't die, not now... Lajos!"

I cast wildly around for him, but he was already beside me, crouching down by the old man, placing his fingers at the base of the scrawny throat. His hand fell away. Slowly, his eyes lifted to mine, and he stood, drawing me with him.

"He's dead, Katie."

I closed my eyes tightly. My grandfather was dead. His fierce, stubborn old heart had finally stopped beating, and he was dead. He would never know now that I hadn't meant the awful things I had said last night, that I loved him in spite of everything, because of everything...

"Don't, Katie," Lajos said gently, and my hands twisted in his. I gasped, letting the wetness loose on my face, burying it in his shoulder.

I don't know how long it was — only a few moments, I think — before he let me go.

"Katie, I have to try and sort this out before the soldiers come."

"Yes," I agreed quietly. "I'll wait here, with him."

István and Mattias found me there an hour later. By then it was quiet outside. The soldiers had come, the fires were out, and the dead were mourned in silence. White-faced, the old Count's sons came to take his body home, and my grief inevitably paled before their greater loss.

His body was carried outside by his old valet and Mark. The three of us followed, wordlessly. The sunlight blinded me as I stepped outside the church, taking me by surprise. I stopped, letting them go ahead to the waiting carriage while the full awfulness of the day flooded through me.

We weren't the only bereaved family today, I thought drearily, not by a long way. Some soldiers were marching past me, momentarily blocking the sun; and I saw that they had prisoners, mostly the Romanian strangers, their shoulders drooping in defeat. I took the last step, and then paused again. Two more soldiers were passing now, and between them, they held Lajos Lázár.

Oh no, I thought stupidly. Oh no, not this too. Looking up just then, he saw me, and his lips moved in a rueful smile, even as he was pulled on.

"Wait!" Almost involuntarily, I was running after them, placing myself in their path so that they had to stop. "What are you doing?"

The soldiers stared at me, but I suppose my dress proclaimed rank, even without a hat, for after a stupefied pause, one of them said, "Arresting ringleaders, madam."

"Ringleaders? But he didn't lead them! He was trying to stop them!" I could hear the tears of rage in my own voice, but I no longer cared.

"It's all right, Katie," Lajos was saying, his voice ridiculously calm, even gentle, despite the hoarseness that would be with him for days yet. His eyes were calm too, quite unconcerned. "I can deal with this, you know."

"But...!"

"Orders, madam," the soldier said brusquely, and they pulled him on, regardless.

After all the rest, this was intolerable. Looking around me wildly for an officer to put an end to this final injustice before it was too late, I was too determined to feel more than relief when I saw Colonel von Avenheim standing gravely beside István and Mattias while my grandfather's body was laid in the coach.

I went up to him at once, barely registering his gentle words of condolence, or the old feeling for me which still lurked behind his normally cool, blue eyes.

"Your men have arrested Lajos Lázár," I said without preamble.

"Not before time," István said tightly. "I swear I shall never forgive him, not for this."

I turned to stare at him. "But this isn't his fault, István! He was trying to *stop* the violence! He was risking his own life to stop it! And when my grandfather became ill, he protected us..."

"Don't upset yourself," the Colonel said soothingly, already beginning to move away. "I'll look into it."

Impetuously, I caught at his arm. "I mean it, Colonel! He is innocent...!" My voice cracked. "Has there not been enough tragedy without this injustice too?"

"I won't allow any injustice," he said gently, and so sincerely that my agitation began to subside. He even smiled slightly. "On the other hand, it will do Lázár no harm to cool his heels in prison for a while and contemplate the consequences of popular unrest!"

CHAPTER THIRTY-FIVE

My grandfather was laid to rest with his ancestors in the family vault. Despite the troubled times, his neighbours turned out in force to honour him. The peasants, silent, sullen, watched from a distance: few of them — if any — had loved the old Count; he had been the representative of an unjust regime under which they had toiled all their lives, a tyrannical and irritable lord. And yet, I had the impression that they were shocked, as if his death had left an empty space. Something stable had left their lives — even if it was only a symbol of hate. They had lost the major scapegoat for all their ills.

Though in his grief István threatened it, none of them, Hungarian or Romanian, were blamed for the old Count's death. It was as well, for they had troubles enough without that. Only three people had died in the end — Lajos had managed to calm them down before the arrival of the soldiers, which had almost certainly prevented further deaths — but one of the victims was a child, and many men, including Zoltán Lázár, had been severely injured. Crops had been destroyed, animals killed, livelihoods ruined. Wounds had been opened up in the community so deep that I didn't see how they would ever heal.

The day after my grandfather's burial, Alex paid a visit to the castle. In the confusion, he was conducted directly to Katalin who was, fortunately, alone with me in the drawing room at the time. I remember feeling stifled by the heavy atmosphere of death which still hung around the house, oppressed by my own and other peoples' griefs so that it was almost a relief to see an outside face, even one which should not have been there.

Katalin flew straight into his arms — while I gazed tactfully out of the window — and wept when he told her he was leaving for Blaj in the morning. There was to be another national congress there next month.

"Perhaps this time it won't be a long parting," Katalin said at last, a note of eagerness in her woeful voice. "I believe István will eventually give us permission to marry."

Alex hugged her tightly but I, turning thoughtfully towards them, saw that his expression was far from joyful. On the contrary, it was anguished. When he left, I made sure it was I who conducted him to the front door. His face was haggard as he took my hand.

"You will look after her, won't you?"

I met his tragic gaze squarely, quietly withdrawing my hand. "I understood that was to be your job — as her husband."

"Things do not — always — work out — just as one plans," he said with difficulty.

"Are you telling me you no longer wish to marry her?"

"Of course I do!" he burst out. "I wish it more than ever, with all my heart! But how easy would that be, Katie, if there was *war* between her people and mine?"

Cocooned in your own troubles, it is easy to forget the world. My eyes fell away from his. "There must not be war," I said determinedly. "You and Lajos must see to it."

Alex smiled sadly. "Lajos and I are mere drops of rain in an ocean. I'm afraid we shall have as little effect. Look what happened even here, where they know him. He asked me to tell you, by the way, that he is leaving tomorrow too — for Buda-Pest."

I swallowed that without too much pain. It was not unexpected, and though I would have liked to see him before he went, I had no right to keep him here, not after I had refused to marry him. I thought the wider arena of Buda-Pest would be a relief to him now. I knew he was grieving for the old tyrant, his enemy. He had wronged my grandfather in the past, forced his financial help and fought him at every turn, without gratitude, and yet there had been love there too, on both sides. I had seen it, almost unbearably, in that little village church.

And of course the inter-racial violence so close to home — even his own brother had not been an innocent victim — he must regard as a personal failure. In the end, he had spent two nights in prison at Vanora before Colonel von Avenheim had let him go. I could only guess at the thoughts with which he had passed the time. The peasants looked on his release as a victory, but from the one glimpse I had had of his face on the day of my grandfather's burial, he had not been in the least triumphant.

Sighing, I put out my hand again. "Good-bye, Alex — and whatever happens, I wish you luck."

Towards the end of August, István seemed to snap quite suddenly out of his grief. The news he received continually from Buda-Pest and Vienna began to penetrate again to the active part of his mind, and he became anxious to return to the capital, for as revolutionary fervour was fading, the Court in

Vienna was gradually recovering its nerve, just as Colonel von Avenheim had foretold, flexing its muscles after General Radetzky's great victory over the Italians at Custozza. And if Hungary was not to be a victim of this revival, strong, sound heads were needed at the country's helm.

So on the first day of September, we all left together for Buda-Pest in the usual cavalcade of coaches. For the first time, Margit came with us; excited yet almost frightened by her new freedom, she twittered unbearably till everyone's nerves were shrieking and I began to realize why my grandfather had so often lost his temper with her. The journey had never seemed so awful.

However, there was worse to come, for even before we reached Buda-Pest we heard of the King's Memorandum: with one blow, he had rescinded the April Laws, demanded the surrender of the separate Hungarian ministries and ordered the Hungarians to end military preparations against the Croats. I was not really surprised to discover Buda-Pest on the verge of a second revolution.

Pest quay was more crowded than I had ever seen it, but unexpectedly the sight of it brought back all the pleasure I had taken in the scene when I had first arrived from Vienna. Everything was still busy and dazzlingly colourful, but added to that now was an air of suspense and excitement.

In common with half the city, we had turned out to see the return of Batthyány and the Assembly's delegation, who had gone to the King in a last ditch attempt to have the infamous Memorandum revoked. The milling crowd parted easily for us — our obvious station guaranteed that. Revolutionary equality, I thought drily, was only on the surface; it would be a long time before anyone regarded the balding little clerk on my left in the same light as Count Szelényi on my right.

I heard the whistle of the incoming steam-ship, and the answering blast from Pest quay. I could see the ship coming closer, but the sun was in my eyes and it glinted red and fuzzy. Taking my spectacles off, I cleaned them on a handkerchief and put them back on rather slowly.

If I had not already known, the tension of the waiting crowd would have told me how much depended upon the answer these men were bringing. The King's simple refusal would force his Hungarian people from legal opposition to rebellion. And rebellion meant, inevitably, war.

Other eyes were sharper than mine, even with the benefit of my spectacles. The noise and babble of the crowd faded slowly. Silence fell. Beside me, I heard István make a sound that was almost a groan. I had allowed myself to hope, but even that was gone now, for the steam-ship sailing into the harbour was flying a red flag which cried out defiance bravely and distinctly against the hazy paleness of the river and the sky and the hills.

And the men on board, who were leaning on the rails watching as the ship pulled in to the quay, all wore red feathers in their hats and red kerchiefs round their necks or wrists. That was what had caused the red haze in the distance.

The King had refused. He had gone back on his word, and God alone knew what dangers the future now held. I looked up at István, to ask for confirmation or reassurance, but then, some way beyond him, my eye was caught at last, and held by the figure of Lajos. He was with Petöfi and Vasvári and some others, looking as sombre as I felt, but I could see in his stance no loss of vitality, only a tension about to burst into action.

And inevitably it was their little group who broke the silence. "Long live the revolution!" one of them shouted. "Long live Hungary and liberty!" And gradually the cries were taken up, and the shouting swelled until the quay was ringing with it. The men on the ship waved, joining in the cheers. And this time, no one added the previously obligatory "Long live the King."

Unbidden, a line of Petöfi's much-reviled poem swam into my mind: 'There is no *beloved* king any more...' Today, I could almost imagine it was true.

The next day, Teréz Meleki was 'at home'. Since it was to be a quiet, select gathering, Elisabeth decided we could go with propriety, despite our mourning state. I was reluctant at first but in common with everyone else in the city, I was restless, so in order to distract my mind I went, dressed all in sombre but stylish black, and in the end I even enjoyed myself, renewing acquaintance with one or two congenial spirits.

The gathering was already beginning to break up when István arrived with Baron Mirányi. I presumed they had come from the Assembly. Their entry was quiet, and in the brilliance of the guests with whom Teréz surrounded herself, they should have been unobtrusive, but something took my eyes straight to them, and my attention was caught and held.

Perhaps it was the gravity of their expressions, contrasting with the witty, brittle light-heartedness of the guests; or perhaps it was the fact that they never spoke to each other or to anyone else. Whatever it was, I was not the only one to sense it.

Conversation died away. For a second, the room was perfectly still. Then silk rustled, sweeping along the floor as Elisabeth went forward to her husband.

"István," she said, and there was enough dread in her voice to speak for all of us. "What is it? For God's sake, what has happened?"

István took her hands, but he did not look at her. His eyes went over her head and found his brother, as if in some kind of silent communication I had never seen between them before. But when he spoke, it was quite clearly, and to all of us.

"Jelacic has crossed the Drava with 40,000 men. Hungary is invaded."

War

September 1848 — January 1849

CHAPTER THIRTY-SIX

Buda-Pest was changing again. People were flooding into the city to answer the call to arms. New soldiers were everywhere, until I began to think that we were living in a military camp.

I saw some very odd sights too. The one that sticks most in my mind is of two Imperial soldiers, armed with knives, following each other in circles and hacking off the tails of each other's frock coats. I was walking with Margit and the children, on the way to buy a new dress for Anna — it was her birthday at the end of the week and Elisabeth had promised her the treat of a dinner party with the adults — but as I stopped to gape at this peculiar spectacle, they drew ahead of me.

"Staggering, isn't it?" remarked a voice in my ear. I jumped, and looked straight up into the eyes of Lajos Lázár. I had not spoken to him since returning to Pest, and this unexpected meeting threw me off balance. However, the antics of the soldiers soon distracted me again.

"What in the world are they doing?" I asked.

"Cutting the tails off their coats," said Lajos helpfully, and when I glared at him, added mercifully, "To show that they are no longer Imperial soldiers, but Hungary's. They have just been persuaded to transfer to the *honvéd*, our new national defence force, and since there are no uniforms for them yet, this is their way of declaring their allegiance."

I looked again at the men, who had finally achieved their goal to the amused applause of passers-by.

"Who," I asked resignedly, "persuaded them?"

"I did," said Lajos modestly, and drew my attention to a group of tail-less soldiers swaggering about in the square opposite. "In fact, I got several with one shot."

I couldn't help laughing, and his lip twitched responsively.

"Is this your new mission?" I enquired.

"Yes; Buda-Pest needs to be defended if the Croats get this far."

I shivered as reality broke in once more. "Do you think they will?"

"If those idiot generals Batthyány was foolish enough to send against them have their way, then yes. Neither Ottinger nor Teleki will fight Jelacic. They tiptoe up to him and retreat till it's tantamount to treason, for Jelacic still has no authority from the King. Legally, he is still only a rebellious subject, but our generals seem to regard him as an old comrade."

"I suppose he is," I said sadly, thinking of Colonel von Avenheim.

Lajos flicked my cheek with one finger. "Don't worry. The people will rise and throw the invader back out again."

I flushed under the careless caress. "You sound very sure."

"I have faith," he said flippantly, "in the people. I'm also on my way to stir them up."

I frowned. "What do you mean?"

"We need the peasantry to join the army en masse."

I smiled grimly. "You're taking March the fifteenth tactics to the country for a recruiting campaign?"

"It works," he said confidently, and I thought of Szelényi a year ago, when he had persuaded the peasants to risk their necks in his demonstration. That had not been armed conflict, of course, and they had been his own people he was dealing with, but I had little doubt that he would be just as effective anywhere — especially now that the peasants had something worth fighting to save.

Ahead I could see Margit, standing still and forlorn, looking around her rather wildly while the children danced on the ends of her arms. Quickly, I glanced up at Lajos.

"I must go — they will think I'm lost. Do — will you be gone long?"

"I don't know. Will you miss me?"

"No," I said crossly, "but if you help to keep Jelacic away from our door, I suppose I shall be grateful."

His lips moved slightly, but his eyes were unblinkingly on mine. Dropping my gaze, I could only mutter, "Be careful," before I hurried away from him to catch up with Margit and the children.

*

To add to the national chaos, there was new friction at the Szelényi palace, for Mattias was wild to join the *honvéd* and save his country from the invader, and István would not hear of it.

"You know nothing of soldiering!" István said impatiently. "You are training to be a *lawyer!*"

"But I never cared for the law above half, you know that. Besides, this is an emergency!"

"Precisely, and as such it will be over before you have had time to buy a uniform!"

"There will be other emergencies. When we fight the Austrians..."

"We shall not," István interrupted deliberately, "fight the Austrians."

Mattias slammed out of the room. He resumed the argument at fairly regular intervals but, interestingly, it seemed he would not join without his brother's permission.

Considering the turbulent state of the city at this time, I suppose it was unwise of me to wander about unattended, but the habits of a lifetime are hard to break, and I was, besides, terribly interested in all that was going on. I watched the people building fortifications around Pest. I saw a hundred French-born inhabitants of the city march off to fight Jelacic singing the Marseillaise. And if that seems odd, imagine more than one thousand Viennese coming to support the fight for Hungary's freedom, for that happened too.

It was while wandering in this way that I discovered Lajos was back in the city, for I came upon him unexpectedly addressing an impromptu gathering in the street near the City Hall. Inevitably, my breath caught at the sight of him; just as inevitably, I stayed to hear him.

"Well, our people have risen up behind Jelacic," he was saying in his conversational tone, "picking off his men and cutting off his supplies. I think they even captured his mail!"

The crowd cheered delightedly till Lajos held up his hand.

"No; save your enthusiasm. Such action is brave and no doubt valuable, but frankly, it is a drop in the ocean compared to what is needed. Armies are not defeated by being worried around the edges. We need an army of our own to fight the Croats! An army so full of spirit and patriotism that any lack of training does not matter. Today, Hungary needs all her men." He paused, his mobile face changing again. "But you know that already. To save the Fatherland from any invader is reason enough to join the *honvéd* and fight. But I have recently made the acquaintance of *this* invader in particular."

He looked around the crowd. "Have you ever seen the Croat *Grenzer?* They look exotically noble, with their beautiful scarlet cloaks and their vicious Turkish weapons hanging from their belts. They even have warrior women who march side by side with the men! The *Grenzer* are awesome; but don't be fooled. There is nothing noble about these savages. They are merely licensed thieves and freebooters. Loot is their only object in war, and believe me, they have pillaged across Hungary, leaving a trail of carnage in their wake that even their own officers are powerless to prevent."

With growing horror, I listened to his graphic description of the atrocities committed by the Croat army. I had heard him speak many times by then. I knew he was calculating as well as passionate, and I tried to tell myself that this was merely his way of rousing the people to action before it was too late; but as his quiet, angry voice went on and on, I could no longer doubt the genuineness of his words.

The crowd were silent at first. Like me, they were feeling the sudden, awful

236

closeness of the war. Then someone gasped and exclamations of horror and outrage followed. They too were angry.

At last Lajos paused. He pushed his hand through his hair and said, "So you see, we must avenge the destruction, the murder, the rape; we have to prevent it happening anywhere else. They are heading for Buda-Pest now. I have seen thousands of peasants enlist in the *honvéd* to stop them. Join your brothers and prove the city as patriotic as the countryside."

A buzz of assent and determination swelled gradually to a rousing shout. But into it someone said, "Will *you* go, Lajos?" And a new fear began, one I should have been prepared for, and was not.

"Yes," said Lajos at once. "When I have done what I have to here, I will join." He smiled faintly. "I have a personal stake in our revolution — I will defend it to the death."

I shivered, for there was truth in his voice, and his words hit me like some evil prophesy: *I will defend it to the death.* Jelacic had started the killing, but God alone knew where it would end now.

I was so lost in these fearful thoughts that I was actually startled when Lajos suddenly appeared at my side, looking down at me, his face unusually serious. "Katie. What are you doing here? Are you in the habit of wandering around like this, alone?"

I shrugged, slightly piqued by his attitude. "From time to time."

"At the risk of offending," Lajos said slowly, "I don't think you should."

I stared at him. "Why ever not? You sound just like István, you know."

"This isn't like March, not any more. There is too much fear now, too much anger. You wouldn't — you really wouldn't — like to be caught up with a mob when it turns ugly, when it erupts into violence."

"Then why do you stir them up?" I asked flatly. "If you're not prepared for the consequences—"

"*I* am prepared," he interrupted. "You are not."

I regarded him sceptically. I was not unmoved by his sudden concern for my safety, but I would not let him see that. He took my arm, drawing me away from the dispersing crowd. "Come, I'll take you home."

"There's no need," I said drily. "I remember the way."

"I'll find you a fiacre."

"I'm sure you have more important engagements."

"None that can't wait. I'm only on my way to lead the good citizens in some howling outside the Assembly."

As Lajos waved down an empty fiacre, I roused myself to observe provokingly, "István says the crowd at the Assembly consists only of undesirables hired by your friend Madarász, and no respectable townspeople at all."

"István would say that."

Katalin's great trouble was that she had had no letters from Alex since he had left Szelényi in August, and by now she was beginning to make herself ill with worry. So, in a disastrous attempt to distract her, I enticed her to drive out with me across the river to admire the view from Buda Hill. We took one of the town carriages, but Katalin vetoed my last-minute suggestion of taking the children too. Thank God she did.

It seemed to me as we drove out towards the bridge of boats that the city was growing ever angrier. Of course, the King's autocratic and highly unpopular appointment of Count Lamberg as Commander-in-Chief had fuelled the excitement of the populace to the point at which I was sure it must soon somehow explode...

As usual, the streets were swarming with people: sullen, discontented, furious. In fact, when we reached the quay we found the way to the pontoon bridge blocked by a large group of people — workers, students, a scattering of peasants who had come into the city to join the army, grasping their agricultural implements like weapons. More seemed to be running to join the throng from all directions.

Something about the nature of this crowd made me remember Lajos's warning; and when Katalin demanded to know what was happening, I said only, "Who knows? We can't pass through this though — I'll tell László to turn back."

However, before I could do so, we were hailed by a familiar-looking youth whom I recognized with an effort as one of Mattias's friends. I returned his greeting and took the opportunity to ask what was happening.

"We're waiting for Count Lamberg. He arrived in Buda today, and someone said he was coming to Pest in search of Count Batthyány."

"Batthyány isn't in Pest," I said, amused. "In fact, I understand he has left in search of Count Lamberg!"

Just then, a shout went up on the bridge. I saw that a fiacre was rumbling across it. Suddenly the people surged forward on to the bridge, and Mattias's friend laughed, raising his hat and dashing off after the crowd.

"Idiots," said Katalin roundly. "What do they think they are doing?"

"Howling at Lamberg probably," I said uneasily. *This isn't like March, not any more.* Suddenly I didn't want to see. "Let's go, Katalin..."

But Katalin did not hear me. Before I had finished speaking she was exclaiming, "Katie, they're going to push his carriage over!" And my eyes flew involuntarily back to the bridge. The fiacre had stopped, surrounded by the crowd, and was swaying perilously under the fists hammering on it.

"No," I said helplessly. "They mustn't..." They didn't. Instead, some enterprising person wrenched open the carriage door and I saw a man being pulled out. "Perhaps it isn't him, and they'll let him go... Katalin, is that Count Lamberg?"

"I can't tell over this distance — he isn't in uniform — ah no!"

This last exclamation came as someone struck the unfortunate man. And as if this was an invitation, everyone within range was hitting and kicking until, sick with horror, I saw the victim fall.

"My God," I whispered. "They're killing him..." I felt a clutch of ice around my heart, a heavy paralysis spreading through my body. I could think of nothing except the unspeakable brutality taking place upon the bridge. And then, just for a moment, I felt a wave of profound relief, for the victim was on his feet again; but still the mob did not let him go. They were pushing and pulling him along the bridge towards Pest.

Lajos, I thought wildly. Where was Lajos now? The radical press had been shouting for Lamberg's head since the appointment was announced — this was *their* responsibility, they had to stop it. My eyes were desperately searching the mob for a face I knew, but none of them were here.

"Sweet Jesus," Katalin said in a low, sick voice. "They're coming this way."

And as the howling mob converged upon us, I seemed to be only a jumble of feelings, of revulsion and hatred and pity and fear and anger, and wild thoughts of dragging the poor victim into the carriage and saving him. But as they pressed against the side of the coach in their hurry, I could not even have opened the door if I had tried. The people were inhuman in their single-minded brutality. They paid no attention to us whatever, and my own abject fear became diluted with a miserable, guilty gratitude.

But my eyes were riveted to the figure being dragged along in their midst. Bloody and dishevelled, he stumbled by us in the grip of his merciless captors, and I had one clear glimpse of his face, of the sheer, hopeless terror, and the bewildered anguish of a man in a nightmare where people are no longer recognized as members of the same species. Since that day, I have seen much suffering, but I have never forgotten that look, or the savagery of those who inspired it.

Katalin whimpered as a particularly heavy body caused the carriage to sway and the horses to sidle unhappily. And then I saw another face pass, the alarmed, uneasy countenance of Mattias's friend, remonstrating with those around him. Somewhere, I was glad of his effort, though I knew he could do nothing. The people either ignored him or pushed him away.

"It's Lamberg," Katalin whispered. "That is Count Lamberg. Oh how can they *dare*...?" And suddenly her head was buried in my shoulder and I clutched her convulsively while the vicious alien shouts of the mob surrounded us and then began slowly to fade, and the prayer went round and round in my head: "Lajos, Lajos, save him..."

"Poor man," Katalin kept moaning. "Poor, poor man." By then László, without waiting for instructions, had whipped the horses into motion and we were galloping away from the murderous scene as fast as the horses could take us.

CHAPTER THIRTY-SEVEN

Some National Guardsmen eventually prevented the mob from hanging Count Lamberg. There was no point: by that time he was dead. While we had driven away to inform the soldiers, the mob had slashed him to death and dragged his body through the streets.

I think the whole city was dazed with shock by this atrocity — even those who had perpetrated it. An aristocrat, a respected man, had been brutally murdered by a mob made up of ordinary people — workers, soldiers, students, men who went home to their wives and families. It made everyone feel unsafe. As for the mobs themselves — these monsters brought into being by Lajos and his friends — I hated them with a fierce, fearful loathing.

Naturally, Katalin and I were both deeply shaken by what we had witnessed. It seemed to drown even fear of the nearing Croat army. Katalin refused to go out the next day, while I desperately tried to keep myself busy, to avoid thinking about Lamberg's bewildered face. In this I was not entirely successful, so I was quite relieved when, halfway through the afternoon, Mattias strolled into the drawing-room, offering a welcome distraction to both of us.

"I'm off to the Pilvax for an hour' if you'd like to come," he said handsomely.

"The *Pilvax?*" Katalin repeated with loathing. "Not for anything! I blame your radical friends for what happened yesterday!"

"Oh come, that's not fair," Mattias protested. "None of the radicals were there! No, the fault lies with Vienna."

"And the killing instincts of mobs," I added. I considered for a moment, then stood up, dropping my unread book on the chair. "*I* shall come with you, Mattias."

Katalin's head turned quickly towards me.

"Fetch your bonnet," Mattias commanded. "Five minutes!" And he wandered out again while Katalin jumped to her feet.

"Katie, if you see Lajos...?"

"I shall ask him about Alex," I said resignedly.

"Do you think — do you think he might arrange to send a letter to him?"

"Shall I ask him before or after I tell him your views on Count Lamberg's murder?"

"That isn't fair, Katie! You said yourself it was the radicals who first stirred up the mobs."

I sighed. "I know. Give me the letter."

"Bless you!" said Katalin fervently, almost sweeping me out of the room and upstairs.

* * *

We found the café fairly quiet, though I could see some intense debates going on. At first I thought Lajos was not there, and was unreasonably annoyed with him, especially when Mattias fell into conversation with a couple of his friends, rather callow youths whom he invited to join us. But then, while I was idly admiring the skill of a waiter carrying a positive mountain of crockery towards the kitchen, I suddenly saw the back of Lajos's head leaning out from behind a pillar to call after the waiter.

In acknowledgement, the waiter raised one hand, causing the pile of plates on his arm to rattle precariously.

I glanced at Mattias and his friends. "Excuse me one moment," I murmured, and without waiting for their response I stood up and made my way towards the pillar, hearing the startled scrape of their chairs on the floor behind me as they made a hasty, if futile, attempt at courtesy.

Lajos was writing busily, a frown on his tired face. He was surrounded by papers and open books, and his free hand was turning the pages of one even while he wrote.

"Good afternoon," I said calmly. I saw the quirk of his lips before he looked up.

"Katie Kettles," he said, dropping the pen and rising to his feet. "Have you come to join me?"

"Briefly," I said, taking the chair he held for me. He sat down opposite and regarded me.

"What is the matter?" he asked. I had forgotten his perception.

After the faintest pause, I answered, "You must have heard about Count Lamberg's murder?"

A shadow crossed his face and was gone. I might have imagined it. "Yes; I have heard."

"Katalin and I saw it. At least we saw the start of it."

Lajos's eyes were searching mine. "I'm sorry," he said briefly. "Sorry it happened at all, sorry you had to see it."

"And that is it?"

"I'm not a policeman. Do you expect me to find the culprits and hang them too?"

"No, I expect you to own to some responsibility! You and your friends brought the people on to the streets, and *this* is the result!"

"No," Lajos said coolly. "It is *one* result, weighed against all the good we have achieved. What you saw yesterday was horrible; no one deserves to die that way. But keep it in proportion, Katie. Lamberg was one man; he's not even the first casualty of the revolution. How many do you think are dying at the hands of the Croats? How many *will* die before this is done? Do you put the blame for all of that on me? Because I and my friends dared to try and help the people?"

"No." I met his gaze ruefully. "I think I blame you for not being there to prevent it."

241

His face moved in quick response. "I can't be everywhere at once."

Then, as if on some hidden cue, I heard the café door burst open and several young men erupted inside, breathless with excitement, yet all talking at once. The room was suddenly silent around them. Lajos pushed his chair back and swung on it to see round the pillar.

"We've done it!" cried one of the newcomers triumphantly. "The Croats are defeated! We have won!"

Lajos's chair landed back on all four legs with a bump. I felt my breath catch in my throat. Lajos leapt up, and I stumbled to my feet with him while people demanded, "Are you sure?", "What has happened?" and "*When?*"

"This morning," replied one of the young men, bubbling over with enthusiasm. "At Pakozd, only thirty miles south of the city. Jelacic attacked us with *thirty thousand* men, far outnumbering us! But General Moga was ready for him! They say the Czech artillery men who fought on our side were brilliant; and the *honvéd* themselves were wild and angry and fearless! In two hours we had won!"

There was a moment of silence, of disbelief, and then a ragged cheer began somewhere around Mattias's table, and grew to an uproar. I found I was swaying. The great fear which had overlaid all the others, even during yesterday's awful scene, was finally lifting, leaving me weak and strangely exhilarated, so that every other trouble, even poor Lamberg's murder, faded into insignificance.

Lajos was laughing silently beside me. Wonderingly, I gazed up at him, and in the midst of the triumphant tumult surrounding us, he threw one arm around my waist, hugging me close to his side. He didn't speak, but I suddenly knew the depths of his relief. More than most, he had a stake in the revolution which Jelacic would have squashed. Apart from the shattering of his hopes, I realized with an echo of fear, not only his freedom but his very life had depended on the Croat defeat.

"Where are the Croats now?" he shouted to the youths who had brought the news.

"On their way home, via Austria, with Moga snapping at their heels!"

That raised another cheer. "Give us a toast, Lajos!" someone shouted, and as people's attention, including Mattias's, turned our way, I became uncomfortably aware of Lajos's arm resting so warmly around my waist.

Unobtrusively, I moved away as Lajos retorted, "Can't you think of your own toasts at a time like this?" But he snatched up his cup from the table and raised it high. "To liberty! And the confusion of tyranny everywhere!"

"Liberty!" they echoed, and, "To hell with tyranny!"

Lajos almost threw his cup down. "I'm off to see Petöfi, in case he hasn't heard — will you come?"

"Yes," I said at once, although I knew I shouldn't. I excused myself with the reminder that I hadn't yet carried out Katalin's request.

Mattias had definitely seen my indecorous stance with Lajos by the pillar. I think he put it down correctly to understandably high spirits, but he was not entirely happy when I told him I was going with Lajos to visit friends. I was irritated, perhaps unreasonably, but it was Lajos who spoke, a challenge as well as mockery in his glinting eyes.

"What's the matter? Don't you trust me to look after your niece?"

"Not this niece, no," said Mattias bluntly.

"You can come with us if you like."

"No thank you!" said Mattias indignantly. "I'm not getting involved in any more of your hair-brained schemes, even if the old man's not here to pillory me for it! And if you take my advice, Katie, you won't either!"

"It's sound advice," I confessed, my irritation melting away. "But I have already agreed. I'll be home in time for dinner."

Outside, I could feel my exhilaration growing. I didn't care about the unwisdom of being with Lajos, only about the pleasure of his company, and my freedom to enjoy it. Escaping with him like this reminded me inevitably of the evening of the fifteenth of March, but today I was determined to shut the past out and live only in the glorious present.

"What did he mean?" Lajos interrupted my exalted thoughts. "About being pilloried by the old man on account of my schemes?"

We were walking fast, and almost without knowing it, my hand was in his arm.

"Didn't you know? We were found out, about the trip to Nagyzseben. My grandfather almost raised the roof — in fact, I helped him. I'm surprised you didn't hear us in the village. I was still trying to apologise to him when..." I broke off abruptly.

"When he died," Lajos finished calmly.

"Yes." I cast a fleeting glance up at him. "I said some awful things to him. I didn't wish them to be the last..."

"They weren't," Lajos said, touching my cheek in a quick, gentle caress, causing my eyes to fly back again to his, and this time he held them. "He would have known you helped him; he heard your voice when he was dying."

"I told him not to die." How arrogant, and how useless.

"I think that said everything to him, don't you?"

I smiled a little hazily. "Perhaps," I murmured, and surreptitiously winked away a tear. For the first time, a little warmth about my grandfather's memory was seeping into my heart.

Petőfi himself opened the door to us, and we could see at once that he had heard the news. He was exuberant and delighted to have someone else to discuss it with, to gloat with. The victory of the inferior Hungarian army largely made up of peasants defending their homeland, had made a profound impact upon his imagination.

Julia Petőfi and Jókai were discovered in the sitting-room. The talk was at first all about the victory at Pakozd. But at last Lajos looked quizzically at Jókai.

"I have hardly seen you since you came back. How was your trip with Kossuth?"

Jókai smiled and Julia explained to me, "He and some of the other youths accompanied Kossuth on his recruiting trip to the Plains — as an armed escort."

"He didn't need one," Jókai said simply. "The people worshipped him everywhere he went. It was incredible, Lajos, beautiful even! He spoke, and they listened, and by the end they would have lain down and died for him at once if he had asked it. Instead, they rose up, thousands of them, to save the Fatherland. And it was *his* words, Lajos, which made them heroes."

"He has been like this since he came back," Petöfi said to Lajos. "I have tried to tell him that we have all persuaded recruits to go to the front, but he insists Kossuth's efforts were greater and holier."

"Jókai, Jókai, you have let him blind you," Lajos said ruefully. "I admit Kossuth has charisma, but he is not a saint! He is not worthy of your *worship.*"

Jókai flushed. "*My* worship doesn't matter. It is the people who worship him."

Lajos regarded him thoughtfully and not entirely sympathetically, but before he could speak, Petöfi had changed the subject, at least partially.

"Were you at the Assembly today, Lajos? Did Kossuth blame the Court for Lamberg's murder?"

"Yes," Lajos said, seeing his point immediately. "He certainly didn't try to stop our street-meetings on the strength of it. Of course, he wants the murderers found."

"Waste of time," said Petöfi, frowning.

"That's what Irinyi told the Assembly — that Lamberg deserved to die, only he should have been tried and sentenced first. A mistake of form, he called it."

I felt a flush of anger rise to my face. "In a civilized country," I snapped, "no one is sentenced to die by being beaten and stabbed by a howling mob."

There was a short silence as everyone turned to stare at me in surprise. Lajos stirred, as if he was about to explain to them. Then he was still and said nothing.

It was Petöfi who spoke. "The people have to learn first to be civilized. Understandably, they have no great faith in present systems of justice; they are only just learning their own power."

"You cannot think the sort of power they exhibited yesterday should be encouraged?"

"It was wild and disorganized perhaps, but it shows they are thinking for themselves, deciding who is the enemy."

"I saw no sign of thought whatsoever," I retorted.

"Katie saw them drag Lamberg away," Lajos interjected at last, and that made Petöfi pause.

"Ah. Then I understand your distress. But in such matters, we must think clearly and dispassionately. The revolution, the people; these are the important things, and to save them, to strengthen them, enemies must be rooted out."

"Does not Lamberg count as a person?" I enquired sarcastically.

"In this case, he counts as an enemy."

"So you would execute all these so-called enemies?" In spite of myself, I was fascinated.

Lajos said, "Blood-thirsty, isn't he? Not so long ago, he wanted to string up the entire Cabinet, including Kossuth."

Petőfi grinned good-naturedly, an amiability I found rather frighteningly at odds with the sentiments he had just expressed. I dragged my eyes away from him, to Lajos.

"Do you think the same way?"

"I've told you: I don't like violence at all."

"Sometimes," Julia said unexpectedly, rising to her feet. "Just occasionally, Lajos, you talk like a sensible man." I gathered from this remark, and Lajos's easy response, that all misunderstandings between them were over. However, I did not have long to reflect on the power of Lajos's charm, for as Julia moved past me, I realized suddenly that she was with child. When I congratulated her, she told me the baby was due in December and smiled so radiantly that for the first time in my life I felt a pang of regret about my own childlessness.

It wasn't until we left Petőfi's that I belatedly remembered my promise to Katalin. Guiltily, I asked Lajos if he had heard from Alex recently.

He looked slightly surprised. "I hear more *of* him than from him. Why?"

"Katalin is anxious," I said. "She has had no letters since he left Szelényi."

"Ah." His eyes rested on my face for a moment. "Alex is well," he said at last.

"Then could he not write to tell her so?"

"To be honest, I think he is afraid to. Matters are not hopeful in Transylvania. He believes he will have to become her people's enemy — and as such, I don't think he knows what to say to her."

I frowned; yet I had imagined something of the sort. "Do you know where he is? Can you send a letter to him?"

He hesitated only the briefest moment, then: "I can try."

I opened my reticule, and by the time I held out Katalin's letter to him, had stopped a fiacre in the road beside us. The letter disappeared inside his coat, and then he handed me into the carriage.

"Can I take you anywhere?" I asked easily, for somewhere in the afternoon I seemed to have lost the restraint which had been between us since March.

I saw surprise flicker and vanish in his eyes, but he said regretfully, "Thank you, no. I'm going to beg my super at Petőfi's."

I nodded briskly, refusing to let my silly disappointment show, but as I settled back something else struck me and I leaned forward again. "What *is* happening in Transylvania that I don't know about? Are you in touch with the Romanians?"

Lajos closed me in. "I've been corresponding with Iancu since we left Nagyzseben," he admitted. "Meet me tomorrow and I'll show you his last letter."

My breath caught. If I agreed to this, I was a fool. I would be letting it start all over again.

I swallowed. "What time?"

CHAPTER THIRTY-EIGHT

That was the beginning of a very strange week, during which I saw Lajos every day. In a kind of desperate dream where I had forgotten the troubles of the past and the future, I existed only for the time I spent with him.

Once, I met him in the street by accident and went with him to the Pilvax. On other evenings, I went to the coffee-house with Mattias and encountered him there. Then, Julia Petőfi invited me for tea once, and of course he was there. And once, he simply sent a servant to tell me he was waiting for me, and we drove out of the city to Rákos in the cool, autumn sunshine.

All of this was, needless to say, indiscreet in the extreme. To Lajos's radical friends, my name very quickly and easily became coupled with his, so it was inevitable that such talk should eventually reach Mattias, who nobly attempted to remonstrate with me over my unwise friendship. Finding me alone in the drawing-room one evening before dinner, he threw himself down on the sofa beside me and said a little doubtfully, "You seem to see an awful lot of Lajos Lázár these days."

"I suppose I do," I said calmly.

"People are talking, you know."

"At times like these, I imagine they have far more than me to talk about."

"Never think it! And if István hears, you..."

"Hears what?" I interrupted, looking at him directly.

He immediately grew flustered. "Lord, Katie, it's nought to me! I spent a whole week in company with both of you, remember? But in your position — and his — you must expect people to talk, even if it's arrant rubbish."

"Let them talk," I said contemptuously.

"You won't say that when István finds out."

As it happened, when István found out, there was no time to say anything very much at all, but for the time being the momentous events occurring around us, as well as the relative isolation which mourning conferred upon the family, seemed to be keeping me safe from hurtful gossip.

Somewhere inside me, I had always known that this dream-life could not last very long. And in fact, it fell apart on the night of the seventh of October. By then, of course, things were looking very bad for Hungary: Count Batthyány had resigned, and the King had dissolved the Assembly, making none other than Baron Jelacic Commander-in-Chief. Under such an insult, even I, in my cocoon of false happiness, knew that Hungary would have to fight. And yet I could think only of when next I would see Lajos, for today was the first day in more than a week that I had not done so...

I had lain awake so long that when I heard the curious yet familiar crack against my bed-chamber window, I thought it was my weary mind playing tricks on me, for it was a sound I had not heard since my first visit to Szelényi Castle last year.

I closed my eyes resolutely, but it came again, and this time I sat bolt upright in bed. My heart was thumping painfully. It's some drunken gallant, I thought, in search of one of the maids... But I couldn't believe that. No maid slept in a room with windows the size of mine.

Without conscious volition, I got out of bed and crossed the floor swiftly and easily, for my eyes had grown quite used to the dark during my hours of wakefulness. Somewhere, I was vaguely surprised by the unsteadiness of my hands as I drew back the heavy curtain and looked down into the street.

There was no doubt as to the identity of the motionless figure standing there, gazing straight up at me. His hands were buried deep in his pockets, holding the disreputable old greatcoat closer around his body.

I had known in my heart since I had heard the first stone strike the glass that it was Lajos. Yet now that I saw him there, I was filled with panic. I knew there had to be something wrong.

Letting the curtain fall back, I sprinted across the room, not even pausing to snatch up a dressing gown or my spectacles before I left. I flew through the darkness, running noiselessly down stairs towards the pale light which burned in the front hall, wondering desperately if he was ill or injured or even in need of rescue from the law — though surely those days were long past now...?

My hands felt clumsy on the large bolts. The front door was heavy as I drew it open. Lajos slipped through when the opening was barely more than a crack, quickly taking the handle from me and closing the door softly. Then he turned to face me in the dim light.

Sick with fear, I searched his face short-sightedly for signs of illness or distress, but all I saw there was tiredness, and perhaps a hint of excitement in his eyes. I felt a puzzled frown contract my brow.

"What is it?" I whispered. His lip quirked slightly, and he moved towards me, taking my hand in one of his while with the other he picked up the lamp, nodding towards the room on the right, where once Alex had waited for me and Katalin, and leading me there. There was a peculiar dream-like quality to this nocturnal meeting. Dazed, I watched Lajos lay the lamp down on a table and straighten, turning to face me again.

"What is it?" I repeated. "What is wrong?"

"Nothing," he said calmly, taking my other hand and gazing down at me. "I came to say good-bye — I'm leaving at dawn."

"Leaving?" I said stupidly. "Why, where are you going?"

But I knew before he answered. His coat had fallen open and beneath it I could see blue and gold and silver. The colours of the *honvéd* cavalry.

The blood sang in my ears. Lajos had always said he would fight for the revolution. I had always known that he would. Only I had not expected it to be *now*...

In the distance, I was aware of his voice saying, "To join Moga on the Austrian border. I'm sorry. I thought there would be more time..."

More time, more time. I had done it again, stupidly assumed that he felt as I did, when if I had troubled to think at all this last week, I would have known that he did not, could not. The feeling was all mine. Again.

Lajos was saying, "It seemed the right moment: the Viennese have begun another revolution, partly in protest against the Court's treatment of Hungary, and our army is on the way to Austria. I've done all I can here. The revolution can't progress until we have made safe what we've won so far — and how better to do that than by helping the Viennese? Who knows? They might just keep the reactionaries out this time and save us a few battles if we can help them now."

This time, I was determined he would not know.

Drawing my limp hands free, I said coolly, "Do you believe that?" And dared to look at him at last. His eyes were unblinkingly on mine, and I saw there a strange, sad smile.

Instead of answering me, he said, "Katie, don't shut me out again. This is hard enough."

And abruptly, I was ashamed. My heart was breaking, but he was going to *war*, where the risks were unthinkable... Desperately, I forced the fear out of my mind, allowing him to take my hands again. I even smiled, tremulously, and felt him relax as if in relief.

"You must make a very smart hussar." My voice hardly shook at all.

"You always said I should find another tailor." His eyes were smiling properly now as his hands slid up my arms to my shoulders. I became suddenly aware of how little I was wearing, and the breath caught in my throat for reasons quite other than fear.

He said softly, "I wonder if you know how beautiful you are like this?"

My whole body began to flush. I didn't know if it was with embarrassment or pleasure, but I recognized the delicious ache that spread through me when his thumbs began lightly to caress my shoulders. I had thought of a clever reply, but now it flew out of my head. He moved one hand, gently pushing my loose hair back from my neck, his eyes all the while holding mine.

"Tell me the truth this time, Katie," he murmured. "Will you not miss me, even a little?"

I miss you every moment you are away from me. I cannot bear it if you go... But I didn't want to speak those words, and no others would come. I gazed up at him mutely. I suppose he read my answer in my eyes, while his clever, sensitive fingers were tenderly stroking the side of my neck.

Slowly, his head bent towards me. Amazingly, I felt his lips on my neck, where his fingers had been, and a shudder of purely sensual pleasure ran through me. My arms moved of their own volition to hold him, then fell weakly back to my side. His fair head moved, tracing a line of kisses, warm and sweet and downwards. With a little gasp, I caught his face in my hands, and he straightened, his dark eyes clouded, his cheeks hollow in the pale lamplight. I was so consumed by love that I wanted to weep.

"No words, Katie?" he whispered, touching my lips with one finger. "Not even a simple yes?"

I made an effort. "What was the question?"

He gave a low, warm breath of laughter. "Will you miss me?" he repeated, and his finger moved caressingly from my lips to my chin, sliding slowly down my neck till it was stopped between my breasts by my carelessly laced nightgown. "Will you?"

I could not move, could not breathe. There were more fingers now, his whole hand moving, caressing, softly closing. I could not even think of being outraged: I melted under his touch, and sensing it, knowing it, his other arm went around me, sweeping down my back and drawing me hard against him. My breath caught, and sighed at the devastating touch of his body. I was lost in delicious weakness.

"Will you?" he whispered, his lips almost touching mine.

"Yes..."

And then his mouth sank on mine in a slow, unbearably sensual kiss, at once infinitely tender and deliberately arousing. Without my knowing it, my arms had gone around him, my hands clinging to his neck, his back, while I gave myself up to the kiss and to my own, naked desire. It had been so long...

When his lips finally left mine, they were smiling.

"One truth," he murmured. "Here is another: you have no idea how much I have wanted this... But you... you won't live with me, you won't marry me; sometimes you won't even speak to me. Yet tonight... tonight you are mine."

His fingers were caressing my cheek. My head fell back against his shoulder. I could not deny it. I had always been his, if he had only known it.

"Why?" he said gently. His eyes were holding mine, and in spite of the wild, barely-controlled passion in him, I could see that he wanted an answer. His finger was lightly tracing my lips. "Is this pity, Katie? Because I'm going away to join the army and you think I might be killed, you will give yourself to me for one night?"

Bewildered, and yet sensing some truth in the words which I barely comprehended for the longing in me, I gazed up at him dumbly.

He smiled, a tender, rueful smile. "I don't want such a gift, Katie, generous as it is. I have no intention of dying, and I don't want one night of love followed by months of recriminations and misunderstandings. We have had all that already. This time, it should be forever — and you still can't risk that, can you?"

I didn't understand him then. I only sensed his withdrawal, although he still held me in his arms, close against his body. Helpless desire still flared in me, but I could see from his eyes that I was rejected. Humiliation rose quickly; in a moment of blind passion, I had offered myself again to this man as clearly as if I had spoken the words, and I was being refused.

I tore my eyes free, making sudden, desperate movements to escape him; but oddly, his arms tightened, and this time he would not let me go.

"Hush now," he murmured. "Don't pull away; don't leave me just yet."

"What are you doing?" I whispered brokenly. "What are you...?"

"Hush." He laid his warm, rough cheek against mine. "I came to say goodbye, remember?"

Abruptly, I relaxed against him, and for a long moment we held each other in that strange embrace; and gradually, a kind of peace settled over me. I don't know which of us it came from, but I think he felt it too.

At last, he stirred. His lips brushed my cheek, and then he straightened, loosening his hold.

"And now, I should go."

Softly, I touched the shadowed skin under his eyes. "Will you go home first and sleep?"

"No. I shall ride wildly round the city, practising being a hussar."

I smiled, stepping back out of his arms to see him better. "You *look* the part."

"I have plenty of gold braid," he said lightly. "Unfortunately, no weapons. I must be expected to win those from the enemy."

I couldn't bear to think of that. I picked up the lamp, carrying it with me as we passed back into the hall, and placing it carefully in its proper place. Then I turned to find him watching my face. I moved closer.

"Lajos?" I breathed. "Will you write to me?"

His hand lifted to my cheek. "Yes, if you wish it." I thought he sounded surprised.

"And you will be careful?"

He smiled. "I promise."

For a fleeting moment, his eyes strayed to my lips. Then quickly he bent and brushed them with his. And that was his good-bye. A second later, he was gone, and I had nothing except the cold air which he had let in to show that he had ever been.

Slowly, I made my way upstairs to bed. Alone.

"Do you ever think, Katie," Katalin said drearily, "that some things are just not meant to be...?"

We had just heard that General Puchner had declared martial law in Transylvania, and in alliance with the Romanians and Saxons was taking over the country in the name of the Emperor. The implications were not lost on neither of us.

I sighed helplessly and thought of Lajos on the Austrian border, and waited patiently, yet intensely, for the letter he had promised me.

Yet when the letter finally came, it was only a light and humorous description of his journey and his early days with Moga's army.

"The men in my charge are a motley crew of heroes and villains," he wrote. "At the moment, fortunately, they stand rather in awe of my name and seem to be immensely proud of me. Of course, we have not yet been in action, so they have not been made aware of my complete military ignorance!

"We are waiting, apparently, for an invitation from the insurgent Viennese to help them. But only the radicals there are prepared to welcome a foreign, revolutionary army, and our conservative commanders don't care for such communistic types. The real authorities are afraid to call on us in case, would you believe, that by so doing they offend the Emperor! It would be laughable if there were not people dying in Vienna for the same freedom we have been shouting about since March. And as you know, I have friends there whom I would give much to help..."

Despite the light-hearted tone he had adopted, his anxiety came through to me, as did his anger against the commanders who would not take the decision to relieve their allies. But it was not until I reread the letter that I realized what was causing my vague dissatisfaction: nowhere was there a reference to our last meeting; he did not say he missed me or looked forward to seeing me again; there was no softer language at all, no endearments save for the standard "My dear Katie" at the beginning. It was as if that last night in Buda-Pest had never been.

Naturally, pride compelled me to reply in the same vein. I wrote as amusingly as I could, describing life in the capital, telling him, if he did not already know, that Petőfi had joined up too and had been sent to Transylvania on a recruiting trip.

Then, a week later came news that shattered the buoyant optimism in Buda-Pest. After defeating two Croat armies, I think we had begun to believe ourselves invincible, but we were not. Too late, the Hungarian army had finally marched to Vienna's rescue, and lost.

"At a place called Schwechat, just outside Vienna," István reported, tiredly rubbing his forehead. He was doing all he could to aid Hungary's efforts to arm, but the price on his conscience was painful to watch. However, I had another, more immediate fear.

"Were many killed in the battle?" I asked anxiously.

"About five hundred, they say, killed, wounded or imprisoned. Moga himself was injured."

Surely, if Lajos had been among them, István would have heard. Lajos was a prominent figure in Hungary after all...

Yet it was several days before I could be free, however temporarily, of the gnawing dread in my stomach. Lajos's second letter, written in retreat after Schwechat, told me only that he had fought in the battle, though he had come to no harm; but despite its lack of words, I could almost feel his agony for the Viennese he felt he had failed, and I was left with the impression of disenchantment and bitterness.

*

One morning, just after I had joined István, Margit and Katalin for breakfast, Mattias came cautiously into the room, looking considerably the worse for wear.

"Inebriate," said Katalin, taking in the situation at one glance.

"Not any more. I eschew the brandy for ever more."

"Don't make promises you can't keep," I advised, and he grinned goodnaturedly.

"That reminds me," he said. "Met that fellow Jókai last night — you know, the writer, Petöfi's friend."

"You should keep better company," István interrupted irritably.

"Then you should let me join the army and get out of here, where I can do nothing but avoid my lectures and drink myself to death!" Mattias sat down, holding his head, and eventually rediscovered his point. "Jókai said Lajos Lázár was here but has gone again now."

I kept my eyes on my coffee for several seconds before I slowly raised them to Mattias. I wanted to weep with hurt and disappointment.

"Gone where?" asked Katalin.

"Transylvania, apparently. He's been transferred to Bem, who has just been put in charge there. Here, did you know some Pole shot Bem the other night?"

Josef Bem was our latest recruit, a Polish soldier of fortune and champion of liberalism who had just arrived in the city from Vienna. A larger than life figure, he had instantly become the rage in Buda-Pest, where wild stories about him abounded: it was even said he had escaped from Vienna when it fell, dressed as a female fruit-seller. But I wasn't interested in Bem, only in Lajos's neglect. I discovered I was angry too. How dared he treat me as if I were of no account?

By mid-day, I was in a truly filthy temper which neither Miklós nor Anna had been prepared to risk. As a result, I was in no mood for company and it was with singularly bad grace that I joined the family for luncheon.

"Oh there you are," Katalin said vaguely as I came into the room, taking something from her pocket and handing it to me. "This came for you — I meant to give it to you before..."

Over the letter, our eyes met, and I realized she had been hiding it this morning from István who would have recognized the writing. I took it, smiling with quick gratitude, and stuffed it hastily in my pocket.

When I finally escaped to my room, I all but tore the letter open with fingers that trembled like those of some schoolgirl receiving her first love letter. Yet no one could have called this a love letter. It was a note from one friend to another; not from the man who had thrown stones at my window and held me in his arms in the dark, early hours of an October morning. He said he had been sent to Buda-Pest with dispatches for the National Defence Committee.

"I tried to see you at the palace," he wrote casually, "but you had gone out. In any case, I had very little time, for I had to see Kossuth as well as War Minister Mészáros; and it seems one of the documents I had so gullibly carried was a complaint against me by my Colonel — I had apparently driven him so mad that he wished me to be transferred as far away from him as possible. Naturally, I incline to the belief that the Colonel should transfer instead — preferably into civilian life — but I shan't bore you with details. The upshot of it all is that I am now bound for Transylvania under the command of a mad Pole called Bem..."

Not a word about looking for me, beyond that one call. I had to face the fact that Lajos had more important things on his mind. It wasn't surprising. I just wished it didn't hurt quite so badly.

*

It was the sheer scale of the catastrophe at Mór which caused the absolute silence in the Szelényi Palace. It was I who broke it.

"What now?" I asked, low-voiced.

That day, the thirtieth of December, only fifty miles west of Buda-Pest, an army of six thousand, under the command of the radical General Perczel, had been annihilated.

"Now, Mattias will take you out of the city," said István. "Go to the estate north of Debrecen, and wait for me there. Who knows? Perhaps we shall be able to go home to Szelényi soon, since Bem seems to be winning back Transylvania."

"I won't go without you," Elisabeth said unexpectedly, and won a surprised, very tired smile from her husband.

"You must. There are the children..."

"Katie can take care of the children. She must go with Margit and Katalin..."

"No," István said firmly. "You must all go."

"Why won't you come?" Katalin asked in a small, oddly childish voice.

"I should be here. When the Austrians come, perhaps I can help salvage something from this mess..."

A lost cause, I thought with anguish; surely now a lost cause...

CHAPTER THIRTY-NINE

It seemed the Assembly agreed that Buda-Pest at least was lost, because the next day, after reputedly stormy sessions and fierce, raging arguments, it was decided, despite all past talk of defending the capital to the last man, to evacuate the entire government to Debrecen in the east.

For us, this certainly solved one problem — István would come with us. We would take the train as far as Szolnok, which was the end of Hungary's one railway line, and find some other, slower form of transport from there.

In a mad flurry of activity, we packed only what could be carried by ourselves and the few servants who would accompany us. Then we said good-bye to the Mirányis, who were to stay behind. Mirányi was not compromised in Austrian eyes to the same extent as István, and I believe they thought that with one part of the family on either side of the fence, they could somehow preserve the whole in the end. I found myself wondering if I would ever see Maria's disapproving face again; but Maria herself was naturally more concerned with the painful parting from her brothers and sisters.

The children had picked up their elders' fear, but they were resilient creatures, and by the evening when we set off for the new railway station, they were as excited as they had been about boarding the Danube steam-ship.

We bade good-bye and good luck to Ferenc and Frau Schmidt, who stood by the door, upright and brave, to wave us off. As the horses pulled us away from the palace gates, I wondered dismally if I would ever see them again. The white faces by the door receded into the darkness; the house itself grew hazy until I realized I was looking through tears. For all that had happened to me here, I knew I had never been happier anywhere, and now I doubted I would ever come back.

The railway station was full of people crying and complaining, adding considerably to my depression. But there was worse to come: Teréz Meleki suddenly appeared with a maid, a footman and a trunk.

"*There* you are!" Elisabeth exclaimed.

"Indeed I am," Teréz drawled. "And more to the point, here is Kossuth..."

Elegant and dignified, with his family about him, the great man entered more as if he were in a triumphal procession than an ignominious retreat.

Perhaps it should have been laughable, but it wasn't. In fact, I noticed something very strange happening.

With his appearance, every face in the crowded station lightened perceptibly; the dismal complaints died away, and a quite unfounded optimism began to grow. Orders and commands began to fly round the station; the miserable, clinging bundles of people began to split up and spring into activity. Incredibly, someone was soon mixing huge bowls of punch in the middle of the station.

I could hear Kossuth's voice saying that this was not the end, but a new beginning, that Hungary would rise again out of her eastern city of Debrecen, and throw the invader from the capital. I almost found myself believing it.

By then, Kossuth was the centre of our little world, and when I looked at him my spirits lifted in irrational new hope. Someone thrust a glass of punch into my hand, and I realized that all the evacuees, Kossuth and his family, the Lords and Deputies and their families, were all clutching cups and glasses.

It seemed a pointless, meaningless extravagance, until quite suddenly, I remembered what day it was. It was the thirty-first of December, Hogmanay, New Year's Eve. A year ago I had danced at the Szelényi ball and flirted with Karl von Avenheim, who was now our enemy, and my only care had been whether or not Lajos loved me. I felt ashamed of the triviality of that, for now a nation had risen in arms to fight for its liberty, its very existence, and young men were dying.

The clock in the station told me it was nearing midnight. Everyone had their punch now. The noise abated, and Kossuth seemed to tower above his fellows.

"Ladies and gentlemen," he said into the silence, raising his glass high. "I give you the new year, and new hope."

Solemnly, fervently, we drank to that. Families kissed and embraced, raised their glasses to friends on the other side of the station. If ever they were united, it was in that one simple toast.

And I, duly embraced, kissed, toasted, accepted as part of that union, felt suddenly and sadly outside it. A grain of loneliness began to grow. I wanted to see my own people again; and my longing for Lajos's presence became suddenly so fierce that I could imagine him beside me, close to me as I raised my glass, smiling back at Kossuth who could still recognize me despite his new greatness.

That was the high point of our exodus. From then on, it only got worse. To begin with, we had to wait another three hours to board the train, and then the riotous clamour to find space in the carriages was positively degrading. Despite the Szelényis' rank, we were pushed and herded along with the rest. Elisabeth and Katalin were flabbergasted, Margit utterly bewildered, though Mattias and István did their best to protect them.

It was Zsuzsa and I, carrying the children, who found space for us all together. Unfortunately, Teréz joined us too, but I could hardly prevent that. With difficulty, we struggled to make ourselves comfortable in our cramped conditions, while all around us was noise and upheaval and constant movement.

And only when the train began to pull slowly forward, did Katalin say suddenly, "Where is Mattias?"

I knew before I saw him. There was a rush to the window facing the platform, and there, inevitably, was Mattias, walking forward with the train, a faint, sad smile of apology on his young face as he lifted his hand in silent farewell.

*

The journey itself was a nightmare. It was cramped and noisy and bitterly cold, and the locomotive broke down three times. I had never been so glad of the extravagant sable cloak which István and Elisabeth had given me for Christmas last year. Miserably, I huddled inside it. I thought we would never reach Szolnok, while Debrecen itself was just a distant dream.

It was around dawn, during one of the breakdowns, that I went to the door of our carriage for some air. At least temporarily, I could be alone there. Shortly afterwards, I saw Teréz leave too, and wander up and down the crowded train in search of her friends and acquaintances. I contented myself with staring out on to the vast flatness surrounding us. With the pale sun just coming up, there was something very grand about the *Puszta*, the Great Plain — perhaps its sheer size, its massive, unchanging space, made all the more impressive by the whiteness of the winter snow covering everything as far as I could see.

After a while, Teréz passed me, going the other way this time. Politely, I stood aside for her, but at the precise moment I moved, the locomotive chose to do the same. The train lurched forward for barely a second, and then the brakes slammed on again, stopping us with a painful jar. I flung my hands out, reaching instinctively for support, and managed to grab at the wall, but my reticule flew away from me, landing open on the floor at Teréz's feet.

Teréz was one of those intensely irritating women who never seem to lose their balance or do anything remotely clumsy. As a result she was in a far better position than I to retrieve my fallen reticule first, even though I, seeing with dismay what had spilled out of it, made a determined effort to beat her.

By the time I had bent and reached out for the fallen letters, Teréz had picked one up and was casually standing on the others with one elegantly shod foot. I hesitated, then, deciding not to make a fuss, I quietly picked up the ignored reticule and the few coins and bits of rubbish that were lying around it. When I straightened, she was looking at me, her expression unreadable.

"Are you a frequent correspondent of Lajos Lázár's?" she enquired lightly, turning the letter towards me so that I could see his name and direction written across it. It was a letter I had written yesterday and never sent, because there had been no time. I was annoyed to feel the colour flooding into my cheeks, but I met her mocking gaze squarely.

"I don't believe that is any of your business," I said evenly. "Excuse me, you are standing on other letters of mine."

She smiled. "So I am," she said, and bending, picked them up, insolently studying the address of all three. "Now, I believe I know that writing — it betrays his lack of breeding, don't you think? Tell me, dear Katie, do you carry all your correspondence so close to your person?"

"If you wished to supervise my packing, you should have called yesterday," I said tartly.

"Ah, but you wouldn't have let me see these, would you? You are hiding them from prying eyes — I wonder why?"

My temper was rising, but I controlled the hasty words which sprang to my tongue, merely holding out my hand for the letters. Teréz ignored me.

"Let's see," she murmured, and actually opened up one of the letters before my astonished, outraged eyes. "'My dear Katie,'" she began, with quite deliberate ridicule, and suddenly I could not help myself. It was not a calculated act, but one of utter spontaneity born of sheer fury at her insolence, at her unbearable invasion of my privacy. Before I knew I was going to, I had raised my hand and dealt her one sharp, ringing slap full across her smooth cheek.

At any other time, her expression of open-mouthed amazement would have been ludicrous. Now, I barely noticed it. I saw only that her grip had slackened with shock and, seizing the opportunity, I quickly twitched the open letter and the two others out of her fingers.

"Thank you," I said calmly, and walked away, tucking the letters back into my reticule as I went.

By the time I rejoined the others, I found I was shaking. Partly, I was appalled that she should even touch anything I shared with Lajos; partly, I was enraged that she should despise me enough to dare to read my letters in front of me. But on top of that, I felt sudden shame that I had hit her; civilized, decent people did not resolve their differences by such methods, whatever the provocation. Remembering her look of ludicrous dismay, I felt guilty, and then, as I recalled also the last flash of venomous, unforgiving hatred in her eyes when I had turned away, I felt uneasy too. She could make trouble for me very easily, if she chose, with the knowledge of these letters, for she knew how István felt about Lajos and how uncertain everyone's temper was in the present crisis.

"Are you well, dear?" came Margit's anxious voice beside me.

I forced myself to smile at her. "Of course. Just tired. Ah, at last! We are moving again."

In fact it was Margit who looked increasingly ill as the dreadful journey continued. The children, on the other hand, bore it remarkably well. They liked the bustle and the fascinating crowds of people. They shrieked with joy every time the whistle blew and ran from side to side watching for the clouds of steam puffing past us. By the time we reached Szolnok, they were the only ones not totally exhausted.

However, we had another impossible task ahead of us: procuring a vehicle to take us the rest of the way to Debrecen. Everyone else from the train was trying to do the same thing, for naturally, no one wanted to walk — though in the end some poor souls had to. István eventually managed to buy a horse and cart at a vastly inflated price, and hired a singularly shifty individual to drive it for us. It was hardly the warmest or the most comfortable mode of travel, though the children thought it great sport, but at least it meant we could all stay together with the luggage.

Inevitably, Teréz came with us since, despite my prayers, no one offered her a seat in a better vehicle. She seemed to have decided to remain silent about the letters, and the slap, but she did not have the look of a woman who has been worsted. Instead, I kept finding her eyes upon me with a sort of predatory satisfaction, almost like a cat playing with a mouse. I couldn't help feeling uneasy, but I tried to ignore it, and to concentrate on quieting the children and trying to make poor Margit more comfortable.

Gradually, the children became more bearable as their usual travel-listlessness began to overcome them. Margit, on the other hand, was beginning to worry me.

"I think she is really ill," I murmured to István. "She should see a doctor."

But István was tired and irritable. "Yes, yes; when we reach Debrecen."

This didn't seem likely to be soon. We lost a wheel off the awful cart, and though it happened fortunately close to a village, it still took several hours to repair. Darkness had fallen again before we were even in sight of Debrecen and, despite the clear moonlight, István was furious — largely because, I suspected, all the best lodgings in the city would be gone before we reached them.

And it was then that Teréz chose to take her revenge. As we turned a corner in the road, the moon obligingly illuminated the edifying sight of a soldier and a girl making love in a ditch. They must have been freezing, I reflected practically. Primly, we averted our eyes. Even the shifty driver did not say a word, but Teréz suddenly laughed.

"Dear me," she remarked. "What do you think, Katie? Another silly little trollop who can't resist a uniform?"

"I am unacquainted with her history," I said drily.

"But is it the uniform which is so attractive?"

"I'm sure we could go back and ask the young lady, if you really want to know."

"No, no, I'm asking you personally. Did *you* succumb to the uniform in the end, or were you always hot for him?"

"Teréz," Elisabeth said warningly, mindful of the children — who were actually asleep — and of the servants huddled together for warmth, silent but interested nearby.

"Sorry, but my question is still unanswered," Teréz mourned.

"Is it surprising when no one has the least idea what you are talking about?" István snapped.

"Oh, Katie knows — don't you, Katie?"

"I haven't the remotest idea," I said calmly.

"Yes you do. I'm talking about your sordid little affair with Lajos Lázár."

Her words fell across the night with disastrous clarity; but even then all might have been well, because Teréz was so obviously being spiteful, and because by now everyone had the suspicion that it was Lajos and not she who had ended their affair. But Katalin, my loyal, stupid friend, immediately fired up in my defence.

"You know nothing about it!" she cried indignantly. "Katie and Lajos love each other!"

I closed my eyes. "Thank you, Katalin," I murmured, and tried to concentrate only on the ache in my head. There was nothing else to concentrate on, for everyone was silent. Then István's voice came, icy cold.

"What is she talking about?"

"Nothing," I said tiredly. "Like Teréz, she is talking rubbish."

"Didn't you know?" Teréz said to him, provoking, pitying.

"Stop it," Elisabeth said, suddenly sharp, but Teréz could not stop till she had caused the maximum damage.

"Well, he has to be told. He must be the only person in Buda-Pest who doesn't know!"

"Know what?" Still that icy command in his voice. I couldn't look at his face.

"About Katie's affair with Lázár, of course," said Teréz innocently. "I imagine those letters she's hiding in her reticule will provide more than enough proof."

Slowly, I dragged my gaze round to István's face. His eyes were glittering in the darkness; his mouth seemed only a thin, hard line. I had the oddest feeling that this was the last straw for István, that what would follow was somehow inevitable now.

"Well?" he said coldly. "Deny it. Deny that you, a Szelényi, would ever let yourself be touched by that vile, base-born, murdering peasant scum."

Whatever happened, I couldn't allow that. "I know of no vile, base-born, murdering..."

"Deny it!" he said harshly, and suddenly I was indescribably weary of deception and games and hiding what was surely the most important part of my life. I lifted my head.

"Deny what? That I love Lajos? I can't. I do love him. I have loved him since I first came to Hungary. I would marry him, if only he wanted me to."

I had only a moment in which to feel the rushing relief of confession, for

István moved faster than I thought he could. Suddenly he was looming over me, and my only emotion was blind, startled fear. The mad, blazing fury in his face, in his icy eyes, was terrifying. It was no longer István.

"Damn you," he uttered between his teeth, grasping me by the front of my clothing and hauling me to my feet. "Damn you, you fornicating little bitch!" And then his grip tightened. I caught wildly at his hand as we reeled precariously on the bumping cart, but he didn't steady me. Instead, before I could even think of saving myself, he swept me off my feet and threw me.

I heard Katalin's scream. I heard Elisabeth's horrified, "*István!*" By then the road was flying up to meet me. I was too stunned to make a sound, but as I crashed on to the road, and rolled, and fell down into nothing, I heard Teréz's laughter chasing me. There was pain and breathlessness and snow in my mouth, and then a sharp, blinding crack on my head. And nothing.

CHAPTER FORTY

When I opened my eyes, I thought I was blind, for everywhere was darkness. Spots danced in front of me, my head was thumping painfully, the singing in my ears grew and faded, but still I could not see.

Frightened and bewildered, I reached out and felt icy, wet grass under my fingers. I realized that I was freezing, and that I was outside. There were perhaps five seconds of pure, terrified panic before I remembered what had happened. István, enraged beyond endurance, had thrown me out of the cart and driven on.

I moved, struggling to sit up, and for several moments the dark world reeled again. I cried aloud in shock at the pain in my head, reaching instinctively for the source. It was unbearably tender, and my fingers came away sticky. I had hit my head on something when I had rolled into the ditch.

I stumbled to my feet, feeling my hip sore and bruised, then reached down searchingly into the snow and found, unmistakably, my spectacles. Wiping them haphazardly on my wet skirt, I put them on, but one of the arms had broken and they lay askew on my nose. It didn't matter. I couldn't see anyway.

I had to all but crawl out of the ditch and forward towards the road. But still, there was only snow and grass and dirt under my hands. I paused, climbing slowly and painfully to my feet. My eyes were beginning to clear now, but the moon had gone, covered by thick cloud which blocked out all its light. Even with my spectacles, I could not see the road. I took a few more steps, then I began to run wildly. Panic filled me again — I had to get back to the road, for I knew they would come back for me.

I knew István; and though I had never seen it before, I knew his rage too. It was the same ungovernable passion which had consumed me in the confrontation with my grandfather after our return from Nagyzseben, so I knew it would not last. Eventually, he would calm down, be ashamed of what he had done, as I had been ashamed of what I had said. He would come back for me, even without the others to force him.

Whether or not he would forgive me for my confession was another matter, but I couldn't worry about that now. I was alone in the darkness, cold, injured, dizzy, lost...

Lost. I had lost the road. I stopped and peered round me, but in every direction the darkness was invariable, almost opaque. I decided I must have been walking in the opposite direction to that of the road, and began to walk back in what I hoped was the way I had come, carefully feeling ahead of me for the ditch in case I fell into it again. I didn't. I didn't even *find* the ditch.

In despair, I began to run. How would they ever find me if I was not on the road? Would they be able to see me? I didn't even know how far I had come — the timeless darkness and the woolliness of my head saw to that. The night was silent, though I strained my ears for shouts, for the sound of wheels rumbling on the road.

"István!" I shouted desperately. "István! Katalin, can you hear me? Please! I'm here! István!"

On the last cry, I stopped running to listen, but all I could hear was the thundering of my heart and my ragged, uneven breathing. I raised my face to heaven, as if pleading silently for help, but the only response was a large, fat snowflake on my cheek. A fearful laugh caught in my throat. Another snowfall was all I needed.

Although my bonnet had vanished, I still had my fur cloak to keep me warm and dry, and oddly enough my reticule too was still dangling from my wrist, quite secure in spite of the trouble it had caused by falling open on the train. Things could be worse, I told myself sternly, drawing the hood of my cloak up over my thumping head and trudging on. Surely, in whatever direction I went, I would eventually reach habitation and help.

I walked for the rest of the night through light, intermittent snow. When the sky began to lighten, the snow stopped, but still I could see nothing but the huge plain stretching before me in all directions. There was one dot in the distance which might have been a house, but I could see no roads, no villages, and certainly no town the size of Debrecen.

Exhausted, I finally lay down under a bush and fell shivering into sleep. I can't have slept for long however, for the sun had not moved very far when I awoke. It was probably as well, for I was wet and freezing cold. For the first time I began to see clearly that I should have stayed as close as possible to the place where I had first wakened. I could only blame the bump on my head for my stupidity in moving so far, but looking back I think sheer panic probably had a lot to do with it too.

Shivering, I stood up and stared at the bleak, empty landscape which surrounded me. There was nowhere to go, nothing to do except walk — so I walked, growing more and more desperate, feeling more and more as if I were part of a nightmare. The only people I encountered throughout that exhausting day were an old woman who spoke neither Hungarian nor German and who seemed never to have heard of Debrecen, and a rude peasant in a sheepskin cloak leading a donkey and cart, who only laughed when I asked him for directions. I began to think I was mad. If I wasn't, I felt I soon would be.

Of a town, or even a village, I saw no sign at all.

Then, just when I was beginning to sink into despair, I saw two soldiers resting their horses in the distance. My heart lifted, for this surely was a sign of habitation. Perhaps I was even close at last to Debrecen. The soldiers were sitting on their saddles in the snow by the side of the road while their horses snuffled around them rather dejectedly in search of sustenance.

I hurried up to them, smiling, for though they were an alarmingly villainous-looking pair, I saw that they wore uniform of the same colours as Lajos's — the blue, gold and silver of the *honvéd* cavalry — and was foolishly cheered. They watched my approach sullenly at first. Then one spoke to the other and they both grinned, showing rotten teeth.

For the first time, I began to feel uncomfortable about addressing them, for close to they were an even less prepossessing sight: unshaven and dirty, their uniforms askew and badly stained with something I didn't care to think about. But just then, they were the only hope I had.

They did not bother to stand when I stopped in front of them, just regarded me insolently. One of them, a raven-haired, stocky man with an ugly scar across his forehead, smirked in a way I found positively repulsive, his eyes sliding beyond me to the road, as if to see who was accompanying me. However, I asked them civilly enough if I was anywhere near Debrecen.

"Debrecen?" repeated the scarred man, genuinely amused. "Lord love you, lady, you're way off the road. Debrecen's miles away!"

My heart sank. I could feel my shoulders drooping, but still determined, I said, "Then could you possibly tell me how I might get there?"

The soldiers looked at each other.

"Please," I said desperately. "It's very important that I get to Debrecen."

"Well," said the previously silent one, taking a piece of dead twig from his mouth. "I don't think we can rightly go *there*."

The other kicked him, grinning. "Of course we can, Béla. For the young lady. For a price. Or least ways, we can take her somewhere as good."

I regarded him coldly. "Unfortunately," I said scathingly, "it has to be Debrecen. I do not ask for your escort, merely your directions; but if you gentlemen cannot help me, then I shall simply thank you for your time and find someone who can."

With which words, I turned sharply on my heel, relief at being free of them struggling with frustration at being no further forward in my interminable quest for Debrecen. But suddenly a hand closed like a vice around my ankle, and before I could even cry out, I was on my face in the snow again, my spectacles flying away out of sight. I heard their crude laughter, but at that time I was too angry to be frightened.

"How dare you?" I spluttered, kicking myself free of the obnoxious hand, and struggling to rise to my feet; but almost casually, the other soldier grasped my arm and pulled me sprawling towards him. His dirty, grinning face leered over me, and quite instinctively I lashed out at it, dealing a wild blow to his chin that hurt my hand. It was a mistake, for there was nothing chivalrous about this gentleman. He simply swore and hit me back with deliberate brutality, full across the mouth.

I cried out, tasting blood and fear through the black dizziness that threatened to engulf me. The scarred one was holding both my hands spread out above my head. The other, the one called Béla, had straddled my body, and only then did I realize what they had intended all along, ever since they had seen me walking alone towards them.

I had never known this sort of fear before. I still don't think there is a word for it. I lay on my back, paralysed with shock while the man above me hurriedly pulled open my cloak and hooked his fingers into the neck of my gown, and ripped. But as the material tore, I was suddenly propelled into action. I wrenched my hands downwards, bucking with all my strength to dislodge my violator.

I think the abruptness of my retaliation, after the stunned stillness, must have surprised them, for I had my hands free and Béla fell sideways. I struck out with my feet and my hands, and a truly terrible struggle ensued.

I had the strength born of pure desperation. I scratched and bit till I drew blood; I fought with my knees and my feet, and once I even connected my elbow sharply with the place Aunt Edith had recommended in such situations. I don't imagine, however, that in her wildest dreams she ever foresaw this sort of silent, vicious struggle. She had been thinking of gentlemen who, perhaps under the influence of wine or spirits, became a little too amorous; rape by two brutal soldiers was an entirely different matter, and I was punished for my elbow's accuracy when my victim, doubled up and howling, struck me hard across the face again.

Now I barely noticed the dizziness, or the cold beneath me, so intent was I upon the fight I had no hope of winning, or any chance of escape or rescue from. Bruised and bloody and powerless, I was crying inside as their lecherous hands grabbed at my body, pulled at my clothing. Exhausted beyond belief, yet still exerting every feeble, useless muscle against them, I closed my eyes to shut out the filthy, bright-eyed face above mine. I smelled his sour, hot breath, felt it quicken as he reached forcefully under my skirts, and the cry became a silent scream that I knew would never stop.

I remember thinking, somewhere deep in my mind where I could still think, that this perhaps was what Lajos had really feared for me at the hands of Aaron Klein's attackers in the bookshop. But there was no Lajos to rescue me now, no Lajos to prevent violation and rape by the mere sound of his voice, his name.

"Lajos..." I whispered, without meaning to, and my attacker paused, though only to laugh.

"Is that your man?" he sneered. "He won't want you after this, so better not tell him!"

His hands were at his trousers now, while the scarred one held me still.

"Lajos Lázár," I said desperately, because his name had acted like a charm upon Aaron Klein's attackers. "Lajos Lázár will punish you for this."

The words sounded silly and childish, even to my own ears, for these were unknown soldiers, not the mobs of Buda-Pest, familiar with his name and his actions. I was actually surprised when Béla paused again. I saw him exchange looks with his partner in crime, and suddenly I was afraid to hope.

At last he said uneasily, "What do you know of Captain Lázár?"

"He will punish you for this, I swear it," I said brokenly.

"Is *he* your man?" the other demanded. "Are you Captain Lázár's woman?"

"Yes!"

They looked at each other again. Slowly, my crushed hands were released. Béla heaved himself off me, moving a little apart with his friend.

"Stay there," he said over his shoulder.

I obeyed because I couldn't do anything else. My whole body was throbbing and trembling. I felt utterly weak, but I could think no further than gratitude for this temporary relief. I managed to sit up, dragging my skirts back down over my legs, trying to hold the bodice of my dress together with thick, useless fingers. Eventually, I remembered I was lying on my cloak and drew that around me instead. I had never been so cold in my life. Fascinated, I watched my clutching hands shake as if someone was pulling strings attached to them.

The soldiers were beside me again. I flinched away, and was surprised when they did not touch me. The scarred one knelt down beside me.

"Captain Lázár isn't in Debrecen," he told me.

It took me a while to understand that, and then my lips could not form the words for weakness. "I know," I managed at last. "I'm going to my family."

They looked at each other again. The scarred one said, "The thing is, we can't go to Debrecen: there's a camp there."

"I know," I said again, my mouth still trembling. "I don't want *you* to go..."

"The road is dangerous. You'll need protection, wherever you go."

I couldn't quite believe I had heard that. I raised my head from my knees and stared at him. To my amazement, his eyes slid away from mine.

"We'll take you to Captain Lázár," he said. "He's *our* Captain."

I closed my thickened mouth. I tried to make my fuddled, hurt head think. I licked my bleeding lips and flinched.

"Why?" I looked from him to Béla. Their reluctance to go to Debrecen because of the military camp there suddenly made sense. "You're deserters."

"No!" they said together, then the scarred one shrugged. "We went off without asking, but the truth is we don't care much for the free life any more..."

"You mean you've spent all your pay," I said contemptuously, then wished I hadn't, for I wasn't safe yet, not by a long way. If I had had the strength to cringe, I would have cringed. However, the soldiers were immune to such insults.

"We have. But it's hard to go back. If we take *you* to the Captain, he'll be so grateful to us, he'll let us off."

"*Grateful?*" Either they were mad or I was. "For *this?*" I touched my cut lips — they were all I could recognize, so far, as damaged.

"Well," said Béla, and suddenly they were threatening again. "You tell him we found you, and saved you."

As if fascinated, I gazed at him. "Why in the world," I asked gently, "would I do that?"

"Because unless you do, we'll cut your throat now," was the candid answer. It was a persuasive argument, but it had severe flaws, as I strove to point out.

"You can't know what I shall tell Captain Lázár. You can't believe me. I doubt he would believe me either if I told him such a tale."

"You swear," the scarred man persevered, almost casually producing a wicked knife from his belt and inspecting its sharpness. "You swear on your mother's grave, and by the Holy Bible, that you'll tell him we saved you. And if you ever go back on that, we'll find you and kill you just the same."

I was sure there was still a flaw, but my mind was too tired and pained to grasp it. It could only grasp the knife, and what I knew they would do to me before they used it.

"Very well," I said stiffly. "I swear. On my mother's grave, and by the Holy Bible."

"And you'll make him believe it?"

"If I can."

The scarred man nodded, and put away his knife with decision. "Good. Then let's go. We can ride ten miles before nightfall." He rose to his feet, holding out his hand to me. I was weaker than a kitten, but I wasn't yet as desperate as that. I managed to get to my feet, unaided.

"My spectacles," I said with vague unhappiness. Amazingly, Béla trotted away and picked something up off the road which he brought back to me. I took them carefully, without touching his fingers, and placed them awry on my nose. It helped the world to swing a little more into focus.

The next ordeal was getting on the horse, not just because of my weakness or the pain I was becoming aware of in every part of my body, but because I was obliged to ride in front of Béla. I shuddered with uncontrollable repulsion, trying in vain to keep any distance at all between us; and new jolts of pain shot through me with every stride the horse took.

When it grew dark, they found shelter under some trees and lit a fire. They had no food, but I didn't want any. I felt sick, with a deep, corroding sickness that seemed to affect every part of me. In a fit of generosity — or perhaps because he imagined I would tell Lajos of his care — the scarred man, who was apparently called Tamás, gave me a blanket, saying with pride in his sacrifice that he would share his friend's.

I lay down, still shaking under my cloak and my blanket, despite my closeness to the fire. Somewhere, I thought I could hear the mournful howling of a dog, or a wolf, but the cry might only have been in my head.

I couldn't quite believe that I was safe now from their violation — if they could make me keep quiet about the last attack, why would they worry about others? I thought I would wait until they were asleep on the other side of the fire, and then slip away. I would take one of their poor horses if I could...

CHAPTER FORTY-ONE

I woke at first light to the sound of their talking. I was cold and damp, and every bone in my body hurt. There was a scab of dried blood on my thickened lip, a swelling on my cheek that pained me whenever I opened my mouth, but incredibly I had survived the night without being further molested.

As we carried on our way, I gave up the idea of escape, partly through inertia, partly through the realization that they were not going to hurt me further if I did as they asked. At the first village we came to they bought bread and milk which was shared out scrupulously. Although I had done nothing, I was ashamed and averted my battered face from the curious stares of the villagers.

When the overburdened horse grew tired, Béla granted me the respite of riding alone while he walked at the beast's head. At first I didn't pay much attention to our surroundings, but then I realized we were escaping the flatness, approaching hills that became the mountains dividing us from Transylvania.

It had begun to snow by the time darkness fell, and the temperature plummeted even further, so when we reached a village with an inn, I made my first decision of the journey.

Stopping and sliding painfully off the horse, I said, "We'll stay here."

"We can't. Inns cost money," said Tamás, as if explaining to a retarded child.

"I have enough money, and I refuse to spend another night outside in this cold. I have no intention of freezing to death to oblige you." With which I marched straight into the inn.

After a pause of sheer astonishment, they followed me. The innkeeper gaped when he saw me, then drew himself up to his full height — all of five feet — and began to tell me in tones of outrage that he ran a respectable house.

"I sincerely hope so," I interrupted. "I would not otherwise care to stay in it." However, I did not blame him for his attitude. The sight of so bedraggled and damaged a figure as I, in company with two of the most villainous looking soldiers anyone is likely to meet, must have told its own tale. "I require two rooms."

"Do you?" said the innkeeper, looking from the soldiers back to me. Perhaps he saw something of the desperation in my self-control; perhaps he pitied me for my bruises. Whatever the cause, his expression of self-righteousness faded, and his face softened slightly.

"What happened to you, Madame?" he asked, more gently. I was stuck for an answer, but my companions were not.

"She was attacked," said Tamás.

"By violent soldiers — bad men," said Béla.

The innkeeper, whatever else he was, was no fool. He took a step nearer me. "Did they...?" he began, low-voiced, but my escort broke in indignantly.

"*Us?* Why, we saved her! This is our Captain's lady — we're taking her to her husband!"

I met the innkeeper's gaze. "You wouldn't think it to look at them," I agreed, "but beneath those hideous facades, apparently, lurk creatures of quite startling chivalry. I presume there *are* rooms free?"

The innkeeper shut his mouth. "Yes, of course — I'll show you at once. Perhaps you'd like my wife to attend you?"

"No, thank you," I said at once. Even without the soldiers' warning stares, I did not want anyone to see the state I was in. But on the stairs I paused. "Perhaps I could have a bowl of soup in my room?"

"Of course."

When I was alone, I stripped off the torn dress with some difficulty, for my limbs were stiff and covered in bruises from the violent struggle with my escort. My shoulders and my breasts were black and blue too. Slowly, I moved towards the cracked mirror on the chest, and examined my face. The left side was badly discoloured and swollen still. My cut lip was beginning to heal, though inside my mouth there was a more severe wound where my own teeth had bitten.

Gazing at myself I felt a sense of unreality. How could I have come to this so quickly? Only days ago I had lived in a palace, pampered, cared for, respected. And now... this.

I wondered rather vaguely what Lajos would say when I turned up. His men had promoted me to wife, which was, I supposed, supremely ironic. I wondered what István had thought when he could not find me. I wondered what the others felt or feared for me — whatever it was, it could not be worse than what these two had tried to do to me.

Abruptly, tears started to my eyes and flowed over my aching face.

"Self pity, Katie," I told myself angrily. "Pull yourself together..."

The nightmares ensured I did not have an untroubled sleep, but nevertheless I felt a little better in the morning. I dare say the innkeeper and his good lady thought it odd that I came down for breakfast with my cloak wrapped securely around my person, but they said nothing. I thought of asking for a needle and thread to sew up the tears in my dress, but it was too late by then — the soldiers were anxious to get on their way.

The mountain road was treacherous in the snow, and as we crossed the pass the wind howled ferociously, hurling armfuls of snow into my frozen face. I barely noticed it. Transylvania. I had never thought to enter it in such a way as this.

One night, I remember, we found a deserted, ruined village in which to sleep — the war had been here — and I lay awake for hours just listening to the pitiful baying of wolves in the darkness, while Béla and Tamás whispered nervously together and edged as close as they dared to the fire.

In the morning we rode on, travelling by devious routes, no doubt to avoid both Hungarian and enemy soldiers, but most of the time I wasn't really aware of my surroundings. I hardly even heard my escort occasionally asking questions of people they stopped on the road.

At last, Béla dismounted and walked at the horse's head.

"This is the Captain's camp," he said with some satisfaction, and reality jabbed through my daze of pain and disgust and humiliation. They were really taking me to Lajos. I was about to meet him for the first time in three months, in this state, and masquerading as his wife of all things.

I only hoped he would see the joke.

My unease was hardly lessened by the way my escort answered the challenges flung at them by armed soldiers who seemed to know them.

"This is Captain Lázár's lady," they said grandly. "We're taking her to him."

The camp was a group of farm buildings around a courtyard. A young officer, striding across from one building to another, glanced at us incuriously, then looked again. He paused, and changing direction abruptly, came towards us. My escort stopped.

"What's this?" snapped the officer. "What is going on? You two have no permission..."

"This is Captain Lázár's wife," Tamás interrupted respectfully. "We've brought her to him."

The officer stared. "His *wife*? I didn't know he was married!" Then, looking suddenly harassed, he swept off his hat and bowed a little jerkily. "Forgive me, Madame — this is unexpected, you'll agree! I'm Nyergesz, Captain... I think perhaps I should get the Colonel." And he shouted to a passing soldier who ran off to do his bidding.

I sat where I was. I couldn't think what else to do. Captain Nyergesz looked at me, opened his mouth to speak but thought better of it. I had tidied and pinned my hair as best I could, and my cloak covered the ravages beneath, but I still must have presented an odd sight, to say the least.

An older man was striding across to us now, a thin, straight-backed individual with fine, military moustaches.

"Colonel Drényi," said the Captain, with relief. "This is Madame Lázár, Lajos's wife..."

Tired of hearing it, I opened my mouth to deny it, but as I moved I caught sight of my escort and was silent. If I was not Lajos's wife, I had no business being here. What was I doing here?

The Colonel looked as amazed as the Captain, but he recovered better. "Why, how is this, Madame? But won't you dismount? You must be tired."

Obediently, I came down, but the sudden twinges caught me by surprise, and the Colonel must have seen the pain in my face. His kind hands helped me the rest of the way, while I held my spectacles on to my nose.

Colonel Drényi was looking concerned now. "Madame, you are hurt. How come you to be in the company of these rascals?"

The rascals were staring at me fixedly. I took a deep breath.

"They saved me," I said, "from attack. They thought I should come here — but I can see it was a mistake. I was upset, you understand. Perhaps you could direct me...?"

"Madame!" The Colonel clasped my hand. I tried not to wince. "You cannot go anywhere without seeing Lázár! I'm afraid he is not in camp just now — he is leading a reconnaissance party — but we expect him back before nightfall."

"Oh," I said inadequately

Colonel Drényi offered me his arm. "Come. I'll take you to Lázár's quarters. I'm sure you would like to rest. Nyergesz — set these two to something unpleasant until Lázár sees them."

Meekly, I took the Colonel's arm and walked stiffly with him towards one of the outhouses. It was a low-ceilinged, bare building of two rooms.

"Nyergesz sleeps there," said the Colonel, indicating one door. "And Lázár is in here."

He opened the second door, showing me a room with a low, narrow bed and a small, open trunk, untidily scattered with books and papers, his disreputable old bag and a discarded shirt. My heart jumped into my throat. I wanted to cry.

"Thank you," I managed to say. "I shall just rest until Lajos comes."

"Can I send you over some food?"

"No. No, thank you. I'd just like to lie down."

He still looked worried, but my uninviting manner seemed to quell even the kindliest questions. He left me. I went across to the window, which looked out onto the courtyard, and watched him stride across to his own quarters. Slowly, I sat down on the bed, touching the shirt that lay there.

Involuntarily almost, I lay down with the shirt under my cheek. If I closed my eyes, I could breathe in the distinctive, clean, male smell of him which clung to the blanket and the shirt. After a while, I realized that the shirt was wet, and threw it away from me, angrily wiping my eyes.

I could not think how to deal with this situation. After all that had passed between us, what in the world would he think of me turning up like this, pretending to be his wife? I could already tell from the officers' attitudes that my presence here was a considerable inconvenience. To Lajos, I would be an embarrassment, a pest, a burden of surpassing insolence. I, who had refused in July to marry him, was now claiming that privilege falsely, and getting in his way. Unbearable humiliation.

I don't know how long I lay there, going over and over everything in my head. Only the sound of horses' hooves clattering into the courtyard brought me out of myself. I heard shouting, laughter, orders being barked out, the clank of weapons. My heart was beating faster again as I knelt on the bed to look out of the window.

I saw him at once. In the smart hussar uniform I had only glimpsed on him before, he looked unexpectedly splendid against the white background of the snow. He sat astride a large, grey horse, dashing, almost magnificent, but somehow a stranger. Issuing commands with a briskness I found quite alien, his posture seemed more erect, more inflexible; and his face, half-turned towards my window, was at once heart-rendingly familiar and frighteningly changed. It was as if his natural watchfulness had grown sharp, his calculation ruthless. And yet I couldn't possibly have seen so much in that one, brief, distant glimpse. It was my imagination, my fear, my guilt playing those tricks.

Now he was speaking quietly to the man beside him. A faint smile crossed his lips, and I recognized it with relief. Then, as the man saluted and rode off, his attention was caught by Colonel Drényi. Dismounting with his quick, casual grace, he released his horse to another waiting soldier and went to meet the Colonel.

With dread, I watched him listen to the older man. I saw the sudden frown furrow his brow. He looked quickly towards me, and I dropped underneath the window. I didn't want to be seen, not yet. Instinctively, I reached up to make sure my hair was tidy. I pulled the sable cloak more closely around me, and settled with what calmness I could to wait for Lajos.

He was not long: perhaps five minutes. I heard his footsteps under the window — even they sounded more determined than they used to. The outer door opened and swiftly closed. Then the door opposite me opened quietly and Lajos stood under the lintel, his cloak hanging over one shoulder, a sword swinging at his belt.

Across the space between us, our eyes met, and I was glad of the shadows and the failing light.

"You," he said.

One word. It didn't sound like an accusation, but it did nothing to comfort me. He came into the room, closing the door firmly. Without meaning to, I stood up.

"I'm sorry," I said, and my voice was little more than a whisper. I couldn't look at him. "I know I should not have come here. I wouldn't, if only I could have thought of another way..."

"Oh, don't misunderstand me." There was a touch of the old humour in his voice now. "I am, of course, delighted to see you, but I'm afraid I missed the wedding. In fact, I was under the impression you did not wish to marry me."

As he spoke, he crossed the room towards me; the light moved, and suddenly I heard his breath catch. But my fearful mind was still on his last words.

"Lajos don't," I pleaded. "This is hard enough to..." I broke off abruptly, for his hand had reached out to my chin, turning my ugly, bruised cheek towards him, and I cringed inside. Slowly, he let me go. His eyes sought and found mine.

For the first time I could see him properly now. He looked tireder, a little tougher than I remembered; there was a new hardness around his eyes that frightened me, and there was a sharp, angry-looking scar running from his left eye to his ear. He was a soldier now, a veteran of several battles, no longer the idealistic, compassionate youth I had so unwisely fallen in love with.

And yet his voice was dangerously gentle as he said, "What happened, Katie? What brought you here?"

"Two of your men..."

"So I understand. They deserted more than two weeks ago."

"They merely left without permission," I corrected wryly. "They brought me here."

"But why? Where is your family?"

"Debrecen, I think."

"You *think*? Why aren't you with them?"

"I — we became separated," I said vaguely, unwilling to throw István's iniquity in front of him.

"I see. But how did you come by this?" He touched my bruised face with fingers that were butterfly light.

"I was attacked."

"I can see that. By whom?"

My eyes fell. I passed my tongue over my lips. "It doesn't matter."

271

A moment longer I felt his eyes upon me; then abruptly he turned away, striding to the door. I heard him calling some order into the yard, and found the time to be surprised again by this change in him. I had never heard Lajos command before: he asked, persuaded, cajoled, never ordered — except with Aaron Klein's attackers, I remembered. He had always been capable of it...

He came back into the room, and I saw that his face was grim. "I've sent for the ruffians in question."

"No, Lajos," I said agitatedly. "Please..."

"Are you afraid of them?" he asked at once. "Did they hurt you?"

I gazed at him dumbly, unsure how to respond to his questioning.

"Did they do this?" he asked, again touching my cheek, and the broken end of my spectacles.

"I was attacked. They brought me here."

"I know that, Katie." His voice was still gentle, but I could not trust the new hardness in his eyes. I could not confide in this strange, commanding Lajos who interrogated me.

I jumped as their hesitant footsteps sounded under the window. Lajos moved away from me to let them in. I drew back as far as I could, but I needn't have worried — under his watchful gaze they did not dare to look at me. They stood stiffly to attention in front of him.

"I suppose," he said briefly, "you have a good reason why you should not be hanged?"

"We came back," said Tamás.

"And we rescued your wife," Béla added modestly. "We brought her to you."

"Two good reasons, in effect. I presume you would not have chosen to come back had you not, providentially, happened upon my wife?"

They hung their heads. I felt revulsion rise again like bile.

"We knew we'd done wrong," Tamás whined, "so it was a real bit of luck that we could do you this service to make up for it, Captain — we hoped..."

"You think I shall forgive you on account of what you did for me?" Lajos said softly, and there was a clearly dangerous note in his voice now. The soldiers looked daunted, uneasy in the extreme.

"Knowing your justice and generosity, Captain..."

"Justice," Lajos repeated. "Yes. Perhaps you can explain to me, since my wife is still upset, how she came by this brutal mark on her face?"

"She was attacked," came the prompt reply, "by wicked soldiery, when she was trying to get to Debrecen. We rescued her, and thought she'd be better off here with you."

Lajos said drily, "You mean you were afraid to go to Debrecen." He turned to me. "Is this true, that they rescued you?"

Now they were free to stare at me, and they made it as intimidating as possible. My eyes flickered to them, and back to Lajos.

"Yes..." After all, I had sworn on my mother's grave.

"Dismissed," said Lajos, without looking at them. "I'll deal with you later."

When they had gone, I sat down rather abruptly on the bed. After a moment's hesitation, Lajos came and sat beside me.

"Katie."

Reluctantly, I raised my eyes to his face.

"Will you tell me how, exactly, you were hurt?"

They tried to rape me. It should have been easy to say, truthful, and breaking no vows, however worthless, but I couldn't. I knew what had happened was not my fault, but shame seemed to rise up from my toes and spread all through my body which still ached from the assault which had occurred, the assault that would have been the lesser...

I said nothing. His eyes were searching my face. I saw a slight frown, and then his fingers moved quickly to my throat. The suddenness made me flinch. Immediately, he dropped his hand.

"Come, Katie," he said quietly. "You know I could never hurt you."

Tears rose in my throat. I tried to swallow them. Slowly, his hand lifted again, unfastening my heavy cloak. I knew that the bruises on my shoulder and neck still showed dark and disfiguring. He looked at them, then back to my eyes.

"Do they still give you pain?"

"A little. Not much. Really, I am fine..." I moved uncomfortably; his eyes fell again. Slowly, he raised his hand, and I saw that my cloak had gaped open. But by the time I was clutching agitatedly at it, he had already drawn the torn pieces of my bodice together and held them there on my shoulder.

"I'll only ask you this once," he said, still with that quiet, controlled gentleness, "and then we need never talk about it, or think about it, ever again. Katie, did they rape you? Do you know what I mean?"

The shame flooded me, yet I could not draw my eyes away from his. I closed them instead, and that was easier.

"I know what you mean. They did not rape me, though they tried to."

He didn't speak. I didn't expect him to. On the other hand, he hadn't moved away from me either. His fingers were still warm on my shoulder. I opened my eyes.

"How did you prevent them?" he asked quietly.

"I spoke your name. I said you would punish them."

Of course, he knew who I meant. There had never been any real doubt in his mind. "And they came up with this alternative plan to return to the army's good pay, and keep me sweet by bringing me you and a cock-and-bull story of a rescue."

"I swore on my mother's grave not to tell you. I also swore on the Bible..."

He said softly. "I promise you, you needn't be afraid of them again. Ever."

I swallowed. "Will you hang them?"

"Not with my own hands."

Some difficult thoughts were struggling to form in me. "They didn't do it, in the end... In their own way, they even cared for me, afterwards..."

"What they did was more than enough."

I heard the intensity, the implacable anger in his gentle voice, and strangely, it warmed me, shifting some of the unreasonable shame. But I was thinking of Mattias, defending the indefensible at Buda-Pest, of the ruined village we had slept in last night, of the six thousand dead at Mór.

Slowly, I shook my head. "There is enough death, Lajos. Please."

There was an arrested expression in his eyes. Almost abruptly, they softened, till I could barely see the new, disconcerting hardness.

"If you don't want them hanged, I'll go along with their tale. But I shall also make sure they never frighten you — or anyone else — again. You know there is nothing they can do to you here?"

"I'm not afraid of them any more." I wasn't. At least, not while Lajos was with me.

He picked up my hand with the same, slow gentleness, and lightly kissed it. "I don't suppose you care to eat with the officers. Shall I bring some dinner over here for us?"

"Yes, please." Wonderingly, grateful for the sheer normality of his words, I gazed at him; he was not angry with me in the least. "Lajos...?"

He had stood up, but paused now, looking back over his shoulder.

"I'm sorry," I said with difficulty, "about the — lies. They — they asked if I was your woman, and I said yes, through panic, and they seemed to think it meant wife. I thought it would be safest if they believed it to be true."

"I think you were right," said Lajos grimly.

"Then — you are not angry? I'm afraid I didn't tell your Colonel the truth either — it would come better from you."

His lip quirked. "I don't think it had better come from either of us. For the moment, you have to stay here, and the only way we can manage that is for you to be my wife. We can arrange the discreet annulment later."

CHAPTER FORTY-TWO

While we ate, Lajos told me that this unit under Colonel Drényi was detached from Bem's main army with the special duty of mopping up the resistance of the Romanian guerrillas who would otherwise have plagued the Hungarian rear.

"We move forward again tomorrow. Will you be able to travel?"

I nodded, and he regarded me, asking after a moment, with a deceptive casualness, "How did you manage to become separated from your family?"

"I — fell out of the cart we hired in Szolnok."

Lajos blinked. "Didn't they notice?"

"István was — angry."

Lajos went very still. "He *pushed* you?"

"You know what his temper is like," I said uncomfortably. "Everything recently has been such a strain on his nerves, making him worse. And you know, it was just bad luck that I bumped my head and knocked myself out. They probably passed me several times while I lay senseless in the ditch. They'll be worried sick by now."

"Good," said Lajos succinctly, rising restlessly to his feet. "Christ, I wouldn't have believed this of István — of someone like Acsády, perhaps, but not István. Has he lost *all* control? What on Earth set him off?"

"Teréz was with us," I said neutrally. He paused in mid-stride, and I met his gaze for a pregnant moment.

"Ah."

"I'm afraid I upset her. She found the letters you wrote me, and when she began to read one — she is quite astonishingly vulgar sometimes — I slapped her. I suppose that makes us both vulgar."

Lajos's lip twitched. "I have the picture."

I didn't think it necessary to tell him Teréz's accusations or my own confession. Instead, I sighed and said, "I should write to them at once."

"No need," said Lajos distastefully. "I'll ask the Colonel to send a message."

"Thank you."

For a moment, he stood looking down at me enigmatically. Then, so gently that the tears threatened again, he said, "You should go to bed and sleep. I have some things to attend to, so I won't disturb you."

"I didn't mean to deprive you of your bed..."

"These days, beds are a luxury I shouldn't allow myself to get used to!" He moved to the trunk then and pulled out a shirt which he threw casually on the bed. "It's the best night-gown I can offer you. If you wake in the night and hear someone in the room, it will only be me."

A moment longer he looked down at me. Then he said, "Good night, Katie," in the soft voice now so at odds with the new soldier in him, and left me.

The nightmares didn't come that night, though I did wake up once. Opening my eyes, I saw Lajos sprawled on the floor on the other side of the room, his tunic loosened, his head resting on his hand while he read by the light of the pale, solitary candle. I felt a rush of aching tenderness, a strange, relieving comfort. I closed my eyes again, and the last clouds of confusion seemed to drift away from my brain, leaving it calm and receptive to the healing sleep.

We had an early start in the morning. It seemed odd, yet rather wonderful, to be woken at dawn by Lajos bearing a cup of strong coffee.

"How are you?" he asked, as I struggled to sit up, blushing and drawing the blankets about me.

"Much better."

"Good. I have things to see to, but I'll come back for you in half an hour."

It gave me time to drink the coffee, sew up my torn gown more securely, and dress myself. I was putting the last pin in my hair when Lajos returned, asking briskly if I was ready to go.

"This is Oszkár, by the way," he added, as a young soldier came into the room. "He will look after the trunk — and you, when I can't be with you. You can trust him implicitly."

Oszkár gave me a shy smile on his way past, banishing my inevitable doubts, and seized the trunk before hurrying away. Lajos came towards me.

"You look much better," he observed. I smiled, a little uncertainly, and he smiled back into my eyes, casually brushing my cheek with one finger. Involuntarily, I moved at his touch, a very small, evasive gesture as the breath caught suddenly in my throat. At once, his hand fell to his side and he stepped back.

"I'm sorry," he said contritely. I flushed, for the truth was, my evasion had not been inspired by fear but by the old remembered feelings his slightest touch had always aroused in me. But he was brisk again. "Come; I've found a horse you can ride. I'll introduce you."

But first there were other introductions. As we stepped outside, a group of officers seemed to appear from nowhere, smiling amiably and expectantly. Lajos paused, an expression of amusement lightening his face.

"Very well, let's get it over with," he said wryly. "These idle, nosy fellows desire to be presented to you, Katie. Captain Nyergesz I believe you have met already. These are Lieutenant Lukács, Lieutenant Király and Major Jászi."

They all bowed and professed themselves delighted to make my acquaintance.

"I can see now why Lázár has kept so quiet about you," Major Jászi said gallantly. "You are much too beautiful to associate with these low fellows. You must allow me to look after you, Madame!"

I laughed — with genuine amusement when I considered the state of my poor face — and Lajos said drily, "She'll let you know if she needs you — but I don't advise you to hold your breath."

"I hate jealous husbands," the Major complained.

"Then take yourself off," Lajos recommended insubordinately.

Just then, Oszkár appeared again, leading two horses: the big grey which I had seen Lajos riding last night, and a slightly smaller chestnut, which Lajos took from him.

"Katie, this is the best mount we could find — he's rather large for you, but he's a gentle beast. And Oszkár spent last night altering the saddle for you."

He had indeed. I was to have the dignity of a lady's saddle. Touched, I shifted my gaze from the placid horse to the shy young soldier who had brought it.

"Thank you," I said sincerely. "You have no idea how grateful I am for that kindness!"

Oszkár blushed, but he managed to return my smile, and I believe that from then on he would have done anything for me, even if he had not imagined me to be his Captain's wife.

When he had carefully lifted me into the saddle, Lajos said, "Oszkár will stay close to you, whatever happens. Do as he says, and there will be no problem."

Sudden panic rose in me. "But where will you be?" I asked urgently. The fleeting smile touched his lips.

"Not far away," he said soothingly, if vaguely.

"Lázár is our expert Vlach tracker," Major Jászi said jovially. "Very well, gentlemen — let us mount up and be gone!"

He herded his subordinates away as he spoke, leaving me alone with Oszkár and my huge chestnut horse. A moment later, I saw Lajos ride out at the head of a troop of soldiers, and I couldn't help the wave of desolation which swept over me. Everyone else was forming up in the courtyard and on the road beyond. Soldiers on horseback, carts bearing baggage and provisions, and one containing five women. I blinked at this last spectacle.

"Should I not travel with these ladies?" I asked innocently, and Oszkár blushed uncomfortably.

"Lord, no, Madame — that wouldn't do at all! They are not *wives*. But we can't shake them off, so they hang around and help out with the cooking and — er — other things." He urged his horse forward, and I, duly abashed and obedient, followed him. We took our place in the column close to the baggage carts.

"If the women give you any insolence, let me know," Oszkár said, as we rode past them. But for the moment the women seemed to be struck dumb with amazement — or curiosity — at the sight of me.

Colonel Drényi rode down to ask civilly after my health and comfort, adjured Oszkár to take care of me for the Captain, and returned to his place.

As we moved forward, I looked at Oszkár rather guiltily. "I'm taking you away from your real duties. You would rather be with La — Captain Lázár. I'm grateful to you, but truly, I do not need an escort."

"Orders," Oszkár said briefly. "And I don't mind."

"Are you the Captain's — servant?" I asked hesitantly, and unexpectedly he grinned.

"I try to be, but he says he doesn't know what to do with me, so mostly I just look after his horse and his baggage. But I'm very glad he asked me to serve you, Madame. It shows he trusts me."

There was nothing I could say to that. Once we were under way, the cavalcade moved on quickly, mostly at a brisk trot or a canter. I saw no sign of Lajos, or of my two recent companions. I wondered if Lajos had hanged them anyhow. It would have been no loss to humanity, of course, but I felt an inexplicable unwillingness to be even the indirect cause of anyone's death

Oszkár rode beside me, cheerfully enough, his shyness gradually giving way to a pleasantly open, sunny good nature. He was a Plains peasant who had joined up from patriotism, to save the Fatherland from invasion, and he had, apparently, two brothers and three sisters at home. His mother was dead, but his father was still in excellent health, working all the hours God sent.

While he revealed these and other details of his life, I noticed that his eyes were watchful, glancing frequently to left and right, especially when we passed through wooded areas. Something of his tension began to communicate itself to me till I felt distinctly uneasy.

Briefly, I was distracted by one of the women in the cart, who called out to me, "Good morning, Madame!" She was a youngish, untidy woman, none too clean but comely in a rather voluptuous way, and she seemed friendly enough. "They say you're Captain Lázár's lady."

I shifted uncomfortably in the saddle as I inclined my head.

"Never tell me *he* gave you that shiner," she said, awed, and I felt a quick flush of shame and outrage mount to my bruised cheeks.

"Of course not," I snapped.

"Told you," said one of the other women with satisfaction. "The Captain's a *real* gentleman!"

Before I could think of a suitable response, a sudden command brought the whole column to an abrupt halt. I turned quickly to Oszkár, an urgent question on my lips, but he didn't even hear me. He was looking intently the other way, towards the woods, and his sword was drawn.

With a painful lurch of alarm, I looked around me. The soldiers had all assumed defensive positions, but they were still and silent, as though waiting for something. A second later, men seemed to fly out of the trees on the left, some on horseback but most on foot, falling upon our column some yards ahead of where I waited.

More orders were shouted amid a fearful clash of weapons. I remember being amazed as well as relieved that I heard no gunfire — it seemed the fighting was all hand-to-hand. Nevertheless I was appalled; I felt paralysed, for I had never seen such violence before. Beside me, Oszkár's hand twitched on his reins, as if he would go to his comrades' aid, but his instinct to obey proved stronger in the end than his will to fight — for which I was selfishly grateful.

The confusion ahead could only have lasted a few seconds when there sounded another, much more concerted shout which pierced even the terrible din of the fight, and the next instant I saw more horsemen bolting out from the wood.

Oszkár was grinning now. I think he meant it to be reassuring. "There's the

Captain," he said with approval, and indeed the newcomers wore hussar uniform. A moment later, my distraught eyes could even pick out Lajos himself, laying about him energetically with his sword.

It was all over very quickly after that. One moment there was frightful, chaotic confusion — at least in my eyes; the next, our attackers were herded between a circle of hussars, and the dreadful noise had stopped. Into the silence, I heard Lajos give an almost casual order in Romanian. The prisoners dropped their weapons, causing a renewed clanking of steel, and some of our soldiers began to collect the enemy's horses and weapons — which varied, so far as I could see, from broken sabres to farming implements.

The Colonel was riding back from the head of the column. "Well done, Captain!" he said loudly. "Good work, men!"

"Thank you, sir," said Lajos. I watched him wheel his horse around, giving a few orders in his new, natural way, and then he was riding towards us. "Everything well?" he said briskly to Oszkár. My eyes anxiously devoured him, but could detect no hurt, not even the smallest scratch. His eyes were still bright with the excitement of battle; the breath seemed to steam out of him in great streams. More than ever, he was a stranger.

He glanced at me, then. "I'm sorry about the disturbance, but there shouldn't be any more. I think that was the last of them."

I swallowed, still shaken by the recent violence. "Are they Romanian guerrilla fighters?"

Lajos nodded.

"You set a trap for them?"

"We were ready for them," Lajos amended, adding briefly, "We tracked them down yesterday."

"Oh."

He transferred his attention to the silent women in the cart, who had been watching this brief exchange between us with interest. "Ladies, have you room for any more on there?"

One of them, a rather stringy blond, screeched with joy. "Bless you, Captain, are you going to join us at last? Under your wife's very nose?"

Naturally, Lajos was not in the least put out, either by the suggestion or by the ribald, distinctly unmusical laughter which greeted it. "I haven't the excuse," he said mildly. "But there are a few — less able than I — who need a seat in your chariot."

"Oh, wounded," said the dark woman who had first spoken to me.

"Are there many?" I asked with foreboding.

"A couple of the Romanians who can't walk too well, but I expect they'll survive. Ours have only minor scratches."

Already two wounded peasants were being carried towards us. They were dumped unceremoniously on the cart with the women, and then the cavalcade moved onwards, taking the prisoners with it.

"What will happen to them now?" I asked uneasily.

Lajos shrugged. "They will be given the choice of imprisonment, or enlistment with us."

I blinked. "Is that the best method of recruitment you have?"

"No, but sometimes it's the only one possible." He glanced at me. "I'll come back later," he said abruptly, and galloped away again.

Bemused, I gazed after him for a moment, then turned my attention to the wounded. The women, whatever their opinion of 'Vlachs', were tending the two in the cart as if they were their own. Fascinated, I watched them bathe and dress wounds, settle limbs more comfortably, all without being asked. The two Romanians, sullen, suspicious and in pain as they were, seemed to be as surprised as I.

Less than an hour later, Lajos, as good as his word, rode back to us, dismissing Oszkár with a friendly word of thanks, apparently taking over the role of escort himself. I couldn't help being glad, even though there was something new and alarming about him now.

There seemed to be a gulf of difference, a lifetime of experience between the witty, quietly spoken intellectual of the Pilvax café, and this tough, decisive, scarred young soldier. I cast a swift, surreptitious glance at him, and found him watching me.

He smiled slightly. "Tell me about Buda-Pest — has the Government really fled so soon?"

I nodded.

"And István intends to stay with it? That surprises me — I hadn't thought he would go so far along that road."

"It isn't easy for him. To be honest, it's driving him mad."

"Perhaps he'll end up in the asylum with his friend Széchenyi," Lajos said callously.

I cast him a hostile glance. "I'm glad you are amused."

He shrugged. "It wasn't I he threw into the road and deserted. Are the whole family in Debrecen?"

"Except Maria. And Mattias."

"Ah." Now I thought he was genuinely interested, rather than making conversation. "Mattias finally broke free?"

"What is the point of being free and dead?" I retorted. His expression was enigmatic, and for a moment he did not answer.

Then: "He's probably safer in Buda-Pest than anywhere else — it will fall easily. The Austrians are probably there already."

I regarded him curiously. "The prospect doesn't appal you?"

"It's not the end of the war. The Austrians are not invincible — we've proved that here. Bem has taken Kolozsvár and Beszterce, and is currently chasing the enemy out through the mountains of Bukovina."

"Then — then you have won back Transylvania?" I said eagerly.

"Not quite," he replied gravely, "but I suspect we will. Bem is a very clever man."

"Despite being a ferocious lunatic?" I said provokingly. I felt unaccountably irritated by the loss of the old, idealistic, pacific Lajos.

But he only smiled faintly. "I'm glad you read my letters." Those friendly, impersonal letters. I looked quickly away from the face I still found all too fascinating.

"I suppose you have fought in many battles," I said, a little desperately.

"No, not many." He glanced at me quizzically. "Why, do you think I have become a brutish soldier?"

I smiled, rather seriously. "Hardly; but I do see a change in you... Are you happy here?"

"As happy as can be expected," he said drily, and I was obliged to laugh.

"I meant, do you quarrel with this Colonel as you did with your last?"

"Not at all. Drényi is a sensible man."

We rode on for a while in silence, and for the first time I became truly aware of the winter beauty of Transylvania. Everything was white, from the distant mountains to the villages and fields and woods around us. It was still like a fairy-tale, yet breathtaking as the serene summer loveliness of the place was not.

When we stopped to rest, I could not stop gazing into the distance. It was Lajos who, catching me around the waist, lifted me lightly to the ground.

"Give the poor beast a rest," he said lightly, and I smiled up at him apologetically.

"I'm sorry. I have never been here in winter before — it's hard to believe such beauty is real."

But Lajos was real. The lithe, fit body so close to me, the rough, scarred face above me, they were so tangible that I was suddenly afraid — afraid of my own emotion, afraid of his intriguing unfamiliarity. I moved quickly out of his hands.

Despite the snow on the ground, the young officers were strolling around as if they were on a summer picnic, trying to out-do each other in their civilities to me. I didn't know whether to be embarrassed or amused. Eventually I realized they were being kind to me, because of my bruised face and the unhappy state in which I had joined them, and I was touched. Lajos, who seemed to be on easy terms of friendship with all of them, watched the proceedings with a benign eye.

For the rest of the day, Lajos and Oszkár alternated as my escort. Whenever Lajos approached, I felt my heart lift in a curious mixture of comfort and unease. I had to struggle to maintain my front of friendly indifference, yet I was both piqued and depressed by his manner to me.

He accorded me a kind of gentle, half-sardonic civility, so that I felt both protected and distant from him — which was exactly how it should be, I reminded myself. I had placed Lajos in an impossible, embarrassing position where he could do nothing but help me. I was only an added burden, another responsibility to him, and I was obliging him to lie to his fellow officers. The list of my iniquities was endless, and still I had to keep telling myself that even less than before was there any future for Lajos and me together.

"Discreet annulment," I said aloud, startling both of us, and he regarded me with eyes that weren't quite amused.

"Content your soul in patience," he said drily, "at least until we reach Beszterce."

"When will that be?"

"Tomorrow, perhaps." He looked thoughtful. "I suppose from there you might go back to Debrecen with the next despatches — or on to Szelényi, if it is safe now."

Ridiculously, foolishly, I felt a pang of hurt at his eagerness to be rid of me.

"I suppose Szelényi would be best," I said calmly. "I can get there easily from Beszterce." I drew in a breath. "I don't think I have thanked you, Lajos, but indeed I am grateful for..."

"No doubt," he interrupted, and there was an odd harshness in his voice that brought my eyes flying back to his face. "But it was never your gratitude I wanted, was it, Katie? It still isn't."

Mutely, I gazed at him, trying to quell the quickened beat of my heart, for this was the first remotely personal remark he had made to me all day. For a moment, he continued to hold my eyes, then he let out a low breath of laughter and spurred forward, shouting for Oszkár.

As the light began to fade, we came to a village where the occupants, contriving to appear both sullen and obsequious, opened their cottages and huts to the troops. However, I saw a middle-aged nobleman come riding in from the other side, and he was soon in conversation with Colonel Drényi.

I was distracted by Lajos riding up to me, tired but brisk, to confirm that we would be stopping here for the night. "I'll try and find you some decent quarters, but don't raise your hopes too high: these are Romanian peasants, and very poor."

"Good news, Lajos!" called Nyergesz, riding over to join us. "We have a noble host! That gentleman with the Colonel is offering his house to the officers." He grinned good-naturedly and leaned forward to say confidentially — though not quite quietly enough — "Cheer up, my friend, you'll have proper married quarters tonight!"

I quickly averted my burning face, hiding the involuntary panic that had risen with the Captain's jocular words.

Leaving Major Jászi to arrange the quartering of the men, the Colonel led the rest of the officers and myself up to the house of our host, whose name was Reményi. He gave us wine while the rooms were being prepared, and then jovially insisted on personally conducting us to each.

"How romantic your story is!" he beamed at me, as he threw open the door of the room I was to share with Lajos. "To come upon your husband so unexpectedly!"

I managed to smile — for if he was a buffoon, he was also extremely good-natured — and to thank him for his kindness. I stepped into the room, trying not to see the huge bed which dominated it, concentrating instead on the valuable rugs, on the curtains, on the view from the window. I pronounced it charming, and he beamed again and left Lajos and me alone.

The tension between us was suddenly so tight I thought it would snap. My head had begun to ache — very slightly, but warningly.

"I'll leave you to wash," Lajos said abruptly, moving towards the door again, "but don't be long or we'll start without you."

The meal was plentiful and pleasant, if a little greasy, and I ate considerably more than I had since leaving Buda-Pest. Buda-Pest. It seemed a lifetime ago. Talk was cheerful and friendly, punctuated regularly by oddly boyish banter between the officers. Lajos was quiet at first, but after the second glass of wine he began to exert himself to entertain, and before long everyone was in gales of laughter, while our host had to wipe away the tears that poured down his merry cheeks.

"Lázár is in form," Major Jászi said to me, still grinning. "Your unexpected arrival has obviously been good for him, Madame! Have you been married long?"

"No," I said with difficulty. "Not long."

"No? Well, he's a capital fellow, young Lázár. I won't say I didn't have my doubts about him when he first came to us — well, *you* must know his reputation for agitating and scribbling! But we soon saw that was nonsense."

I smiled, sipping my wine with some amusement. "I don't believe it was *all* nonsense, Major."

"Well, he has never been any trouble to us," said the Major jovially. "In fact, damned useful, on the whole — begging your pardon, Madame. Cleared up no end of Vlachs for us, haven't you, Lázár?"

Lajos looked at him. "Romanians," he said gently.

"Whatever," was the careless response, and Lajos cast me a very speaking glance. "They're still dashed traitors!"

"Not by their own lights."

Jászi looked uneasy. "Here, you're not going to start philosophizing again, are you? And here was I telling your charming wife how little trouble you are!"

When the meal was eventually over, Lajos rose to his feet. "Excuse me," he said politely. "I have a few things to see to."

"Good man," said Colonel Drényi, amusement lurking in his grey eyes. "But don't be too conscientious."

I had no doubt he was referring indirectly to my presence, which embarrassed me considerably, and when Lajos had gone, I fled rather cravenly to my own room for the night.

CHAPTER FORTY-THREE

I woke to a beam of pale, early light drifting into the room. Instinctively, I looked towards the fire. It had gone out and the chair beside it was empty. For a moment, I felt disappointed, but even as I berated myself for idiocy, I became conscious of someone breathing beside me.

Slowly, I lifted my head, turning over on the bed; and there, beside me, lay the motionless, sleeping figure of Lajos Lázár. Dressed in his shirt and trousers, he was lying on his back on top of the coverlet, one arm flung up across his forehead. I had never seen him asleep before. Wonderingly, I gazed down on the still, impassive face. There was a faint frown between his closed eyes that I wanted to smooth away, along with the deep, weary lines that made him appear so much older than his years. But despite these things, he looked almost boyish in sleep, touchingly young and vulnerable. Even the alien scar on the side of his face filled me now with tenderness. Asleep, there was no difference between the old Lajos and the new. They were the same man underneath, and I still loved him unbearably.

I watched him for a long moment, almost afraid to breathe in case I woke him. Then a sudden draught made me shiver, and I thought he would be cold. Carefully, I lifted the blankets off my own body, folding them back till they covered him. Then, of course, *I* was cold — cold and exposed.

I slid quickly out of bed, padding round it in search of my clothes; but as I reached out to pick them up from the chair, I could not resist one more glance at the man who had been sleeping beside me. I turned my head towards the bed, and looked straight into his open eyes.

For a heartbeat, neither of us moved. Then I caught my breath, painfully aware of my undressed state, of my bare legs visible from well above the knee. Foolishly, I clutched at the neck of my shirt.

"I'm sorry," I stammered. "I covered you — I thought you would be cold."

His eyes moved, resting for an agonizing moment on my legs. I snatched up my clothes, holding them protectively in front of me. Abruptly, Lajos sat up, throwing back the blankets.

"Thank you, but I should be up already," he said distantly, swinging his feet on to the floor. When he stood, it brought him too close to me. I stepped back in panic, but by then, a genuine smile of amusement had crept into his dark eyes, and he followed me, picking up a strand of my loose hair and twisting it around his finger.

"Poor Katie," he said, with gentle humour. "Don't look so terrified—I shall neither eat you nor seduce you. I promise." He let the lock of hair unwind, then pushed it carefully behind my shoulder without touching my skin. His lip quirked.

Then he turned away, picked up his coat and was gone, leaving me bemused, confused, and peculiarly disappointed.

The headache hung around me all of that day, which was remarkably like the one before it except that we were not attacked. Lajos, again his brisk, controlled self, and Oszkár took turns to escort me on our swift progress.

"Bem is back in Beszterce," Lajos told me as we started out. "Apparently he soundly defeated the enemy in Bukovina, and now he is waiting for us to join him. We should be there by nightfall."

I felt miserable. In Beszterce we would separate — our 'discreet annulment' would occur, and I would no longer have his disturbing, unsettling, *necessary* company... And he would no longer be plagued by a burdensome 'wife'.

When we rode into the town, General Bem himself came to greet us. At that time I rode at the front of the column with Lajos, Colonel Drényi and Major Jászi, so I was given an excellent view of him. He was a squat, elderly gentleman with fine white whiskers and extraordinarily bright, cheerful eyes. Sitting comfortably in the saddle, he greeted Colonel Drényi with jovial friendliness, congratulating him on the success of his troop, and cordially welcoming him back to Beszterce.

"But what have we here?" he demanded, before Drényi could reply, for his quick eyes were devouring me. "Surely it is a lady, Drényi?"

"Precisely, General. This is Madame Lázár, Captain Lázár's wife, who has become separated from her normal protectors..."

The General spurred forward to me, and I met his curious gaze with some trepidation. However, I soon saw that his eyes were twinkling with kindness, and he only bowed over my hand, gallantly kissing it.

"Enchanté, Madame! Lázár, you dog! Why did you never tell me of this ravishing creature? Surely a wife such as this could not have slipped your memory?"

"Hardly, sir," Lajos agreed, holding without difficulty the gaze which had swung suddenly upon him. "But I was not expecting to introduce you!"

"You shall tell me all about it later! Tonight, we forget that the enemy is in Buda-Pest; we eat, we drink, we dance! Tomorrow, we shall make more serious plans."

Lajos and I were allotted a room of our own in the house of a decent but unfriendly Saxon burgher. When we had settled in, Lajos went off again to look after his men, promising to return in time to take me to Bem's headquarters for dinner.

This he duly did, and we discovered there a prevailing atmosphere of jollity. Bem's officers, who had been with him in Bukovina, were exhausted, and those of them who could get to the dinner needed this relaxation after their dreadful journey in the mountains — I heard a little about it as the evening wore on, and I was horrified.

I saw at once, with some relief, that at least I was not the only lady present. One or two officers' wives ate with us, as did some prominent, respectable ladies of the town, together with their equally respectable husbands. At first, I was rather apprehensive about the local people, fearing that they would recognize me and ruin my reputation for good with the startling information that whatever I was, I was *not* Lajos Lázár's wife. However, they barely looked at me. I presumed the wife of a peasant-born Captain was in a similar category to a governess, and thought no more about them.

General Bem, who was a fascinating and rather charming old gentleman, came over to meet us as soon as we entered the room. He kissed my hand again and beamed upon Lajos, throwing a fatherly arm around his shoulders.

"So! Once more I hear you have done very well, my Lázár!" he said affectionately. "Drényi has been telling me. Of course I said, 'Nonsense, you cannot mean Lázár. Lázár does not like to fight.' But he insisted it was you." He turned to me appealingly, his eyes twinkling with friendly mockery. "How is it, Madame, that I am saddled with a soldier who hates violence?"

"You asked for me," Lajos said drily.

"So I did. I expect I was temporarily insane. Come, Madame, you shall sit by me! Let us eat!"

We ate. During the meal, I overheard snippets of other people's conversation, about the late, arduous campaign, about the evacuation of Buda-Pest which some considered to have been premature, and about the Austrians marching into the capital over Count Széchenyi's new chain bridge — ironic that this should be its first use.

The General questioned me subtly, and I or Lajos answered as briefly and as honestly as was possible in the circumstances. Not by the smallest hint did he appear to disbelieve us, but once, just as the meal ended, I saw his eyes resting on my bare left hand. Instinctively, I hid both hands in my lap. I saw him smile faintly, but he said nothing.

Afterwards, there was dancing. Some gypsies were commanded to provide the music, which they did extremely well, and I danced with General Bem and with Colonel Drényi, after which I was delivered back up to Lajos with a twinkling apology for depriving him of his bride. I expect I added to their misconceptions by blushing, but Lajos took it all in good part, merely snatching an untouched glass of wine from his Lieutenant and giving it instead to me. Király only laughed, and begged to be allowed to dance with me later.

The talk at that moment was on the subject of Kossuth's power. Although only part of the National Defence Committee, it was always on Kossuth's shoulders that all the decisions — and all the work — appeared to fall. He had made numerous vain efforts to form a proper Cabinet to help him, but in spite of this, accusations of tyranny and power seeking were provoking him to fury.

"He was grumbling about it even in October," Lajos remarked. "In fact, he was so incensed by the injustice of such accusations that he told me he would rather be a dog than the Prime Minister."

I had only been half-listening up until then, but now, without warning, I suddenly found this image of the suave, elegant Kossuth longing to be a mere dog, exquisitely funny. As the amusement bubbled up inside me, Lajos met my gaze, his own eyes sharing my laughter. But the others, who didn't seem to appreciate the joke, were already discussing something else. I never discovered what, for Lajos was still looking at me fixedly, a disconcerting new intensity in his dark eyes.

"What is it?" I asked with an attempt at lightness. "Are my spectacles crooked?" These, I had discovered by my bedside that morning, mysteriously repaired with an odd but functional spare arm.

Lajos's lips quirked. "Not in the least. I am a skilled workman. I was just thinking, people will find it very odd if we don't dance together at least once."

"As long as it's not a czardas," I said involuntarily, and then blushed as the laughter sprang back into his eyes.

"Don't you like the czardas? Now, that is odd, because I had the impression that you liked it very much."

My blush deepened, but I said sweetly, "Appearances may be deceptive."

"Obviously. However, I'm prepared to settle for this waltz."

And suddenly his arm went around me, whirling me on to the floor, and I was held in an embrace at once soothingly familiar and disturbingly new. He held me too close. I could feel the hardness of his body against me; his face was only inches away from mine. Delicious excitement rose in me as I spun with him around the floor. I wasn't even surprised that he could waltz.

The other dancers swept past us in a haze, never too near. I could feel his arm like steel around my waist. I was desperately afraid of my own aroused feelings, perversely triumphant about the desire I could sense in him, and yet over it all, I simply enjoyed the exhilaration of waltzing, Viennese style, in the arms of the man I loved.

And then, abruptly, he dropped my hand. The arm around my waist swept me out of the room into the deserted, draughty hallway outside. Gasping, I found my back against the wall. One of his arms still held me to him while he leaned the other across the wall over my head in an attitude quite clearly predatory. Dazed, I was held by his dark, glittering eyes which devoured me.

He bent his head slowly. I felt my stomach melt with anticipation; my eyes began to close of their own volition. And then I heard his breath catch, and my eyes fluttered open again. His gaze was now on my bruised cheek. For a moment he did not move, then, gradually, his hold slackened, his arm dropped to his side as he straightened.

"There," he said, and though his voice was light, it was not quite steady. "That's rough soldiery for you. I'm sorry. Let's rejoin the party."

Confused by this sudden change, I let myself be led back to the dance. I could not think why he hadn't kissed me — it had been so obviously his intention. Perhaps he had been repelled by the ugliness of my bruise... Or had been reminded by it of my treatment at the hands of his men. He thought I was afraid to be touched; or perhaps he simply would not take advantage of me when I was so vulnerable, so dependent on him.

"It's your decision, Katie. I'm damned if I'll make it for you..."

The ache in my head began to grow. Instinctively, I lifted my hand, pressing it to my right temple.

"What is it?" Lajos said at once, and his voice was normal again, concerned as he would be for anyone.

"Nothing." I forced myself to smile. "I'm a little tired."

"I'll take you back if you like — but Király will never forgive me if you don't dance with him first."

I couldn't help wishing that he did not relinquish me to his Lieutenant with quite so much relief. However, as I danced with the amiable Király, I pulled my self together, recovering my refuge of pretence and sociability.

When we finally said our farewells, I intercepted a few stray winks aimed at him by his friends. General Bem merely smiled benignly upon us, and we departed, walking the short distance back to our lodgings.

"This is ridiculous," I fumed. "We're being treated like a pair of newlyweds! What have you said to them?"

"I? Nothing," said Lajos, faintly amused. "I believe it was you who told them we were only just married."

"Rubbish!" I said indignantly. "Major Jászi asked if we had been married long, and I said 'no'! It seemed nearest the truth."

He glanced at me enigmatically. "Poor Katie. But I'm afraid this particular bed is of your own making — you'll just have to lie in it for a day or so longer. Which reminds me: Bem doesn't think you should risk going to Szelényi just yet, but he will send you with the next couriers to Debrecen, if you like."

"I don't care," I said tiredly, and that was the truth. If I couldn't be with Lajos — and I couldn't — I did not care where I was. Then, with a pang of guilt, I remembered Margit's illness, and the untaught, no doubt neglected children, and belatedly, I began to worry for them all again. "I'll go to Debrecen," I said quietly.

It was the bedroom door closing behind him which woke me in the morning. There was a cup of coffee beside the bed, but I was completely alone. Impulsively, I threw off the heavy blankets and ran to the window. I could just see him striding down the street alone, his sword swinging at his side.

I touched my aching head ruefully, and went back to my coffee. Half an hour in bed did not lessen the pain. I felt almost resigned to what I knew must follow. Still, I went through the motions of trying to prevent it. I got dressed and went out into the fresh air. I stayed out for hours, in spite of the cold, until the drilling soldiers, and even the conversations of passing towns-people, became too painful.

And then I thought I had left it too long. It took me some time to recog-nize the house we lodged in, and when I did, I found my way to our room more by feel than by sight. With relief, I pushed open the door and went in; but my trials were not over yet. A bright, uniformed figure sprang up at once.

"Katie? Where have you been?" It was definitely Lajos's voice, unusually anxious, and when I peered in the direction of the blue, I could even make out his face.

"Just out," I said vaguely. "Taking the air..."

There was a slight pause, as if he was examining me. Then: "Are you well, Katie?"

"Quite well," I said politely.

"I was worried. I thought you had tried to do something silly, like going to Szelényi on your own."

The idea of going anywhere on my own in this condition was so exqui-sitely humorous that I laughed.

"Why should I do that?" I asked, surreptitiously feeling my way along the wall to where I remembered the other chair to be. I didn't look at the wall as I went, for it would not stay still.

"You didn't seem to like the idea of Debrecen." His voice was unnaturally loud in my head, yet interestingly enough, it didn't hurt me any further.

"Debrecen," I repeated. It was very hard to follow conversations now.

"Katie, what is the matter?"

"Nothing," I said mechanically. I reached out to where the chair should have been — it wasn't. I dropped my hands to my sides, sent a quick prayer to the Almighty, and launched myself away from the heaving wall into the room.

But I had only taken three uncertain steps before I was caught and stead-ied. Lajos's arms were around me, his hand in my hair.

"Stop," he said, urgently yet with wonderful gentleness. "Stop. You can't see."

"I can. I can see."

"Katie." His hand lifted my chin, but though I peered, I could no longer make out the features of his swimming face. "You don't need to hide this from me. It doesn't matter. I'll help you."

I wanted to cry, but not with the pain. There was the old, childhood shame, mixed up with unspeakable relief. I closed my eyes. His chest was in-vitingly available, so I let my head rest there.

"Is it a migraine?" he said, and since he seemed, incredibly, to understand, I didn't bother answering. Instead, I just allowed myself to stay where I was. His presence, his strength were indescribably comforting. I felt myself lifted in his arms like a baby, and for a moment, my stomach heaved. I clung to him as he carried me to the bed. A moment longer I tried to wrestle with the pain and concepts of dignity, and then I gave in, letting the pain crash round me and through me.

Somewhere, I realized he was loosening my dress, covering me, and then his hands left me. My aching eyes flew open; I reached out to him wildly.

"Don't leave me, Lajos," I whispered foolishly. "Please don't leave me."

My hands were taken in his. I felt him sink down on the bed beside me.

"I won't leave you," he said distinctly. "I'll just draw the curtains, and then I'll be back."

Satisfied, I let him go. Some of the piercing light disappeared, and then he was beside me again. In the haze of agony, I felt him take my hand.

"Is there anything I should get for you?" he asked.

"No..." The word was less painful than shaking my head. I turned carefully on to my side, ignoring the nausea, and tucked his hand under my cheek to help me weather the storm.

It went on for the rest of the day and all of that night. It didn't enter my shrieking head that he might have duties to attend to, and he never tried to go. He just sat there beside the bed, letting me hold his hand like a talisman against the pain. Around dawn, I felt it begin to recede, and gradually I slipped towards the sleep of exhaustion.

Vaguely, I heard a knock on the door. My hand was freed. I opened my eyes and watched him cross the floor. The room was blessedly still again. I heard his voice, and another in the hall outside, and then he came back.

"Are you awake?" he asked softly.

"Yes... It's better now."

"Will you sleep now if I go out for a while?"

"Of course. Yes. I'm sorry..."

"Hush. Would you like anything before I go?"

Humbly, I asked for some water, and he lifted the glass I had not seen beside the bed. His arm passed around my shoulders, lifting me, holding the glass to my lips. I gazed up at him wonderingly as I drank. It was so intensely soothing to be helped like this, to be treated as something fragile and precious instead of as a silly girl with a sore head.

I smiled, and saw him smile back. Then he lowered me on to the pillows, lightly brushing my forehead with his lips. And then he rose to his feet and was gone.

*

I think I was asleep before he left the house. And I suppose it was the most valuable sleep I have ever taken, for I woke from it with my mind quite marvellously clear.

Naturally, the first person I thought of was Lajos. He was not in the room, so I spoke his name aloud, hearing the wonder in my own voice. I said it again, and this time there was joy. The woolliness, the confusion, the contradictory arguments of the last year, all had fallen away, lost somewhere in the haze of pain which Lajos had shared with me through the long night. What was left was blindingly simple.

I loved Lajos. And he loved me. Whether or not his love was greater or lesser than I wished it to be was suddenly irrelevant. It is in the nature of women, I thought, to be more obsessive, more exclusive in their love. I would always have to share Lajos with his cause, but that did not matter, because the exquisite tenderness he had shown me in my weakness proved his feeling for me, forced me to recognize it.

Marriage or non-marriage; these were irrelevant too. It was he and I who mattered; and our being together, whether for a month or for the rest of our lives, was surely vastly, immeasurably more important than the petty reasons which had been keeping me from him. Suddenly, I *knew* that an instant of this love was worth every risk, every heartbreak I could incur.

I had been wasting time, I thought in panic. The opinions of the world were insignificant beside this one huge, incontrovertible fact: I loved him. And he could be taken from me, violently, at any time.

Slowly, I got out of bed and took off my dress and underclothes. I bathed myself all over, shivering as I rubbed myself dry with the Saxon lady's towel. I put on Lajos's shirt, and then sat down before the glass to comb out my dishevelled hair. By the poor, fading light, my bruises hardly showed. My face looked soft and contented from sleep, my hair tumbling loose around my shoulders.

"*It's your decision, Katie.*" It was; and I had made it.

Even so, I jumped when I heard the door slam below. I stayed stock still until I was sure it was his footsteps running up the stairs. Too soon, I thought in panic. I threw down the comb, ready to bolt back into bed and assume the alluring pose I had been dreamily planning. But I had only stood up and taken one hasty step before the door opened and he came quietly in.

"Katie?" he said softly, his eyes going immediately to the bed. Then they moved and found me. If I was mesmerized, I had the comfort of knowing that his breath was caught too; nor could he look away from me. After a moment, his lip quirked.

"Is it time for bed again?" he asked lightly.

"Yes," I said, and smiled back, trying to hide my nervousness. My heart was hammering as I moved towards him. I saw many expressions flit across his unguarded face in that instant: hope, desire, suspicion, desperation, concern...

"Is the pain quite gone?" he asked with rare difficulty.

"Yes," I said again. "All the pain." I had come to a halt before him, afraid to touch him and yet longing for him to touch me. *It's your decision, Katie...*

His eyes had dropped to my mouth, to my breasts rising and falling too quickly beneath the stiff cotton of his shirt, then down to my legs and at last, determinedly, back to my face. He tried to smile, and when he spoke it was meant to be humorous as well as a warning.

"Katie, if you don't wish to be ravished, for God's sake cover yourself."

And suddenly the words came easily. "But Lajos," I said softly, "that is exactly what I wish." And at last I could lift my arms and grip his shoulders. I stood on tiptoe, raising my head to his, and daringly, achingly, kissed him on the mouth.

At once, his arms came up, holding me, but lightly, loosely, although I felt them tremble. His voice too was unsteady.

"Katie, what is this all about? Do you know what you are doing?"

"I love you," I whispered. "I have always loved you, only too many things kept getting in the way... When I woke up just now and the pain was gone, I suddenly realized the truth. I knew what was important and what was not. I love you."

His arms tightened convulsively. One brown, rough hand covered with tiny, healing cuts, touched my face caressingly.

"There can be no going back for us this time, Katie; do you understand? Is this really what you want, what you are asking?"

Slowly, I took his hand, cradling it against my cheek, softly kissing it; and then I carried it to my breast and held it there.

"I want you," I said simply, and then at last he bent his head and his mouth found and devoured mine. For a long, wild moment, I was swept hard against him, as closely as in the village dance. And then, once more, he lifted me in his arms and took me to bed.

*

In my innocence, I had thought that life could hold no greater physical pleasure than that which Lajos had given me on Erzsébet Island. All through that long, January night, he showed me how wrong I was. And when I awoke at dawn after a short sleep of pure exhaustion, there was a happiness inside me so intense that it was almost pain. I was afraid to open my eyes in case my memories were only a dream. But no, I could still feel his arms around me, his naked thigh heavy against mine, and my body still ached pleasurably with the night's love. Smiling, I opened my eyes and gazed directly into his. He kissed me.

"Good morning," he said softly.

I touched his cheek caressingly. "You look as if you haven't moved. Didn't you sleep at all?"

"No. I've been watching you sleep, which is much more enjoyable." His finger traced a line around my fading bruise to my lips. "This time, Katie — no regrets?"

"None," I whispered. "I have been the biggest fool, Lajos..."

"Oh I think we both share that honour. In some perverse way, I believe I have enjoyed the game — in parts at least — but I'm not sorry it's over."

"Over?" I repeated, suddenly stricken with alarm, and he laughed softly.

"The game is over. A new life is beginning."

I buried my face in his neck. I couldn't quite believe that one person could be this happy. Surely, it wasn't allowed.

Toward Peace

January – July 1849

CHAPTER FORTY-FOUR

The question of my going to Debrecen or to Szelényi was never raised between us again. Instead, I followed the army as far as I was allowed, and shared Lajos's lodgings whenever I could, whether they were in a stately home, a barn or a tent. We were in the middle of a war; fighting, blood and death were all around us. I suppose in such circumstances those months cannot have been unadulterated bliss. And yet I remember only the vital, intense joy, the rare moments of peace and contentment that we both jealously protected from the ills of war.

And if the war had added to Lajos a new, commanding character, I soon discovered it had not altered what lay underneath. This was brought home to me forcibly after the Battle of Gualfálva, only days after my migraine had cleared my head of all its foolish inhibitions.

It was the first of many occasions when I sat alone in some inhospitable habitation with the boom of gunfire ringing in my ears and my imagination busy with visions that could not have been more horrendous or more gory than the actual battle. I tried to face the prospect of life without Lajos, told myself how unfair it would be if he were taken from me now when we had only just discovered happiness. And yet at the back of my mind was always the nagging doubt that I did not deserve such happiness, and that sooner or later it would be taken from me. I could only pray for later, and live through the agonies of apprehension, waiting with dread and with fierce impatience for the battle to end.

And then it was even worse, for wounded men trickled back into the camp with tales that set my teeth on edge. Those left behind in camp — the doctors, the camp followers and servants as well as the wounded, took what comfort they could from each other.

That first time, I heard their voices, but I could not join them. I couldn't even look out of the window of the hut I had shared with Lajos the previous night. I heard men riding in, heard the clank of steel and weary, marching feet, but still I could not watch. A simple monotonous prayer was repeating itself over and over inside my head until my lips moved with the words, "Let him live, let him live."

And when his shadow eventually darkened the hut, I was afraid to look at him. But I did. His shoulders sagged with exhaustion; there was blood on his uniform, and a strange, weary desperation behind the smile in his eyes. At first I could not move. I could only speak his name as a question, and it was he who came in all his dirt and other men's blood, and put his arms around me, holding his cold, rough cheek against mine in proof that he was still alive.

"We won," he reported mechanically. "I'm unhurt. Bem is alive by the skin of his teeth after some Austrian hero attacked him. All is well."

Despite the unbearable relief, I knew that all was *not* well. When Lajos went away from me again, about his duties, I found I was afraid of what the battle had done to him. I also felt ashamed now of my selfish inertness, and impulsively I went to the surgeon to offer my help.

The doctor and his assistants seemed to be working in a noisy hell: I thought I had somehow stumbled into a mediaeval evocation of the underworld. The makeshift hospital was full of pitiful groans and screams of agony. The stench was sickening. There seemed to be blood everywhere. Men sat or lay where they fell, with shattered limbs and terrifying head wounds. I saw soldiers with such dreadful injuries that I didn't understand how it was that they were still alive. Some of them were not, of course, for very much longer.

Dazed by the sheer scale of this suffering, I picked my way through the carnage till I finally came upon the harassed surgeon — a hard-eyed, middle-aged man called Tedényi — examining what was left of an unconscious soldier's chest.

"Sir," I began, and he cast me such a fierce glance of astonishment that I was silent. A particularly vile oath escaped his lips, but then he paused and I saw recognition in his tired eyes.

"You're Lázár's wife, aren't you? Go away, for God's sake, this is no place for you. Your husband isn't here."

"I know," I said quickly. "I came to offer what help I can — I know nothing, but I can obey instruction."

He stared at me. The he wiped his hands on his bloody apron and turned back to his patient, saying shortly, "I'd laugh, except I need any help I can get. You can start by washing that fellow's head so that I can see where his wound is — but be warned, Madame, if you faint, I shall simply step over you."

Humbly, I moved to obey him. One of the assistants gave me an apron. I needed it. I didn't faint in the end; nor was I sick, though more than once I felt both dizzy and nauseous. I had never thought of myself as particularly squeamish, but then battle-wounds, the sawing of limbs, such sheer human agony had never come my way before. Doctor Tedényi treated me as he did all his assistants, who included two of the camp followers I had encountered on my first day with Colonel Drényi's detachment. We exchanged only curt nods, though I was pleased enough to see them — it was impossible to smile in such a place.

By the time the doctor sent me away — which he did with rough words and a surprisingly gentle push — there was a real haze before my eyes. When I closed them, I could see only gory wounds, but in a vague, undisturbing sort of a way, for I was just a little proud of myself and tiredness had, in any case, overcome the horror by the time I left.

*

It had, of course, been a great victory for Bem. With a force of only seven thousand men he had beaten an Austrian army of twice that number — or so they said. Puchner was in flight, and the Hungarian camp was celebrating.

It was late at night when Lajos came to me at last, bone-weary, almost asleep on his feet. I didn't speak, just helped him out of his clothes, pushed him gently into the make-shift bed, and pulled the blanket over him, while he watched me with a tender, half-amused smile. His eyes were already closed when I lay down beside him. We slept.

But not for long. The sudden jerking of his body brought me startlingly awake. He was still asleep, but I could see at once that he was dreaming, and not pleasantly. Though I tried to soothe him, the restless, violent movements got worse, and though he didn't actually shout, he kept muttering incoherently and making strange, heart-rending sounds of anger and distress. His face became contorted with anguish until I could not bear it, and even as I determined to wake him, I saw the wetness on his cheeks.

"Lajos," I said loudly. "Lajos, wake up!"

At once, his eyes flew open. His body was still. Half-frightened, I smoothed his forehead caressingly, until he said, "What is it? What's the matter?"

"You were dreaming. I think it was a nightmare." With pity, I brushed the tears off his face with my fingers. There was another pause.

Then he said, "I'm sorry. I've had nightmares since Schwechat. A new fight always seems to bring it back."

"Are they very dreadful?" I asked softly.

"Not as dreadful as the battles. They don't hurt anyone."

"Oh Lajos..."

But he was speaking again, as if he couldn't stop himself. He didn't distress me with horrific descriptions of the battles themselves, but quietly, intensely, he told me of his physical fear, of the depths of his hatred for the violence and the killing, of his utter compassion for everyone involved, enemies as well as friends, of the awfulness of attacking men who had been or should be friends, countrymen.

"Then why do you do it?" I whispered, stroking his hair. "There are others who can fight."

"I can't leave others to protect what I began."

"Then it is still the revolution you are fighting for?"

"What else?" he said simply. "What else is worth this?" And suddenly his eyes were desperate again. "Sometimes, sometimes I even wonder if the revolution is..."

I held him close to me. Almost afraid to ask, I said quietly, "And is it?"

"I'm still here," he said for answer. He moved, rolling me over so that it was he who now leaned over me. "Don't you despise me now, for my cowardice?"

"It's not cowardice to overcome fear," I said quietly. "Or to admit to it. Besides, I could never despise you."

For a moment his eyes were intent on mine, then his lip quirked slightly, and I realized that subtly the nature of his embrace had changed. It was something more urgent than comfort which he sought now — or perhaps the love was comfort. At any rate, he made love to me that night with a new, fierce abandon that drove the anguish away and left us both exultant.

And despite the awful suffering I saw in him that night, part of me was glad to see the idealistic youth still beneath the soldier. I could only admire the steely strength that forced him to go through with the business of war, not only with adequacy but with efficiency and bravery, inspiring his men and impressing his superiors with his intelligence and flair. Lajos did nothing by halves, and if he was occasionally wracked by conscience and doubts, only I ever knew of it: Bem and his brother officers, I noticed, treated his assertions that he disliked fighting as a rather good joke.

When I woke from heavy sleep the next morning, Lajos was already up and dressed, sitting on the edge of the bed, watching me. I reached up at once, winding my arms around his neck, but though he held me to him, his fingers kept my chin up so that he could look at me.

"I have one more confession," he said lightly.

"You drank all the coffee?"

"Would I be so selfish? No, it's about your friends who brought you to me."

I felt myself grow still in his arms. I searched his eyes, but they were guarded, watchful. "What about them?" I said at last.

"They are both dead."

In spite of myself, I sagged against him with relief.

"They died in the battle," he went on. "Or at least Tamás Nagy did. Béla Vahot was severely wounded; he died later in the hospital."

"In the hospital?" I repeated, startled. "But I was there..."

Now it was he who was surprised. "What in the world for?"

"I felt guilty after you came back. I went to help Doctor Tedényi."

His eyes softened. For a moment he did not speak, then abruptly he pressed his cheek to mine and murmured how proud of me he was. My heart swelled; basking in the warmth of his praise, I didn't notice until after he had left me that he had begun the conversation by using the word 'confession'.

The remembrance made me pause. For a long moment I stared unseeingly in front of me, but in the end I knew I did not care how responsible Lajos was for their deaths. I had never been told and I had never asked what punishment, if any, Lajos had inflicted upon them, but I had always been aware that only my plea had preserved them from the ultimate penalty. Lajos disliked violence, but in his heart he could never forgive what they had done, nor what they had tried to do to me.

We chased Puchner's army back to Nagyzseben, but here, although all the towns we had passed through on the way had fallen into Bem's hands, we suffered a reverse; Bem would not wait for the reinforcements he was expecting, but attacked at once and was soundly beaten. It was the first of a series of defeats.

These were dark days. The spirits of the men drooped, and I was conscious of a constant, ever-deepening frown on Lajos's face. I remember four whole days of unrelenting fighting as we retreated from Vizakna to Deva, until the snow seemed to have turned blood-red.

I think we kept each other sane in those days, each gaining strength from the other in the short times we could spend together. Trudging through burned villages, dragging carnage with us, somehow the vital force of our personal happiness carried Lajos and I through the shattering defeats unscathed.

And then we had an unexpected visitor. From the doorway of our farm lodging I was anxiously watching Lajos's company ride into the yard after a scouting expedition, but even as I felt my heart lift as it always did at the sight of him, I heard a sharp command shouted across the camp.

"Captain Lázár! Place yourself under arrest!"

Indignation and alarm warred within my breast as I turned to see who had dared issue such an order. A young officer on foot was swaggering over from the Colonel's quarters towards Lajos who, still mounted, was frowning in the newcomer's direction. Slowly, the frown cleared, but his men still watched the scene in silent, sullen hostility.

"On what charge, Captain?" Lajos enquired, and he did not sound bothered in the least.

"Utter failure to write a single letter in four months, you bastard!" was the astonishing answer, as the young officer grinned and threw up his hand to Lajos. Under the men's astonished gaze, Lajos bent in the saddle and gripped the proffered hand. And then suddenly he was all but pulled from his horse in a boisterous display of affection, and only when they both began to walk towards me did I recognize Petőfi.

The poet greeted me with delight and civility and absolutely no surprise. "I thought it must be you, Miss Katie, when they told me Lajos had got married — though I admit you could have laid me out with a feather when I first heard the news! How are you? You look wonderful!"

I laughed. "Why, thank you — I return the compliment! How is your wife? And are you a father yet?"

"My wife and son are both well," Petőfi said, with no attempt to conceal his pride. We congratulated him, of course, and learned that his son was called Zoltán and was in Erdod with his mother and grandparents.

"But what are you doing here?" Lajos demanded.

Petőfi grinned. "I asked to come. Bem is the only General worth serving — so here I am. I'm Bem's new adjutant."

"Isn't Vasvári somewhere around here too? We should start a new branch of the Society for Equality." Lajos spoke sardonically, but underneath I could sense his pleasure in having Petőfi now so close. He got along very well with his brother officers and with his men, but I think he had felt the lack of soul-mates.

As the retreat went on and on, I helped to care for the wounded, and rather to my surprise I found I was beginning to be looked upon as a source of comfort, and not just by Lajos. In all, I was valued in ways, and in degrees, which I had never known before, and in the midst of disaster and suffering I drew my own strength from that knowledge.

Only once, in the hospital, did I break down and weep, and that was when they brought Oszkár. A friend from the same village, who had joined up with him, carried him in, tears streaming unashamedly down his plain, rough face; but there was nothing Tedényi could do — Oszkár was already dead.

For days afterwards, I expected to see his shy, smiling face as he trotted up to join me; and sometimes I would turn impulsively to the man who rode beside me, meaning to say something to Oszkár, and it would be a shock to discover the sharp, sly features of the soldier who had replaced him as Lajos's servant.

This was a bright-eyed individual called Zrinyi. He was light-fingered in the extreme, and no amount of threats or punishments could stop him stealing. He robbed officers, prisoners, priests, any village we happened to pass through. And yet he never stole from Lajos or from me. In time I came to appreciate his sharp sense of humour, his unexpected kindness, and even his honour which was of its own, peculiar brand but quite as rigid as any honest gentleman's.

At last, things began to turn again in Hungary's favour. At Marosvásárhely, where once we had secretly spent the night at a run-down inn with Katalin and Alex, Bem won a decisive victory, and now it was Puchner who fled before our pursuing army. And then, suddenly, we were travelling north again, for another Austrian force had attacked from the Borgo Pass, and taken Beszterce, killing Colonel Riczko, with whom I had danced at Bem's impromptu party that night in January.

Petőfi did not come with us on this journey. He was ill, and Bem had sent him to Szalonta to recover.

We retook Beszterce, but after this victory Lajos and I suffered our first parting in more than a month. Bem wished to pursue the fleeing enemy into Bukovina, and Lajos refused to take me. I pleaded, cajoled, shouted, sulked, but he was quite adamant, so in the end, seeing that I was only distressing him by my demands, I was silent.

I didn't even cry when he left me in Beszterce. I waited until he had gone.

CHAPTER FORTY-FIVE

While Lajos was away, I took the opportunity of doing house-wifely things: mending shirts and stockings — to the best of my poor ability — and trying to make myself a new gown from material I had bought cheaply in the town.

I also wrote to Aunt Edith in Scotland, though I had no idea if the letter would reach her through the current confusion, and to the Szelényis in Debrecen. The latter was a short note, for I could not guess how they regarded me now. I only knew how my mother had been treated for marrying beneath her, and how much greater was my own crime in their eyes. Colonel Drényi had already sent them word that I was alive and well, and I was sure they would have heard from the same source that I was Lajos's wife. I couldn't bring myself to mention this, for I could neither lie to them nor apologise for what I was doing now. So in the end, I only told them where I was and asked after everyone.

And then, suddenly nostalgic, I wanted to add that I wished we were together again, but I hesitated. It was not entirely true, for my first desire was to be with Lajos; so I said nothing about that either. In fact, it was a dissatisfying letter to me, whatever it was to become to them, and I had found that I did miss them, particularly Katalin and Miklós and Anna — and Mattias, who could be a prisoner of the Austrians now, or even dead...

When the shout went up that the Hungarians were coming back, I was out buying food. I dashed home with only half of what I needed.

This time, we were lodged with a Saxon widow who was the complete opposite of the sour-faced couple who had put us up the last time. She smiled benignly upon my panicked return, laughing at my frantic efforts to tidy myself and the sitting room, which she had been generous enough to lend us along with the bedroom.

I am not surprised that she was amused, for Lajos was hardly the stern, fault-finding husband who would berate me for poor housekeeping. The truth was that I was nervous for quite other reasons. I was afraid he would not come back at all, that he would be ill or injured — after all, the death toll on the last pursuit into Bukovina had been horrendous. And if he did come back, would he still want me? Might he not have found the freedom from me quite a relief? And how would I know if he chose to keep it from me...?

At last, my landlady, who was looking out of the window, said, "Here he comes," and trotted off to let him in. For a second, I closed my eyes with relief; and then, abruptly, I took off my spectacles, polishing them thoroughly so that I would be able to see his every expression as soon as he came in.

But I ran out of time. I heard Lajos's voice, his firm footsteps coming too quickly to the door. I jumped to my feet as the door was flung open, and my spectacles tumbled onto the floor.

It was only a beloved blur which stood in the doorway. I smiled uncertainly in its direction, and then dropped to my knees, frantically searching for the glasses. I was aware of him coming towards me, of the very odd nature of the welcome I was giving him, but somehow it seemed imperative to see him clearly at once.

"I've dropped my spectacles," I said nervously to his boots as they came to a halt in front of me. They moved. I felt Lajos crouch down and reach across me.

"Here," he said gravely, holding the spectacles out to me. I took them, risking a glance at his face. He was close by me now, so I didn't need the glasses to see the tender amusement in his eyes, the rueful understanding. With something approaching wonder, I continued to gaze up at him, and slowly I returned his smile.

"Hallo," he said.

"Hallo."

He took my hand, but rather to my surprise, he did not kiss me. Instead, he helped me to my feet.

"I have brought you a visitor," he said, and at once I crammed the spectacles on to my face. I had not even realized there was anyone with him, but now, standing just inside the room, I saw an officer in Austrian uniform. I smiled enquiringly from Lajos to the stranger — and at last recognized Colonel Karl von Avenheim.

He had been observing this strange passage between Lajos and me, and I saw amazement, pleasure, bewilderment all chasing each other across his face.

"Colonel!" I went forward at once, my hand outstretched. Almost dazed, he took it in both of his.

"Why, Katie — Miss Kettles! How is this? What in the world are you doing here? Surely there is no one at Szelényi?"

I laughed. "I haven't been to Szelényi since August! What interests *me* is what *you* are doing here! Are you a prisoner-of-war?" These days, the unbelievable had become almost normal.

"I'm afraid I am," said the Colonel, charmingly rueful. "This young man has captured me — curse his impudence! — and offered to lodge me under parole." He glanced at Lajos as he spoke, and I saw to my surprise that some sort of friendship had sprung up between them. The last time they had met, Lajos had been his prisoner; before that Avenheim had tried to shoot him. Yet now it seemed they had found something in each other that they liked.

"What a coincidence," I said inadequately. Remembering my manners, I asked him to sit down. He did so rather mechanically, for his mind was obviously still taken up by the oddity of my presence here.

"Are these *your* lodgings, Mademoiselle? I wish you would tell me how you come to be here! Are István and Elisabeth with you?"

"No," I said calmly. "They are in Debrecen so far as I know. We became separated during the evacuation of Buda-Pest."

"But are you all alone here?" he asked, astonished. I looked quickly away from the concern in his eyes, seeking help from Lajos, for clearly the Colonel knew nothing about our relationship. Almost with a jolt, I remembered his declaration to me last summer.

Lajos was unbuckling his sword belt, throwing it casually across the nearby chair as he caught my eye. He paused for a second, then looked at Avenheim.

"No. She is not alone. She is with me."

The Colonel frowned, uncomprehending. Involuntarily, I had moved closer to Lajos, and suddenly it seemed things fell into place in his mind. For a second he looked blank, then, abruptly, he stood up, turning away from us. "I see," he said jerkily. "Then am I to understand that *this* is the man you told me of in the summer?"

"Yes," I said quietly.

"Perhaps I should have known. Yet your stations were so unequal that it never — of course, there has been a revolution." He gave a short, unnatural laugh, turning back to face us. Despite the touch of revulsion which he could not quite keep out of his eyes, I felt a wave of sympathy and pity, but there was nothing I could do. With an effort, he smiled. "So, how long have you been married?"

My eyes flew again to Lajos, questioning, pleading, for suddenly it was impossible to lie so deliberately to a friend. This was something I had not considered before, so isolated was I in my new happiness, but now, resolutely, I had decided that honesty was my only possible course, despite the inevitability of the Colonel's reaction. I could stand his scorn; I could stand the world's, if Lajos was with me.

Lajos met my gaze. He shrugged, almost imperceptibly. I drew in my breath, and looked steadily at Colonel von Avenheim.

"We are not married," I said calmly.

"Not married?" Frowning, his eyes moved from me to Lajos and back. "I don't understand. I took Lázár to mean he lodged here with you."

"He does."

The Colonel's frown had become ferocious. Gradually, his gaze travelled to Lajos, who met it steadily, but before either of us could explain further, he began to speak rapidly, with an intensity I had never heard in his voice before.

"Do you know, Lázár, over the last few days I began to think I had been wrong about you, that you were, in fact, a man of sincerity and principle, however misguided. But now..." He broke off. I saw his lip curl into an uncharacteristic snarl, and when he resumed, his voice was louder, more emphatic and full of angry contempt. "Now I discover you have callously abused the trust, the affection of an innocent girl! You have seduced and ruined her for nothing more than your own pleasure! You, who are not fit to be ground under her feet, have taken what no man has the right to, not without marriage! My God, you should be *dead!*"

On the last word, he leapt without warning for Lajos's sword, and in a trice it was out of the scabbard and brandished before him. There was no trace left of the calm, civilized gentleman I thought I knew. His eyes were wild, glittering murderously.

"Dead," he repeated, and lunged. Lajos stepped nimbly aside. I let out a gasp of fear and distress.

"Stop it!" I commanded. "Put down the sword, Colonel!"

"Oh no. You persuaded me to that once before, but *this* I cannot forgive!" He lashed out at Lajos again and again. Each time, Lajos evaded the weapon till at last he snatched up a chair and held it before him for protection.

"Colonel, you're on parole," he said, almost conversationally.

"I do not regard as binding the promises made to peasant scum."

"That's the trouble with the world," Lajos observed, parrying a vicious thrust on one of the chair's legs, which Avenheim sliced off, sending it crashing to the floor. "No one ever regards as binding the promises made to peasants. Nevertheless, I think you should put down my sword."

"I'm sure you do; but for what you did to Katie, Lázár, I'll kill you first!"

Another leg was hacked off, and another, just as the door opened and our landlady stuck her amiable head into the room and screamed.

"Fetch help," I cried to her. "Fetch the soldiers!"

Lajos was laughing breathlessly. "Katie, we *are* soldiers," he said, leaping for safety over the sofa. Avenheim followed him, crashing the sofa on to its back as he went. The whole scene was insane; it would have been hilarious had it not been for the deadly blood-lust in the Colonel's eyes.

I could only think wildly how unfair it would be if Lajos were to be killed like this, for nothing. Angry now, I followed them, catching Avenheim by the arm — just as he hacked off the whole back of Lajos's chair.

"Colonel, stop it! What do you imagine he has done to me?"

His answer was a cry of pain and rage as he shook me off and went after Lajos. I tried to explain, to bring him back to reality, but he was beyond understanding or even listening. In no time, it seemed, he had backed Lajos into the corner and raised his sword to strike. I looked desperately around for a weapon, and seized the first thing that came to hand. It happened to be a vase of flowers — thoughtfully provided by my landlady to welcome Lajos back. I advanced purposefully, just as the door flew open and the landlady and Petöfi fell precipitately into the room, and Lajos, an expression of resignation on his face, hit the distracted Avenheim over the head with the wooden seat of his chair.

There was an instant of total silence. Then the sword fell out of Avenheim's hand and he slid easily to the floor. Lajos met my gaze.

"For the Colonel?" he enquired breathlessly, indicating the vase in my hands. "How useful — we can use the water to bring him round. Don't you ever knock, Petöfi?"

"Ungrateful lout," said the poet without heat. He still looked rather pale and ill. "You wouldn't have heard me if I *had* knocked. What on Earth are you doing? Besides not welcoming me back."

"Oh, fighting the good fight," said Lajos vaguely. "Madame, I'm sorry about the chair. I'll pay for it, of course." He had stepped over the recumbent Austrian, and now, under my fascinated eyes, he and Petöfi were setting the sofa back on its feet. Then Lajos walked towards me and took the vase out of my still hands, replacing it firmly on the table.

I swallowed. "I thought we were to bring him round with the water?"

"There is no hurry," Lajos said, looking significantly at the landlady, who gulped twice and fled. He turned his repelling gaze next upon Petöfi, but his friend, immune to it, threw himself on to the sofa.

"Not I," he said resolutely. "I want to know what's going on."

"So," Lajos said, "do I. Katie, why should the good Colonel feel so obliged suddenly to spill my blood?"

"He wanted to marry me once. I turned him down at Szelényi. You were in Buda-Pest at the time."

"I thought so." He sighed. "Ah well, so much for friendship with the enemy. Where's that vase?"

"Hold on," Petöfi interrupted. "I don't see what right the fellow has to try and kill you just because Katie preferred to marry you rather than him."

"Haven't you worked it out, Petöfi?"

Petöfi stared.

"I am not married to anyone," I said calmly.

"The Colonel chose to take moral exception," Lajos added.

"I don't blame him," said Petöfi frankly. "It's none of my business, Lajos, but Katie deserves better than that."

"No," I said quickly. "I couldn't have better. I came to Lajos for protection and that is what he has given me, that is why he pretended to be my husband. But I love him, and I shall stay with him, whatever anyone thinks."

Calmly, I picked the flowers out of the vase and lifted it, moving towards the prone figure on the floor.

"I'm not sure either that *you* deserve *her*," Petöfi remarked.

"I don't," Lajos said, and I heard the smile in his voice. "But I shall keep her just the same."

I knelt by the Colonel, picking up the fallen sword and handing it to Lajos who stood looking down at me enigmatically. After a moment, I dipped my hand in the vase and splashed the water on Avenheim's face. He groaned, so I repeated the process and his eyes opened. They focused on mine, bewildered. I waited until intelligence — and anger — began to show in them, and then I spoke.

"Before we go any further, Colonel, you should understand that I am here willingly, through my own choice. It was I who came to Lajos in my trouble, and to protect me he agreed to pretend we were married. But I have never been happier in my life, and if you think Lajos should die for making me happy, then I suggest you are given other lodgings. On the other hand, if you accept that our lives are our own business, then I am delighted to see you again."

The deliberate, matter-of-fact calmness of my voice seemed to have an effect. The unnatural fury began to fade from his face. He stirred.

"That is quite a speech," he said, struggling to sit up. I helped him. As he looked at me the bitterness began to die out of his eyes, leaving only a sadness which I recognized all to easily. Then his eyes were veiled by a kind of rueful amusement that I thought was not all pretence. "I believe I *should* stay somewhere else, but to be honest, Lázár, you're fiendishly heavy-handed. My head is splitting."

Without a word, Lajos examined the cut; and suddenly I heard Petöfi laugh.

"Oh God, I'm leaving this madhouse!" he said, springing to his feet. "Lajos, good luck. Katie, I salute you! And sir — whoever you are — I shall really take it amiss if you put a period to my friend's life. I should be confoundedly dull without him."

"A masterly exit," Lajos approved, as the door closed behind the poet who, I remembered irrelevantly, had once been an actor.

"Who is the puppy?" Avenheim demanded.

"Sándor Petöfi."

"That bloodthirsty, Jacobin scribbler?"

"You," said Lajos, "are too free with your criticisms, especially when you are at my mercy. Katie, can you find some fresh water?"

We left the still bemused Colonel von Avenheim behind us in Beszterce a few days later, and travelled southwards.

Petöfi caught up with us again at Kolozsvár, breezing into our lodgings one evening and looking much more his old self than he had at Beszterce. On the other hand, he was wearing civilian clothes, his eyes were glittering and his movements were restless with dissatisfaction. Dropping into the rather rickety chair I offered him, he thrust a piece of paper under Lajos's nose.

"Here, read this," he commanded. Lajos took the paper, quickly perusing it. I saw amusement tug at his lips and demanded to know what it was.

"I suspect," said Lajos, "that it is Petöfi's disrespectful reply to Mészáros's request that he wear a necktie with his uniform."

"Precisely," Petöfi said approvingly, "though why I should be respectful towards that silly old windbag...!"

"He is the Minister for War," I said with mock severity.

"Minister for neckties! I ran into him in Debrecen, and he had the *gall* to censure me for being improperly dressed, implying that I had no right to wear my captain's uniform without it! Naturally, I preferred to resign my right to the uniform than bow to such tyranny."

"You didn't," I said positively, but Lajos knew him better.

"He did," he corrected me, and turned back to Petöfi. "Couldn't you have been satisfied with *this?*" He waved the paper in the air till I stood up and plucked it from his fingers.

"No," said Petöfi uncompromisingly while I read his latest poem, a withering verse called *The Necktie* which ridiculed Mészáros's insistence on proper dress and ended with the lines: 'If you have no tie, stay off the battlefield. Long live Mészáros, and long live the necktie!'

"Oh dear," I said faintly, and Petöfi grinned at me. Lajos balanced his hip on the arm of Petöfi's chair, regarding his friend with a mixture of affection and irritation.

"Why do you let this sort of thing upset you? No one would have been any the wiser if you had been polite to Mészáros and still left off your tie. It makes no difference to world liberty, you know."

"*Someone* has to make a stand over their nonsense!"

"At the expense of wasting your talents as a private soldier?"

"If that is what it takes. I've been one before, after all."

"You're mad," said Lajos without emphasis. He stood up again. "Still, I'm sure it's only a temporary demotion — Bem will return you to your old rank before you can blink."

"I expect he will," Petöfi said complacently, for a strange friendship had grown up between himself and the Polish General, based on Petöfi's rather surprising but quite immovable hero-worship, and Bem's fatherly affection.

"Still," Lajos said thoughtfully, taking the piece of paper back from me, "it's a very good poem."

"I was rather pleased with it," Petöfi said modestly, "especially the bit about Mészáros's men running away — which they did! — but all wearing their neckties."

"Well, let's hope he doesn't run into *you* again."

"Amen," said the poet devoutly.

CHAPTER FORTY-SIX

At the end of that month, I finally rode into Debrecen. Transylvania was quiet at last, and Bem had chosen to send Lajos with his latest despatches.

"Why you?" I had asked discontentedly.

"Apparently," Lajos had replied thoughtfully, "because Kossuth requested it."

I had looked at him suspiciously. "Why should Kossuth want to see you?"

"I don't know. Shall we go and find out?"

I had been quick to pounce on the 'we'. "You mean I may come too?" My discontent had vanished like a spring shower in sunshine. Lajos had watched me with some amusement.

"Of course. I can't leave you here on your own, can I? Besides, I thought you might like to see your family." His eyes had been rather guarded then. I wondered, incredibly, if he had actually imagined that they could turn me against him.

For some reason, I had expected Debrecen to resemble Buda-Pest, but I could not have been more wrong. It was just like a huge village, without pavements or street-lights or, judging by the smell, proper sewers. Many of the houses were little more than mud cottages.

As our horses slowly picked their way through streets running with mud, my mind boggled at the thought of my aristocratic relatives living in this comparative squalor, and I said so to Lajos, who only smiled faintly. His eyes were resting on a figure wading along the side of the road ahead of us.

Eventually, he called out, "Hallo! Jókai!" and the figure turned quickly, narrowly avoiding crashing into a large citizen with a ridiculously long beard. His eyes searched wildly, and when they eventually found Lajos they lit up with instant pleasure.

"Lajos!" He plunged heedlessly into the road, splashing mud everywhere, and Lajos leaned down from the saddle to shake his hand. "How are you? You look the same as ever! And Miss Katie!" He shook my hand too. "But what are you doing here?"

"Messenger-boy," said Lajos disparagingly. "But since we have run into you, perhaps you can point us in the direction of reasonable lodgings?"

Jókai did not appear to be in the least surprised to find us together, from which I presumed that he had heard something of our situation from Petőfi. When he led us to a decent inn, I left him and Lajos alone and went up to my room, where I washed and changed into the gown I had made so badly that Lajos had laughed and taken it himself to a dressmaker in Beszterce to be re-made. It now looked quite unexceptionable, and the deep wine colour I thought was quite becoming. I brushed and re-pinned my hair, and then doubtfully satisfied, I rejoined Lajos and Jókai downstairs.

"Well yes," Jókai was saying uncomfortably. "The Society still meets, but to be honest, there isn't much point with the war still going on. And since this trouble with Madarász..."

"What trouble is that?" I asked, sitting down beside Lajos.

"The 'Diamond Affair'," Jókai said contemptuously. "A chest full of jewels and money, confiscated from a traitorous nobleman called Zichy, was in Madarász's keeping, since he is Police Minister. Now they're accusing him of having embezzled the diamonds for his own purposes. It's all rubbish, of course, but mud, as they say, sticks. I suppose he should have been more careful to account for everything."

"I heard that the Peace Party was out to get rid of him," Lajos said casually, and Jókai began to look unaccountably uncomfortable. "I heard that Pál Nyári had gone over to the Peace Party — and that you had gone with him."

Jókai met the mild but watchful gaze of his friend rather defiantly. "Yes, I want peace. *Nothing* can be more damaging to the country than this kind of war and uncertainty."

"You would go back to the old ways? After March?" Lajos's voice was still quiet. He had never spoken of this to me before, and I still had no way of telling how he regarded Jókai's defection.

Jókai said jerkily, "March — the April Laws — may be salvaged. We need peace more than anything, Lajos."

"I dislike the war as much as you — more, probably. But I don't like the idea of peace at any price either."

"Neither do I!"

I saw Lajos's lip quirk. "Join us tonight, if you care to, and we'll fight it out."

There was relief as well as pleasure in Jókai's smile. "Of course! And now, Miss Katie, I have been asked to escort you to the Szelényi residence."

Startled, I looked at Lajos.

"I thought you would like to go at once," he remarked. "And I have to go to the City Hall to see Kossuth. Jókai knows where they are."

They lived, it seemed, in a large, comfortable house. It was not quite the Szelényi Palace, but neither was it a mud hut. My heart was beating uncomfortably fast as I thanked Jókai for his escort and knocked nervously on the door.

Of course, it was a strange servant who answered, and when I asked for any of the family, he only admitted me grudgingly to the hall, enquiring my name almost as an afterthought. I didn't know whether to be amused by his ill-manners, or outraged. In the end I just stood meekly in the hall and waited — but not for long.

I heard them before I saw them, louder than I remembered and running on the stairs faster than they should have been allowed. I began to smile, for

I knew the game they were playing. They skidded almost together around the corner at the foot of the stairs, and came to an abrupt halt, staring at me.

There was a tiny moment of amazement, but I did not even have time to register my fear of rejection before Miklós roared, "*Katie!*" and Anna squealed, casting herself upon me with what I can only describe as glee. Miklós was not far behind her, and I realized suddenly how much and how badly I had missed them.

As a result, when I emerged from their crushing embrace and straightened, my vision was a little hazy; but then, vaguely seeing the still figure of a woman at the foot of the stairs, I quickly brushed my fingers across my eyes, and smiled uncertainly.

"Katalin."

"Katie...?" A couple of hesitant steps and then a rush towards me, and she too was hugging me convulsively. "Dear God, Katie, where have you been? *How* we have missed you!" she pushed me away, crying unashamedly even while she smiled till I thought her lips would split. "And you look so well and happy, you wretch!"

"I am happy," I said shakily. "And so glad to see you again... Oh dear, I hate emotional scenes..."

Laughter gurgled up from within her and she threw her arms round me again. "Oh I *have* missed you! But, Katie, is it really true that you have married Lajos Lázár?"

At that crucial moment, the slovenly servant returned, announcing reluctantly that the Countess would receive me.

"Of course she will, bubble-head!" Katalin cried indignantly. "This is our niece, and she will always be received!" With which she swept me upstairs, and I entered the Countess's drawing-room with a laughing, chattering, wildly excited escort.

I saw at once that both Elisabeth and Margit were there, and felt a surge of relief. I had really feared that Margit might have died after that dreadful journey eastward from Buda-Pest. However, it was Elisabeth who first drew my full attention. She stood facing me, pale but erect in a heavily flounced gown of sky blue silk. She looked as calm and composed as she ever had, so it was something of a shock to hear the hesitance in her voice.

"So it is you... I, I could not quite believe it... Are you, are you — well?"

"I am very well," I said gently. "Did you not get my letter?"

"Letter!" Katalin exploded, with her first sign of anger against me. "A pathetic, distant little *note!*"

"I'm sorry," I said ruefully. "I didn't really know what to say — or what you would want to hear." I looked at Elisabeth. "To be honest, I didn't know if you would be prepared to receive me."

"*We* be prepared to receive *you*?" There was a rare flash of honest feeling in Elisabeth's voice and in her suddenly flushed face. "Dear God, Katie, we pushed you into the road in a strange country on a freezing cold night and *lost* you! Is it not you who should hate us?"

"No," I said, distressed. "No."

"It was István," Katalin reminded everyone, "who pushed her into the road. It was ages, Katie before we could even make him listen to us, and then we could not find you, though we scoured the road over and over till morning..."

"I know. I bumped my head when I fell — I don't know how long I lay unconscious; and then I stumbled around blindly in the dark instead of standing still and waiting for you..." My eyes were on Margit, still sitting by the fire, staring at me as if stunned. Quickly, I crossed the room to her, and saw the tears streaming down her face.

"I thought you were gone. I thought you had gone too..."

"Oh Margit." I bent and hugged her. "I was afraid for you too: you seemed so ill..." Hastily, I dashed a hand across my eyes. "Oh dear, shouldn't we have tea or something?"

An unexpected snort of laughter was wrung from Elisabeth. "Oh, God, Katie, I'm glad you're back! Ring the bell beside you, Anna."

"And István and Mattias?" I asked, casting my cloak carelessly on the side of the chair which the children put me in before sitting on either arm. I could neither breathe nor see past them with any ease.

"Mattias is with Görgey's army," said Katalin. "He seems to have taken to soldiering like a duck to water! He thinks the world of Görgey too, for some reason."

Relieved, I looked at Elisabeth. "And István?" I prompted.

"István," she said carefully, "has a lot of guilt on his conscience. You know he has never been happy about this war; and then, when he realized what he had done to you in his awful temper..."

"But I am fine," I interrupted. "Did Colonel Drényi not send you a message which said so?"

"István had a message which said that Madame Lázár desired him to know that she was safe and well; and since Eszter Lázár has never in her life sent a message to István of any description, we could only conclude — though doubtfully — that it was you."

"Your second message confused us even more," Katalin added, "because you never even mentioned Lajos. Did you really marry him?"

I took a deep breath. "No."

Elisabeth's shoulders, I noticed, sagged with relief, but Katalin was frowning.

"I don't understand. Why all this *Madame Lázár* nonsense? And where in the world have you been for the last three months?"

I sighed. "It's a long story." I told it prosaically, explaining without fuss how the world had come to regard me as Lajos's wife. "Which for the last three months," I finished, primly sipping my tea, "is exactly what I have been. To all intents and purposes."

Katalin stared at me. "What do you mean?"

"She means," said Elisabeth drily, "that she is Lajos's mistress, though pretending to be his wife. How lowering to admit to Teréz that she was right and I was wrong."

I flushed and laid down my cup, meeting Elisabeth's challenging eyes over Anna's head.

"I would be grateful if you did not discuss me at all with Teréz. I'm sorry, since she is a friend of yours, Elisabeth, but the woman is nasty, ill-natured, malicious and vulgar. I may have loved Lajos since I first came here, but I never indulged in the sort of affair she imagines — or pretends to imagine — either with him or with anyone else. What is between us now just *happened*, but you had better know that I shall stay with Lajos until..." I broke off.

"Until what?" Katalin prompted, almost awed.

I gave a quick, unnatural laugh. "Until one of us dies." Or until he tires of me...

Katalin, still a lover of romance in any form, smiled mistily at me, trying her best to come to terms with the shock. Margit looked as uncomprehending and as happy as the children. Elisabeth was gazing at me with the curiosity one accords a particularly foreign insect.

"You are a very odd girl," she observed. "And I honestly don't know whether István will consider it worse for you to be his wife or his mistress."

"Oh, I think either condemns me," I said lightly. I regarded her. "Should I stay and see him or not?"

"But of course you must stay!" Katalin exclaimed. "You don't imagine we shall let you go again?"

The children picked up the gist of that. They stopped playing with my hands and stared at me accusingly. I avoided their eyes, glancing a little sadly at Katalin.

"But I have to go. When Lajos goes back."

Katalin swallowed. "Can't you wait for him here till the war is over?"

"No. I have done all the waiting I intend to. Besides," I added, aiming for lightness, "I would embarrass you horribly among your friends."

"Speak to István," Elisabeth recommended. So I waited.

It was an unexpectedly jolly party which István discovered upon his return. Katalin and I were kneeling on the floor with the children, playing a boisterous game of jack-straws with them while I caught up with their news and told them something of my adventurous life since January, including an edited version of my encounter with Colonel von Avenheim.

He saw me as soon as he opened the door. I glanced up, still laughing at Miklós's antics, and slowly, the laughter died on my lips. I saw the awful guilt written clearly in his eyes, a guilt he could barely live with; and I knew instinctively that if there was to be any reconciliation with him, I would have to begin it.

I rose quietly to my feet and went towards him.

"István," I said, holding out my hand. He took it mechanically, almost blindly, and I reached up, briefly kissing his cheek. Abruptly, his strong face crumpled, his arms closed round me like a vice.

"Katie, Katie, I didn't mean it, I'm so sorry..."

"I know," I said, swallowing the tightness in my own throat. "I know. It doesn't matter; it's all forgotten. István, I forgive you — I have the same temper!" Smiling, I drew back a little, watching the beginnings of hope gradually lighten his tortured eyes just a little. "But wait — *you* still have to forgive *me*. Teréz Meleki was telling lies that night, but I do love Lajos Lázár and I always have. And though it began as a fiction to protect me, I now live with him as his wife."

Even at the time, I thought it a remarkably concise and neat confession. Of course, it needed time to sink in. As his arms fell back to his side, I stepped away, and Elisabeth led him to the sofa, sitting down close beside him. I sat opposite and waited. Somewhere, I was surprised by the importance I was according his reaction. Two years ago, this family had meant nothing to me; now I wanted their friendship very badly.

Istvan's eyes looked blank with incomprehension. No one spoke, and the silence went on and on.

Then: "Why?" said István unexpectedly, and we began to talk. Oddly enough, he seemed to think his own bad behaviour had pushed me into this situation against my will, but I soon disabused him of this notion.

It was, on the whole, a surprisingly peaceful discussion, though it was not without its moments of anger on both sides. He didn't like it — none of them did — but he was still very conscious of the unforgivable injury he had done me, and this, perhaps, helped him to keep the peace. His arrogant self-assurance had suffered badly recently, over the war and over me, so that he seemed now somehow diminished. He was no longer the same István who had employed me, and he was no longer sure of his ground about anything. Pity welled up inside me, yet even so, I knew that the old István would never have forgiven me for what I had done; now, there was a chance.

The other factor that calmed him was that the world believed we were married: despite Lajos's birth, and despite István's hatred, it seemed wife was still preferable to mistress, and I spent a long time emphasising the honourable nature of Lajos's conduct throughout. He could appreciate the dilemmas which had led to our pretence, even if he could not understand why I now clung to it. In the end, we called a truce, and I saw with relief that I had not yet managed to lose this new family of mine.

I even stayed for dinner. As a treat, the children ate with us, but afterwards they were reluctant to go to bed in case I disappeared again. I was touched by the strength of their affection; I even felt guilty about leaving them, but, I re-minded myself, they were not my children.

When I said that I should go, Katalin tried again to persuade me not to, and István frowned rather ferociously; but eventually he said, "Where are you staying? I'll take you."

I smiled with surprised gratitude, but before I could answer, the sour-faced servant came in and announced that Captain Lázár was here to collect me. I saw a spasm cross István's face. I saw Elisabeth hesitate helplessly.

"Don't worry," I said lightly. "I am ready to leave. Thank you for your offer, István, it was appreciated. May — may I come again?"

"Of course," he said, a little stiffly and then, as I smiled farewell at the oth-ers, already moving towards the door: "Katie? Do you have money?"

"Yes," I said gently. "I have money. Thank you."

Lajos was waiting for me in the hall, pacing idly up and down. He smiled when he saw me, and took my cloak from the servant, advising that morose individual to cheer up before he soured the milk; and I was swept out of the house.

I felt his eyes on me as we walked away, but for a long time he was silent. Then, as if he could bear it no longer, he said lightly, "Well? I presume every-thing is fine?"

"Almost." My voice was unexpectedly small, and at once he put his arm around my shoulders, still gazing down at me. There was another pause.

Then he said, "I wondered if they would persuade you to stay."

I smiled. "They tried, which is very flattering in the circumstances."

"Were you tempted?"

"No," I said truthfully. "I'm so glad to have seen them, and I realize now how much I have been missing them — especially the children — but no. I don't want to lose them, that's all." I nestled into his arm more comfortably. "And you? What did Kossuth say?"

"Something very interesting. He asked if I was still in communication with Avram Iancu."

I blinked. "How did he know you ever were?"

"Madarász told him, apparently. Certainly I never mentioned any names when I spoke to him before about the Romanians. Anyhow, I told him — again! — the gist of our meetings last summer and this time he began to look quite animated. The upshot is, he wants me to make contact with Iancu to try and win him over to our side."

"But that is wonderful!" I exclaimed. "It's just what you always wanted — a gesture from our government to them."

"Yes, but *I* am the only gesture," Lajos said wryly. "I can't pin him down to any concrete concessions, and without those, Iancu just won't play. He has been shut up in the Apuseni mountains, surrounded and unassailable, for months now! He won't give in for nothing."

"Did you tell Kossuth this?"

"Yes." Lajos's lip twitched. "He told me I could promise them anything that did not compromise Hungary's political or territorial integrity."

"Does that leave you much scope?"

"No. I warned him he could lose all of Hungary, when all he needs to do is give up a little piece over to the autonomy of the Romanians; but he thinks it will encourage all the nationalities to demand autonomous areas and he won't hear of it."

"So what will you do?"

"Go and see him again tomorrow to receive my final orders."

"Then you have agreed to do it?"

"I don't have any choice. Besides, we should never have stopped trying in the first place."

"*You* didn't," I said, and he hugged me to his side.

"Wonderful creature. Would you care to get drunk tonight with Jókai and me?"

"That is not a very proper suggestion. I couldn't possibly accept."

"Then perhaps I can entice you to join us in a glass of wine?"

"One glass," I said graciously, "and then you and Jókai may get as drunk as you please without me."

They did.

After Lajos had seen Kossuth in the morning, he came back to the inn with a parcel under his arm.

"Are these Hungary's concessions?" I asked humorously.

"No, these are Lázár's clothes." He tore the paper off and revealed shirt, trousers and coat. "I'm to travel as a civilian. I suggested a couple would be beyond suspicion, and he agreed to that quite happily. He even congratulated me upon my marriage."

I smiled doubtfully. "How kind. I suppose a civilian would be safer in Romanian territory than a Hungarian officer... Or is he making sure your visit is unofficial? Lajos, is this dangerous?"

"No, I don't see why it should be. I know Iancu, and his word will be good enough for the others."

I sat down on the bed, fingering the material of his new coat. "Do you still think Alex is with Iancu?"

"It's possible."

"Would a letter from Katalin to him compromise us? Always supposing she still wishes to contact him, of course."

He shrugged. "So long as it is personal."

I regarded him with disfavour. "Like your passionate letters to me?"

He smiled faintly. "I was protecting your reputation — and István's for what it's worth."

"What a selfless, heroic fellow you are," I marvelled. "When do we leave?"

"Tomorrow. Do you want to go to the Szelényis' again today? I'll walk with you, if you like — there are some old friends I want to see in that direction."

*

The Szelényis had visitors when I arrived, so I crept cravenly up to the nursery to see the children and to renew my acquaintance with Zsuzsa, who positively grinned at me when I came in.

"I *knew* there was something between you and Lajos!" she cried gleefully. "I'm so glad you married him!"

I only laughed, feeling ridiculously touched as well as uncomfortable. An hour later, Katalin came to find me, with the news that the visitors had gone.

"I was afraid Teréz would be one of them," I said bluntly.

"Oh, she and Elisabeth don't visit any more. To be frank, even Elisabeth could not stomach her deliberate malice in using you and István to satisfy her own spite. Do you really have to leave tomorrow, Katie?"

"Yes," I said, taking her arm and leading her away from the children who were currently quite happy with each other. "Which is why I want to speak to you. I didn't have the chance yesterday to ask you about Alex."

Immediately, she looked dismal. "I have not heard a word from him since Buda-Pest."

"Lajos thinks he knows where he is. It's just possible, even, that we might see him."

"Oh, Katie...!"

"Do you want to give me a message for him, just in case?"

"Yes, oh yes! Oh, Katie, you *angel!*"

Katalin's love, it appeared, was not yet dead from lack of nourishment. Before I left, she slipped a letter into my hands.

This time, I did not stay to dinner, for we planned an early start in the morning, and there were things I had still to do. Again, István offered to drive me to the inn, and this time I took up his offer.

The carriage was quite a luxury to me now. I settled back to enjoy the short drive, while we discussed impersonal things, such as the latest news of a Hungarian victory, which had just reached István.

"Now it seems retaking Buda-Pest may soon be a possibility. I won't deny I didn't believe we could win this war, but it seems I was wrong — thank God."

When we arrived at the inn, István insisted on conducting me inside. Lajos was sitting there in the coffee-room with Jókai who, I had discovered last night, was now a journalist in Debrecen, and a few other men who looked faintly familiar to me. They were obviously entertaining each other.

István stopped dead, just as Lajos looked up and saw us. He came to his feet at once.

"István was kind enough to bring me back," I said lightly.

"Thank you," Lajos said to him, and I saw a spasm cross István's hard mouth. Their eyes were locked like the horns of warring bulls, but Lajos at least was prepared to be friendly. "Will you join us?"

István's lip curled. He didn't even bother to answer, just turned to me, saying, "Good-bye, Katie — keep in touch," and left the inn.

"Rude fellow," said one of Lajos's friends.

"No, not normally. He just doesn't like me."

CHAPTER FORTY-SEVEN

Spring had come to the western mountains. The snows had melted, the trees were budding into new, green life, and the wild hill flowers were beginning to scatter their bright colours all around the slopes.

As Lajos and I walked hand in hand in the hills around the town of Abrud, I could imagine that the war had never been, that he and I were just two lovers enjoying the peace and incomparable beauty of the mountains — except, of course, that the whole area was ringed by Hungarian soldiers whom we had been able to pass only with Kossuth's written authority, while in his high mountain fastness, Avram Iancu led his men in the most stubborn resistance of the Transylvanian war.

In those early April days, Transylvania was quiet. Bem was trying to win lasting peace through clemency to the rebels, and now it seemed that Kossuth and the Hungarian government were prepared to stretch the hand of friendship to their former enemies, and I was glad, for without at least Romanian neutrality, I was sure the country would not stay quiet for long.

In fact, I had high hopes for Transylvania and for Hungary, which did not seem so very far-fetched, for we had just heard that Hungarian armies had won two major victories over the Austrians and were advancing upon Buda-Pest.

But I did not want to think about the war. I didn't even want to think about the stubborn warlike youth whom Lajos had come to win over. I wanted to concentrate only on the sweet smells of spring, the cheerful singing of the birds, and the man striding silently along at my side.

For a while, I managed it, but we were not the only people in the hills — that was why we were here — and Lajos was heading steadily in the direction of the path which led eventually to Iancu's stronghold. Not that he intended to knock on the door: he was simply looking for a man to carry a message to Iancu. As yet, Kossuth did not want Lajos's visit to seem official.

Foolishly, my heart sank when I saw the two dots appear on the hill and grow ever closer. I wanted the day for us, not for the business of war and politics and negotiation. I tried to slip my hand free but Lajos held on to it, though I was under no illusions as to why. Simply, the sight of two lovers was quite unthreatening.

The men were Romanian peasants, thin, malnourished. They couldn't be anything but malnourished, for no food but what was grown there had come to this area for months. They looked at us suspiciously, exchanging low-voiced mutters in their own language which I was rather glad then not to understand.

As I expected, Lajos greeted them civilly in Romanian. They replied reluc-tantly, and then Lajos surprised me by passing with no more than an amiable smile. I regarded him fixedly, questions forming on my lips, but before I could voice them, he had nodded his head forward significantly. Following his gaze, I saw what had distracted him from the two peasants — another, solitary figure; and this one, so far as I could tell over the distance, wore a coat and appeared to walk with a very upright, gentlemanly carriage.

Abruptly, Lajos dropped to the ground, into the long grass, pulling me with him.

"What are you doing?" I demanded. "Lajos, I am not prepared to take the role of lover any further!"

His lip quirked appreciatively. "Content yourself. At the moment I have no designs upon your body. Rather, upon his. Hush now."

We lay still, side by side, though I could not imagine we were hidden from the approaching man.

We waited silently as the quick footfalls came nearer and nearer, and then Lajos moved, hurling himself at the man's legs and toppling him easily to the ground. In a trice he was leaning over him, and I, bewildered and not a little angry, heard him say happily, "Hallo, Alex."

There was a pause, and then I laughed. Now I could see the dazed face of Captain Zarescu staring up into Lajos's, and slowly, a smile of intense pleas-ure spread across it.

"Lajos, you — you..."

"Hush, my friend; we have company."

"Well, get off me then, you oaf," Alex said, dislodging Lajos and sitting up in the grass.

"Alex," I said, smiling, and he clutched his head.

"I'm dreaming. First Lajos, and now you! What in the world are you doing here?" Suddenly, the pleasure died out of his eyes altogether, and I saw a flash of quick suspicion. "Lajos, the Hungarians have not broken through?"

"No," Lajos assured him, but Alexandru's black eyes were still more watch-ful than I had ever seen them, and they were locked unamiably to Lajos's.

"And yet I heard you were an officer in Bem's army."

"I am."

"I don't see your uniform. Do you want to be taken as a spy? Is that what you are?"

"No; I'm a negotiator."

Some of the suspicion died, but now I could see that Lajos's own eyes were veiled and almost piercing. He must have been aware of the suspicion he would arouse, even in the breast of a friend as close as Alex. He had known he would no longer be trusted. I didn't know how much he trusted Alex.

I hated the war anew for what it had done to friends.

"Ah. You have come up in the world," Alex said lightly. "On whose authority do you negotiate?"

"That of the Committee of National Defence — in effect, Kossuth."

"And you come to negotiate with...?"

"Iancu, of course."

Alex pulled the head off a tiny, yellow flower and examined it minutely. "Iancu is not aware of any negotiations."

"He wouldn't be. They haven't yet begun. You can begin it, if you like."

Abruptly, Alex looked up again, meeting the other's steady gaze. "What are you up to, Lajos? This is no way to begin formal negotiations — a junior officer out of uniform, indulging in schoolboy pranks with an old friend! And why in God's name is Katie here?"

"She wanted to come with me. As for the rest, perhaps we should clear a few matters up at once. First of all, although I have been fighting in the Hungarian army since October, my views of Romanian rights have not altered. I am not here to betray you, Alex."

Alexandru's eyes flickered and fell. His smile was slightly sheepish as he said, "I don't see how you could betray us, unless you ask for a cease-fire?"

"I have no authority to request or grant cease-fires. At the moment, this is all secret, presumably in case Kossuth looses face over it. He asked me to see Iancu privately. He wants you on our side; and you know Hungary needs you."

Alexandru's fading smile twisted. "She doesn't seem to. These mountains are all that's left of your opposition, so far as I can find out."

"Then now is a good time to negotiate, don't you think?"

Alex drew his hand through his hair, beginning to speak jerkily, quickly.

"You know I never wanted this war, but it's easy in the circumstances to become bitter and full of hate. Over the months I have had plenty of opportunity to hate. I have not always been here, you understand — I move from place to place, training peasants to be soldiers and leaders, burying them and training some more. I have seen the results of Hungarian atrocities — and Romanian, I admit — and I have seen the way our allies despise us."

There was a pause, then his voice dropped. "If we can end it, *with honour*, I would be happy."

"So would I," said Lajos quietly. Slowly, Alex put out his hand and Lajos took it, though he said, "There's no need. I never counted you an enemy."

"Save your flannel for Iancu. You'll need it. Where do you want to meet him?"

"Anywhere he chooses. We're staying at the inn by the Orthodox Church. Any message will reach me there."

Alex nodded, but Lajos's words had reminded him of my presence. "I still can't believe *you* are here," he remarked. "And I still don't understand why! Looking at you now, I almost expect you to produce Katalin from under your cloak..."

"I can't do that," I admitted, "but I can give you this, if you wish to have it."

I took Katalin's rather crumpled letter from my reticule, and held it out to him. His thin face became suffused with colour. I think his hand was actually trembling as he took the letter from me.

"Then — then she still thinks of me?"

"Obviously."

"I don't deserve her."

"I have often said so," Lajos remarked ambiguously.

Now, it seemed, we had nothing to do but sit and wait for a message to come from Iancu. Lajos had no doubt that one would come, for Romanian aims were in reality far closer to those of the Hungarian revolution that to Austrian absolutism, however benevolent.

In the meantime, I was content to enjoy our time alone together, for in many ways, this trip was like a honeymoon for us. As the darkness closed in that evening, we ate our pitifully frugal meal in the inn's quiet coffee-room, sipping sweet, local wine, talking of things that had nothing to do with the war and thinking, as our eyes met more and more often, of the delightful night to come.

I didn't hear anyone arriving at the inn. When the quick footsteps approached us, I assumed it was the landlord.

"You would make an easy target for guerrilla fighters," said a mocking voice I remembered.

I knew from his stillness that Lajos was as surprised as I, but he looked calmly up into the stern young face of Avram Iancu and observed, "None of them ever said so before." Casually, he held up his hand to the other man. "How are you?"

Iancu blinked. Then suddenly he laughed and seized Lajos's hand, gripping it hard.

"Only you would wander into the lion's den and behave as if we are meeting at a tea party!"

Lajos's lip quirked. "I don't believe the lion will eat me — or not yet. You remember Katie?"

The bright, hungry eyes turned on me. "Of course. The lady from Scotland."

Calmly, I gave him my hand. I remembered him too, but he had changed even more than Alex. He reminded me of a coiled spring.

"Won't you join us?" I said politely.

He smiled, and slid like a cat into the empty chair beside me. "You must forgive me for disturbing your meal."

"We've finished, but I'll fetch you a cup..."

"No need," said Iancu, producing one from nowhere. "I have brought my own."

Lajos's lip twitched, but he poured wine into the rough cup and pushed it across to him gravely enough.

"To peace?" he suggested. Iancu inclined his head, and we all drank.

"So," said Iancu, "what have you come to offer me?"

At that point, any receding hopes I still harboured about keeping some of the evening to ourselves vanished completely. Iancu had come to negotiate tonight.

And so the serious talk began. It went on all night. The innkeeper cleared up and locked up around them, and went to bed as discreetly as a shadow, while in the coffee-room the two young men negotiated for peace and friendship, as if they held the fate of nations in their hands; and yet they were not rulers, nor even members of a parliament.

By the time I left them and went to bed, they had both grown passionate and dishevelled, and I could see that Lajos's points were going home.

When I rose in the morning, early, they were still there, as if they had not moved. Iancu stood as soon he saw me cross the room.

"I must go," he said, "or my men will come and kill you!" He held out his hand to Lajos. "So, we are agreed? Your government will send a peace mission, and we will talk under cease-fire. If they bring the same promises as you, we shall lay down our arms, and gladly."

His words warmed me, but nevertheless it was with some relief that I shook hands and watched him go. Lajos was heavy eyed, but still full of energy.

"Success, I presume?" I said, sitting down opposite him.

"Providing Kossuth does not let me down."

"Then we go back to Debrecen today?"

He smiled. "Whenever Iancu sends us an escort."

The escort turned out to be Alex, who took us out of Romanian-held territory, and hesitantly gave me a letter for Katalin before parting from us with ill-concealed reluctance.

Lajos's desire for a speedy end to the Romanian-Hungarian conflict was frustrated by the simple fact that Kossuth had left Debrecen to spend some time with the army. Lajos would have gone after him, except that he was expected back any day now.

So Lajos threw himself into a fever of activity while he waited. He wrote pamphlets in favour of the rights of so-called subject races, and sent articles on the same theme to all the newspapers in Debrecen. No one printed them. He met with the Romanian Deputies of the Assembly, and was particularly impressed with one called Ioan Dragos, whom he brought to eat dinner with us one night.

I spent a lot of time with my family, taking the children for outings and trying to quell the indiscipline into which they had fallen since my unexpected departure in January. I suggested to Elisabeth that they needed a new governess, but she only shuddered and said, "Don't speak of it! I shan't be strong enough until all this trouble is over."

I frowned. "But doesn't István object to abandoning their education like this?"

"To be honest, Katie, I don't think he cares a hoot any more. He has plenty of other things to worry about. Though, of course, if *you* were to come back..."

"*I?* Would he let me teach them now?"

"Oh yes. I don't suppose you want to?"

"I don't think I can," I said, with a hint of true regret. "We expect to return to Transylvania any day."

She regarded me. "You wouldn't consider leaving him? No, I thought not. The trouble is, Katie, I don't see a way out of your predicament, even if you did leave him."

"Am I in a predicament?" I asked, amused.

"Of course you are. How can you get married if everyone believes you are married to Lázár? And if you admit that you are not, then you are ruined and no one will want to marry you! In fact, when things get back to normal, you may find yourself socially ruined in any case, being married to someone so far beneath you."

"Or not," I added provokingly, and she cast me a glance of dislike.

Kossuth finally saw Lajos that evening. He thanked him for his efforts which he praised effusively, and promised to send a formal commission to Iancu immediately. In the morning, we left again for Transylvania.

There, we found that Bem had already left, taking Petőfi with him. However, Colonel Drényi's troops were among those left behind to keep the peace, and they had been sent to occupy the mountain garrison of Vanora, which had once been Colonel von Avenheim's responsibility.

It was tempting to make a detour via Szelényi, but in the end, Lajos decided that we should go straight to Vanora — it was what the army expected of him, and he did not propose to imitate Petőfi's revolt against military tyranny. His own rebellion was internal and much deeper.

Vanora was a well-equipped garrison town, only a little damaged by the fighting which had dislodged the Austrians, the Hungarians and again the Austrians. Colonel Drényi welcomed us with unfeigned delight, and the next day held a little ceremony which I watched from my bed-chamber window. The men paraded in the square below, and then Drényi pinned a medal to Lajos's breast, with the words that it had been Bem's wish before he left for Hungary, that Captain Lázár receive this commendation of his resource and valour. I could not see Lajos's face as he accepted the award, but I imagined quite clearly the mixture of pride and cynicism, impatience and self-depre-cation that would be swirling beneath his guarded expression.

Because of Lajos's special experience, he was considered to be the best man to pacify the Romanian irregulars who were still causing trouble in the region. So, with a sword in one hand and a carrot, as he sardonically ob-served, in the other, he led frequent patrols out of the fortress while waiting impatiently for news of Iancu's truce.

One morning, as I lay in bed, watching him shrug himself into his coat, he said abruptly, "We passed through Szelényi yesterday — did I tell you?"

"No," I said, hiding my surprise. "You didn't tell me."

Uneasily, I waited to hear the news, while he turned to buckle on his belt and sword.

"The village is still standing, just. So is the castle, although it's being guarded for us by some peasant enthusiasts under the command of a retired officer."

"Thank God," I said, for it had been unbearable to imagine Szelényi gone the way of so many other villages in Transylvania: deserted, savaged, ruined by war; but Lajos had not finished.

"The neighbouring villages are decimated. The Acsády lands are almost completely ruined, their villages razed to the ground, the people gone or dead."

I sat down, distressed as much by the new tone in his voice as by his words. "Who?" I asked at last.

"Do you mean who did it? Does it matter? The war did it."

I swallowed, meeting his gaze rather warily. I didn't know this mood and I didn't trust it. "Did — did you see your parents in Szelényi?"

He nodded.

"Are they well?" I asked, and then felt ashamed of the common politeness of the question, but I couldn't think how else to ask.

"They're alive. Most of the village stores have been taken by passing ar-mies, but they are not yet starving; and Károly has, so far, avoided impressment — though Zoltán could be anywhere, they haven't heard from him in months."

"Lajos..." I began pleadingly, for I couldn't understand the brusque dis-tance he was suddenly achieving

"Father Ránoczy sends his regards," Lajos interrupted. I stared.

"I — how does he know I am here?"

Lajos shrugged. "He was never a fool. They're waiting for me — I have to go now." And he went, leaving me feeling confused and bereft, for the first time in months, of the smallest crumb of affection.

I lay in bed for a long time, distressed by his odd humour. Gradually it came to me that it stemmed from guilt. He had begun the revolution for Szelényi, for Transylvania, and now the country lay in ruins from months of civil warfare; Szelényi itself was worse off than it ever had been, and his own brother was missing, possibly dead, his family distraught. He had always said he was prepared for the consequences of revolution; for the first time, I doubted it.

It was a long, difficult morning for me. I could settle to nothing, so it was a decided relief when I was interrupted at midday by Lieutenant Király looking for Lajos. Seizing my opportunity, I enticed him inside, determined to find out if anything untoward had occurred in Szelényi.

However, I had not got further than the most vague enquiries, when the door opened and Lajos himself came in. I saw at once that his mood had altered drastically since the morning. In fact, what I saw in his eyes made my heart leap.

Király said hastily, "You have news? What is it?"

Lajos seized the wooden chair by the desk, and swung it round beside us, sitting astride it with his arms resting along its back. He smiled at me and at his Lieutenant. I remember thinking irrelevantly that he was actually no older than Király.

"Lajos," I said threateningly.

He was still smiling at me as he said, "The Hungarian army has re-entered Buda-Pest. The fort of Komarom is ours too. The Austrians are bolting for the border."

I think it was only then that I realized how completely I had come to regard Hungary as my home. Breathlessly, I stared at him.

"Truly?"

"Truly."

Király let out a violent whoop of joy, and then, from all over Vanora, I could hear cheers breaking out.

"Then we have won?" I demanded of Lajos. "We have really won?"

"It's beginning to look rather like it."

"*Look* like it?" Király exclaimed. "Rot you, Lázár, we *have* won! We must have! What remains?"

"Castle Hill in Buda," Lajos said apologetically. "A small and isolated stronghold, I admit; and one or two other minor fortresses. And as I understand it, dealing the Austrians a good drubbing as they leave would be a good thing."

"Easy!" Király said enthusiastically. "My God, this is wonderful! Madame, your servant!" And with that, he was gone, rushing off to find someone to celebrate with.

Lajos continued to look at me with that light of quiet triumph in his eyes. "It seems it has all been worth while after all," he said softly. I went to him, and he stood up, taking me in his arms. "Soon, with luck, it will all be over and we can get back to the important things in life..."

I smiled into his shoulder. "The revolution?"

"The revolution," he agreed, "and you." Suddenly his mouth was on mine in wild, urgent passion, and with joy I yielded.

CHAPTER FORTY-EIGHT

April turned into May, and the mood of triumph and optimism continued at Vanora, even after the news had come about Dragos.

Ioan Dragos, the Romanian Deputy whom I had met in Debrecen, had been Kossuth's chosen commissioner of peace to Avram Iancu. How their talks would have turned out, we shall never know, for although they negotiated in Abrud under a cease-fire agreement, the Hungarians had broken the truce and stormed the town in the grandiose hope of capturing Iancu himself.

I was appalled. "Did they succeed?" I demanded, even as I searched Lajos's eyes for the answer.

He shook his head tiredly. "No. Not that it matters much, the Romanians repelled them. But then Iancu's men decided that Dragos was part of the plot, and executed him without bothering to ask questions."

"Oh no..." I felt both distressed and frustrated by this unexpected turn in events. A man I knew, a good man, was dead, his life snuffed out by the hysterical unreasonableness of this war; and by that one foolish, treacherous act, the Hungarian soldiers who had broken into Abrud had undone all Lajos's work, all Kossuth's and Dragos's, and doomed the two races to further pointless conflict and suffering.

I put my arms around Lajos, cradling his head on my breast. There was nothing I could say to comfort him. Later, perhaps, he would try again.

In the meantime, General Görgey, instead of chasing the main Austrian army back to Vienna, was ignoring it and concentrating the best part of his own army on reducing the fortress on Buda Hill.

Colonel Drényi and Lajos were united in contempt for this madness. Military strategy not being one of my best subjects, I could see nothing wrong in trying to eject the Austrians from the Castle.

However, Drényi fumed. "The whole country is under our control, save a few puny little fortresses like Buda, which would have to surrender anyhow when they are completely cut off from Austria and the Austrian army is all but annihilated!"

"Avram Iancu," I pointed out, "is completely isolated too."

"Iancu is mad," Drényi said firmly. I looked enquiringly at Lajos.

"He has lunatic tendencies," Lajos allowed. "Otherwise called stubbornness, or heroism. But the Colonel is right. What Görgey should be doing is wiping the floor with the fleeing army, following it back to Vienna, where at least, we would be in a position to negotiate for an honourable peace."

"The April Laws and return to the Monarchy," Drényi nodded. Lajos smiled fleetingly.

"Well — the April Laws," he conceded pointedly, "as a start," and Drényi regarded him with affectionate amusement.

"Damned radical — your pardon, Madame!"

Then, shortly after Castle Hill finally fell, Lajos had a very furtive-sounding letter from the radical Deputy László Madarász. I could not make head or tail of it.

I looked enquiringly at Lajos, who said, between gulps of coffee, "I think he wants me to help overthrow the Government."

"He *what?*"

"Not just the two of us, you understand. I imagine 'our military friend' must be General Perczel. As far as I can understand it, he seems to want Perczel to occupy Debrecen with his troops while the radicals seize power."

I stared at him, feeling suddenly haunted. "Oh, Lajos, you wouldn't consider it, would you?"

"It won't happen," Lajos said flatly. "Perczel knows we don't have the support now for a move like that. If we were going to do it, we should have done it last September when revolution was still in the air. Now, I suspect people are just weary of strife." He took the letter from me and threw it in the fire. For a moment he stared into the flames. "Still," he said slowly, "I can see his point. Kossuth and Görgey are making a mess of this between them..."

After we had almost grasped success, disaster seemed to fall upon us very quickly, step by step, leap by leap. At first it was simply faint, gnawing unease, because soldiers and civilians alike were tired of the war; but then we heard what Lajos had always feared since he had encountered Russian troops at Nagyzseben in March. At the invitation of the Emperor, a massive Russian army was marching on Hungary; and in Transylvania, tragedy was no longer creeping, but galloping with terrifying speed.

The Russians came through the Borgo Pass in huge numbers. A large detachment marched on Vanora, and only then, with the choice of death or retreat, did I finally contemplate the possibility of disaster.

In the bed-chamber I had shared with Lajos since April, I lay alone, face down with my hands over my ears to blot out the awful, shattering noise of the guns. For once, I let the clouds of fantasy and wishful thinking roll back, and forced myself to face the consequences of defeat. If Lajos were captured, the Austrians would hang him. Killed or captured, there was no way out for him, not from this...

Whatever happened now, it seemed to me on that cold, comfortless dawn that my happiness was over.

Of course, there was a way out, at least in the short term. Bem came back to Transylvania; and orders reached Drényi to abandon Vanora and join him. At dead of night, we left the fortress in the hands of a few volunteers and wounded men, who would surrender it in the morning, and crept off into the darkness.

I found I was silently, unstoppably weeping. Once I discovered Lajos beside me in the darkness. As if he knew, he reached out and touched my face.

"Sweetheart, don't cry," he whispered. "Don't cry. We'll come about again; we always do. Don't cry..."

I couldn't tell him then that I was weeping for him. At best, his dream was in ruins.

Meeting up with Bem and the men retreating from the Borgo Pass, we turned back upon the enemy, and when I heard that we had retaken the Pass, I knew a moment of jubilation. Lajos had been right — we would come about again! I didn't know now if I was laughing or crying; in the end I had the energy for neither, for it was a trap, and our men limped back into camp wounded and dispirited, carrying their dead comrades and wearing the unmistakable signs of defeat.

Lajos too came back, with a bloody cloth tied around his arm. He was limping, but more from tiredness than anything else; tiredness and the thought of the retreat to come.

Even now, I can't think of those ghastly days without wanting to weep in fury and pity. Our army suffered defeat after defeat, and the Russians gradually over-ran the country. They were aided, of course, by the Romanian rebels, who now renewed their fight with a vengeance. It seemed as if everything was tumbling down around us. I went through it in a daze made up of noise and horror, living with the roaring of the guns as if it were as normal as bird song.

I grew inured to the sight of the carts carrying the wounded back for treatment in steady streams. I helped Doctor Tedényi, when he would let me — it was the only way I could be useful in this carnage — but all too often now he sent me away again with his peculiar, curt kindness. He said I looked too ill myself; but I wasn't ill — I was only concerned for Lajos.

Then, one day when we had a moment's respite from the unwavering pattern of retreat, fight, retreat, and Lajos and I had a few precious hours to spend together, General Bem sent for him. I almost wept with frustration, for I badly needed that time with him. However, I had learned something during my months with the army. I forced myself to smile; I even passed him his coat, while my heart ached for the weariness and grief behind his eyes.

He was back surprisingly quickly, and my spirits suddenly lifted again, for the spring was back in his step and there was a new light in his eyes that might have been hope.

"Is there news?" I said at once. "What is it? Have the Russians been beaten in Hungary?"

He grimaced. "No one will fight the Russians in Hungary. Our armies retreat and manoeuvre to avoid them. They only want to fight the Austrians. No; Bem told me something quite different — Kossuth has authorized contact with the Romanians."

I felt my eyes widen. "You mean he will give them the autonomy they asked for? At last?"

"It would be criminal if he didn't," Lajos said intensely. "It's the only thing that can save us now. If the Romanians rise and help us throw the Russians out of Transylvania, then at least we will have a chance..."

"But did Bem send for you just to tell you this?"

Lajos sank down onto the makeshift bed, and lay full length upon it, the back of one hand across his forehead while he gazed at me.

"No. There is a Colonel called Simonffy, in charge of some Hungarian troops in the Apuseni Mountains. He managed to contact Iancu."

A tiny jolt of hope went through me. "Then Iancu too is willing?" I said, almost breathlessly.

"He must be. He shouldn't have been able to hold out beyond April, yet he's still there, quite cut off. He probably doesn't even know about the Russians. The thing is, he wouldn't commit himself to Simonffy: he wants to speak to me."

I went slowly towards him, sitting on the edge of the bed to search his eyes. "You will tell him," I said finally. "You will tell Iancu about the Russians."

"Iancu knows I will tell him the truth — that's why he asked for me."

"But Lajos, he won't negotiate if he knows he will be relieved at last!" I touched his face, as if trying to smooth away the deep lines etched around his eyes and forehead. "When will you go?" I asked calmly.

"Tomorrow."

I looked away.

"I don't suppose I can come?" I said hopelessly.

"I don't see why not. It can't be more dangerous than facing the Russian onslaught every day."

I closed my eyes with thankfulness. I moved, and lay down beside him on the narrow bed, treasuring his nearness, his warmth, the almost physical pleasure his mere presence always brought me. These days, I let myself feel these things with every intense fibre of my being; for each time he left me, I had to face the prospect of loosing him forever.

In the morning, we rode westwards for the Apuseni Mountains and what I knew full well was our last hope. There were reminders of the war all around us — burned villages, scarred landscapes, wary peasants, fortified buildings, marching soldiers; and yet somehow, we became light-hearted — not forgetful of the danger, but careless of it. The late June sun shone down upon us as we rode, warming my skin with new-born hope and faith in the future.

Now, with that in my heart, I was able to say, "What will happen, Lajos, if we lose?"

He shrugged. "Everything will be as before the revolution, I suppose, only worse."

"But what will happen to you?"

"Me? I shall escape," Lajos said flippantly, "probably disguised as an opera dancer."

"That should confuse the enemy." I glanced at him from under my lashes. "But perhaps it won't be necessary. Perhaps, when General Haynau executed those Hungarian officers for treason, he was just making an example of them, to frighten us." If so, he had succeeded dramatically.

Lajos met my gaze. Unusually now, I could not read his eyes. Then they cleared, and he said quietly, "Katie, they planned the gallows for me long before I put on this uniform. For people like Petőfi and Táncsics and me, there can be no clemency, no choice."

I had known that too, but to hear him say it suddenly made my throat hurt unbearably. I swallowed and stared between my horse's ears, feeling his gaze still on my face.

"No," he said at last, his voice carefully light once more, "it has to be escape."

Bravely, I tried to play the game. "Escape to where?" I asked, and he appeared to consider.

"London, I think. All political exiles go to London, or Paris."

"And may I come?" I asked casually. "Or would I be a burden to a political exile?"

He smiled at that, a quick, spontaneous smile. "A burden? You? Haven't I told you, you are my only joy and comfort? I should find it very hard to leave you behind! And yet..."

My heart twisted. Carefully, I stared expressionlessly at the road ahead.

"And yet... I can give you little enough here, Katie, if we win. In exile, I would have nothing. I couldn't ask you to share nothing."

The pain died away into calmness. I turned my head and looked at him. "You don't need to ask, Lajos."

He met my gaze as I spoke, and some sort of deeper, wordless communication passed between us. At last his lips quirked upwards in the familiar half-smile I loved so well.

"Do you know, I hoped you would say that? It's settled then. We shall go to London together, and I shall give music lessons. The violin, I think."

"You don't play," I pointed out, then added doubtfully, "Do you?"

"I shall learn. I feel it's the thing to do as a poor exile. *You* will have to take in washing, of course, and sewing..."

"Oh, not sewing, Lajos. I hate sewing," I objected, for I found I could play easily now.

"You must sew," he said firmly, "to keep me in gin."

Laughter bubbled up at that, but then a serious thought suddenly interrupted the nonsense. "What if we become separated?"

"Then I shall meet you in London. You'll find me quite easily: I'll be the only Hungarian giving and receiving violin lessons in the same room."

Perhaps it was significant that we talked so much of exile on that journey; yet at the time I was only aware of the optimism that let us laugh. Iancu and Lajos were friends, natural allies. Surely it was inevitable that in the end they should unite their peoples in the last stand against tyranny.

This time, I was not present when they met. On Colonel Simonffy's recommendation, I was left in a run-down but respectable inn with Zrinyi to guard me while Lajos, under a temporary cease-fire, went to negotiate.

When he left me, I gave way to the nausea which had been haunting me, and was vilely sick. Anxiety was praying upon me in physical ways; no wonder Doctor Tedényi was reluctant to let me near his patients.

I know what happened at the meeting, because Lajos told me. They met in the open this time, and on horse-back, while their people watched from a wary distance. Though he looked for Alex among Iancu's followers, there was no sign of him, and Lajos found himself hoping that Alex had *chosen* to stay away. The alternative was unthinkable.

Lajos was shocked by the change in Iancu: continuous privation and hardship had made him gaunt and ill-looking; but his carriage was still erect and his eyes still shone with life, however grimly.

"I'm glad you're still alive," was his greeting; and Lajos responded frankly, "I'm astonished that you are. I don't know how you have held out here for so long."

"Between you and me, Lajos, I shall be glad to end it. One way or another. What is it you want?"

"Alliance. Against the Russians and the Austrians."

Iancu's eyes lightened. His smile was slightly twisted. "I wondered if you would mention the Russians. Now, you need us."

"We have always needed you. It's Hungary's tragedy — and yours — that she hasn't always known it. Are you prepared to do it?"

"If it happens quickly, Lajos, I'll try. I can't wait for long, though, not with the Russians coming. And I'll need what time there is to convince my people — you can't turn loyalties on and off like a tap..."

"I know."

"Will Kossuth agree to autonomy?"

Lajos hesitated.

"I don't know," he said truthfully. "I can't believe he'd be foolish enough not to now."

Iancu drew his hand tiredly across his eyes. "I can't do it without guarantees, Lajos. We've come too far to give up for less."

"I know." He met the other man's gaze without secrecy. "It's all gone wrong, Iancu. We should have been allies in this. Perhaps we started it all too early, before people were ready, before the country was *capable*..."

"Perhaps we can still salvage something. Third time lucky." Iancu reached out across the space between them, and Lajos leaned forward and gripped the Romanian's hand. He thought a sigh of relief came from both sides, so loud that the whisper of it reached the two negotiators.

"Put it in writing," said Lajos, "for Simonffy and Kossuth."

Iancu nodded. Their hands parted reluctantly; and as Lajos straightened in the saddle, he had to tear his eyes away from Iancu's. He could think of nothing to say except, "Good luck," and then they both smiled at the woeful inadequacy of the words. Lajos wheeled his horse and rode back to the Hungarians.

"I had the oddest certainty that I wouldn't see him again," Lajos said to me later, when he had come back to the inn. "I'm not sure I care to leave such fatuous last words between us — and yet what else is there but luck now?"

In the morning, I was sick again, but I hid it from Lajos, for I didn't want to add my illness to his troubles. We rode eastwards to rejoin Drényi and the slow retreat, and as the day went on, I felt better.

A week later, word reached us that Kossuth had again refused to grant Romanian autonomy.

"There is nothing left," Lajos said; and nothing so far had frightened me so much as the defeat in his resigned, quiet voice. "There is nothing else left."

"There is always a miracle," I said with forced lightness. "An act of God."

He looked at me, unsmiling. "I don't believe in God."

CHAPTER FORTY-NINE

Now, when I think about the month which followed Lajos's wasted interview with Avram Iancu, I'm sure everyone was just going through the motions. Nobody believed any more that we could win.

Lajos grew more and more silent and grim. The light-heartedness of our journey to the western mountains vanished completely. Only with his men did he preserve the front of optimism and enthusiasm; and yet he wouldn't give up. Wherever we were, he deliberately sought contact with Romanian units, regular and irregular, trying to establish the alliance so nearly made with Iancu. He was supported in his efforts by both Drényi and Bem, and in the end, when it became obvious that the Hungarians were hopelessly outnumbered, Bem revived the spirit of adventure by leading us into Wallachia to try to recruit the Romanians there.

It was an exhausting and futile trip, and by the time we returned no one imagined that Bem could still pull off one of his startling, daring victories to change the course of the war. Buda-Pest, we heard, was again in the hands of the Austrians and their Russian allies. The Assembly, after only one meeting in the capital, had decamped once more, this time to Szeged. I wondered if István and the family had gone with it. I wondered about Mattias.

One of the few events that lightened the darkness of those days was the return of Petöfi. His faith in Bem undiminished, his desperate, nervous energy infectious, he managed to lift Lajos's spirits as I could not. Talking far into the night just as they used to seemed to calm them, refresh them, as if they needed to remind each other of what had actually begun this fight, at least for them. The fight was all but lost; yet the cause was still good.

The biggest shadow that hung over them was the death of Vasvári, barely twenty-four years old, killed by Romanian guerrillas. More than anything else could have done, this grief shattered them, for apart from the awful personal loss, it proved that the old lifestyle of the Pilvax radicals was over for good, whatever the outcome of the war. The 'March Youth' had disintegrated, one way or another.

"Still," said Petöfi with forced cheerfulness, "trust in Father Bem!"

Then came the day when Lajos refused to take me any further. We had spent the night at a country inn some miles from Segesvár. The Jewish innkeeper was one of Lajos's friends, and upon first meeting, one of the most morose individuals I had ever encountered. However, behind that bearded, lugubrious exterior lurked an extremely sharp sense of humour, betrayed only by an occasional twinkle in his heavy, hooded eyes. Marta, his wife, smiled a lot and said little, but her black eyes were unspeakably sad.

We ate with József and Marta in their private parlour that evening. They bemoaned the war at length, praying for its end and the return of trade and decent living. Lajos's smile was twisted as he told them they would not have long to wait. József eyed him seriously.

"What will you do, Lajos?"

Lajos shrugged. "Fight as long as I can, I suppose. There will be a major battle soon now — I expect that to be the end, for Transylvania at least."

József leaned forward, his eyes flickering to his wife and back. "You know we can hide you here, if it comes to that."

Lajos smiled, sincerely this time. "Thank you. I may yet have a favour to ask you." He changed the subject then, and shortly afterwards I went to bed.

Although I knew he was exhausted, it was some time before Lajos came to me; but I wasn't asleep — something wouldn't let me rest.

"Old times again?" I said lightly, and he sat on the edge of the bed, looking down at me enigmatically.

"No," he said, after a moment. "The future this time. The immediate future. Katie, I want you to stay here for a few days."

"No," I said at once.

"Yes. It's comfortable here, and József and Marta are friends we can trust. There is no point in your coming further yet — we shall probably fight at Segesvár. I'll come and fetch you after the battle."

Abruptly, I sat up, seizing him convulsively by the shoulders.

"Lajos, don't!" I whispered. He touched my cheek.

"Don't what, sweetheart? Protect you? I can't help it. I want you safely here where I can find you."

"No. You think you won't come back."

"It's possible. It was always possible, but I've always survived. Listen: did you know that the Szelényis were at Kolozsvár three days ago?"

My eyes widened. "No," I said, bewildered. "Why are they there?"

"I expect they were going home, to sit out the rest of the war. Also — they had Mattias with them. Apparently he was ill."

"No, oh no," I said distressed. Lajos's arm was around me, holding me.

"He was alive. I don't even know if it's a fever or a wound he is suffering; but he's strong, Katie, he always was. It's István who should worry you — he has been too close to the Committee of National Defence. The Austrians may well be looking for him."

"Lajos, why are you telling me this?"

"Because, if I don't come back, you should try to find the Szelényis. József will help you."

I clutched at him, burying my face in his neck. I had to face the possibility of a life without him, and I couldn't. It was unthinkable now in ways I couldn't even have imagined in the months when my only misery had been the prospect of having to leave Hungary. Death was the final parting. No fate or kindness could intervene after that.

I almost told him then. Pressed to him, feeling the warmth of his body seeping into mine, and the hard buttons of his uniform digging into my flesh, inhaling the male fragrance of his body for what could be the last time, panic nearly unsealed my lips; but this was not the time to give him new anxieties. It would not have stopped him fighting the last battle of his revolution. It would merely have distracted his mind when he needed to concentrate on staying alive. So I was silent.

There was a desperation in our lovemaking that night, a fierce yet gentle intensity that made me weep; and when it was over he held me close and kissed away my tears, soothing me like a baby until I slept. He didn't sleep at all. He lay awake beside me, watching me until dawn, and then he left me and went to join his men.

I was lost when he had gone. I had nothing to do and nothing to think about except what would drive me to madness. I spent hours with Marta and József, talking and talking: about how they had met Lajos — they had used to run a tavern near Szelényi when Lajos was an adventurous, roving boy — and about how I had met him; about their children and their pride in them. I smiled at that, hugging my own secret to myself.

And all the time I felt as if my ears were wide open, waiting for the distant roar of guns that would tell us a battle was under way. We didn't hear it that day, so I went to bed, able to sleep.

The next day was different. We stood at the inn door listening to the guns. They were far away, but that sort of noise carries for miles. I watched the peasants pass by, indifferently going about their business. They were tired of the war; they no longer cared who won.

I was shaking so that I couldn't stop. This was the worst waiting I had ever done, worse even than the first time in January. When the guns died away, the knot in my stomach tightened and twisted unbearably; and now the real waiting began — waiting for news, waiting for Lajos.

It was dark when the two soldiers banged on the inn door. József opened it, reasoning that if he didn't the soldiers would simply break it in. They were Hungarian *honvéd* troops, dirty, bloody, dispirited, threatening; but when József drew them in and gave them wine before he was asked, the dangerous look passed from their faces and they began to answer questions.

"Where was the battle?" József asked them urgently. "How did it go?"

"We lost, of course. We always lose now — old Father Bem has lost his touch."

I closed my eyes to gather strength. I think I had always known we would lose. Certainly I had known the truth as soon as I had seen them, but hearing the words did not make it easier to cope with.

"It was at Segesvár," said the other soldier tiredly, "A rout, a massacre. Our men are all scattered or dead or taken. Me — I've had enough. I'm going home to my wife, and no King or Emperor or President will ever make me leave again..."

I licked my dry lips. "Do you know Captain Lázár?" I asked them. "One of Colonel Drényi's officers?"

"No, can't say I do," said one.

"I know him," said the other. "He's the radical, from Buda-Pest."

"Yes," I said eagerly. "That's right. Do you know where he is?"

"Dead most like," was the chilling, almost indifferent answer, and then, encountering some look of József's, he glanced back at me. "That is, I don't know. I never saw him today."

"Then you can't tell me if — if...?"

"No." The soldier glanced at me again with a hint of compassion. "Is he your husband? I'm sorry, Madame, I don't know."

"And the enemy?" József asked quickly. "Are they coming this way?"

"Not yet," said the soldiers, "but first thing in the morning, we're off, anyhow."

József gave them beds for the night, and food. There seemed no point now in labelling men as deserters. I thought briefly of Tamás and Béla, and shivered. How many men had died since they had?

To please Marta, I went eventually to my own room, but I didn't even bother to undress. I sat by my window all night, staring fixedly at the inn yard and the road beyond, and clasping my shaking hands together so tightly that all my muscles ached by morning.

When I went downstairs, sluggish with tiredness and fading hope, József told me that the two soldiers had gone.

"But," he added, "I got them to admit that they didn't see the end of the battle. In fact, they bolted when their officer was killed, which, so far as I can gather, was pretty near the beginning — I thought they'd made pretty good time from Segesvár!"

I caught hold of that eagerly. "So it may not have been as bad as they said?"

"Pray not," József said grimly. I did.

As the morning wore on, the news dribbled into us via fleeing soldiers and travellers and peasants. Segesvár had indeed been a rout and the number of dead was staggering. All that day I sat outside the inn while my hope faded with every passing hour. There had been something in his manner the night before he had left me, which had seemed to imply that he had known he would not return.

I polished my spectacles incessantly, so that I could see as far and as clearly as possible, but the tiny dots which emerged in the distance only became peasants or dogs or strange soldiers, none of whom could give me news of Lajos. I got to know that scenery very well. On the other side of the road was a wood which spread outwards to the right and up the side of the hill. I think I knew every tree intimately by mid-day.

The sun was at its hottest when I saw a travelling carriage lumbering down the hill. I was not remotely interested in such vehicles, for I was sure that was not how Lajos would be travelling. However, as the sun glinted off a nobleman's crest on the side of the coach and I realized that it was being followed by a second carriage, I remembered that I should not advertise my presence here. The whole area would soon be crawling with Austrians and Russians, and if Lajos was still alive, I had no intention of being used to trap him.

If he was still alive...

He must be, I thought. I would know if he were dead, know it by more than this numb fear... wouldn't I?

I waited inside the inn for the carriages to pass. However both pulled into the yard and stopped, so after a warning glance at me, József went bustling outside to meet them. Standing well away from the window, I strained my ears for German or Russian accents, but I heard no voices at all. Restlessly, I began to move towards the stairs, intending to go to my room to watch the road from there, but suddenly I paused in mid-step, for a child's cry filled my ears.

In fact it was not a particularly loud cry and penetrating across the yard and into the house had faded it further. Perhaps I would not have noticed it at all, except that there had been a time when my ears had been attuned to that particular sound. That particular child.

For a moment I was paralysed, and then, suddenly terrified that the coach would leave again before I could get to it, I ran to the door, pulling it open wildly and dashing out into the yard. István was standing beside the first coach, giving his orders to József. I glimpsed his face, pale and drawn, and then my eyes were searching the windows.

It was Katalin's shriek of "Katie!" which brought an abrupt end to Anna's wails, but by that time István had turned to stare in surprise at the small, demented figure I must have presented. Katalin almost tumbled out of the carriage and into my arms, and then Margit and the children, with Zsuzsa peering in disbelief from the door. I saw Elisabeth look out of the second carriage, and then everyone was hugging me at once, and I think we were all crying with sheer pent up emotion. Poor József, brushed aside like a large, sad fly, waited with exaggerated servility until we were finished.

At last I met István's eyes.

"Mattias?" I asked, suddenly afraid again, and he nodded towards the second coach. Katalin took my arm and led me to it.

"He is very weak," she said seriously. "But the doctors say he will live — if he isn't moved." I only stared. I did not need to point out that he *was* being moved, and over some of the worst roads in Europe. "I know," she said, replying to my look. "But what else can we do? He said he wanted to go home to Szelényi..."

Mattias was lying across one seat in the coach, propped up on pillows and cushions. I knew it was him, but only because they had told me. He seemed at once bigger and more wasted than in January: his shoulders had broadened and filled out, his face become less boyish and more manly; and yet he seemed to have shrunk to haggard skin and bone. His face looked almost transparent, deathly white apart from the hectic flush in his cheeks. His eyes too were glittering feverishly as they stared at me in disbelief. Then, slowly, a smile, pitiful in its weakness, spread across his face. His hand made a feeble movement towards me, and I was on my knees beside him.

"Oh, Mattias, you *idiot*," I whispered, because I couldn't think what else to say.

"I know," he murmured. "Soldiers are meant to die gallantly in battle, not in sick-beds like old women..."

"You," I said more firmly, "are not going to die." *Don't. Please don't.*

334

"Yes, Mademoiselle," he said, smiling still; and then his eyes closed again with frightening exhaustion. By then the others had joined us. Margit had slipped her hand timidly into my arm, chirruping faintly in my ear.

"But you, Katie?" István said at last. "What are you doing here?"

"Waiting for Lajos. There was a battle, at Segesvár..."

"We know. We have been avoiding the results all day."

"I suppose you know you are going in the wrong direction for Szelényi?"

"We gave up that idea. We're making for Turkey now."

I laughed until it became unsteady. "Are you? Lajos and I are going to London — wouldn't you be more comfortable there too?"

"Where is he?" Elisabeth asked bluntly.

"I don't know. He fought in the battle. I'm waiting for him."

She met my gaze for a moment, then nodded decisively. "Very well. We shall wait with you."

My eyes were uncontrollable that day. Clumsily, I took off my spectacles, staring fiercely down at them while I wiped them.

"You must get to safety yourselves," I reminded them.

"We are not in danger," Elisabeth said calmly.

"István is."

"Not yet; and they say the Russians are very gentlemanly."

I began to say that I didn't know how long I would have to wait, but though I felt I had to make the protest, I was not sorry when they cut my objections off with the curtness they deserved.

They stayed. József and Marta were glad of the wealthy custom and took my word without question that these aristocrats were friends.

As darkness fell again, István tried to tell me with unwonted gentleness that Lajos was not coming, and that I should leave with them in the morning. I suppose it must have seemed to him an ideal solution to the problem of my relationship with Lajos.

"I can't," I said simply. "I have to know what has happened. Don't worry — I know you cannot wait longer, but I have to."

Elisabeth said, "What did Lajos want you to do?"

István could not help his derisive snort, but at least he had the grace to cut it off.

"To wait for him here," I said firmly. Then my eyes fell before her suddenly piercing blue gaze. "And if he didn't come back, I was to leave with you. If I could find you."

"He hasn't come back, Katie."

"He is not dead. I would know if he were dead."

"Katie, how *could* you know? We cannot wait for official news to reach you here, and you cannot stay here alone."

István said awkwardly, "You know what would happen to him if he were captured?"

I nodded dumbly. There was nothing else to say.

When the others went to bed, crammed into the inn's small available space, I sat up. I was a little stupid from lack of sleep, and in truth I felt none too well; but I knew I would never be able to sleep. Oddly enough, it was Elisabeth who stayed with me, distracting me with her own anxieties over István — which no longer concerned his imagined infidelities, but his very real nervous exhaustion. Recent events had made us all grow up.

"To be honest, that is one reason we are leaving," she confessed. "I have no idea whether or not he is in any actual danger from the Austrians — after all, he is not nobody and he has many friends at Court..."

"Lajos thought he should go, at least for a while. To be on the safe side."

Elisabeth looked surprised that such a thought had entered Lajos's head, but she only said, "Perhaps. At all events, he needs to get out of this country to get his strength back. I've never seen him like this before."

"He will get over it," I said, trying to sound both authoritative and comforting. "I'm sure he will."

Her voice went on, strangely soothing, until it merged with the tired singing in my ears and the sound of the wind in the trees outside. The next instant, I was jerked awake by her touch on my shoulder.

"What...?" I began.

"Hush," she breathed. "I think there is someone outside."

"I'll fetch József," I whispered, but already it was too late. The window casement was pushed up with a quiet rush, and instinctively, Elisabeth and I drew together again. I still don't know why one of us did not scream — paralysis seemed to have grasped us both.

A boot, a soldier's boot, came over the sill; the blue of the *honvéd* cavalry danced before my eyes, and for a moment I could not quite believe it was Lajos.

CHAPTER FIFTY

I was across the room before his name had moved from my brain to my lips, and his arm was around me, wonderfully hard and real and strong, and I was clutching him as if I could never bear to let him go. For a moment all I felt was a relief so powerful that everything else was blotted out. I was dizzy with it; and then I realized that he was only holding me with one arm, and that the other was just hanging at his side. His sleeve was stained dark, even through the mud and dirt.

"Lajos?" I said fearfully.

"Scratches," he said, but mechanically, for over my head he had seen

Elisabeth; but he did not release me, only moved with me towards her. "Madame," he said civilly.

"I suppose it is a silly question," Elisabeth drawled, "but what is wrong with the door?"

"Nothing — at least when I last used it. I thought the window would be quicker and quieter — and unlocked. I didn't expect to see you here."

"While we, on the other hand, have been expecting you any time these last ten hours." It was her usual, social voice, languid and slightly amused.

"I'm sorry to have kept you waiting," said Lajos drily. "By 'we', I take it István is here too? If he is waiting to fight with me, I beg you will take him away again before he finds out I am here. I'm heartily sick of fighting."

"You, Lajos?" she mocked. "Surely not."

"Oh, I shan't retire for good," he said vaguely. His eyes had drifted down to me again for I was searching his face anxiously. It was etched with fatigue, the black shadows indistinguishable from the streaks of dirt and blood. Under the mud, I had the impression of deathly pallor, heightened by the flickering candle-light, and I couldn't tell whether the agony I could see behind the darkness of his eyes and in the tight, drawn line of his mouth was physical or spiritual. Under my probing, frightened gaze, his face softened slightly; his lips even twitched upwards in a semblance of the old smile so that I wanted to hug him to me in pity and gladness.

"Well," Elisabeth said drily, "I am going to bed."

Lajos was roused to glance at her. "We should go early tomorrow — first light. Even then I suspect we shall be barely ahead of them."

"Ahead of whom?"

He shrugged. "Cossacks. Austrians. Romanians. They're all out there. Sleep well."

"What a comfort you are to us all, Lajos. Good night."

"Good night," I said, already drawing Lajos to the sofa by the fire. I fetched him wine and the remains of our supper. He drank the wine in a convulsive gulp, but the food he barely picked at. By then I had seen the rough bandage under his hat, wound around his forehead, as bloody as the one on his arm which daunted me when I helped him out of his coat.

I forced myself to ask calmly, "How badly hurt are you?"

"My arm is pretty useless — there's a rifle ball lodged in it somewhere. This on my head is only a shallow sabre cut, but it bled so much that I couldn't see until I wrapped it up." Again came that awful effort to smile. "I was lucky."

I looked at him steadily. "Some soldiers were here. They said it was a massacre."

"Yes." He was staring over my head, while I knelt at his feet. "It's the end, now. Transylvania is lost; Hungary itself is only a matter of time."

I reached up and touched his shadowed, unshaven cheek. "And we are going to London."

This time, the smile managed to touch his eyes. "So we are." Then the light died again. I took the glass from his nerveless fingers, laying it on the floor beside me.

"What else, Lajos?" I said quietly. "What else happened?"

His lips parted, and closed again. There was another pause, and then he said, "Petöfi is dead."

Not Petöfi. Surely not Petöfi too... Unthinkable that *he* should be no more... And yet was it not symbolic that he should die with the last hope of the revolution he had personified for so many? Was it not he who had made the first call, *"Arise, Hungarians..."*?

Slowly, while the disjointed, flickering thoughts spun through my head, I reached up and put my arms around Lajos's neck.

"I'm sorry," I whispered. "So very sorry."

His sound arm held me. His bowed head was buried in my neck. This was the unkindest cut of all, and it would be open and bleeding long after the others had healed. There was nothing I could say, nothing I could do to compensate him for the loss of such a friend.

My throat ached for his grief, and they were my tears, not his — for he was beyond them then — which rolled down his face. They made him lift his head.

He said, "That is why I was so long — I was looking for him in the rout. He shouldn't even have been there — Bem was trying to protect him, to keep him away from the battle and possible capture, but he came anyhow. I met a doctor later on who had seen him, fled with him. He told me Petöfi didn't even have a horse. There is no way he could have escaped from there without one... The Cossacks cut him down..."

My grip tightened; then, after a pause, I asked, "Did Bem escape?"

"Yes; his luck held that far. He told me to get out of the country — I must be the only licensed deserter in Europe." He stopped for a moment, looking at me without seeing me, then added with something cold and terrible in his voice, "I think Drényi made it, too, but Jászi is dead, and Király and any number of our men — even Zrinyi, though I had thought he was indestructible. Too many. Too many lives snuffed out... and it seems it wasn't worth it after all."

"Lajos, don't think that." The words tumbled out of me in a distressed whisper. I would grieve for the dead later, when I had time. "Please don't ever think that..."

His hand cupped my cheek. His eyes were still fathomless, intense, but something had altered; the awful grimness had faded a little, leaving them strangely glowing.

"My Katie..." he murmured softly. "Do you know what I thought of when I was on the battlefield, when I ran from it, when I was searching for Petöfi? I thought of you being here for me when I returned."

I swallowed, holding his hand against my face. "I can't compensate, Lajos, but I'll always be here..."

But he was shaking his head, almost impatiently. "No, Katie, you're not 'compensation' — that's what I'm trying to tell you. Politics, revolution, ideals — they have always taken up such a large part of my life. They were what I lived for, and the people I cared for lived for them too..."

I hadn't expected this to be quite so painful. I hadn't thought my heart could hurt so much and still be with him.

With desperate, hopeless honesty, I said, "I can't care for abstracts, Lajos; I never could..."

"I don't want you to." He sounded surprised. His hand was behind my head now, holding me still as his eyes gazed down at my confusion, willing me to understand. "I just want you as you are. Revolutions come and go, governments rise and fall and change — we've seen it all in the last two years; but in the end, it is *you* who are still here, Katie. It's you I *want* to be here, not just to come back to, but to *be* with me..."

I stared at him, still a little bewildered, and afraid to take him seriously.

"That's battle fatigue," I said with a catch in my voice. "You'll feel differently in the morning. You know revolution is the breath of life for you."

His fingers touched my lips. "It won't go away," he conceded, "and I don't think I want it to; but perhaps my — priorities have changed. I'm sorry it took so long, Katie — not to *feel*, because I always did, but to *know*."

For a moment I listened to the steady beat of my heart. I was afraid of disappointment, but I could live with it.

I asked, "Know what, Lajos?"

"That I love you. Beyond everyone and everything I have ever known; beyond life itself, I love you."

Despite all that had passed between us, I still tried to hide the intensity of my feeling, bowing my head on to his lap. But he knew me. Lifting my head, holding it still, he forced me to meet his eyes, and then he bent and kissed me, gently, sweetly. For a time, the world receded; and then I remembered his wounds and his exhaustion and his grief. I stood up, drawing him with me, and led him upstairs to bed.

It wasn't quite light when I woke, but Lajos was already drawing back the blanket to get up.

"What is it?" I asked, alarmed.

"Nothing, but we should make an early start." I watched his naked back as he walked to the window and looked out on the misty dawn. Suddenly I didn't want to go anywhere. Glancing back at me, he caught my expression, and his lip quirked. "Oh no. If I come near you, we won't leave for hours."

I smiled, feeling as if I hadn't a care in the world. He was wounded, defeated, hunted most probably, but we were escaping together. It was only the beginning of another adventure.

Yet the danger, I reminded myself, was real. I sprang out of bed and dressed quickly. I had to help Lajos, for his arm, clumsily bandaged, was useless.

"Has a doctor seen that?" I asked hurriedly.

"Lengyel — the man who spoke to Petöfi — looked at it for me. It needs the ball dug out, but we don't have time now." He dropped a kiss on my head. "Go and wake your ridiculous family, if they are all to come with us in cavalcade."

I obeyed, but they were up and moving already. I thought Mattias looked slightly better for his night's comfortable rest, and the news that Lajos had come back won a grin and a feeble cheer from him.

The reaction of the others was ambiguous. I think they actually believed that life would have been easier for me if Lajos had had the grace to die on the battlefield. Now, if we were all to stay together, they would have to cope with this peasant, this serf's son, as a member of the family. I did not underestimate their difficulties.

He joined Katalin, Margit and me in the parlour long enough to gulp down a cup of coffee, but then, as if he was not yet ready to face the inevitable confrontation with István, he said quickly, "I'll see to the horses," and went towards the door. However, before he could reach it, it opened and István paused there, staring at him.

As if to forestall trouble, I went to stand beside Lajos, but neither of them seemed to notice me.

"So you're alive," István said neutrally, and Lajos's lip quirked.

"Yes. I even brought you a present."

And under everyone's astonished gaze, he felt in his coat pocket and produced a fat pamphlet which he held out to the other man. István took it mechanically, flicking through the pages as if he didn't know what else to do. Over his elbow, I looked too; I had never seen it before; I didn't know where he had got it. My eyes had time to focus briefly on some words which I remember very well.

"Let the ruling classes tremble at a Communist revolution. The proletarians have nothing to lose but their chains. They have a world to win. Workers of the world, unite!"

"I thought," Lajos said blandly, "you might pass it on to Acsády."

I glanced rather anxiously at István. His eyes were on Lajos, suspicious, but Lajos was still smiling, openly inviting him to share the joke, and at last I saw his lips twitch. His breath caught in what might have been a laugh.

"You were always impossible. I care nothing for your filthy, communistic pamphlets. Will you survive the journey?"

And Lajos, unmoved by the sudden change of subject, said briefly, "Oh yes," and went quietly out.

It was only as the door closed behind him that I realized I was holding my breath. I expelled it in a rush. They might not have been friends, but at least recent events had changed them enough to call an unarmed truce. It seemed a good omen.

A piece of bread settled my queasy stomach, though I still felt a trifle unwell. I wanted nothing else, so I accompanied József outside — just as a troop of Austrian soldiers rode down the last of the hill and into the yard.

Oh no, I thought stupidly. Not now...

"Don't," József said quickly, as I began to look anxiously towards the stables. Immediately, I stilled the impulse, and instead regarded the soldiers reining in before us. There appeared to be two officers, but only some twenty men. One of the officers, expertly controlling a frisky, dancing grey mare, gallantly swept off his hat and bowed to me.

"Major Conway, Madame, at your service," he said in German, and then, indicating the other officer at his side, "Lieutenant Kohlberg."

I inclined my head warily. "Conway does not sound a terribly German name," I observed, because it seemed something worth remarking upon and I was desperate to appear normal.

He smiled faintly. "As a matter of fact, I'm English."

"Are you really?" I said cordially. "I am Scottish. I didn't know we were involved in this war."

"Oh the British army is not, of course. I am, as you might say, a soldier of fortune. There are many of us in the Imperial Army."

"That must be comfortable for you," I said inanely, just as István and Katalin came out of the door, arguing. They stopped in their tracks, mouths still open, when they saw what greeted them, while I found myself performing polite introductions, and József, obscured by so much aristocracy, effaced himself, moving casually towards the stables.

"I see you are busy," István said, looking directly at the Major. "Don't let us keep you from your duty."

"Oh, we're just rounding up the scattered foe," Conway said, with a rather charming mixture of apology and humour. He was a handsome, dashing officer with very fine whiskers that gave him an almost piratical look. "Civilians," he added casually, "are not our concern."

By which I took it we were free to go. Of course Mattias was not technically a civilian, but he had not fought at Segesvár. I didn't suppose that either of these gentlemen knew his history.

Lajos, on the other hand, was a different matter. I didn't see how he could get out of the stables without being seen by at least one of the soldiers.

"Have you stopped for refreshment?" I enquired desperately

Conway smiled. "Hardly. We had reports that several Hungarian soldiers passed this way. We hoped to catch a few at the inn."

"Is that not rather a lowly task for such senior officers?" I asked pleasantly.

"It depends on the soldiers," Conway said easily. "For example, old Bem himself escaped the battlefield — he has to be somewhere. And we hear the revolutionary poet, Sándor Petöfi, was there too."

Petöfi is dead. A wave of grief struck me so unexpectedly that I had to drop my eyes. Poor Julia. Poor little baby, who would never know his vital, intense father...

I heard myself say, "Well, if they were here, they have been very quiet. I never heard that either of those gentlemen were quiet."

"Lajos Lázár, though, is a more subtle creature, I'm told."

My stomach jumped unpleasantly. It was left to István to say sneeringly, "He's not as subtle as all that."

Conway smiled faintly again. "To be frank, sir, we hardly hoped for such a fine haul. Besides, there are still bodies on the battlefield to be identified. Still, one must be systematic." With those words, he dismounted, signalling to the front row of men to do the same. Just as they did so, I became aware of a gentle clip-clop behind me. I didn't dare look until Kohlberg did, and then I saw József leading a big carthorse across the yard. Oddly enough, it was saddled, though riderless, and for the life of me, I couldn't think why József was leading it to the back door of the inn — which was the only place, so far as I knew, it could go...

"Where's the rascally landlord?" Conway demanded loudly, attracting Kohlberg's attention again.

"Here, your honour!" called József morosely. "I'll be with you directly." He and the horse had reached the back door, which was open. József paused, petting the huge, placid animal on the nose and ears. Then, with a lugubrious and quite audible sigh, he turned the horse around and walked it back to the stables.

I felt insane laughter rumbling inside me, for I had glimpsed the shadowy figure leaping off the side of the horse and disappearing inside. It was gone in a trice, so perhaps it was not surprising that the soldiers had seen nothing. Lajos must have been balanced on one stirrup, hidden from everyone's view as he crossed the yard. An air of unreality was settling over me.

"*Now*, landlord!" yelled Kohlberg over his shoulder.

"Coming, your honour." The horse was abruptly abandoned, saddle and all, while József scurried up to the officers.

"Show us your inn," Conway advised. "Lieutenant Kohlberg will look at your outhouses and stables."

"Please, your honour, go right in..." But Conway was already inside — and brought up short by the breathtaking spectacle of Elisabeth smiling at him.

"Madame!" He bowed, recovering quickly. "Yet more beauty in a rustic setting!"

"Countess Szelényi," murmured Jozsef respectfully.

"And my sister, Countess Margit," István added sternly.

Margit barely glanced up. She was endeavouring to put a coat on a very recalcitrant Miklós, while Zsuzsa held him still.

The soldiers were swarming all over the inn, under József's gloomy supervision. Marta came out of the kitchen, and I met her eyes questioningly. Imperceptibly, she nodded. A soldier brushed past her on his way into her domain. She bridled quite obviously and sailed back in after him.

I began to think uneasily of anything that Lajos could have left in my room, but surely he had come with nothing but what he was wearing now? I thought of his belt and sword and kerchief, but I could almost see him collecting all these things before we went downstairs. I was sure there was nothing left. In fact, it was something less solid that he had left behind.

A soldier came clattering downstairs, presenting a pillow to Major Conway, who removed his eyes reluctantly from Elisabeth in order to look at the exhibit. His gaze lifted again to the soldier, and I felt a twinge of serious alarm.

"Where?" he asked, and the soldier answered, "The first room on the left."

The world reeled a little, but I steadied it again.

"Who," enquired Major Conway, "occupied the first room on the left last night?"

István opened his mouth, but at this stage it seemed better to tell the truth. "I did," I said quickly.

"*You*, Mademoiselle?" He sounded astonished. "How strange. Perhaps you can explain to me how there comes to be so much blood on your bedding?"

I dropped my eyes, for I had just discovered his amiable orbs to be uncomfortably penetrating. "Really, Major, that is not something you should ask a lady."

I heard Katalin's tiny, shocked gasp. The soldier blushed furiously, but Conway was made of sterner stuff.

"On your pillow?" he said in blatant disbelief.

I lifted my head and stared at him. "Certainly. I had a nose-bleed."

"She is subject to them," Katalin said helpfully. "Nose-bleeds and headaches."

"Unfortunate lady."

"I could have more distressing ailments," I observed judiciously.

Another soldier shouted something over the banister.

"Ah yes," said Conway. "The young man in the second room on the right?"

"My brother," said István. "He is very ill..."

Smiling unhappily, József went upstairs to watch the soldiers ransacking his bed-chambers. I went too, to look in on Mattias. Then, restless and curious, I wandered out into the passage. One of the soldiers, a sergeant, I think, was asking József, "You got attics here?"

The innkeeper shrugged. "No, I don't think so."

"You should have, under a roof like that."

"Yes?" József didn't sound very interested. "We have enough space without attics."

The sergeant was poking around in a cupboard, in search, I presumed, of an attic stair. József watched him with a lugubrious serenity which calmed my sudden alarm.

"Come on, Jew, you know damn well you have attics!" the sergeant said impatiently. "How do I get in?"

József shrugged elaborately. "Why ask me? If I have attics, I have never seen them! I don't like heights. My wife hates spiders. Why should we bother with dirty, old attics?"

Too much, I thought suddenly. József was saying too much. I knew with certainty then that there *were* attics, and that Lajos was there. Perhaps the sergeant felt the same; or perhaps he just liked to cause as much trouble as possible. At any rate, he summoned three other soldiers and set them to prodding at ceilings all over the upper floor.

Suddenly an exclamation of triumph escaped him, and something inside me twisted with an almost physical pain, while the sergeant pushed a part of the hall ceiling upwards.

"Here!" he shouted. "Here it is!"

He poked his head in rather warily, peering inside. Carefully, he reached up through the hole and hauled himself upwards. At his snapped order, a soldier passed him up his rifle. My throat was dry. I couldn't hear anything but the frantic thundering of my heart: it seemed to be saying, "Not now, not now, not now." It would be too cruel, too unfair if they took him now... Surely he had suffered enough in the last two months to satisfy the most merciless judge...?

I found I was alone in my own room — it seemed to be the only one not full of soldiers. My fingers twisted together uselessly. This was intolerable. Don't let them find him... please, God, be generous, now... He didn't believe in God.

I barely heard the movement above me. I think it was the shadows that made me look up, and then I saw that there was a door in my ceiling too, and Lajos was noiselessly easing himself through it, one-armed and awkward.

Fear made me act swiftly. Silently, I seized the upright chair from the corner, placing it under the hole for him to drop on to. He landed with some relief, carefully drawing the door closed again so that no hint of the opening remained. His face was white with pain — or perhaps strain — but to my amazement, there was a demon of mischief dancing in his eyes.

Lajos, Lajos, this is not a game!

His lips quirked when he saw the expression on my face. He touched it briefly, comfortingly, then lifted the heavy chair, moving it back to its corner. Helplessly, I watched him, and then, with a jolt, I realized quick footsteps were moving along the hall towards us. Lajos heard them too. Swift and light as a cat, he ran along the wall to the closed door, so that when it opened, he would be behind it. He held his sword close to him in case it fell against either the wall or the door. Petrified, unable to breathe, I stared at the closed door, praying for the decisive footsteps to pass.

They stopped. The door was pushed open impatiently.

CHAPTER FIFTY-ONE

Smoothing my face just in time, I gazed upon Major Conway. He held my bloodstained pillow in his hands.

"I beg your pardon," he said in English. "I didn't think anyone was here."

I moved quickly to take the pillow from him, but he was already advancing into the room, passing me and placing the pillow on the bed. Lajos used the opportunity to slip silently round the open door and out into the passage. I made an instinctive, anguished movement after him, waiting for the cries of discovery; but strangely, none came. I tried to school my features into cool disdain as I turned to face the Major.

"Thank you," I said briefly.

"I didn't know if you would need it tonight. Perhaps you are staying here?"

"No. We have other plans."

Conway smiled faintly. "I'm sure they are for the best," he said, and his voice was not unkind. Above us sounded the heavy clumping of soldiers' boots. Conway looked amused. "What in the world are they doing up there?"

"I believe they have discovered attics which József never knew existed," I said indifferently. I regarded him directly. "Exactly what — or who — is it you are looking for, Major?"

He never answered me, for István was standing on the threshold, glaring icily at him.

"Whatever it is," István said coldly, "I doubt you will find it in my niece's bed-chamber. I really think my family have been put to enough inconvenience."

"I have told you, sir — you are quite free to go," Conway said gently, and for the first time I thought our lingering here so long must look suspicious to him. And yet how could I leave without Lajos?

"Come, Katie," said István. Then, to the officer: "By the by, is my friend Avenheim still in command of your regiment?"

"Yes, sir. He was imprisoned for a time by the Hungarians, but when we retook Beszterce, he rejoined us."

"Give him my regards," said István, and that at least he meant sincerely, even if it doubled as a warning to the Colonel's subordinates. István and I left the room. In the passage, the soldiers who had been disappointed and frustrated by their futile search of the attics, were accusing József of lying to them.

"Of course you knew of them!" one exclaimed. "They're packed full of stuff!"

"Not mine," József said at once.

I no longer knew where Lajos was. More to hide my nervousness than anything else, I went downstairs, where chaos reigned. Marta was screaming at the soldier in her kitchen, and through the open door I could see that she and Zsuzsa were about to belabour him with saucepans. The children, meanwhile, were shouting with laughter, chasing each other in circles around Katalin, who seemed to be about to tear her hair out.

With relief, I reverted to a role I knew.

"Miklós! Anna! Come here this instant!" said the governess severely, and was surprised when they still obeyed her.

Katalin cast me a glance of pure gratitude, and as I took them outside — manageable now, if not quite docile — she followed me. I avoided her questioning gaze, for I was terribly afraid we would be overheard if we discussed anything of importance.

Under the eyes of the soldiers — some cold, some amused — who stood around by the gate and the stables, I persuaded the children to play ball with each other, inventing a series of complicated rules to keep them interested. Katalin and I stood together watching them, with our backs pointedly to the soldiers whose remarks, judging by the ribald laughter in the yard, had grown crude and lascivious.

"This is intolerable," Katalin said in a low, shaking voice. "If they don't want István, what in the world are they looking for?"

"Lajos," I breathed. "I'm sure of it... And the truly damnable thing is, we only bring suspicion on ourselves by staying here..."

"Mattias's illness is a good enough excuse... oh God."

I glanced at her in quick alarm, and saw that her eyes were fixed on something ahead of her. I tried to be discreet in following her gaze, but I couldn't prevent the breath from catching in my throat. Lajos was climbing out of the window of Mattias's room.

For several seconds it seemed as if my heart did not beat at all. I couldn't breathe.

"Sweet Jesus, they'll see him," Katalin whispered.

"Don't look, don't look. Their attention is all on us. They won't be able to see from the stables... Perhaps we block out the view of the others?"

It was a feeble hope. I was terrified he would fall, clinging on with only one hand. I was angry with him for doing it at all, as if it were a game... Surreptitiously, I cast my eyes, not my head, in the direction of the window.

He had moved to the right, balanced on the edge of the sill, his back hugging the wall. I saw why too. There were soldiers in Mattias's room. József was there also, and Margit. My God, I thought wildly, could he think of no safer place to hide than outside the window where he could be seen by at least five soldiers?

He had seen the soldiers. He saw us too. He looked ridiculously casual in such a dangerous position. He even gave me a slight, resigned shrug; and I saw with blinding, dreadful certainty, that he would be caught in the end. He was only prolonging his freedom minutely by such starts — there was no escape possible for him.

Beyond everyone and everything I have ever known...

Oh God, oh God.

For once, I was glad of the squabble which inevitably broke out between the children. It attracted the soldiers' interest, kept their gaze low, and it gave us something to do, to rebuke them; but we were afraid to go to them in case that would provide the soldiers with a clearer view of Lajos. Yet our very inaction must have looked suspicious.

It seemed that God had heard my inarticulate prayer, for the soldiers were leaving Mattias's room. Incredibly, Lajos was going to be able to go back, unseen.

Perhaps he would have done it too, if Elisabeth had not chosen that moment to come outside and walk towards us. Elisabeth was the sort of woman who always drew male eyes to her. There was no question but that the soldiers' eyes were now on her. I held my breath. Lajos was edging back towards the window; and then the cry I had been dreading went up.

"Christ! Who in hell is that up there? Look, lads!"

Of course they looked. Elisabeth turned too. The soldiers further round, at the stables, came forward to see better. And Lajos, sliding one leg over the sill, paused and glanced at them; and then, for all the world as if he was at a Buda-Pest rally, he lifted one hand and waved to them.

A choke of laughter that was at least half anguish caught in my throat.

"Captain Lázár!" said a quiet, commanding voice behind us.

I jumped, but I had no need to turn to recognize Colonel von Avenheim. I felt despair rise inside me like a tide.

"Why, Karl," said Elisabeth, flint behind the languor of her charming voice. "How delightful."

Avenheim spared her — and us — a glance and the briefest of bows. "Forgive my informal manners, ladies. I'm afraid I have a duty to perform before I can give into social pleasures. Where are my other good fools? Inside, I must suppose." He turned and barked an order at the soldiers, one of whom went running into the house as if all the fiends in hell were after him. Avenheim, avoiding my pleading gaze, returned to the contemplation of Lajos.

"Do you intend to stay there all day?" he enquired, moving nearer to the house.

"No," Lajos called back, "but I can do, if you'd care to join me. How are you, Colonel?"

"All the better for seeing you again, my dear Lázár. And this time it would appear our roles are reversed."

"Not quite," said Lajos. "The Hungarians have never killed their prisoners of war." I saw Avenheim's faint twitch of distress. Lajos had always known

347

where to hit for maximum effect, but this time, I doubted its lasting influence.

The Colonel said drily, "His Majesty believes you have other charges to answer to."

"Poppycock," said Lajos affably. "His Majesty has never heard of me."

"I assure you, you are too modest."

Breathless with fear and helpless fury, I watched Lajos's glance flicker back to the room behind him. The soldiers were coming back in.

"I'm not known for it," Lajos said, almost casually drawing his sword.

"Oh Lajos, don't," I whispered aloud.

"Don't be a fool, Lázár," Avenheim said sharply. "You'll only be killed."

"Well, I've never cared for the idea of the rope," said Lajos resignedly; and then he moved with startling suddenness. One moment he was poised, at ease on the windowsill; the next, he had catapulted himself into the room.

I heard the soldiers shouting, steel clashing on steel, disordered crashing, as if furniture were being tumbled over.

"Colonel, stop it," I pleaded. "You must stop it!"

Avenheim swore under his breath. Still he would not look at me, but he strode off into the inn. The children were clinging to my hands. Margit came precipitately out through the door, accompanied by Zsuzsa and Marta. Katalin put her arms round me, but there was no comfort she could give me now.

It took them nearly ten minutes in the end. He broke through the soldiers in Mattias's room, and I could have sworn I heard the invalid's delighted encouragement. From there, the fight moved on to the stairs and into various rooms on both floors, with Lajos not above simply turning tail and fleeing to a better position when he could. Once, I even heard his rare, unmistakable laughter, breathless but genuine.

It was Lieutenant Kohlberg who finally captured him when he was trapped in the kitchen. I saw the sword-point pressed to his throat, saw the soldiers disarm him and Kohlberg push him outside to where the Colonel now waited with me and the other women. At once Lajos's eyes sought and found mine. They still held the exhilaration of the ridiculous hide-and-seek fighting, but behind that, I saw the love, the grief and the desperation. And yet I could have sworn he was still planning, still calculating.

"So you are Lázár," Kohlberg was saying, half-contemptuous, half-fascinated. "I must say, you don't look much."

"I brush up tolerably well," Lajos returned. He was still looking at me.

I broke free from Katalin and ran to him. He caught me in his good arm, hugging me briefly to his side. For an instant I felt his lips in my hair, and then he was pushing me away. I found Kohlberg staring at me.

"Didn't you know?" Avenheim said wryly. "This is Madame Lázár." It seemed he was preserving my reputation, though such things had no importance now.

"Then," said Major Conway, emerging from behind with István, "it *was* his blood on your pillow."

"Yes," I said indifferently. My eyes were fixed on Lajos. He was still breathing fast, and his face, I noticed, was unnaturally pale. Blood dripped from a fresh cut on his hand. I wondered if he would faint, and if that would inspire pity in his captors...

"Where are you wounded?" Avenheim demanded.

"All over," said Lajos. His eyes had locked with István's. I saw the struggle in the older man's aristocratic face.

With difficulty he said, "Karl. He is with us. He is — family."

I couldn't imagine what it cost him to say that, but I saw the flicker of surprise in Lajos's eyes before he veiled them again. I felt a rush of warmth and admiration for István then, even though I knew from Avenheim's face that his efforts were futile.

"I can't take account of families," Avenheim said harshly.

"Then why don't you take me, and Mattias too!"

"I have no orders to arrest you."

"Yet. Only because no one knows I am here."

"That suits me very well, István. I don't want you on my conscience too. For God's sake, bring Mattias down and leave here!"

"I should go, István," Lajos said quietly. "Take care of Katie..."

István flushed, but not at the insolence of the request, only, I saw with wonder, at his remembrance of the shameful time he had *not* looked after me.

"No," I said hoarsely. "I'll come with you."

"You can't," said István and Avenheim together, but I ignored them, staring only at Lajos. His hand reached up, and at once the soldiers raised their rifles threateningly, but Lajos disregarded them, touching my cheek caressingly, as if he was absorbing the unbearable emotion in me and trying to give me his new calmness.

He said softly, "Sweetheart, this is one time I don't want you with me. I'll be better alone, knowing you are safe..."

"I can't, Lajos..."

At a nod from Avenheim, Kohlberg stood between us; and at that deliberate cruelty, my fury erupted.

"This is ludicrous!" I fumed. "What charge can you possibly have against him that may not be brought against half the male population of Hungary?"

"Very good," Lajos approved, his mood appearing to swing again. "Yes, gentlemen, what *is* the charge?"

"One you won't talk your way out of," Kohlberg said drily. "Treason, and raising rebellion against your King."

Lajos's brows lifted.

"Against my King? But haven't you heard? *There is no beloved king any more!*"

One for Petöfi. Inevitably, Kohlberg struck him, full in the face with the butt of his pistol. The force sent him reeling before he fell. I cried out, pushing my way to him.

"Enough," Avenheim snapped, as I fell to my knees beside Lajos.

Blood was oozing from a cut on his cheek, but his eyes were open, summoning me nearer. I was surprised only for the briefest moment. I put my head down to his.

"Give me one more chance," he breathed in my ear. "When the time is right, try to distract them..." Then he was silent again as the soldiers came to haul him to his feet. One had seized him by his injured arm and I saw all too clearly the pain that caused him to catch his breath.

Katalin lifted me to my feet. Avenheim sent two soldiers to carry Mattias downstairs. József himself, no humour now behind his miserable eyes, was sent to arrange the coaches and horses. I too still had a task to perform. To gain time, I turned to Avenheim.

"Colonel..." I pleaded, and at last he met my gaze. I saw tiredness, disillusion, pain in his handsome face, but nothing that gave me any hope. Part of him even wanted to hurt Lajos, because of me. "Colonel, they won't let him live, you know that. Please, don't arrest him now — it's as good as killing him yourself."

His smile was mirthless, twisted. "No, Katie. This time I *will* do my duty."

I stared at him. I hadn't expected any other answer. There was no pity left in the world. Abruptly, I turned away, just as Mattias was carried out of the door by two soldiers, supervised by István.

"Hallo, Karl," Mattias said weakly; and then, after a quick, desperate glance around me, I fell heavily against one of the soldiers who held Lajos.

Instinctively, he released his prisoner to support me, and the same instant, I saw Lajos heave himself free of the other. Before anyone could even glance at him, he was running like a hare across the yard. I couldn't look: for one thing, I had to keep up my pretence and distract as many people as possible; for another, I was afraid to.

While people clustered around me, the shout went up. There were boots pounding on the ground, orders and advice being cried out, and Mattias laughing delightedly and shouting with fierce exultation.

"Go, Lajos, go!" he cried, sounding stronger than I could have believed by looking at him. I decided to abandon my faint, and sat up, cramming my spectacles more firmly back on to my nose.

"He jumped the wall!" somebody exclaimed. "Like a damned horse!"

And now he was running for the woods on the other side of the road; but rifles were already being aimed at him, and it was only a matter of time. I lunged to my feet, launching myself at the nearest soldier, thrusting his rifle up just as he fired.

Avenheim plucked me off angrily. "Be still! You little fool, he's as good as dead now!"

I stared at him. Without warning, I was choked by tears. "Do you really not see it, Colonel? He was as good as dead as soon as you took him. He would *rather* die this way..."

Another shot sent my attention flying back to the chase. Lajos had reached the woods now, and was dodging between the trees, heading for the hill. He's going the wrong way, I thought wildly. That way is back to the enemy... Several soldiers were chasing him, one on horseback, spoiling the aim of the marksmen behind.

But with fresh anguish I realized that climbing the hill was making him an easier target for everyone, even with the protection of the trees. I saw the soldier nearest to him stop and take aim. Inside, I was crying so loudly they should have heard me; and then a movement at the top of the hill caught my eye. There were men there too. He was trapped. Lost.

A shot rang out, and then several others, and without grace, without theatre, Lajos fell. I could no longer see him. For a space of absolute stillness, I waited for him to get up, to move, but there were only the men at the top of the hill, and the soldiers behind, all running to where he had fallen.

There was a roar of rage, coming, oddly, from István; there was a voice in my head drumming monotonously, "No, no, no, no, no." But perhaps I was saying it aloud, for Katalin hugged me to her, tears streaming down her own face as she whispered, "Hush, Katie, hush."

I pulled away from her, intent only on reaching Lajos, but they all held me back with pitying, immovable hands.

"Wait," Avenheim said quietly. I was blind then to the compassion in his face and his voice. "They will signal."

But I knew before the signal came. I couldn't take my eyes away from the place he had fallen. I couldn't see his body, but I knew it was there, without vitality or thought, still at last.

I first saw him in Vienna, young and full of life, preaching a revolution I had not believed in; and then, two years later, when the revolution was over, and I no longer knew how to live without him, I saw him die.

They were Romanians, the men on the hill who had helped to kill Lajos. I remember that being explained; and I remember thinking before my mind closed down, that it was an inevitable part of the whole tragedy, that he should have died in the end at the hands of those he had tried so hard to befriend. My family objected at first to the escort of such men to the Turkish border, but Colonel von Avenheim insisted.

And as they bundled me into one of the carriages, silent and helpless and uncaring, I thought distantly that it would have been easier to bear if he had died in the battle. It didn't seem right that he should die now, after what he had said to me last night...

The Colonel's head appeared briefly at the carriage window, his eyes troubled, pitying.

"Katie..." he began gently, but I looked away. There was nothing he could say that would make any difference. It was over. Everything was over.

I think he and István shook hands before they parted. I didn't care. And then we were moving, away from Lajos's body. I stared out of the window, back at the hill where he had fallen, but all I could see were rough, ill-dressed men on horseback, closely surrounding the carriage. They were dirty and unkempt, armed to the teeth, but riding two to a horse in some cases.

"I've never seen such a set of ruffians," Elisabeth said uneasily. "They'll murder us all as soon as we're out of Karl's sight!"

I didn't care about that either. I withdrew further into myself, barely aware even of Katalin squeezing my hand in compulsive sympathy. She was grieving too, but I couldn't think of that then.

I don't know how long it was or how far we had gone before a shouted command outside brought the carriage to a halt.

"I told you!" Elisabeth exclaimed, fear dilating her eyes. "They're going to kill us!"

It seemed she was right, for the carriage door was wrenched rudely open, and one of the Romanian riders stared in. I frowned at him. Something elusive tugged at my memory. Behind the beard, and the dirt and the privations of war, I knew him.

With an effort, I forced myself to remember. It wasn't Alex; it wasn't as bad as that, though it was bad enough.

"Petru," I said aloud, and the man bowed slightly, solemnly in the saddle. The others were staring at me in surprise, but all I could think of was that this was Iancu's friend; he hadn't liked Lajos at first, though later they had laughed and drunk together...

"Is this necessary?" came István's voice, cold and haughty. "We may be obliged to travel with the enemy; surely we need not converse with him?"

"We are no longer your enemies," Petru said. I remembered his voice now too: serious, precise. "We have concluded a truce with Kossuth. It's too late to ally with you, but we are neutral."

Now they were neutral; now, when he was dead...

"*Neutral?*" István exclaimed, and later I would be pleased by his anger on Lajos's behalf. "Do you call what happened on the hill neutral?"

There was a pause. Then Petru said, "No. That was not neutral." He looked directly at Katalin. "Be so good as to sit on the other side. We have a wounded man who needs your place."

I could tell from her face that she would have liked the courage to refuse, but Elisabeth was already pulling her across, and under Petru's instructions two men were lifting another into the coach. I forced myself to move over. I hoped with vague distaste that I wouldn't have to touch him. I kept my eyes on Petru, wondering dispassionately if he felt any remorse for what he had done. He met my gaze, and then he managed to surprise me. His lips stretched into a smile — twisted, but a smile nevertheless.

"Madame Katie," he said. "Take care of my comrade." And then, while I was still trying to take in his recognition and the significance of his words, he had slammed the door on us.

"Petru, wait!" The abrupt command was more of a plea; it came unexpectedly from Katalin, half out of her seat to pull down the window while she cast a glance at István that was both scared and defiant. Petru waited calmly where he was. "Petru — do you know anything of Captain Zarescu?" she breathed.

"Your fiancé," he remembered. It might have been a sneer. "I know he was alive when I saw him last, but that was a month ago."

She had never doubted it. "Petru... Petru, will you tell him where we have gone? Will you tell him I... tell him..." She broke off, floundering in the impossibility of saying all that she needed to through such a message, and such a messenger. But Petru surprised me again.

"I'll tell him," he said flatly, and rode ahead. As the coach began to move forward again, Katalin fell back into her seat, almost blissful under Elisabeth's sardonic gaze. Later, I thought, later I shall try and be glad for her; much later, when we are clear of *them*...

Involuntarily, I glanced down at the wounded man lying beside me — and my eyes widened in shock, for beneath the dirty cloak they had wrapped him in I could see a patch of blue and gold and silver. Slowly, fearfully, I reached out and drew the rough wool away from his face. It was deathly white, but the tight lines of pain around his mouth told me he was not only alive but conscious.

For a moment, I couldn't believe my own eyes. I couldn't see how it was possible. I don't think I even breathed. And then I heard István's soft, amazed laughter, Katalin's exclamations of joy, and I knew it was true. I realized at once the severity of his new wound, the frightening frailty of his whole body, and yet, in spite of everything, I was suddenly, unreasonably, certain of our future together. I drew a long, shuddering breath that was more than half a sob.

His eyes opened directly into mine. His voice little more than a whisper, he said, "I hope you remembered to pack my violin."

And somehow I was on my knees on the carriage floor, my face buried in his neck, his hand in my hair; and the tears that wouldn't come when I had thought he was dead, were threatening to drown us both.

"He's delirious," Katalin said uneasily, and now I didn't know if I was crying or laughing. I lifted my head to let him breathe; and I saw his eyes go beyond me to István. Uncertainly I looked from one to the other.

"You bastard," István said unsteadily. "You never would just lie down and die, would you, Lajos?"

"Sorry," Lajos said weakly. I thought he was trying to laugh. "I've always had too much to do... I still have."

Ruefully, remembering the pamphlet he had given to István, I smoothed his blood-streaked brow, murmuring, "The world still to win."

"And you." His eyes had begun to close, but his fingers were strong as they gripped mine, lending me courage. "For you..."

I took a deep breath.

"And the baby," I said casually. My voice didn't even tremble. Not surprisingly, his eyes flew open again, widening into mine with astonishment, and fear, and wonder, and finally, so that it almost obliterated the pain, a slow, intense joy.

Satisfied, I smiled serenely upon him and sat back on my heels, fixing my truly invaluable spectacles more securely on to my nose, the better to enjoy my family's shock.

About the Author

Mary Lancaster was born in Glasgow and now lives on the Fife coast with her husband and three young children. She graduated from the University of St. Andrews with a degree in history, the subject which remains the chief inspiration for her writing.

Despite earning a living over the years as Editorial Assistant, Researcher and Librarian, Mary Lancaster has managed to retain her love of books, particularly old and dusty ones. Her interest has always extended to writing - though, for many years, only for her own amusement. Her first published novel was *An Endless Exile*.

Also by Mary Lancaster...

An Endless Exile

An Endless Exile is the story of the eleventh century hero, Hereward "the Wake", the only Englishman to have defied and defeated William the Conqueror.

Torfrida is thirty-two years old, cynical, secretive, confident of her own wisdom and learning. Yet even she is taken by surprise when Hereward is brutally killed by his Norman guests.

Lonely and embittered, it is with reluctance that she remembers the past, from her first childhood meeting with the tumultuous Hereward, through their stormy courtship and Hereward's military adventures as mercenary and as patriot - which she shared - up to the unforgivable betrayal which parted them. Even more reluctantly does Torfrida begin to question Hereward's murder, eventually seeking the elusive truth with a desperation that mirrors her own unacknowledged need to believe in him and the value of their marriage.

But the truth only leads her into greater danger, threatening her unexpected new happiness in the very moment of its discovery.

Please see *www.mushroom-ebooks.com* for more information.

www.ingramcontent.com/pod-product-compliance
Lightning Source LLC
Chambersburg PA
CBHW022246020726
47496CB00004B/1092